D0404395

Victoria Hislop

Inspired by a visit to Spinalonga, the abandoned Greek leprosy colony, Victoria Hislop wrote *The Island* in 2005. It became an international bestseller and a 26-part Greek TV series. She was named Newcomer of the Year at the British Book Awards and is now an ambassador for Lepra. Her affection for the Mediterranean then took her to Spain, and in the number one bestseller *The Return* she wrote about the painful secrets of its civil war. In *The Thread*, Victoria returned to Greece to tell the turbulent tale of Thessaloniki and its people across the twentieth century. Shortlisted for a British Book Award, it confirmed her reputation as an inspirational storyteller. It was followed by her much-admired Greece-set collection, *The Last Dance and Other Stories*. Her fourth novel, *The Sunrise*, was published to widespread acclaim, and was a *Sunday Times* number one bestseller. Victoria Hislop's last book, *Cartes Postales from Greece*, is fiction illustrated with photographs. It was a *Sunday Times* bestseller in hardback and one of the biggest selling books of 2016.

Victoria divides her time between England and Greece.

To find out more, find Victoria on Facebook
f/OfficialVictoriaHislop
follow her on Twitter **🐦** @VicHislop
or go to her website at www.victoriahislop.com.

Praise for Victoria Hislop:

CARTES POSTALES

'Hislop's passionate love of the country
breathes from every page'
Daily Mail

THE SUNRISE

'Intelligent and immersive . . . weaves a vast array of fact
through a poignant, compelling family saga'
The Sunday Times

THE THREAD

'Storytelling at its best and just like a tapestry, when each thread
is sewn into place, so emerge the layers and history of relationships past and present'
Sunday Express

THE RETURN

'Executed with verve and sensitivity'
Sunday Telegraph

THE ISLAND

'A vivid, moving and absorbing tale . . . At last – a beach
book with a heart'
Observer

By *Victoria Hislop*

The Island
The Return
The Thread
The Sunrise
Cartes Postales from Greece
Those Who Are Loved

The Last Dance and Other Stories

Victoria
Hislop

Those
who
are
loved

REVIEW

Copyright © 2019 Victoria Hislop

The right of Victoria Hislop to be identified as the Author of
the Work has been asserted by her in accordance with the
Copyright, Designs and Patents Act 1988.

First published in Great Britain in 2019 by
HEADLINE REVIEW
An imprint of HEADLINE PUBLISHING GROUP

First published in this Trade Paperback edition in Great Britain in 2019 by
HEADLINE REVIEW

1

Apart from any use permitted under UK copyright law, this
publication may only be reproduced, stored, or transmitted, in
any form, or by any means, with prior permission in writing of
the publishers or, in the case of reprographic production, in
accordance with the terms of licences issued by the
Copyright Licensing Agency.

All characters in this publication are fictitious
and any resemblance to real persons, living or dead,
is purely coincidental.

Cataloguing in Publication Data is available from the British Library

ISBN 978 1 4722 2323 4

Typeset in Bembo by Palimpsest Book Production Limited, Falkirk, Stirlingshire
Printed and bound in Great Britain by Clays Ltd, Elcograf S.p.A.

Headline's policy is to use papers that are natural, renewable and
recyclable products and made from wood grown in sustainable forests.
The logging and manufacturing processes are expected to conform
to the environmental regulations of the country of origin.

HEADLINE PUBLISHING GROUP
An Hachette UK Company
Carmelite House
50 Victoria Embankment
London EC4Y 0DZ

www.headline.co.uk
www.hachette.co.uk

Those
who
are
loved

For my beloved uncle
Neville Eldridge
15 June 1927 – 19 March 2018

Prologue

2016

I N A SMALL apartment in Athens, four generations gathered to celebrate a birthday. A diminutive woman with silver hair smiled as great-grandchildren ran giddily around the outside of the group and adults sang:

Pandoú na skorpízis,
Tis gnósis to fos,
Kai óloi na léne,
Na mía sofós.

May you spread out the light,
Of all that you know,
So everyone says,
How wise that you are.

Though she had heard them a thousand times, Themis Stavridis listened to the words, and reflected on all the wisdom she had shared. Her family were familiar with her 'secret' recipes, her technique for building a slow-burning fire and how to tell an edible berry from a poisonous one. In practical terms, she had taught them all that she knew.

Tightly packed round an old mahogany dining table were eighteen family members, and several of the children had been seated on their parents' laps in order to fit. The meal was over, the cake devoured, and now, in the late afternoon, the younger generations were becoming restless, furtively looking at their phones to check messages and time. The two-bedroomed home could not contain the energies of children, small or large, for much longer, and under their mothers' instructions they formed a queue to embrace the nonagenarian.

In a frayed but favourite armchair sat Themis' husband, present and absent at the same time. Before leaving, the children queued to kiss him, mostly on the top of his head or on a cheek, wherever they could reach. He appeared not even to acknowledge that they were there. His face was like a dark house. In the past five years, the lights had gone out one by one and today his wife's radiance accentuated the contrast between them. Giorgos Stavridis had no idea that most of these people were blood relations who owed their very existence to him. At certain moments, their presence even baffled and alarmed him, now that all were forgotten and unknown.

Kisses and goodbyes and well-meant promises to meet soon took some time but eventually the apartment was quiet. Half-finished dishes of *pastítsio*, *spanakópita* and *dolmadákia* were spread across the table. There was still enough to feed every guest all over again. There was only one empty platter, on which remained a few crumbs and smears of icing from the creamy chocolate cake. It had been deftly divided and parcelled on to paper plates, the last of which now balanced on the arm of the old man's chair.

Two grandchildren stayed behind: Popi, who lived close by, and Nikos, who had come from America to celebrate his grand-mother's birthday. Nikos sat in the corner of the room working on his laptop while Popi gathered dirty glasses on to a tray.

'I'm going to help you with all this, *Yiayiá*,' she said, beginning to pile up the dinner plates and to scoop untouched food into plastic containers.

'No, no, Popi *mou*. There's no need. I know how busy you young people are.'

'I'm not busy, *Yiayiá*,' she said, adding the words 'if only' under her breath. Popi was a translator, but her hours were part-time and her salary low. She was looking for bar work to supplement her income.

The chaos created by the party was too much for the old lady and she was secretly glad of the help.

Her youngest granddaughter was long-legged, almost thirty centimetres taller than her grandmother, but she had inherited the same cheekbones and fine fingers. Her hairstyle had upset her *yiayiá* when she had first arrived. It was the first time Themis had seen Popi since she had shaved her head on one side. The other side, still shoulder-length, was now streaked purple. She also had a small stud in her nose, but that was a few years old.

'Look at all this food we couldn't eat!' she exclaimed with disapproval. 'Maybe we shouldn't be wasting so much in this crisis.'

'Crisis?' repeated the old lady.

'Yes, *Yiayiá*. The crisis!'

The old lady was teasing her, but it took Popi a few moments to realise it.

'I know. I know. Everyone talks of "the crisis". But today I wanted to celebrate the plenty that we *do* have, rather than what we *don't* have.'

'I just feel guilty, that's all. I can't help it.'

'Just for my sake, *agápi mou*, try not to feel guilty. Even if it feels a little wasteful.'

There was just enough space in the tiny kitchen for one person to wash and dry the plates and for another to put them away. The long-limbed Popi did not need to stand on a chair to reach the high shelves.

Once they were finished with the chores, and the kitchen was spotless, they went out on to the balcony, stepping over Giorgos' legs to do so. Nikos joined them.

Nikos and Popi were in their late twenties but there the similarity ended. The contrast between them was startling, with Nikos dressed in a suit and Popi in leggings and a T-shirt. The pair had met only a few times in the past decade at family events, but usually gravitated towards each other when they did. Popi always wanted to grill her cousin about American politics, and on recent visits Nikos had been full of questions about Greek society. Their childhoods had greatly contrasted in terms of privilege and opportunity, but they had both enjoyed good university educations and talked to each other as equals.

Having grown up in a detached house surrounded by lawns, Nikos found plenty of things alien about Greek life. Several of them confronted him now. Open windows and ill-fitting shutters meant that everyone was familiar with intimate details of their neighbours' lives: raised voices, babies crying, televisions blaring, a radio left playing, the relentless drone of angry teenage music. Silence was as rare as privacy here.

The 'American cousin', as Popi thought of him, was also unused to the way in which personal details were announced by washing lines. The number, age and size of family members was often evident; even the kind of work they did and perhaps their politics too were displayed.

Themis Stavridis caught her granddaughter scrutinising the balcony opposite. An unbroken row of black T-shirts confirmed her own fear.

'Do you think they're *Chrysí Avgí?*' asked Popi, a note of alarm in her voice.

'I am afraid so,' Themis answered sadly. 'The father and all three sons.'

'*Chrysí Avgí?*' queried Nikos.

'They're fascists,' said Popi. 'Anti-immigrant, violent fascists.'

Themis had seen on television that the far-right party had been demonstrating the previous day, and she found it deeply disturbing.

For a few moments the three of them continued to look out. There was always something to watch. Some small boys kicked a ball, while their mothers sat on a bench nearby, smoking and chatting. Three teenagers mounted the pavement on their mopeds, parked and ambled into the café close by. One man stopped another, apparently to get a light for his cigarette, but both Popi and Nikos noticed him taking a small package and sliding it into his pocket.

Themis could not sit down for long. There were dozens of plants that needed watering, then there was sweeping to be done, and finally the tiles of the balcony itself to be hosed down.

While she was bustling about, Popi asked if she could make some coffee.

'Should I make some for *Pappoú* too . . .?' asked the young woman quietly.

'He doesn't drink it any more,' Themis answered. 'It just sits there getting cold.'

'You know it's almost twenty years since he last went to the *kafeneío*? It was just after my birthday – which is how I remember it. He came back that day in such a strange mood. I knew he would never go again. I think it was the last coffee he ever drank.'

Nikos looked at his grandfather with sadness. Even he understood the significance of a Greek man ceasing to visit his *kafeneío*.

'He lives in his own world now,' said Themis.

'Perhaps it's as well. Things aren't so great in the real one, are they?' said Popi.

Themis gave her a look of sorrow.

'Sorry to sound gloomy, *Yiayiá*. I can't help it sometimes.'

Themis took her granddaughter's hand and squeezed it.

'Things will get better,' she reassured her. 'I am sure of it.'

'Why are you so sure?'

'Because over time life just does. Sometimes it gets a little worse again. But on the whole, things improve.'

'Are you serious? You can say that even now? When there are people queuing at soup kitchens and sleeping in doorways!'

'I agree that things are bad at the moment. But everyone is so preoccupied with the present day. They should look back and remember how much worse it used to be.'

Popi looked at her quizzically.

'I know I seem a bit extravagant to you, dear, but I promise you we wouldn't have thrown anything away when I was your age. I know I shouldn't now, but because I can . . .'

'I didn't mean to be critical,' said Popi.

'I know, I know.'

'You've lived for so many years, *Yiayiá*. I sometimes wonder how all those memories fit in!'

'It's busy in there,' the old lady said, tapping her forehead. 'When I look down into the street, I don't just see how it is now but how it was before.'

'In what way?' asked Nikos. 'Nostalgically?'

'Not always. Good things happened in the past – but bad things did too. And looking down there reminds me of so much.'

'Such as?'

'You know that photograph on the dresser in there? The one on the right?'

From where they sat, Popi could see through the open glass doors that led back into the living room. Silhouetted on the dresser was a row of framed photographs.

'You mean the one of you and your sister?'

'That's not my sister, actually. It's Fotini. We were best friends at school. And like sisters. Perhaps even closer than that.'

The old lady pointed through the railings to the corner of the square.

'She died. Right there,' she said.

Popi looked at her grandmother in disbelief and then turned her eyes to where she had indicated. She had never heard this before and the blunt revelation shocked her.

'It was during the occupation. There was a famine, *agápi mou*. Hundreds of thousands died.'

'That's terrible,' said Nikos. 'I didn't realise things were so desperate here.'

When he was a child, his father had given him only the broadest outline of Greece's history. All he knew of it then was the Fall of Constantinople in 1453 and the Greek Revolution in 1821 but he could not name even one prime minister (though he could recite the name of every American president in date order, a party trick since he was precociously small). In his teens, however, his interest had grown and he had even taken intensive Greek lessons, so keen was he to connect with his roots.

'Yes, Nikos. It was terrible. Really terrible. She was so young . . .' Themis paused a moment to collect herself before continuing. 'We were hungry *all* the time in those days. When there is more than enough, as there is now, I like to cook plenty – simply because I can. It probably looks like extravagance.'

'It feels like it to me, *Yiayiá*,' said Popi, squeezing her grandmother's arm and smiling. 'But can I take some home?'

'You can take all of it,' replied her grandmother firmly.

Leaving her grandparents' home laden with leftovers was a ritual. They would see her through to the end of the week and be enough for her flatmates too.

Inside the apartment, her grandfather now snored quietly, occasionally muttering.

'What do you think he dreams of, *Yiayiá*?' asked Nikos.

'I don't think he has many thoughts or memories,' she answered. 'So it's hard to imagine.'

'I suppose things live on in the subconscious,' he mused.

'Sometimes I envy him having space in his mind,' said Themis. 'I imagine it might be quite peaceful.'

'What do you mean?' asked Popi.

'I can remember too much, perhaps, and it gives me a headache sometimes. Perhaps memories can be too vivid.'

A few minutes passed. The sun had gone down now and street-lamps were coming on. Themis then leant across to touch Popi's hand.

'Why don't we go out for coffee?' she whispered. 'Then we'll go into the little church. There's something I always do on my birthday.'

'Pray?' Popi said with surprise, knowing that her grandmother was not especially devout.

'No, *agápi mou*. I light some candles.'

'Didn't you have enough on your cake?' teased Popi.

Themis smiled.

'Who are they for?' Nikos asked keenly.

'Come with me and I'll tell you,' she said, looking at Nikos, as ever mildly thrown by the strong resemblance to the man after whom he had been named.

During the course of that day, with her family crammed into

the small apartment, Themis had reflected with some regret that she had nothing to bequeath her children and grandchildren. There was little of any worth except the battered table around which the family had been eating for generations.

Or was there perhaps another kind of legacy? She suddenly realised, now that Giorgos was absent in all but body, that there were things she would like to tell them. Her life story was not an heirloom, but it was all she had and she would give it to these two young people. She loved all of her grandchildren equally but had special affection for Popi because she had seen her almost every day since she was born. For Nikos, she had a particular soft spot, even though he only visited once a year.

They quickly got ready to leave, Nikos helping his grandmother into her cardigan while Popi threw on her faded red thrift-shop coat.

Nikos would be getting a plane back to the US the following morning and Themis insisted he have some fresh baklava and proper Greek coffee before he left. They had all eaten copiously at lunchtime, but he could not refuse and soon they were at the local *zacharoplasteío*.

Once they were seated, Themis began to talk.

Chapter One

THE SWISH OF a hem against her cheek, the vibration of floorboards as her siblings ran around, the clatter of china from somewhere unseen and the sight of her mother's brown, buckled shoes, moulded around misshapen feet. These were Themis' early memories.

With a small mansion, a husband at sea for months at a time and four children, Eleftheria Koralis was constantly engaged in domestic tasks. She had no time for play. The little one spent her early years in a state of happy neglect, and grew up believing she could make herself invisible.

Eleftheria already owned the two-storey neo-classical house in Antigonis Street when she married Pavlos. It had been her late mother's dowry. The exterior had been designed to impress, with no thought for restraint. It had a grand balcony, ornate pillars and a row of baroque embellishments along the roof-line. The ceilings were finished with cornicing, some floors were tiled and others made with polished wood. The day the craftsmen had packed up their tools, with the plaster only just dry on the moulded caryatids that decorated the upper windows, was its moment of greatest glory and grandeur. From that day on, the house had seen a long and steady journey to decay.

The family's lack of resources for making any repairs meant that cracked stonework and rotten floorboards proved a constant danger to them all. The once-prosperous family was now a struggling one. Seventy years earlier, Themis' maternal ancestors had been part of the growing merchant class, but unwise investments meant that only the house remained. Many of the contents, including paintings and silver, had been sold off over time and only a few pieces of antique French furniture and some jewellery were spared.

Themis knew no different and imagined that all families lived in a state of warfare with a crumbling building. Cracked windows let in the dust, flaking plaster sometimes fell from the ceiling in chunks and roof tiles were sent crashing to the pavement in high winds. During winter and spring, she was kept awake by the steady *ting ting ting* of raindrops landing in one of a dozen buckets. It made an almost musical sound and the ever-growing number of receptacles catching the water was a measure of the building's steady progress towards dereliction.

Another house in the street was already boarded up. In reality, it was fitter for human habitation than the mouldy building lived in by the Koralis family, who cohabited with a growing population of bacteria that even now were beginning to form spores. The ground floor was decayed, with a smell of rot rising through the floor and seeping into the walls.

The children had free run of their home, oblivious to the dangers presented by its state of decay, filling it with noise and boisterous play. Though Themis was too small to join in, she sat at the foot of the stairs and watched as her siblings ran up and down the big central staircase and slid down the smooth wooden banister rail.

Three of the posts had split, leaving a hazardous gap with a sheer drop to one side.

She watched with great delight as Thanasis, Panos and Margarita flew towards her. Their mother rarely kept watch and only appeared when one of her children lost control and landed on the hard, stone-tiled floor. She responded quickly to a howl of pain and always came to make sure that the injury was no more serious than a bruise to the head, cradling the injured child for a moment but returning to her chores the moment the sobs subsided. At the foot of the stairs lay a rug still spotted with blood from Thanasis' most recent accident. Eleftheria had done her best to scrub it clean and soon the marks would blend into the mostly faded browns and reds of the weave.

Themis ignored a ban on going under the dining table. She loved this secret place where she could hide beneath the solid mahogany and the drapes of a heavy, embroidered cloth and listen to the muffled sounds of what was happening above her. It was a place of both safety and danger; in truth, nowhere in this house was without hidden peril. A section of floorboard beneath the table had rotted away, leaving a hole big enough for a small foot to slip through. When she grew another few centimetres, her leg would appear in the room below. 'And then you will fall through,' said her mother. 'And die.'

For Themis, her mother's voice was associated with instructions and warnings.

Pavlos Koralis made an occasional appearance when the merchant ship he captained docked in Piraeus. He was a giant of a man and could easily pick up both his daughters at once. Themis could never understand why Margarita was even meaner to her than usual when their father was at home, not knowing that the older child had felt displaced the moment she arrived. She hated sharing anything, least of all paternal affection. When he returned from one of his journeys to a far-off place, Pavlos' bag was full of strange and exotic gifts for them all. From China there were tiny embroidered slippers, a knife each for the boys and an uncut gem for his wife (fake or real, she never knew). And from India he brought carved elephants, incense sticks and pieces of silk. These were the 'artefacts' that added occasional glimpses of colour to the house in place of the more valuable but dour family heirlooms that had been sold to buy shoes.

When Pavlos was on leave, the anarchy in the house increased. Eleftheria Koralis tried to keep on top of domestic demands but her husband's presence added to her duties, not just in the bedroom, but with meals and laundry. Themis associated her father's visits with her mother being more harassed than normal and a dirtier than usual floor.

During these days, Themis spent as much time as she could in her favourite hiding place. When her father was in town, there were visitors to the house and when they ate there was constant banging on the wooden roof above her, as they thumped their hands on the table. From an early age she was familiar with certain words and names, always spoken in a raised voice and rarely without cries of outrage: 'Venizelos!', 'George!', 'The King', 'Turks!', 'Jews!'

By the age of three, she knew the word 'catastrophe'. Why had it happened? Who had been responsible? Up until the decade's end and for many years beyond, there were arguments around every table in the land over who had been at fault for the events that led up to the destruction of Smyrna, the most beautiful city in Asia Minor, in 1922. The deaths of so many Greeks would never be forgotten, nor would the million refugees whose arrival had changed the fabric of society.

Themis grew up with the impression that even those who socialised together, such as Pavlos Koralis and his friends, often disagreed. The finale for any altercation, however, was always the clinking of glasses. They tipped back one measure of firewater after another, banging the glasses down hard enough to dent the table. The clear liquid fuelled their passions and their anger before a rowdy song began.

Eventually Themis would be pulled out from under the table by her mother even if she had fallen asleep across her father's boots.

From her hiding place, Themis also overheard muted conversations between her parents and sometimes, when her father was away, between her mother and paternal grandmother, who was a regular, if not always welcome, visitor to the house. Most of these seemed to relate to the dilapidated mansion and how long they might be able to live there. One day, when her grandmother came, she heard something that made an even bigger impression.

'They can't live in this shipwreck of a house *any longer.*'

Her grandmother sounded indignant but the child loved the idea of the house being like a boat. On stormy days, with the wind whistling through cracked windows, it creaked and swayed as if they were out at sea.

Her mother's response was not what she had imagined.

'You have no shame,' she hissed. 'This is our home. Please go. Please leave, *now.*'

Her mother's voice was hoarse with all the effort it took simultaneously to whisper and project her anger.

'I worry so much for them,' continued Kyría Koralis. 'I just think they should live somewhere less . . .'

Eleftheria did not let her continue.

'Don't you *dare* say this in front of the children!'

The older woman's campaign to 'save' her grandchildren was

often conducted more subtly. Themis heard far more than she should and soon worked out the cunning ways of adults.

'I am worried about your wife,' the grandmother said to Pavlos when he was home from sea. 'She works so very hard. Why don't you move somewhere modest but decent?'

It was true that such a house needed two maids to keep it clean, and they could not afford even one.

Her mother-in-law's interfering comments were rarely addressed directly to Eleftheria herself, so in turn she answered through her husband.

'This is our home,' Eleftheria said to Pavlos. 'Whatever your mother thinks, I can manage.'

It was obvious even to Pavlos that his mother was jealous of a wife who had brought such an impressive property to the marriage and he was not surprised that there was mutual dislike. When he and his friends talked of it, they agreed that it was normal for a woman to resent her daughter-in-law, and for a wife to dislike her *petherá*. Eleftheria believed that her mother-in-law's possessive attitude to her only son and proprietorial attitude towards their children undermined her own role, while Kyría Koralis believed these were natural expressions of love and a mother and grandmother's rightful role.

Themis, on the other hand, looked forward to her grandmother's appearances because she always brought something fresh and sweet – usually a creamy pie or cake. Her mother never made such things and the children's exclamations of delight added to Eleftheria's sense of inadequacy and made her resent her cheerful, generous-hipped *petherá* all the more. Kyría Koralis was almost sixty but did not have a single grey hair.

Like his mother's, Pavlos Koralis' visits were always a surprise. This was exciting when he arrived but when he left, also without notice, the children felt bereft. Themis would wake in the bed she shared with her sister and simply know, without being told, that he had gone. The booming voice no longer filled the house and the lofty, crumbling spaces felt empty. Life immediately returned to its old normality: constant squabbling among the children; play-fighting between Thanasis and Panos, which always ended with someone hurt or something broken; mild cruelty perpetrated by Margarita; the grandmother coming by for an hour, not to help in any way but just to watch her daughter-in-law as she ironed, cooked, cleaned and hung out washing, never failing to comment on how raw her hands were from scrubbing out stains from clothes and marks on the floor.

With Eleftheria constantly busy, Themis was often left alone to amuse herself. The child had never known a single hour in her life when her mother was not involved in a pressing task that would need repeating the following day.

One winter's morning, when her mother had left in a hurry for her daily visit to the market, and Themis was under the table (her place of comfort now that she was old enough to know what loneliness was), the four-year-old child heard a bang, like the slamming of the heavy front door. It must be her mother back sooner than usual from her errands.

In fact, amongst all the cracks in the plaster, disguised among the many lines that criss-crossed the flaking paint, were fissures that went from inside to out, from top to bottom. A series of mild seismic movements over the past few decades (and an indiscernible one that day) had been enough not only to crack walls but also to create instability in the foundations.

When Themis emerged from beneath the table, where it was always dark, she faced a brighter than usual light. Shutters usually kept the room in a state of twilight but now there were none.

Nor were there windows or walls. There was nothing to stop the light coming in. She walked to the edge of the room and looked out. She could see the whole of the street, to left and right, trees, a far-off tram, people walking in the distance. She looked down into what seemed like an abyss.

People had begun to gather on the pavement beneath her and were looking up, pointing at the little girl in a pale pink dress, who stood as if in a picture frame. Themis looked down and waved at them cheerfully, moving closer towards the edge of the precipice to try to hear what they were calling to her.

As her mother came hurrying down the street, moving as fast as her burdens would allow her, she noticed the crowd gathered outside her home. Then she saw the unfamiliar sight of a building, opened up like a cupboard, with the small figure of her daughter seated, her legs dangling over the edge.

The floor was unsupported by anything beneath. It was floating.

Eleftheria Koralis dropped her shopping and ran. People moved out of the way to let her pass.

'Themis! *Agápi mou!* Darling!'

These were unfamiliar words from her mother.

'*Mána!*' she called back. '*Koíta!* Look!'

On the street below, a bigger crowd was gathering. It was extraordinary how rapidly people had appeared from their homes.

Even for a grown man, the jump from the first floor might have been challenging, but for a small child the fall into a pile of twisted metal and sections of broken stonework and jagged plaster could prove fatal.

'Stay . . .' said Eleftheria, holding the flat of her palm towards her daughter and attempting to sound calm. 'Just stay still . . . and we will get you down.'

Carefully she picked her way over some fallen masonry, then

turned to the people around her, appealing with her eyes for their help. A man had appeared with a blanket and three other men were already volunteering to hold it out so that Themis could jump. They were scrambling over the wreckage of the façade to get themselves into position. There was another audible crack as one of the side walls fell inwards. With a squeal, mimicking the way in which her siblings sometimes launched themselves off the stairs for a dare, Themis jumped. She landed lightly on her feet, in the middle of the rough wool bedspread, and before she knew what was happening found herself bundled up into a ball and tossed to the waiting crowd as the men fell over themselves to jump clear of the falling masonry.

Once at a safe distance, she was quickly unwrapped from the folds and handed to her mother. Eleftheria cuddled her for a few moments and then everything went still, as the whole house began to crumble. Every wall had supported another and now that the structure had given way the entire edifice collapsed, not piece by piece but in one swift, almost graceful, movement, sending a cloud of dust over the spectators, who now backed away, shielding their eyes from the grit.

At this moment, Thanasis, Panos and Margarita turned the corner into Antigonis Street. They were puzzled by the gathering ahead of them but could not see above all the heads to find out what was holding their attention.

Panos tugged on the sleeve of a man standing in front of them. He had to be persistent.

'Hey!' he yelled above the general commotion. 'What's happened?'

The man spun round.

'A house. It fell down. Right in front of us. It just collapsed.'

The children had all heard their grandmother telling their father on numerous occasions that the house was 'going to fall down around their heads' and had spent their lives dodging the drips and being woken by chunks of ceiling landing on their beds. Their *yiayiá* had been right.

'Our mother,' said Margarita tearfully. 'Where is she?'

'And the little one,' added Panos. Even though she was four, Themis was still known as this by her siblings. '*I mikrí?* The little one?'

'We'll find them,' said Thanasis firmly, aware of himself as the big brother.

Nothing more could happen now. The crowd was beginning to disperse and the view was clearer for the children. The three of them stood, eyes wide, staring at the irregular pile of shattered furniture and possessions, the contents of three floors now sitting on the ground. They all noticed individual objects sticking out from the rubble – some of the gifts from their father, splashes of colour visible even in the chaos, Margarita's favourite doll, torn books, a kitchen cabinet lying on its side spewing out pots and pans.

One of the neighbours had spotted the children clinging to each other with distress and came over. All three were suppressing quiet sobs.

'Your mother is safe,' she said. 'And little Themis. They're both safe. Look, she's over there.'

A short way down the road, they spotted the almost unrecognisable figure of their mother, her light auburn hair covered in white dust. Eleftheria Koralis' clothes were coated with plaster, and the fine rain that now fell made them glisten. She was still fussing over Themis as the other three ran towards her, calling out.

One of the neighbours came out with a jug of water for them all, but no one seemed to have any intention of providing more than that. Their hospitality did not extend beyond a look of concern. The children stood in a huddle staring back at the dereliction, but their mother faced away, too distressed to contemplate the sight of it.

They stood immobile for some time as the rain turned to hail. When their coats began to soak through, they realised that they could no longer stand there. Themis herself was wearing just her thin frock.

'I'm cold,' she shivered. 'I'm really cold.'

'We'll find somewhere to go,' said her mother reassuringly. At that moment, perfectly on cue, the children's grandmother appeared. Eleftheria Koralis had never detested her *petherá* more than at this moment, when she would have to fall upon her charity.

Only an hour later, they were settling into the older woman's newly built apartment in Patissia.

Her mother-in-law's sense of being right was all the more galling to Eleftheria when it was expressed without words. Her manner alone was clear enough. At this moment, they were poor in possessions and destitute of options, and the children needed a roof over their heads.

The following day, Eleftheria walked back to Antigonis Street to survey the damage once again.

She noted that all the beautiful items of furniture of which her parents had been so proud were beyond repair. Fragments of polished inlaid wood and finely chamfered edging were scattered like an unsolved jigsaw, but there in the corner, defiantly unbroken, was the mahogany dining table. It was the only still-whole piece of furniture.

With utter recklessness, Eleftheria stepped over shards of glass, jagged edges of plaster and splintered wood and picked about in the debris until she had found what she was looking for. It was a small chest containing her jewellery, and with difficulty she wrested it from under a beam. She was not going to allow looters such a prize. As well as obvious valuables, she wanted to find a few clothes. Identifying an old wardrobe in the maelstrom, she took out various items and shook off the dust. They were her favourite things.

Several days of fierce debate ensued. Eleftheria wanted to bring the table to their new home and, in spite of it being oversized for the space, stubbornly refused to give in. It was either that or she would take the children to some great-aunt or other in Larissa. With enormous reluctance, Kyría Koralis capitulated and the following day, the table was retrieved, installed and resentfully covered with several layers of lace cloth that even concealed its finely turned legs.

'That's all I'm letting you bring in,' muttered the older woman as her own smaller table was carried out of the apartment.

Her daughter-in-law pretended not to hear.

The area of Patissia where the grandmother lived seemed far from the centre of the city, but as she regularly pointed out to the children: 'It has so many trees! And so many lovely green spaces for playing and sitting.' By emphasising the strengths of the area, she subtly criticised the one where they used to live.

The children soon settled in. They loved going down into the square beneath the house and finding other children to play with, amused themselves on the roof where their grandmother hung out the washing, weaving their way between the sheets to play hide-and-seek, and frolicked up and down the stone staircase, always looking out for the woman on the ground floor who might be coming out with her enchanting dog.

Perhaps what they loved most of all was that when they pressed a light switch, the room was always illuminated and when they slept they did not breathe dust but air. After a few months, when the buds on the trees down below began to uncurl, their dawn chorus of coughs was no more.

Meanwhile, the old house had been fenced off for safety. The authorities were waiting to demolish it.

Eleftheria Koralis and her children now owned no more than the refugees who had fled from Asia Minor almost a decade before. Thousands had arrived with nothing but the clothes they stood up in and the majority still lived in pockets of poverty round the edge of the city. The problem of finding accommodation for such a wave of newcomers was still not resolved and, unless she accepted Kyría Koralis' hospitality, the family would have to join the queue. There was nothing else between them and penury.

'I am sure we can rebuild,' said Eleftheria Koralis to her husband, when he returned from sea. 'We can clear the land and start again.'

Her husband's response was an indifferent nod. He did not express it openly but the collapse of the old house did not bother him and he was happy enough that his family now lived in his mother's apartment. The leaks and draughts in Antigonis Street had never allowed a comfortable night's sleep when he came home from sea.

They had not been with old Kyría Koralis for long, but unhappiness already pumped through Eleftheria's veins.

The apartment in Kerou Street was compact and organised, everything in its place, neatly stacked, impeccably swept, washed, tidied, ordered and aligned in rows. There was a central living room with two reasonably sized bedrooms and a small room previously used as a study by her late husband. She quickly turned this into a bedroom for herself, while Eleftheria shared her double bed with the girls and the boys took the other, twin-bedded, room.

Themis liked the whole family being on a single floor. It gave her a sense of security to hear her grandmother's snores, audible

23

even from behind the closed door, and her mother quietly muttering in her sleep. She was even protected from Margarita's occasional spitefulness. The hair-pulling and pinching had stopped now that there was someone else close by.

Instead of dust and danger, there was the cheerful sound of music from a radio, the fragrant scent of cooking, the gentle glow of an oil lamp on the iconostasis and a sense of calm. The apartment might not have been big enough to run around in, but this meant that the older ones were allowed to play in the leafy square below and even to explore the nearby streets. The city became theirs and they soon got a sense of its limitless possibilities.

Kyría Koralis enjoyed the challenge of feeding them all in spite of continuing austerity. It was she who now disciplined the boys to do their homework when they came home, making them sit at the kitchen table until it was done. Bribery (a candy, more time playing in the square, even the promise of a visit to the sea) was a tactic she willingly used.

Only Eleftheria grieved what had been left behind and dreamed of regaining their lost life. The demands of a crumbling house had given her a *raison d'être* and nowadays she could find little incentive to get out of bed in the morning. Kyría Koralis began to be perturbed by the sight of her daughter-in-law slumped on her pillows at midday.

Whether the grandmother actually took over the family so completely that it eroded Eleftheria's will to live, or whether the younger woman's loss of will meant that the old lady was obliged to step in, would be hard to say. Themis had no sense of what came first. All she knew was that their current situation had been caused by the collapse of their home and her siblings told her that everything was better in their new life.

For many months, no one acknowledged that anything was

wrong with their mother and Kyría Koralis carried on as if her daughter-in-law's behaviour was normal. She sometimes took in a tray of food when the children had left for school, but Eleftheria rarely acknowledged or ate it.

It appeared that she was slowly and steadily starving herself to death. One day when Kyría Koralis came back from her errands, she found the big double bed empty. Perhaps she had finally decided to 'pull herself together', the old lady thought.

Tiptoeing across the hallway, she peeked through a crack in the door to the small room and noticed her daughter-in-law's outline beneath the counterpane. She crept in, removed her own clothes from the cupboard and swapped them with Eleftheria's, which hung in the larger room. The exchange was done quickly. That night, she lay on the big bed with the girls leaning against her, a generous grandmotherly body providing a pillow for the sprawled tangle of arms and legs.

When Pavlos Koralis next visited, which happened less and less these days, it was with his mother that he discussed what should happen to the derelict Antigonis Street house. Themis was sitting in the corner one day doing a drawing when a lawyer came to the apartment. Themis was five now but adults still seemed to believe her either simple or deaf, and although much of the language was beyond her, she understood enough. It seemed that everything was to be decided between her father and her *yiayiá*, and she heard an unfamiliar word being used in relation to her mother. As she later attempted to describe it to Panos, it sounded like 'sick', but longer. The word they had in fact used was 'schizophrenic'.

Eleftheria rarely emerged these days from the room at the back of the apartment. Pavlos Koralis and his mother agreed that the kindest action would be to find an appropriate private institution. It was the only solution for someone afflicted by such ever-deepening depression. A judge had granted power of attorney to Pavlos Koralis and he had managed to sell the site of his wife's old mansion. Proceeds from the house sale would be used for her care.

The children were told that their mother needed to go to hospital for a while. They all understood that she was ill since why else would she stay in bed all day? And the promise that she would be treated, get better and then come home again was believed. Only Themis and her grandmother were there when a nurse arrived to escort her, and the small bag Eleftheria took with her supported the notion that her absence would be short.

Themis was briefly hugged by her mother and was puzzled that even on a cold day she left without putting on a coat. From the balcony, both grandmother and child watched the fragile figure being helped into a car and driven away.

When they returned from school, the other children were distraught that their mother had gone. They had hardly seen her during the past months, but knowing that her small room was now empty caused great distress. Margarita kept Themis awake with her crying that night, and even through the walls she could hear her brothers sobbing.

The psychiatric institution near Drama where Eleftheria Koralis now lived was in a decaying building with high ceilings and cracked walls. It was more than six hundred kilometres away and Pavlos Koralis only visited once, early on in her stay.

'Pavlos thinks it reminds her of somewhere else . . .' commented Kyría Koralis to one of her friends. 'He says he hasn't seen her more contented since they first married and moved into that awful house.'

Twice a year, a letter arrived reporting on her condition. She remained 'stable', but against what measure it did not say. The question of diagnosis was never raised, a fact that seemed not to trouble anyone, and the children accepted their mother's need to convalesce. Even if she had not been so far away, they would not have been allowed to see her.

A wedding photograph of Pavlos and Eleftheria stood on Kyría Koralis' dresser, more or less the only reminder of the absent couple.

Chapter Two

FOR THE NEXT few years, Kyría Koralis' care of her grandchildren was exemplary. She now had the family she had always
wanted. Her husband had been in the Hellenic Navy and had died
at sea when their only child was small. Pavlos had surprised her
by joining a merchant fleet, leaving an empty space in the centre
of her life. Now she had a flock of children to fill her days. She
was in her early sixties but still had boundless energy, as well as
the ability to organise the young.

Every evening, Kyría Koralis enjoyed sitting at the head of the
table and observing her grandchildren. She did not admit it to
herself but the fact that Margarita had inherited her father's large
almond-shaped eyes (and her own round face and plump figure)
made her the favourite. Thanasis also reminded her of Pavlos, with
his chiselled cheekbones and broad shoulders. Panos was slighter
in build, like their mother, and Themis also had Eleftheria Koralis'
skinny frame and an unmistakably reddish tint in her mousy brown
hair. Old Kyría Koralis was privately disappointed that her grandsons were not taller, but blamed this on the poor diet they were
all restricted to.

With her careful budgeting for food, and her skill with a

needle, they 'made do' with what they had but it was not always possible to protect them from the growing economic depression. As they grew into teenagers, Thanasis and Panos often complained that they were still hungry after a meal. Kyría Koralis remained patient with them and made sure there was another loaf the next day.

It was Margarita whose lack of appreciation pushed her into losing her temper one day. For her granddaughter's twelfth birthday she had painstakingly altered an old summer dress of Eleftheria's.

Margarita's eyes glistened with excitement as Kyría Koralis placed the package on the table in front of her, but her expression changed as soon as she opened it.

'But that's not a new dress, *Yiayiá*. You promised me a *new* one,' she said petulantly.

Even with its bright buttons and braided hem, Margarita was not persuaded. The dress sat on her lap in a tangle of wrapping and ribbon.

'There are plenty of girls who would dream of having such a dress, Margarita!' Kyría Koralis told her firmly.

'Yes, Margarita,' interjected Panos. 'You're rude.'

'Shut up, Panos,' snapped Margarita. 'It's got nothing to do with you.'

'What you need to remember, young woman,' said Kyría Koralis, addressing her pouting granddaughter, 'is that new dresses are in short supply these days, even on birthdays. And for plenty of people, food is too. Not just in Greece but everywhere else. So please be a bit more grateful.'

Kyría Koralis snatched her handiwork from Margarita's lap and left the room. Her understanding of politics was not extensive but she knew that the economic depression they were experiencing was far-reaching and it was time that her wayward granddaughter realised it too.

Even with the door of her own bedroom shut, she could hear raised voices between the children and then Margarita shrieking before a door slammed.

Themis had said nothing. In her entire life she had never worn a new dress. Only hand-me-downs from her sister.

Two days after Margarita's birthday, the front page of the newspapers showed a woman bowed in grief over the corpse of her son. The desperation of tobacco workers in Thessaloniki had led them to strike and in an attempt to keep control over the crowd, police had opened fire and killed twelve men.

For some time, social division had been growing and with it an atmosphere of unrest. The threat of a general strike following this violence provided an excuse for the Prime Minister, General Metaxas, to impose a new regime. On 4 August 1936, with the King's permission, he suspended the constitution, declared martial law and established a dictatorship giving him unlimited powers.

In former days, political arguments had only occurred when Pavlos Koralis visited and brought friends to the house. Nowadays they raged between Thanasis and Panos. Even from early teenage years, they had opposing views on how to deal with their country's problems. Thanasis was in favour of the general and even admired Metaxas' own role models, among whom was Mussolini. Panos, on the other hand, did not like the rigid order that Metaxas represented. In fact, he was not keen on discipline in any form. Sometimes Kyría Koralis had to remind them that if their father visited she would have to tell him of any bad behaviour. They were too old and tall now to be disciplined by her but the threat of their father's wrath was enough to make them conform.

One of his rare visits coincided with a bout of rebellious behaviour from Panos.

It was the night of the weekly meeting with his EON squad. *Ethniki Organosis Neolaias*, the National Youth Organisation, was the new movement into which the older three siblings had enrolled. Metaxas had established the organisation shortly after imposing his dictatorship, and soon it would no longer be voluntary to belong.

Panos hated going and had skipped it.

'Why should I go?' he demanded. '*Why?*'

He was now fifteen and almost half a metre taller than his grandmother.

'Because it's a good thing to go to,' she replied. 'You learn some discipline there.'

'Discipline?' he retorted scornfully.

She did not know that Panos had been missing meetings for some time. He detested everything about EON, from the intense right-wing propaganda to the fascistic double axe on the uniform.

By contrast, Thanasis looked forward to the military drills they had to perform and was already aiming to rise up the ranks. Margarita actively embraced it too. She loved the outfit and happily echoed the mantra that the woman's place was in the home.

Panos had chosen an unfortunate day to challenge his grandmother. Their father had come back earlier that afternoon and was taking a rest in his mother's little bedroom. The slamming of the door in the small apartment had woken him.

As he got out of bed, Pavlos Koralis could hear his son's voice, slightly raised, and then his own mother's authority being challenged. Everyone knew what the consequences of rebellion against the Metaxas regime could be. Refusing to be part of EON could result in expulsion from school, reduced job opportunities and who knew what other shame? Fury surged through him.

Themis was sitting at the kitchen table. As soon as her brother had come in, she wanted to jump up and warn him, but it was too late. The bedroom door had already flown open.

It was months since he had seen his children but Pavlos Koralis did not approach Panos from behind in order to give him a surprise embrace. Instead he gave him a mighty shove in the back.

Panos went flying towards his grandmother who, without a moment of hesitation, stepped to one side to avoid the human missile. He fell heavily, his forehead catching the corner of the table before he landed.

Themis shrieked.

Panos had no time to brace himself and his body hit the floor hard. His head seemed to bounce as it made contact with the tiles. Within a second Themis was kneeling down beside him.

'Panos . . . Panos . . . Can you hear me?'

She looked up at her grandmother, who was vigorously crossing herself.

'He's dead, *Yiayiá*,' she whispered through her tears. 'I think he's dead.'

Kyría Koralis was soon calmly soaking a piece of rag to dab at the cut on her grandson's face. A purple lump was already appearing.

After a few seconds of unconsciousness, the boy began to stir.

'He'll be all right, *agápi mou*,' she said, caught between her love for her grandson and her loyalty to his father. 'Don't you worry.'

For Themis, it was a moment of lost innocence. She glared at her father. How could he have done such a thing?

Panos came to, without the slightest idea what had taken place. Even now, he did not know that a hand had pushed him, and certainly not whose. His father had left the room.

Kyría Koralis knelt on the floor to nurse her grandson and tend to the cut on his head.

'What happened?' he said weakly. 'My head hurts. It really hurts.'

'You fell,' his grandmother answered simply.

He closed his eyes and Kyría Koralis made a gesture to Themis, a forefinger held tight against her lips, which instructed the child to say nothing.

Themis understood. The violent action of her father must not be revealed, not to anyone. She must say nothing.

Having established that his son had survived the fall, Pavlos Koralis crept out of the apartment without saying goodbye. He returned to Piraeus from where his ship would be leaving the following day.

When Margarita and Thanasis returned from their EON meeting, dressed in their smart blue uniforms, they found Panos in bed with a bandaged head. Once they had learnt the story of his 'fall' and reassured themselves that he was already on the mend, they gathered at the kitchen table to eat dinner. A plate was taken in to Panos, but it was not touched.

Margarita was full of news about a parade that she had just taken part in.

'I was put right out in the front!' she gushed, rigidly holding out her right arm to demonstrate her ability to hold the salute. 'I was one of the leaders!'

'That's wonderful, darling. You're doing so well,' enthused Kyría Koralis.

'I did something new today as well,' Thanasis interjected, not wanting his sister to be the centre of attention. 'We were taught how to hold a gun.'

There was a note of triumph in his voice, as if he had won a battle.

Themis chewed her food silently but could not swallow. Nobody ever expected her to say much at the table, so it was easy for her

33

to keep her thoughts to herself. She would have to join EON soon but the only reason she might want to be part of such an organisation would be to learn how to use a gun. That sounded interesting and useful. Nothing else about it appealed.

She looked from Margarita to Thanasis to her *yiayiá*, overwhelmed by the sense that Panos had been betrayed.

Anger, fear and shame mingled inside her. In a short space of time, a crack as invisible as the one in Panos' skull had divided her from the rest of the family.

Chapter Three

FOR SOME TIME after, Themis felt a distinct sense of isolation. With five people living in such close proximity this should have been impossible.

It was more than half a decade since they had moved into the Patissia apartment, and in these years the children had grown and now filled the space almost to bursting point, the boys with their lanky adolescent limbs and Margarita with curves and self-assurance that developed by the day. At the generously sized table, they now elbowed each other to snatch second helpings, even though their grandmother cooked three times as much as when they had first moved in.

Relationships between the children were as volatile as those between politicians in the outside world. Panos and Thanasis never stopped arguing and wrestling with each other in an endless fraternal power struggle. In addition to the new scar on his forehead, Panos had a few others, such was his brother's superior strength. It was not only between the boys that battles raged. Margarita and Panos constantly squabbled over everything and nothing. Between Margarita and Themis there was no obvious argument, but the older girl never missed an opportunity to be spiteful. This made life behind the closed door of their bedroom a torture for Themis. Margarita commanded all the space in their room, twisted her little sister's ears until they hurt, careful never to leave a mark, and kicked her so hard that she often ended up sleeping on the floor or creeping out into the living room. Instead of the quiet space Themis craved, she was then kept awake by the eerie sound of her grandmother grinding her teeth. The youngest child of the family was too proud to cry or complain, knowing that doing so would only invite new and cunning cruelty from her older sister.

The place that had felt so secure and homely when they moved in was now full of conflict and discomfort. Themis had no refuge within the home. School became her sanctuary, an environment where she felt safe and free. The high white walls of the school-yard seemed like a prison to some, but for Themis they were like a warm embrace from her very first day. As autumn approached, Themis looked forward to the new term.

The schoolroom itself was austere, with rows of wooden desks, hard chairs and nothing on the walls but a cross and an image of the Virgin Mary. The focus of the room was the teacher, Kyría Anteriotis, on her raised dais, and the blackboard behind her. There was no choice of seats. The surname that fate had dealt her determined that Themis should sit between two boys, Glentakis and Koveos, who teased her whenever the teacher's back was turned. Regardless of their intentions, they failed to distract Themis. Their endeavours only helped her to develop superlative powers of concentration. For the first few years of school, Themis had little competition in the classroom apart from a rather shy boy who occasionally got his hand in the air before her, and whether they were learning algebra or grammar, she rarely gave a wrong answer. She focused her attention on lessons, and had little awareness of anything but the *tac tac tac* of chalk on blackboard.

One day, a few weeks into the term, when the teacher had scratched an equation on the board, and then looked over her shoulder for the answer, it was neither Themis nor the timid Giorgos who was invited to provide it. Another voice called out the solution. Someone else had solved a mathematical problem before either of them. It must be someone new.

Themis looked round to see who it might be.

Past the familiar faces of forty other classmates, she could see a head of dark hair and a pale forehead. Themis craned her neck to get a better view.

Not only was the girl's voice unfamiliar, but she had a strange accent. Themis turned back to her desk and wrote down the answer she had given.

As soon as the bell sounded for a break, all the children poured out of the room. The new girl was already at the far end of the yard by the time Themis got outside. As she approached, Themis saw that the newcomer was engaged in a careful process of picking the needles off a pine cone, fallen from a tree that grew by the wall.

Themis made her way towards her, dodging all the other children who were engaged in skipping routines or games of chase. The girl was alone, but there was nothing lonely in her demeanour. She looked around her as she dismantled the cone, surveying her classmates, contented in her own company, as if she was not even expecting anyone to speak to her. Themis' heart was beating faster than usual, sensing even before they spoke that she would be her friend.

It was autumn, so the girl was wearing a woollen coat. It was dull red, frayed at the hem, with sleeves rolled over several times to reveal her hands. Themis herself was wearing an old brown jacket of Margarita's that was slightly too large for her, but this girl's coat looked like one that she would never grow in to. Just like Themis, she had dirty socks but her footwear was even more scuffed.

From time to time this new girl fixed her eyes on someone, not bothered by how they might interpret her stares. She exuded the confidence of someone older than eleven.

Themis stood a few metres away, leaning nonchalantly against the wall, looking down at her worn, dusty boots. She needed a moment to gather the courage to approach the newcomer.

She loitered like this for some time and then the bell rang. It was time to return to the classroom. Themis grabbed her opportunity, falling into step next to the girl. As they reached the main door, Themis saw her hesitate. Left or right? There were classrooms on either side.

'We go this way,' said Themis, confidently, taking the stranger's sleeve and pulling her in the right direction.

Both girls hung up their coats on the same peg at the back of the classroom and, as they were walking in, there was just enough time for Themis to ask her name.

'Fotini,' came the proud reply.

A moment later the teacher entered and the next lesson began. By the end of the fifty minutes, Themis knew with certainty that someone even more studious than her sat a few rows behind.

When the bell went again at the end of the school day, Themis could not pack her books fast enough and was soon pushing her way past her classmates. She stopped at Fotini's desk and found her still lining up pencils in a wooden box and carefully packing her exercise books into an old satchel.

Fotini looked up. She had blue eyes, very fair skin and almost black hair arranged into two thick plaits that hung down like mooring ropes on either side of her face. She gave Themis a broad smile.

The girls already felt familiar with one another, since they had both spent the afternoon vying for the teacher's attention. Kyría Anteriotis had successfully given them equal chances to answer her questions.

They unhooked their coats, left the classroom together and walked across the yard to the gates. It appeared that they were going in the same direction.

Themis rattled off her questions and Fotini dutifully answered.

'Where are you from?'

'What's your family name?'

'Do you have brothers or sisters?'

'Where did you go to school before?'

When the interrogation finally ended, it was Fotini's turn to find out about Themis.

'And where do you live?' she asked eventually.

They had been walking along the main street for ten minutes and had reached a corner.

'Just up here,' Themis indicated. 'At the end of this road is a square. And we live in the square.'

Fotini smiled.

'We don't live so far away from you,' she murmured.

They said their goodbyes and laughed at their simultaneous chorus of 'See you tomorrow!'

That evening, Themis was bubbling over with the excitement of having a new friend.

'She's *so* clever,' she told her grandmother.

'What, cleverer than my little Themis?' teased Kyría Koralis.

'Surely not possible,' said her older sister sarcastically.

'Anyway, she is called Fotini, she has no brothers or sisters, she's two months older than me and her family comes from Smyrna.'

'So they're refugees?' interrupted Thanasis, suspiciously.

'Why do you ask that?' challenged Panos.

'She just moved to Athens. And before that she was living in Kavala. And now she is my friend,' said Themis emphatically.

'Well, that's nice for you,' said Margarita, cattily. 'You need a friend.'

The evening meal continued with plenty of teasing, some of it kind, some of it less so.

Themis could hardly wait for the next morning. Her brothers and sister went to school in the other direction, so she walked alone. That day she almost ran in order to be in the yard before Fotini got there.

As she turned into a sidestreet, she caught a glimpse of a faded crimson coat. Fotini was ahead of her and her walk turned into a run.

'Fotini! Fotini! Wait for me.'

The other girl spun round.

'Hello, Themis.'

They clasped both hands like friends acquainted since birth and then strode together into the yard.

There was no question of Fotini moving desk to be nearer to Themis. She had joined the class after the start of the year and would stay in the back row. Both girls waited eagerly for the breaks between lessons. Sometimes they joined in with skipping games, and sometimes when the sun shone, bringing unexpected winter warmth, they sat on a bench and shared their stories. Their respective portraits of the past were formed from a mixture of what they had been told by adults as well as sensory recollections of their own. Both of them had experienced dust, hunger, tears, tiredness and loss, but it would not be until later on that they shared the details of these.

'So why did your parents move from Smyrna to Kavala and then here?' asked Themis with the curiosity of one who had never left the city of Athens.

'My parents didn't want to leave Asia Minor,' Fotini said. 'But they had no choice. They stayed in Kavala for a few years because my father had always been in the tobacco industry and there was plenty of work there.'

Themis knew about the Asia Minor Campaign. After all, she had grown up hearing people argue about it and the million or so refugees who had arrived with little more than they stood up in. Most of them were poor – and she remembered her father's resentment at how it had changed his city.

'There's a reason they call it the *catastrophe*,' said Fotini firmly. 'Because it was. They were happy and then suddenly everything changed. Everything that was good just vanished.'

'And is that why you have no brothers and sisters?' asked Themis.

A puzzled look passed across Fotini's face. It was something she had never thought of before.

'They were hungry a lot, so I suppose it might have been worse if there were more of us to feed . . .'

'So what happened after Smyrna?'

'They were taken by boat to Kavala. And one of my aunts was already there so they all lived together. I liked certain things about it.'

'Such as?'

'It was by the sea. A beautiful city. With a huge aqueduct running across it, like a giant bridge. And it had an old castle. And lots of old buildings and little streets.' Fotini's eyes shone as she described it. 'It was nothing like Athens.'

'Do you like Athens?'

'Not yet,' she answered. 'But I hope I will, in time.'

At the point where Themis would go one way and Fotini another, the two girls stopped and sat on a low wall. They hardly paused for breath.

Themis began to share her own family 'catastrophes': the collapse of the old house and the departure of their mother. She admitted to Fotini that, since her parents' wedding photograph had been put away, her mother's image had faded.

'I can't remember her face now,' she said to her friend. 'But *Yiayiá* once told me that I look a bit like her.'

'You have your father, though?' said Fotini.

'In a way,' she answered, saving that story for another day.

The following week, as they walked home, Themis told her more about the mansion that had fallen down.

'I'll take you to see the ruin one day,' she said. 'I think it's still sitting there.'

'There were mansions in Kavala too,' said Fotini. 'But they belonged to bad people who owned tobacco factories.'

'Why were they bad?' asked Themis.

'Well, the owner of the one that my parents worked in . . .'

'Your parents? Your mother as well?'

Themis did not know many people whose mothers worked. Staying at home, as her mother always had, was common even in humble families, where extra money would have been welcome.

'Yes. They worked together. My mother says that they sat together on the sorting floor. Men and women together, Christians and Muslims. Separating the good leaves from the bad and grading them.'

'But . . .'

Themis was open-mouthed as Fotini continued.

'I think it was all right sometimes, but their hours were very long. And they seemed to get longer and longer.'

Fotini paused. 'Didn't *your* mother have to work?' she asked.

Themis hesitated.

'When we were in the mansion she worked all day long in the house . . .'

Themis then casually dropped in that her father was mostly away at sea, so she and her siblings were looked after by their grand-mother.

Themis' mention of her father prompted Fotini to talk about hers.

'My father is dead,' she said. 'That's why we moved to Athens.'

Themis did not know what to say. At least her own mother was still alive somewhere, and her father did make an occasional appearance.

'I didn't see my father very often either,' Fotini went on. 'He always came back late at night from meetings and even when he got home he and my mother carried on talking and writing his speeches.'

'What speeches?'

'To the workers. At the factory. He had big black shadows around his eyes and he never stopped reading newspapers and books. He was always up until late at the kitchen table.

'But then one night, my aunt was looking after me and my mother was even later home than usual. For some reason I couldn't sleep so my aunt made me a cup of warm milk. She seemed anxious too. A bit later I heard the sound of a key in the door. My mother.'

Themis leaned forward. In suspense.

'Her face was dirty and even in the dim light I could see that there was a graze on her cheek, as if she had fallen over.

'She was trying to speak but not getting any words out. Once she calmed down, she told us everything. There had been a demonstration. Workers wanted more pay and better conditions to work in. The police had attacked them. Some had been injured.'

'And your father . . .?'

'He had been killed.'

For a moment, a rare silence descended between them. Themis felt awkward, unsure of what to say.

Finally Fotini spoke.

'All of that was a while ago. We packed up our things again and eventually came to Athens. My mother said she didn't care how poor we would be. She couldn't stay in a place where the bosses killed their workers. She wouldn't be a slave. It was an injustice. That was the word she used.'

Injustice. Themis had heard the word plenty of times but mostly in relation to squabbles among the siblings: unequal portions of cake, or exclusion from a game and, for herself, being Margarita's scapegoat.

Fotini was crying now and for the first time Themis understood what it was to feel sadness for someone she had never met. She too wept for Fotini's loss.

At the dinner table that night, Themis recounted the story of Fotini's misfortunes to her grandmother and siblings.

'So your new friend is a communist?' said Thanasis.

'No,' said Themis, who managed to face up to her big brother in a way that she could not with her sister.

'It sounds as if her father was defending his rights,' Panos retorted, defending his little sister. 'I heard about a trade union in Kavala. They were protesting—'

'Why?' Margarita cut in. 'What's the point?'

Panos was intolerant of his sister.

'What's the point of protesting?' demanded Panos. 'To stop people being mistreated. To make the weak stronger—'

'Well, he isn't strong now, is he?' his sister retorted cruelly.

'He wasn't just acting for himself,' said Panos. 'But that would never occur to you, would it? That anyone might make a sacrifice for someone else?'

'Like Jesus, you mean?' asked Themis, who had recently been obliged to learn parts of the liturgy by heart in religious education.

'Don't compare a communist to the Lord!' Thanasis glared, slamming his fist down and making the table jump.

'They're not so different,' Panos said firmly in support.

'*Theé mou*,' muttered Kyría Koralis, appealing to God to stop the pair of them arguing.

The argument continued viciously between the two boys and Themis wondered if God ever listened to her *yiayiá*'s incessant prayers. She had certainly not noticed it.

'How dare you say that? How dare you suggest that the Church is on the side of those people!' shouted Thanasis.

'You mean trade unionists?'

'They're scum. They'll wreck this country.'

'What? By trying to make sure their families have enough to eat? That makes them scum?'

'Feeding their families? You think this is their main aim? I don't believe it. Most of those immigrants are just troublemakers.'

'The refugees didn't come because they wanted to. You're a fool, Thanasis. They had no choice.'

'You're saying the politicians forced them to come and live here? To crowd us out? To take our jobs?'

'You know it wasn't like that,' Panos tried to reason. 'It was the government that took the decisions that led to the war. So it was their fault that all those people had to leave their homes and everything they owned.'

'And they welcomed them into Greece so that they could make trouble, did they?'

Themis' eyes went from brother to brother. Panos and Thanasis rarely agreed on anything, but the strength of feeling in this altercation was even stronger than usual and she knew that she had been responsible for igniting this particular flame. She looked across the table at Margarita, who seemed to be enjoying the fight.

'Tell me,' Thanasis screamed, thrusting his forefinger towards Panos, with undisguised aggression. 'Do these communists have the right to go against the law?'

Their grandmother had got up to busy herself cutting up fruit for them all, but when Thanasis crashed a fork down on his plate and stormed out of the room, she returned to the table.

'*Panagiá mou*, Mother of God,' she snapped at Panos. 'Now see what you have done. Why do you children have to argue all the time?'

'Because we disagree on things,' retorted Margarita, who felt she had a right to be rude to everyone, including her grandmother. 'Even though Panos is always wrong.'

Panos good-naturedly cuffed his sister round the ear.

'Come on, Margarita, have a heart. This new friend of Themis . . . She lost her father.'

'I mean it, Panos. You're wrong. Anyone would think you don't love your motherland.'

Her brother refrained from answering. He got up from the table and silently left the apartment.

Themis had sat quietly, as one of her siblings described her new friend's family as though they were criminals. She resolved *never* to repeat to Fotini what Thanasis had said. The cleft that had already opened within the family was beginning to widen.

Ten minutes later, Thanasis appeared at the door of his bedroom dressed in cadet uniform, the hat tilted at a jaunty angle. He was soon joined by Margarita, also very smart in her EON blue.

'It's the final practice for Friday's parade,' she said proudly to her grandmother. 'You'll be coming, won't you?'

'Yes, *agápi mou*. We'll be there to watch, won't we, Themis?'

Themis was still sitting at the kitchen table, her books now spread out in front of her. Her mind was far away. Why, she was asking herself, would Jesus not be on the communists' side? Did he not say that the poor should come unto him? Did he not want everyonc to be equal? They had been taken to church often enough and she was sure that this was what the priest had said. Perhaps the world was full of such contradictions and she had simply not noticed them before.

Chapter Four

THE FRIENDSHIP BETWEEN Themis and Fotini grew over the following months. Each morning they met on their way to school and were together for the whole day. One afternoon, as they walked home, deep in conversation as usual, Themis suddenly suggested a detour.

'I want to show you our old house,' she said brightly.

Taking a circuitous route and occasionally stopping to ask someone the way, they finally found themselves in Antigonis Street. Themis had a dim memory of how it had looked, but it did not match what she saw that day. From end to end the street was now lined on both sides with new buildings. Nothing remained of the old houses and all the trees had been cut down.

Themis could not hide her dismay. She rarely thought of her mother, but she came to her mind now and she was glad that Eleftheria Koralis was not there to see the place she must have loved so utterly erased.

'It didn't look like this before,' she said quietly to her friend as they turned away.

She did not breathe a word to her family about what she had seen.

When one academic year rolled into the next, Fotini was moved into her correct alphabetical place, next to Themis. Karanidis and Koralis. The two girls were inseparable, sharing crushes, conversation and copies of books. The only other person in the class who provided any academic competition was the boy called Giorgos. He was especially good at mathematics but his stutter sometimes prevented him getting the answer out. Teased by many of the other children, Giorgos was pleased to be accepted by the girls. If he put his hand in the air, they always gave him the chance to answer first.

Arguments in the Koralis home had intensified. What might once have been simple fraternal competition between Thanasis and Panos had metamorphosed into a war of opposing ideals, bitterly fought and with neither side having any hope of achieving victory, big or small. Perhaps if their father had been a presence in the house he would have been able to douse the flames, but Pavlos Koralis had not visited for almost a year. Some while before, he had sent a letter from America saying that he was planning to stay there for the foreseeable future and would be sending money back on a regular basis. Economic necessity had obliged him to start a new life and the United States was a place of unlimited possibilities.

Kyría Koralis broke selected parts of this news to the children, all of whom received it with *sang froid* except for Margarita, who adored her father and had always eagerly awaited his colourful and exotic gifts. She wept inconsolably for days and took the black-and-white framed photograph of him in naval uniform and put it on her bedside table.

Life continued as before and, from time to time, some American dollars arrived and were divided up by Kyría Koralis with small amounts evenly allocated to each of the children. Thanasis opened a bank account for himself, Panos used the money for books, Margarita always wanted new clothes and Themis asked for something each week so that she could have a few coins in her pocket. Themis was in her last year at elementary school and the others were at the nearby *gymnásio*, with Thanasis considering what to do next. His ambition was to train in the police force.

At mealtimes, Kyría Koralis could not make her voice heard above the raised tones of her grandsons, so she had given up trying. It was not simply a war of words. Their aggression with each other often exploded into something more physical and she was ashamed that she could not control them.

Themis often described to Fotini the relentlessness of the arguments and noise in the apartment, her sister's meanness towards her and the constant slamming of doors. It was no environment for study, and with the pair of them about to move up to the next school, Fotini suggested that they could both go to her place to do their homework.

'My mother won't mind,' she said. 'She doesn't get home until much later, in any case.'

As they wandered towards the street where Fotini lived, they each chewed on *kouloúria*, the fresh buns that Themis had bought with her drachmas. It was a steep climb away from the busy road, past several churches and into a warren of ever-narrowing streets where washing was strung from house to house.

Even the road surface changed. It had been raining earlier that day and Themis' feet slipped in the mud as they walked up the slope. Small children stood in doorways as they passed, looking at them silently, their faces sullen, their feet bare.

Themis had assumed that Fotini lived somewhere just like her, in an apartment building. Now, as they turned into an alleyway, its width only just big enough for them to walk next to each other, she saw single-storey dwellings, very different from anything in Patissia. It was hard to tell if they were old or new, temporary or permanent, such was the flimsiness of their construction.

A few buildings down on the left, Fotini stopped and pushed open a grey door.

Themis watched her friend cross the room to light a gas lamp and the yellowish glow it created was just enough to show her the scale of the single room that was Fotini's home.

At the far end, there was another door, which Fotini opened to let in more light before propping it back with a bucket.

Themis looked out and saw a courtyard, which was clearly shared with many other residents of the street, and noticed a woman pinning up sheets, and a child handing her wooden pegs as she did so.

Close by was a tank of water standing on a metal frame and next to it a flimsy curtain. That must be where Fotini has to wash, thought Themis with embarrassment. Both girls were beginning to feel self-conscious about their constantly changing bodies, and she found herself cringing at the awkwardness of such public bathing.

There was an enamel jug sitting on a small dresser and Fotini carefully lifted the little cloth edged with beads that protected the contents from flies, took some cups from a cupboard and filled them. She held one out to Themis and smiled.

'*Kalós órises*,' she said. 'Welcome to our home.'

Themis' eyes had now adjusted to the gloom and she looked around. It was impossible to conceal her curiosity.

'The carpet,' said Fotini, 'is the only big thing they brought from our home in Smyrna.'

Themis looked down at her feet, conscious of the flecks of mud that had stuck to her shoes. The worn rug she was standing on had an indistinct pattern in shades of brown, not so unlike the one she remembered from Antigonis Street, and she was suddenly anxious that she might have brought dirt into the house. In the Koralis apartment, shoes always had to be left at the door.

'My mother always reminded me it was carried thousands of kilometres from Smyrna,' continued Fotini. 'So there was no question of leaving it in Kavala.'

She pointed to a small picture nailed to the wall.

'And that's a painting of our village. That was the other thing we brought with us. It travelled all the way in my mother's skirt pocket. Along with a photo.'

When they had left Asia Minor, Fotini's parents brought almost nothing with them. And from what Themis could see, they could still count all their possessions on one hand. For her, it was a moment of stark realisation. This was what Panos meant when he talked about refugees. Most of them struggled, even now, almost two decades since they had fled from their homes.

Fotini's mother had made the best of the small space in which they lived. There was a narrow bed in the corner, neatly made with an embroidered cover over it, though Themis could not see where a second person would sleep. Three chairs were tucked under the wooden kitchen table, and on another smaller table sat a metal basin, inside which nestled a jumble of pots and pans. A small set of shelves was attached to the wall with a few plates and cups and, against the wall, there was a low wooden bench, on which rested some embroidered cushions. Beneath the bench there were several piles of books.

Fotini drew a chair out from under the kitchen table for her friend and then sat down opposite her. Above them was a photograph of a couple of indeterminate age, their arms hanging stiffly down by their sides.

It must be the one Fotini had referred to, thought Themis.

'My father and mother. On their wedding day,' Fotini said matter-of-factly.

'Oh,' Themis responded, not quite knowing what to say.

'Let's study,' continued Fotini, eagerly taking her books out of her bag and opening one of them.

For an hour or more they read in silence and then moved on to some mathematics homework. They finished almost simultaneously, noting that they had reached the same solution in each case, but via a different route. As usual, Fotini's workings out were written carefully in the margins. Themis' were messier, her handwriting much bigger, some of her 5s and 6s indistinguishable. She could take up a whole page for one equation, while Fotini could fit three in the same space.

'You're so neat and tidy,' Themis teased. 'Not like me.'

'My father told me not to waste any paper. It doesn't grow on trees, he said!'

The girls laughed together, but Themis knew there was a serious point: that people with little can never afford to waste what they have.

They were still laughing when the door from the street swung open. A very slender woman with translucently pale skin and huge oval eyes, her hair pulled back from her face, came in.

Fotini got up and went over to embrace her mother.

'This is my friend, Themis,' she said proudly.

'Very nice to meet you,' said the woman, smiling. 'Fotini hasn't stopped talking about you since the day she first went to her new school!'

She put a small basket down on the dresser, took out two packages and began to unwrap them. Themis marvelled at the long dark plait that reached well below her waist. She seemed in a hurry to prepare something with the ingredients.

Themis was used to her grandmother's large pan and was conscious that, over the small gas ring, Fotini's mother was using a diminutive saucepan.

'It's getting quite late, you know,' she commented.

Neither of the girls had kept track of the hour. They had no means of doing so.

'Won't your family be waiting for you?'

'Yes . . . I must go home,' said Themis, realising that she might have outstayed her welcome. She started packing her books away as the aroma of *fasoláda,* bean soup, began to drift over her.

Fotini walked with Themis to the main street. She would never have been able to retrace her steps without a guide.

'See you tomorrow,' said Fotini. 'It was nice that you came.'

As she entered her own home, Themis saw her siblings already sitting at the table. Her grandmother was about to serve from two large pans that were almost full to the brim, one of stew, the other of *hórta.* A whole loaf sat uncut on the table in front of them. Themis realised that the small amount that Fotini's mother had been preparing might be all that she could afford. It would certainly explain why they had not invited her to stay.

'Where've you been, then?' asked Thanasis.

'And why are you so late?' demanded Margarita.

As the plates were passed around, any answer that Themis might have given would have been lost in the clatter of crockery and cutlery and water splashing into glasses. She had no wish to tell them where she had been. The past few hours had been contented ones, and she was not going to allow her siblings to destroy the memory.

Margarita was persistent, however, and in spite of her resolve Themis finally shared the truth of where she had been. As she had feared, it immediately provoked rage from Thanasis.

'She is not Greek in the same way that we are,' he said adamantly.

'But she speaks Greek, she is Orthodox, she was baptised . . .'

'Her parents—'

'Her father is *dead*,' protested Themis. 'He was killed! I told you that.'

'Her mother, then. Is she still a communist?'

Margarita joined the onslaught against her little sister.

'So what does the EON slogan mean to your friend? "One Nation, One King, One Leader, One Youth"?'

Themis remembered the conversation with her friend. She knew Fotini's mind almost as well as her own.

Thanasis spoke again, this time more gently. Even he could see that his younger sister's eyes were brimming with tears.

'Who is her mother's "leader", Themis? Is she obedient to Metaxas? Or does she support those who want to pull down the regime?'

Themis had no time to answer before Panos leapt in, not just to defend Themis but all those who objected to the dictatorship they lived under.

'You two just can't see it, can you?' he shouted, waving his finger at both Thanasis and Margarita. 'It doesn't bother you that Metaxas admires a regime like Italy's. And crushes the opposition with his bullies.'

As usual when her four grandchildren were divided into warring camps, Kyría Koralis busied herself preparing food, washing dishes and reordering kitchen utensils that were already in place. She made the occasional plea to them to keep their voices down and sometimes, as she did now, interrupted with a political point that betrayed her own allegiance.

'It's correct that Metaxas looks up to Mussolini, Panos, but I think the admiration is mutual.'

'Hitler admires the Greeks too. And we should all be proud of that!' added Margarita.

'She's right, Panos,' said Thanasis triumphantly. 'Everyone knows that the Germans admire the Ancient Greeks!'

It was true that the Ancient Greeks were depicted in Nazi text-books as their 'nearest racial brothers' but Panos reacted with scorn.

'They no longer exist!' he said. 'We're not the same people. And the sooner we stop pretending we are, the better.'

'Calm down, Panos,' urged Thanasis. 'It's a great thing for Greece that Hitler respects Hellenistic ideals.'

'I can't listen to this. And *don't* tell me to calm down!'

Thanasis rarely failed to provoke his younger brother to anger.

Margarita sat with her hands clapped over her ears as her brothers began to shout.

Thanasis was not to be deterred. Now that he had stirred his younger brother to boiling point, he got in his stride, feeling in command of the debate, all his facts at his fingertips.

'Look what great things Hitler is doing for his country! It's about leadership and discipline, Panos.'

'He even has a youth organisation,' Margarita chipped in. 'Lots of countries are following the same path.'

'That's the only thing you've said that I agree with,' shouted Panos. 'That fascists all follow the same path.' Then a note of despair came to his voice: 'But where will that path lead?'

For a few moments, there was silence. No one seemed to have an answer to this.

Themis wiped her nose on her sleeve. She desperately wanted her brothers to stop arguing.

Margarita sat there smirking. In her view, Thanasis had gained the upper hand. Beneath the table, she swung her leg, occasionally kicking her sister's shin.

Thanasis got up from the table, sighing as he did so.

'You're just so stupid, Panos. You can't see anything clearly, can you?'

Panos did not reply. The argument had played itself out.

Themis was used to seeing this happen and even though it was a mention of her own best friend and her mother that had sparked this particular altercation, she herself had hardly spoken a word. Instead, she had felt the heat from the raging fire that was, as usual, instantly extinguished when one of her brothers left the room.

For Themis, the most important thing she had learnt that after-noon was that not everyone lived as they did. As she lay in bed that night, the image of Fotini's mother carefully measuring out a few dried beans remained in her mind until she slept.

The following morning, her friend was full of chatter.

'My mother was so happy you came to our house,' Fotini said. 'You were the first guest we've had.'

'Can I come again?'

'Of course you can. As often as you are allowed,' answered Fotini quickly.

From that day, a new routine began. Every day, after school, Themis went to Fotini's house in the narrow backstreet and the two girls diligently studied together. Although it was noisy out in the yard, where women gossiped and babies cried, nothing could disturb their concentration.

Themis always stayed until Fotini's mother appeared. They exchanged a few friendly words and then she left as the aroma of cooking began to rise.

Their schoolwork was exemplary, delivered on time and scoring the highest marks. There was only one evening in the week when the pattern was broken and that was when they were obliged to attend an EON meeting. It was now compulsory for girls their age.

'If we just mouth the words of the songs, then we're not really singing them,' said Fotini.

'So we won't really mean them . . .?'

'No. We won't,' said Fotini firmly. 'We'll sing different words in our heads so we'll be thinking the opposite. My mother was annoyed that I had told you what happened to my father,' she went on. 'But I can't forget it.'

'Of course you can't, Fotini. And nor will I, now,' said Themis, still shocked by her own family's antagonism. 'But maybe she thinks it's not safe for you to tell people how he died.'

Fotini shrugged. 'I am not ashamed of it and I won't pretend it didn't happen.'

Fotini's mother's attempts to warn her daughter to be careful about what she expressed were brushed away. It was impossible to knock the rebellious streak out of Fotini.

'I hate this dressing up as a soldier,' Fotini complained one day, as she was putting on her EON hat. 'Are we pretending to be at war? Who am I meant to be fighting? Tell me!'

Her mother did not respond. War was closer than anyone imagined and the question of whose side to take soon became a topic of national conversation. In September 1939, Hitler invaded Poland, and Britain and France declared war on Germany. During the following months, the conflict escalated and it seemed that every country must decide who to support.

Even Margarita, who had always loved her EON activities, found the possibility of war anathema. She blocked her ears when everyone began to talk of it. She wanted a different life. While Themis' closest friend lived in the poorest area of Athens, her own best friend, Marina, lived in the most well-to-do. Marina's mother had beautiful clothes and went to the hairdresser twice a week. Margarita wanted to be like her and nurtured aspirations beyond Patissia. As everyone else in her family debated between left and right and what was happening in Europe, Margarita daydreamed that she belonged to another family, and her destiny lay elsewhere. She began to look for evidence.

One morning in early December, she found herself alone in the apartment, and could not resist the temptation to pry into places that she knew were out of bounds. These pieces of 'grown-up furniture', as she thought of them, included a desk that had belonged to her father. Having riffled through its drawers, she quickly established that paperwork was generally dull and put it all back. It was not in the same order but she could not imagine that anyone would ever notice the mess. Curiosity then led her to a small cupboard in her grandmother's room. When she turned the handle and found it locked, her interest was immediately aroused. It must hold something interesting and secret.

The key, tucked in the drawer of the bedside cabinet, was easy to find and the mechanism, though stiff, eventually turned. The cupboard was full of neatly folded clothes and Margarita carefully picked up the first garment and held it up to herself. The dress was half the width of the plump fifteen-year-old but finding the buttons down the back already open, she stepped into it, pulling it on over her dull green jumper and brown woollen skirt. Her nose was filled with the smell of damp and dust, and catching a glimpse of herself in the mirror she was filled with disgust. An image of her mother wearing this dress, curled up on her bed, lifeless and sad, leapt from somewhere in her memory. Quickly pulling it off, Margarita bundled it up and tossed it back in the cupboard.

She had destabilised the pile of clothes, however, and it toppled forward, to make an untidy heap that spilled out of the cupboard and on to the floor. Now she could see that something had been concealed by the clothing. A box. It was about the size of a large book, but three times as deep. She bent down to lift it out. It was heavier than she expected but she picked it up and sat on her grandmother's bed to open it.

Only in a children's story about Turkish pirates had she seen such a sight: a chest spilling over with gold and silver, pearls and gems. She picked up the first item and found it entwined with another, chains and clasps were knotted together, with bracelets almost impossible to extricate from beads and brooches.

For the next hour she patiently separated every item and lay them on the bed, sorting one from another. She hummed as she worked, happy, excited, her eyes sparkling with joy at her discovery. This was treasure.

Once everything was unravelled she stood back and admired the collection. There were many necklaces (some with pearls, two with diamonds), pendants (one shaped like a snake with emerald eyes and another with a large central ruby) and a gold bracelet with a row of sapphires set in the centre. There were several rings too.

Margarita did not know that they had been part of her mother's dowry, along with the house in Antigonis Street, and at one time might have been worth more than the house itself. When she had left for the psychiatric hospital, Eleftheria had taken just one small bag of clothes and Kyría Koralis had promised her that everything else would follow. The first time her husband visited, he realised that his wife would not need any more of her clothing as she was mostly confined to bed. As a result nothing more was sent.

One by one, Margarita tried on each piece of jewellery and looked at herself in the mirror, carefully putting the item down when she took it off. Then she experimented with different combinations: amber with emerald, ruby with pearls, silver with gold, amethyst with diamonds. The number of permutations seemed infinite and she had no idea how much time passed.

After she had put everything on at least once, she tried more extravagant pairings and then many items at once, until she had almost everything on at the same time – three necklaces, brooches running down like military medals from shoulder to chest, and bracelets from wrist to elbow. She pouted and pranced in front of the mirror, as if being photographed for a magazine, strutting as she imagined that actresses and models might strut, standing with her back to the mirror and throwing glances over her shoulder. And all the time she smiled. All their years hidden in the darkness had not dulled these gems.

Margarita kept catching glimpses of herself in the mirror. Having never owned or even had the opportunity to try them, she now realised that gold and silver and precious stones cast a magic spell. They made her more beautiful. This must be why they were so coveted and why women desired them so much.

Margarita wanted to be like one of the glamorous women who went to Zonars, the new café in central Athens. She had glimpsed them through the gleaming plate-glass windows, sipping their coffee with gloved hands. In the winter they wore mink, and in the summer pastel silks. Their hair was sculpted and without exception they wore heavy necklaces. Like Marina's mother, Margarita would one day have a rendezvous there, and one of the uniformed staff would hold open the door as she passed. Her head held high, she would walk between the tables in her high heels and stockings that made it look as if her legs were bare, even though they were not.

Still wearing most of the jewellery, she went over to the cupboard and tried to tidy the pile of clothes. If only she had some fur . . .

Suddenly the apartment door slammed. Margarita froze as she heard the heavy footsteps of her older brother come to a halt outside.

Thanasis was led to his grandmother's room by the light and pushed open the door. The rest of the apartment was in darkness.

There was nowhere to hide, so Margarita stood up. She had been caught red-handed.

Thanasis' reaction disarmed her completely.

'You look so pretty!' he exclaimed, smiling. 'Look at you, in all our mother's finery!'

He stood back to admire her. Being a few years older than Margarita, he remembered their mother before her illness and held on to memories of her dressing in some of these clothes and putting on her jewellery.

'I always wondered where her diamonds went,' he said, gazing wistfully at his sister.

'You knew she had these . . .?'

'Not all of these. But I remember her wearing some of them. I think you should take them off before *Yiayiá* finds you here.'

It was impossible to put the clothes back just as they had been, but they did their best, confident that their grandmother would not notice that anything had been disturbed. Judging by the musty smell, it seemed as if she rarely opened this cupboard.

'It's such a waste, leaving it all in there,' Margarita said quietly, burying the box beneath the clothes.

'The clothes?'

'No. The jewellery.'

'I am sure you'll be given something when the time is right.'

'How long do I have to wait? Until that woman dies?'

'Margarita!'

'Well, she wasn't a proper mother, was she?' said Margarita defensively.

Thanasis still missed his mother. He had been the one closest to her, with the strongest memories of her love. As the first child, he had been the only one to receive her exclusive attention. He thought of her often, even though letters about her condition had become infrequent.

He noticed a ladies' handkerchief lying on the floor and, unobserved by Margarita, he picked it up and tucked it into his pocket. In the corner was an elaborately embroidered 'E'. Later on he would hold it to his face. There was no trace of his mother's scent but he would treasure the small square of silk.

'But we never see her. We never hear from her. And it's such a waste, all of this just hidden in here,' protested Margarita.

'You're a bit too young for it yet,' he stressed.

Their voices drowned out the opening and shutting of the front door and they were entirely unaware of Themis' entry into the room.

When Margarita caught sight of her she pushed her out again.

'Why are you always spying? Get out!'

Themis fled, but she had heard enough. Her older sister seemed no longer to care whether their mother lived or died. Her heartlessness seemed to have no bounds.

Margarita was furious with Themis for catching her going through their mother's things. As they were about to sleep that night, she sat on her little sister's chest and swore that if she ever gave her away, she would kill her.

Themis did not doubt it.

Margarita regularly returned to the cupboard whenever her grandmother was out and became familiar with every item, lovingly getting to know each piece and putting them in order of their value, which she could only guess. The jewellery gave her dreams and aspirations, and filled her with fantasies about leading a life in which everyone appreciated her beauty and treated her like a princess. Perhaps she might even meet royalty? And if so, which piece of jewellery would she want to be wearing?

While Margarita lived in her dream world, her brothers were watching events in the real but unpredictable one.

Although General Metaxas had been happy to emulate aspects of the German and Italian regimes, he had not supported them on the outbreak of war in September 1939. Instead, he turned towards Britain.

Early one October morning in 1940, just over a year later, the Italian ambassador arrived at Metaxas' residence with a demand that he should allow Mussolini's forces to enter Greece from Albania and to occupy certain territories. Metaxas' response was a blank refusal.

Italian forces crossed the border almost immediately.

'They've invaded,' said Kyría Koralis, wringing her hands. 'What are we going to do?'

The panic in her voice was palpable.

Even at the age of fourteen, Themis had no practical sense of her country's geography, never having been further than the coast twenty kilometres from the centre of Athens. If the Italians were marching south, they would arrive in Patissia by the morning. She was sure of it. The girl had a sleepless night.

The next morning, everything looked less bleak. News reports told them that Greek forces had reacted with unexpected ferocity and power. Over the following months, despite harsh winter conditions, they pushed the Italians further back into Albania and briefly occupied an area in the south of the country themselves.

By then, whether or not the Italians admired the Greeks was no longer relevant.

'I am so glad you two boys aren't there,' said Kyría Koralis tearfully as they gathered round the radio. The conditions in which Greek soldiers were fighting were severe.

'I'm not glad, *Yiayiá*,' said Thanasis. 'I'd be happy to defend my country. They're showing how much they love their motherland. May God bless them.'

'You'll have your time,' said Kyría Koralis. 'I am sure of that. All that EON training won't go to waste.'

The success of the Greek forces was cause for celebration for everyone in the Koralis home. The simple '*Óchi*' to the Italian ambassador had made Metaxas more popular among his admirers, and even those who objected to his dictatorship grudgingly admitted that he had protected his country from humiliation.

'Here's to our brave troops,' said Thanasis, lifting a glass of firewater. All four of the Koralis children were in their EON uniforms that night. They had attended a victory parade that afternoon in front of their proud grandmother. Panos' toast was half-hearted but even Themis had got swept up in the excitement.

'To our general!' she and Margarita chorused in an uncharacteristic display of unity.

The repulsion of the Italians on the Albanian border was a great victory but Metaxas was still trying to avoid getting embroiled in the war.

'He's turned down Britain's offer to send troops!' said Panos. 'Why? They would protect us!'

Thanasis was swift with his answer.

'If we have Churchill's troops in our country, that will be the end of us,' he snapped. 'That's when Hitler will see us as his enemy.'

Everyone around the table was quiet. Their country was extremely vulnerable.

During this time, the repressive measures of the Metaxas dictatorship continued. One January day, not long after they had gone back to school after Christmas, Themis witnessed its brutality. She was at Fotini's house when the police arrived to search the street for suspected communists. She saw a young man around Thanasis' age being dragged from his makeshift home and out into the street. As the group passed, she and Fotini had peered through a crack in the door, shivering with fear. Themis noticed that the youth's face was already bleeding as he was bundled into a van.

Only a week later, they once again heard shouting in the street and the sound of beating on a nearby door. Kyría Karanidis told the girls to hide under the bed in case the police came in. They willingly did so, clasping their hands over their ears to keep out the sound of screaming.

At the end of January, something then happened that no one could have predicted. General Metaxas suddenly died.

'Septicaemia,' announced Panos without sorrow. He was reading from a newspaper. Reactions were mixed, especially in the Koralis household.

Themis felt a surge of optimism. Perhaps the dictator's death might mean the return of other political parties and the end of the sort of police brutality towards communists that she had witnessed so recently.

Thanasis and Margarita mourned Metaxas ostentatiously. There were now more than a million members of EON and many of them felt that the cornerstone of their beliefs had been pulled away. By contrast, Themis felt nothing. Panos even less.

'You wait,' said Margarita to Panos. 'You'll miss Metaxas. You didn't approve of him but you'll be sorry he is gone.'

Panos openly enjoyed doing battle with his siblings, but Themis did everything she could to avoid confrontation, especially with her spiteful sister. Panos knew, though, that she felt the same as he did.

'Look, Themis,' he urged when they were alone together. 'Even if we are not allowed to express them, it doesn't make our views wrong. Perhaps it makes them even more right.'

And so, while keeping their thoughts to themselves, Panos and Themis did not shed any tears for the dictator's death. They hoped it might lead to better times and restoration of civil liberties.

Such a hope was not to be fulfilled. Within a few months, freedom of every kind was lost for each and every Greek, whatever their political beliefs, left, right or centrist, royalist or republican.

Ultimately, neither the Greek nor the British forces who had arrived at the invitation of Metaxas' successor, Alexandros Koryzis, could do anything to prevent a German invasion. At the beginning of April, the Nazis marched in.

Chapter Five

IN THE PAST few years, the radio had brought children's stories and music into the apartment, as well as news, both good and bad. On 9 April 1941, it brought them information that so many had feared. Germans troops had arrived in Thessaloniki.

Even that day, as they sat at the table with the radio turned to full volume, Thanasis maintained that the Germans were more natural allies of the Greeks than were the British.

'I am sure we will all come to see the Germans in a different way,' he said, with his newly acquired head-of-the-family intonation.

There was plenty to back up his view. Goebbels had made a radio broadcast in Berlin just before the invasion: 'The fight on Greek soil is not a battle against the Greek people but against the archenemy,' he had said. 'The archenemy is England.'

'It makes no sense to be on the side of the Allies,' Thanasis continued.

'Shh!' urged Kyría Koralis. She wanted to listen to the details of the announcement being made, but Panos was more interested in challenging his brother.

'Well, that might be your view,' spat Panos. 'But we have been invaded now, and there are foreign troops on our soil.'

Both Thanasis and Margarita felt connected to the Germans and still believed that they shared a cultural identity.

'We have less in common with the British than with the Germans!' said Margarita defiantly. 'Maybe you'll realise that soon.'

'Margarita, *agápi mou*, please don't shout! You are putting my nerves on edge,' pleaded Kyría Koralis.

'But, *Yiayiá*, you know they admire the Greeks,' she pleaded, banging her fork down on the table.

Kyría Koralis shook her head from side to side in despair. Greece had been invaded and the tone of the newsreader's voice was enough to convey that this was a bad thing. Themis said nothing. It was obvious to her that any soldier who came in uninvited was an adversary.

Over the following days, Thanasis used every fact he could find and every statement of Hitler's that was reported in the right-wing press to reinforce his argument. Now, more than ever, he held on to the view that Germany was a friend of Greece, not a foe.

Panos almost gave up disagreeing. He believed one day that Thanasis would see the truth.

Themis, too, found her older brother ridiculous, especially when he raked up facts to prove his case.

'Some say that Rudolf Hess has a Greek mother!' he continued. 'So how can he be against us?'

Margarita supported her brother with enthusiastic nods but the rest of his audience remained silent.

'And the chief of German Military Intelligence is descended from Constantine Canaris!' Thanasis continued. Canaris had been a freedom fighter in the Greek War of Independence and one of the first prime ministers of modern Greece. 'Hardly likely to be an enemy. Eh, Themis?'

Thanasis was always keen to recruit Themis on to his side, and now aimed his comments at her. She stirred her soup round in the bowl and would not look up to meet him in the eye. Being ignored did not deter him.

'You're clever enough to know that facts are facts,' he continued. 'It doesn't make sense to fight these people when some of their leaders share our blood.'

'But we aren't fighting them, are we?' interjected Panos, staring down at his plate and gripping his fork so hard that his knuckles began to shine. He had a vision of it plunged into his brother's neck. 'They're here now, Thanasis, and there's nothing we can do. It's over.'

'Don't be so gloomy, Panos.'

'Gloomy? You tell me not to be gloomy when the Luftwaffe have just destroyed every ship in Piraeus?'

'They were British ships.'

'No, they weren't. You know they weren't. Some were ours. You lie, even to yourself, Thanasis!'

They had all seen the far-off flashes that had lit up the sky when the port of Piraeus was bombed. Even when evidence proved otherwise, Thanasis stuck to his position, with Margarita his trusty echo.

Events rapidly unfolded. Each day, there were fresh and alarming developments that rendered the front pages of the newspapers obsolete by the time they rolled off the press. In the Koralis apartment, the radio was permanently tuned. The two girls and their grandmother were sitting together, white-faced, one evening, when Panos came in. The day before they had all heard the shocking news that the Prime Minister, Koryzis, had shot himself and now they were listening to a report that the King, the government and the majority of the British forces had left the mainland for Crete.

'I can't breathe out there,' said Panos. 'It's so tense!'

The Nazis were steadily advancing south and the terrifying threat of a German presence in Athens hung in the air. Fear was palpable.

Tens of thousands of Greek soldiers had already been taken prisoner and Themis fretted that the whole family would be tied up. Margarita was adamant that the entire city would become a giant prison.

'What do you think is going to happen?' Themis asked her grandmother. 'It's as if we've been abandoned.'

'*Agápi mou*, I don't know,' replied Kyría Koralis, wringing her hands. For the first time in her life, she could not reassure her grandchildren. She could not promise to keep them safe. Her fear and uncertainty were as great as theirs.

'Everything will be fine, little Themis,' said Thanasis, who had just come in. He grabbed his sister and lifted her up so that they were eye to eye.

'Put me down!' she insisted. Now aged fifteen, she was too old to be treated like a five-year-old. 'Put me *down*!'

'What's the matter?' laughed Thanasis.

'What's the matter?' she asked. 'I'm scared. Of what's going to happen.'

'Everything is going to be fine. You know what one of the German generals said? He wants to make the friendship between Germany and Greece even stronger! That's hardly something to fear, is it?'

Even now, the German leadership continued to claim that they had come to bring peace, and within hours of their arrival, the key to the city was calmly handed over to them by the mayor. This symbolic gesture, as Thanasis was quick to point out as they sat at the table that evening, was carried out without gunfire.

They ate in silence for once, too overwhelmed to argue.

'You're not to leave the apartment. Any of you,' said their grandmother. 'I need to know you're all safe.' Nobody wanted to upset Kyría Koralis, but when she briefly went to the balcony to fetch some biscuits that were cooling outside, both boys took the chance to slip out, one after the other. The girls remained at the table.

'They've gone to their room,' Margarita said quickly, before her grandmother had time to ask.

The old lady put an arm round each of her granddaughters.

'I think we should try and find out what is going on,' she said.

She turned on the radio. Even as the voice that crackled over the airwaves gave them the bad news, it also exhorted them to have courage in defeat.

'The valour and victory of our army has already been acknowledged. We did our duty honestly. Friends! Have Greece in your hearts, live inspired with the fire of her latest triumph and the glory of our army. Greece will live again and will be great. Brothers! Have courage and patience. Be stout-hearted. We will overcome these hardships.

Thanasis returned as the broadcast was ending.

'Do you know where Panos is?' Kyría Koralis asked the girls, realising they had both fooled her.

'No,' they said, each looking at the other, slightly abashed.

A while later, another broadcast gave out instructions for the following day. The tone was practical. Transport would be interrupted, civilians should remain at home and soldiers in their barracks. Shops and schools should stay closed.

Panos was not out for long and when he returned he was downcast. For once, he agreed with his brother.

'We must do what we're told,' he said. 'And just wait to see what happens.'

On the morning of 27 April, the first troops marched through the deserted streets.

Throughout the whole day, Themis felt trapped. She wished she could go and find her friend Fotini or at the very least go down into the square. With such options closed to her, she climbed the dark flight of stairs that led from the landing outside the apartment and let herself out through the heavy door at the top and on to the rooftop of the building. Drying sheets furled and unfurled around her like white flags, but she pushed them aside and made her way across to the flimsy metal railing that ran around the edge. Her eyes followed the straight line of Patission Avenue that pointed like an arrow to the Acropolis. Less than three kilometres away, the ancient Temple of Athena was visible against the skyline. Very distinct on this clear spring day, the sight reassured Themis that all was well.

From this vantage point, however, she could not see the Nazi flag fluttering in the breeze. It had just been planted next to the Parthenon. When she went back downstairs she found her grandmother pleading with both boys to stay inside. They were determined to witness what was happening.

'But it's so dangerous,' she cried. 'They have specifically said you must remain *inside*! If your father was here . . .!' There was nothing the old lady could do to prevent them. Like any curious young men eager to witness a drama, they were both determined, and for their own reasons.

Thanasis left first.

Panos went out on to the balcony. It infuriated his grandmother, but he had recently taken up having an occasional clandestine cigarette and she caught him having a puff.

'*Agápi mou*, please don't drop ash on the plants,' she entreated.

Panos did not acknowledge her. He was too absorbed watching

his older brother crossing the square and now disappearing round the corner. He had no doubt that Thanasis would be making for the local EON headquarters.

'Panos!' snapped Kyría Koralis, as she saw her grandson dropping the stub into one of her pots.

'Sorry, *Yiayiá*,' he said, his lips touching his grandmother on her cheek. 'Sorry. I'll be back later.'

Panos ran from the apartment and down the stairs. Once outside, he hesitated before crossing the square. He would find a different route from usual to the centre of the city, taking sidestreets and alleyways to avoid the main road and to make sure he was not seen. On his way, he did not meet another human soul. It was as though the city had been evacuated. Occasionally there was the sound of a voice coming from an open window. Cats still sat in doorways. Soon even they would notice that the restaurants were closed.

He walked quickly, his hands deep in his pockets, his head down. A few moments before he reached Syntagma, he could hear the sound of steady hammering, like metal being beaten on an anvil. The noise grated on his ears. Suddenly he identified the source of the sound. Across the narrow entrance to the street, passing towards the centre down Academia Street, he saw ranks of grey-uniformed soldiers, their boots crashing in unison on to the road. The soldiers' eyes were fixed ahead, but nevertheless Panos flattened himself into a doorway, terrified of being seen.

He worked his way down a parallel street, his heart beating in time with the soldiers' march. Eventually the ranks of soldiers had all passed so he made his way to the end of the street and observed their receding backs. Who knew whether there would be more following, but he had to see. What shocked him was neither the volume of soldiers, nor the swastikas that were already fluttering from the buildings. Much worse was the sight of some Greeks on the pavements waving enthusiastically. Then he caught sight of his brother. Thanasis was with a few of his friends and Panos saw a German soldier stop and take a cigarette from their group. Close by, a small group of women smiled as the soldiers passed and a few others leaned from their balconies waving and calling out their greetings.

Panos felt nauseous. His legs shaking, he made his way back home, almost careless of his safety or his route.

This evidence of mutual goodwill between Greece and Germany sickened Panos but it gave Thanasis new conviction.

'Have you heard any guns?' he asked Panos when he too returned to the apartment. 'Has even one Athenian come to any harm?'

Thanasis was right and Panos could not deny it. Nevertheless, the news that the Nazi flag had been planted next to the Parthenon was now widely known, and offended him deeply.

'War is more than a bloody battlefield,' said Panos wearily. 'We weren't firing guns at the Turks every day, but we were in conflict with them, weren't we? Every day for four hundred years, it was war.'

'Well, this doesn't feel anything like war to me.'

Thanasis would not shift from his position. He had plenty of 'evidence' that Panos was wrong and continually taunted his brother with it. Each of them was as stubborn as the other.

In the first few days of occupation, Themis regularly sneaked up to the roof to make sure that the Parthenon was there, glad that she could not see the foreign flag. Schools were shut for the time being and she desperately missed Fotini. There was no way to communicate with her and she could not defy her grandmother and go out alone.

Kyría Koralis spent even more time in front of her iconostasis than she had in the past and her grandchildren saw her crossing herself vigorously every time some new announcement was made. Themis wondered why she bothered. Every day things were getting worse so clearly God was not listening.

When they heard that a new Greek government had been formed, Themis resented the idea that it would co-operate with the occupying forces.

'We just have to be patient,' her grandmother said reassuringly. 'Everything will be well if we do as we are told.'

'I don't want to do as I am told by Germans,' protested Themis.

'It's not the Germans now, you idiot,' said Margarita. 'It's our own people. We have a government. They're Greek. Why don't you listen to *Yiayiá*? You never listen to anyone, do you?'

'Shut up, Margarita,' Themis responded.

'You're just stupid, that's all. But you always have been.'

Margarita always maintained that her younger sister had been brain-damaged when the old house collapsed. In an ostensibly teasing way, it meant she could dismiss Themis' opinions whenever they disagreed.

Themis' refusal to attend the German army's victory parade a few days after the occupation was met with abuse.

'You're an idiot,' Margarita told her, poking her in the ribs as she left the house with freshly brushed hair and a smear of lipstick. 'You don't know what you're missing.'

Thousands had gathered in the streets, or watched from balconies. Members of the far right and of EON gathered to hail the passing soldiers and a few households had hung out swastikas.

Themis heard her sister and grandmother return from the parade. As was usual now, the two boys were out and Kyría Koralis could not demand explanation. They were nineteen and twenty-one now, and it was no longer possible to control their comings or goings. She was actually grateful when they were not there together. The bickering between the sisters was more than enough, without adding the noise of the boys' constant conflict.

The day after his army's parade in Athens, Hitler made a speech in the Reichstag. Thanasis read a report of it, insisting on repeating his views to the girls as they sat at the table after dinner.

'He blames Britain's Prime Minister for what's happened here, you see?'

'Churchill?'

Even Kyría Koralis could not see the logic of this.

'How can it be his fault?' queried Themis. 'That's stupid.'

'We invited Allied soldiers on to our soil. So Hitler had no choice. Listen. Here's how much he loves Greece!'

Without pausing for breath, Thanasis pulled out a newspaper cutting from his pocket and rattled off a few sentences in which the Führer expressed his regret for attacking their country.

'He says he was born to respect the culture of this country, that the first rays of mortal beauty and dignity emerged from here, that it was a bitter experience to see this happening . . .'

Thanasis had not noticed his younger brother returning as he continued unabated.

'He believes that Greek soldiers fought with the greatest bravery and contempt of death. And they say that he will release Greek prisoners—'

'You just believe what you want to believe, Thanasis!'

The older brother spun round.

'And you just don't want to accept the truth,' he retorted.

'But you don't even *know* the truth! The Germans locked up plenty of people before their parade. The only ones on the street were traitors like you. Hitler doesn't respect this country any more than Mussolini does.'

Kyría Koralis stood silently drying plates until she had almost rubbed the pattern away. She loved the boys equally, and at times was as distressed by the sound of them arguing as by the bleak announcements on the radio. She tried to contain her reactions to both.

She was finding that German instructions to Athenians on matters of day-to-day conduct encroached on all of their lives, and she knew this was making Panos even more rebellious. Orders came thick and fast: the Nazi emblem was to be flown throughout the city; no help to be given to Allied prisoners; no listening to the BBC; no one to be out on the streets after eleven at night.

Many Greeks, especially the young, began to engage in sabotage. When Panos was out for several hours at a time, Kyría Koralis began to expect a knock on the door, and a stranger to report his arrest. Her anxieties increased after the swastika was torn down from the Acropolis. When she heard about it, she even feared it might have been her grandson who had dared to do it and was relieved when she heard that the perpetrators had been caught.

'I wish it had been me, *Yiayiá*,' Panos said, hugging his grandmother. 'I would have been proud!'

'Promise me you won't do anything stupid, *agápi mou*,' she pleaded.

He did not answer.

Thanasis overheard.

'It was a stupid thing to do!' he ranted. 'The Germans will punish all of us. You think they will just forget it?'

'It was courageous!' retorted Panos.

'Courageous?' Thanasis spat the word out with contempt. 'Those idiots who did it – they'll just make things worse for us all.'

The atmosphere between the boys had become more hostile, and between the sisters it was not much better. The new government had disbanded her beloved EON, which made Margarita more bad-tempered than normal so Themis escaped to Fotini's house as often as she could. At the modest Karanidis home she could avoid her sister's moods, study and think about something other than the presence of foreign soldiers in the streets. School, a *gymnásio* for girls, was sometimes shut during these days of occupation, so Themis began to borrow books from her brothers' room and to spend some of the money that she had saved in a local bookshop. This way, she and Fotini were never short of reading material.

Schools reopened mid June for about a month by which time there were not only German troops in the city but Italians too. In late June, Mussolini's battalions had arrived.

During the hot months, largely spent inside Fotini's house, their personal studies of science and mathematics became a passion for the girls. No one could refute the absolute truths of Pythagoras or the certainties of the periodic table. Whether you were rich or poor, royalist or communist, the answers were the same. Scientific formulae were not a matter of argument and both of them were able to forget how much everything had altered in the world outside.

They tested each other's memories on chemical compounds, got through several books of 'problems', always checking their answers in the back, and set themselves the task of learning at least one poem a week. One afternoon, Fotini produced a slim pamphlet. She had found it hidden inside one of her mother's treasured books.

The girls read aloud alternate stanzas. It was *'Epitáfios'* by Ritsos, a lament inspired by the front page photograph of a mother weeping over her son a few years earlier. He had been killed by police during a strike. The girls were too young to appreciate the sincerity of its emotion and found some of it too sentimental.

They were giggling when, unexpectedly, Kyría Karanidis walked in the door.

She saw what was in her daughter's hands.

'What are you doing with that?' she demanded, snatching it away.

Fotini apologised sheepishly.

'It was banned,' said her mother, sternly. 'I hid it for a reason.'

They watched her putting the poem back where Fotini had found it. The girls did not really understand what they had done wrong but realised the subject was closed.

'It's about time you two were back at school,' said Kyría Karanidis, softening. 'If it's open, that is.'

'I do miss school,' replied Fotini.

'I think it's Dimitris you miss,' teased Themis.

All three of them laughed.

Although their schooling was single sex now, several boys from the adjacent *gymnásio* flirted with them at the school gate. Fotini's beauty attracted many but there was only one that really interested her and she blushed at the sound of his name.

The sun never penetrated the shadowy Karanidis home, giving it the advantage of remaining cool. The raging summer temperatures, the fear on the streets and the bitter atmosphere of Patissia all seemed far away as they sat down to revise Ancient Greek grammar before another new term began.

The girls got their wish to return to the classroom but as autumn progressed, although equations still balanced in the classroom, in the real world numbers were no longer making sense: the population had been swelled by the occupying forces and they all had to be fed. Greece was expected to feed them. Simultaneously, food was being shipped out of the country to Germany.

The decision of the Allies to place a blockade on Greece worsened the situation. They could not restrict supplies to the Germans and Italians without affecting the Greeks too. For Fotini and her mother, the consequences were felt almost immediately.

'So there is less food, to feed more people,' explained Kyría Karanidis when she returned from work one day, carrying even more meagre supplies in her basket than usual.

Themis noticed the pitiful amount that she was unpacking on to the table and felt Fotini's eyes on her. She glanced up to see an expression of shame on her friend's face and felt embarrassed that she was there to witness her discomfort.

At Patissia they were still eating well enough but even the Koralis family began to notice changes. For so many years, Kyría Koralis had been proud of the way she had fed her grandchildren: the generous wholesome meals, the fresh loaves, meat most days, vegetables from the market, home-baked baklava. She made her budget go a long way. Within a short period of time all of this changed.

At first she tried to conceal the problem but little by little the menus altered. First the meat became stringier, and then there was less of it. A single chicken could be stretched over several days until there was just a shred of it floating in a soup. Kyría Koralis had always kept a good stock of pulses in big glass jars on the kitchen shelf, but even the levels of chickpeas and lentils gradually went down to zero.

The memory of Kyría Karanidis' paltry handful of beans was still fresh in Themis' mind one cold autumn evening when she, her siblings and their grandmother were sitting at the table.

Margarita was moaning, but her complaint was gratuitous and aimed at her sister.

'*Yiayiá*, it's not fair,' Margarita said, her mouth full of bread.

'What's not fair?' replied Kyría Koralis patiently.

'You're giving Themis the same amount as the boys.'

Margarita was watching her grandmother ladle out equal portions of soup. Once she would have called it chicken stew. Nowadays the pattern on the plate was visible through the unappetising brown liquid. Without the few shreds of cabbage on the surface it would have been little more than hot water.

'I am giving everyone the same, Margarita.'

'But that's not fair,' she replied, pulling a plate towards her.

The boys said nothing as the other plates were handed round.

'You can have some of my bread,' said Themis, tearing her piece in two and subdividing the half for her brothers. They both accepted.

'Happy now?' asked Themis, casting a defiant glance at Margarita.

Kyría Koralis had not given herself a slice of the loaf. Everyone was a little hungrier than usual and it made them all irritable. All of the children, save Margarita, were lean at the best of times but in the first few months of occupation they had all lost kilos. The once-generously padded Kyría Koralis seemed to be half her former size and the boys had to hold their trousers up with belts pulled in to the last notch.

Margarita, too, had lost some weight (though carefully padded her brassiere with old socks to hide it). Her face was still full enough and she learnt how to give herself a healthy glow by constantly pinching her cheeks and biting her lips to redden them. She was scornful of Themis' stick-like legs.

'Your knees are like turnips!' she shrieked one day, prodding them with a fork. 'All knobbly.'

Shortages of all foodstuffs worsened as that year's harvest of olive oil, figs and raisins were all seized. Livestock was also taken from farmers.

The first time that Kyría Koralis was forced to serve a soup without even a trace of offal floating in it, she apologised.

'It's not your fault, *Yiayiá*,' Panos reassured her. 'We'll manage. The bastards have taken our animals to fatten their Fräuleins,' he went on.

Kyría Koralis, who hated any bad language at the table, cast a despairing look at her grandson.

'Just watch your mouth,' scolded Thanasis.

'But it's true,' Panos said. 'My friend's uncle is a farmer in the north. Cows. For dairy and beef. They've all gone. On trucks. And they'd ship us out if we were edible.'

'Panos, don't exaggerate,' giggled Margarita.

'I'm not,' he snapped. 'Why do you think Hatzopoulos has his shutters down?'

Right up to the previous month, their local butcher had always found something, however small, to wrap up for them: some oxtail, lamb's kidney or even a scrap of tripe. These were cuts that Kyría Koralis would have scorned in the past but had gratefully used them to add flavour to the soup. One of the boys had often come home with a spongy package wrapped in wax paper, but no longer. Even for his favourite customers he had nothing now.

Everyone ate in silence. There was no answer to Panos' question and it was true that millions of animals had been exported to Germany.

It was not just food that was plundered by the Nazis. Little by little Greece was stripped of everything else too. Tobacco, silk, cotton, leather and all the other raw materials of industry were pillaged by the occupiers. Forests were destroyed to provide fuel for the Axis and energy production was almost halted. Within the space of a few months, the infrastructure, industry and morale of the country was in tatters. Fear was replaced by desperation.

The effects were immediate and catastrophic: unemployment rocketed and hyperinflation took hold. Kyría Koralis came home in tears one morning when the price of a loaf reached several million drachmas and continued to rise. When rationing was brought in, the amount of bread allowed for each person fell to little more than one hundred grams a day. Thanasis was broader than his younger brother, but they both craved sustenance and hunger kept them awake at night, as if they had stones in their bellies.

Kyría Koralis' task of keeping them all fed was becoming harder by the day. As winter approached, a sense of hopelessness began to set in.

'It's cold in here,' moaned Margarita as she held her hands over a bowl of soup in an attempt to warm them. She then shoved her younger sister, who always sat in the chair closest to the stove, in the ribs. Themis had a full spoon raised to her lips and Margarita's action sent it flying.

'You clumsy . . .' exclaimed Themis, as the soup spattered across the cloth.

'Just move! Why should you have all the heat? Why?'

'Because in the summer, nobody wants to sit there! It's too hot then,' said Panos coming to his sister's defence.

'Well, it's too cold everywhere now,' said Margarita. 'It's just too cold!'

She threw her own spoon down now and stormed from the room.

'I have an idea,' said Panos a few minutes later, when the rest of them had resumed eating. 'Some of my friends went to the countryside last weekend. They found a few bits of wood and brought them back. Why don't we do that? It would be a change for all of us. And we might be able to make this place warmer.'

The following Saturday, putting aside their differences, the four siblings walked from the apartment to the end of the street and waited patiently for one of the very few occasional buses which had not been commandeered by the occupier. Several went by, already full, but even Margarita did not complain. This was how it was nowadays. There was not enough of anything and there was nobody to blame except the occupying forces. Neither Thanasis nor Margarita voiced so much support for the Germans now.

When they finally managed to squeeze on a bus, it was only half an hour until they reached the outside of the city. They got off and had walked only a hundred metres along the road before Panos saw a path that led into a wood.

'This looks like the place that Giannis described.'

The leaves had turned to shades of auburn and gold and some of the trees were already laden with orange berries. For a while, as the siblings followed the path, they were silent. It was a long while since they had been close to nature.

They were, of course, unused to walking on soft earth and Margarita was the first to complain that her shoes were muddy and that the briars were catching on her cardigan.

'We're here for a reason,' Thanasis snapped. 'So stop complaining.'

It was rare for him to reprimand his sister. 'We'll gather some fire wood and go home.'

'It's for you as much as for anyone else!' added Themis. 'You're the one always complaining about being cold.'

'And we must look out for nut trees too,' said Panos. 'Giannis said that he found enough walnuts to fill a bucket when he came.'

'What about acorns?' asked Themis, picking some up from the ground.

'We can't eat those, stupid,' said Margarita.

'Fotini's mother does.'

'So your little communist friends live on acorns, do they?' sneered Thanasis.

'Kyría Karanidis grinds them into flour. I have seen her do it. And then she makes biscuits,' replied Themis.

'Let's pick some up then,' said Panos. 'Why not?'

'You won't get me eating acorns,' said Margarita. 'They're for pigs.'

Panos poked his sister in the ribs.

'But you love your food!' he teased. 'You've always loved your food!'

Margarita raised her arm to hit him, but Panos ducked and for a while they chased each other round the woods, laughing and squealing. Thanasis and Themis joined in, trying to catch Panos, eventually cornering him and pulling him to the ground.

For a short while, on this chilly autumn day, they became flush-cheeked, carefree children once again.

Their need, though, was not a game. It was very real. At the end of the afternoon, the girls each had a basket filled with nuts and acorns and the boys had armfuls of twigs for kindling, as well as the largest branches that they could carry under their arms. They had not needed to venture far into the woodland to get what they wanted and returned home as it was getting dark to present their trophies to Kyría Koralis.

The afternoon had briefly taken them away from the grim austerity of the city and the oppressive atmosphere that permeated its streets. For a few hours they had seen bright colours, breathed in the fresh scent of earth and heard the wild calls of birds that were not caged.

'We want to go again, don't we?'

Themis was the first to express her enthusiasm to their *yiayiá* as they ate that night. Her siblings all nodded. The apartment was warmer that evening and a reassuring smell of walnut biscuits being baked in the oven reminded them of better times.

During this period, school was often shut for several days and the incidences of this became increasingly frequent. The cold was sometimes so intense that it was pointless to try to teach shivering children in a big unheated room. On other occasions the lack of light made it impossible. Themis would go back with Fotini to her house and one day Themis noticed how thin her friend was getting. Her skin had become transparent, as she described it to her grandmother later.

'You can see through to her bones,' said Themis.

'Poor girl,' responded Kyría Koralis sympathetically. 'I wish we had enough to go round . . .'

'I couldn't invite her here anyway, *Yiayiá*,' said Themis. 'Not after the things Thanasis said.'

'That's so long ago, *agápi mou*.'

'I know. But he still thinks like that. I know he does.'

The next day, Kyría Koralis wrapped one of the biscuits she had kept back in some paper and gave it to Themis.

'That's for your friend,' she said. 'And no eating it yourself.'

Later on, Themis watched Fotini slowly chewing each mouthful and then licking the paper to get the last crumb. Perhaps the most painful moment of all was when she had finished it and reached out to hug Themis.

'Thank you,' she whispered. Themis was shocked by the realisation that beneath the red coat her friend was wasting away.

A month later they planned to repeat the outing and Themis asked Fotini to come with them, knowing that she and her mother were struggling more than ever to find food.

A few days before, Fotini fainted in class. She used her 'time of the month' as an excuse, but the real reason was different. Many factories were closing now because of a lack of raw materials, and Kyría Karanidis had lost her job. With no money left for food, Fotini had not eaten for two days. She went home from school early and the following day did not return.

Themis went to her friend's house that evening and, a few moments after she knocked, the door opened a few centimetres. A pale face peered out.

Even when she saw her friend, Fotini showed no sign of throwing the door open and letting her in.

'I just came to see—' began Themis.

'I'm fine,' said Fotini hastily. 'It's just my period. Don't worry about me. I'll be fine in a few days.'

Before Themis had time to wish her well, the door was closed. She was upset not to be able to speak for longer to Fotini. She had even brought a book for her in case she was worried about missing lessons, and a small container of cooked rice that her grandmother had pressed on her. She returned home, downcast, with both.

For the rest of that week Fotini did not appear at school, and Themis vowed to herself that she would go back and see her after the weekend that was now upon them.

Chapter Six

WHEN SATURDAY ARRIVED, the mood of the outing was very different from the previous time. For some while, the four Koralis siblings sheltered in the doorway of an empty shop waiting for a bus. They were infrequent and several did not stop because they were already overloaded with passengers. A cold rain turned to sleet and by the time the bus came, the girls were shivering and as it trundled and coughed its way out of the city, they huddled together for warmth. Themis did not dare to admit that she had already dropped one of her gloves. The streets were almost empty, with many shops boarded up. Occasionally they glimpsed someone in uniform: German or Italian, it was hard to distinguish through the steamed-up windows.

When they reached their stop, they soon realised things had changed. Many trees had been cut down and the remaining ones had been stripped bare of their branches. They returned home, damp and despondent, with only some scrappy twigs that might do for kindling once they had dried out.

Even as they climbed the stairs, the four of them commented on the smell of lamb but imagined it was emanating from a neighbour's home.

As they opened their own door, the intoxicating scent of meat intensified and they saw a table already laid out for a meal. They followed their grandmother's instruction to wash their hands and sit down, then watched wide-eyed as she set a bowl down in front of each of them filled to the brim with a knuckle of lamb, potatoes and carrots. In the middle of the table was a pan of spinach rice. They had not seen food like this in months. They ate greedily, their heads bent down to their plates, breathing in the aroma, feeling the warmth of the stew rising into their faces and opening the pores in their skin. There was even enough for the boys to have second helpings.

Only when their hunger was sated did any of them begin to ask questions.

'How?'

'Where?'

'When?'

The old lady gave an answer that satisfied their curiosity and put an end to any further interrogation.

'Your father sent some money,' she said simply.

'Was that *all* that came?' asked Margarita, hoping that he might have sent a gift as well.

'Just some money,' she answered. 'But I think we should all be grateful for that.'

She crossed herself several times and then began to clear the plates.

'They hardly need washing,' she smiled. Every last trace of sauce on their plates had been wiped clean with warm, doughy bread.

In truth there was no money coming from America.

Rumours had been flying that food shortages were going to get worse, and Kyría Koralis knew she would have to dip into the one reserve that remained to her. By selling the valuables that her daughter-in-law had brought to the marriage, she could purchase things on the black market. What else were those items of jewellery for now but to feed her own children? Kyría Koralis knew that they were not really hers to sell, but she could not even be certain if Eleftheria was still alive. Reports on her daughter-in-law's condition had been only occasional, and she did not dare to imagine what conditions in the asylum must be like. The institution where her daughter-in-law lived was in an area occupied by the Bulgarians and their reputation for barbarism surpassed even that of the Germans and Italians. Before the occupation, Kyría Koralis had felt an occasional pang of guilt about not making some attempt to visit her, but that would be impossible now.

Two days before the children's second excursion to the countryside, she had pulled out the box from beneath the pile of Eleftheria's stale clothes. She was glad she had not discarded them because, with the shops empty and fabric impossible to find on the open market, she would have to adapt them all for the girls. She did not notice their slightly unruly order.

Opening the chest, Kyría Koralis stood in front of her mirror and held up a string of lustrous pearls against the pale, papery skin of her neck. It was the necklace that Eleftheria had worn on her wedding day. The weight of the sapphire clasp on her palm gave the old lady a small shiver of pleasure.

That alone should feed us all for a few weeks, she thought.

There was no sentimentality attached to any of these valuables and she had already heard that there was someone in the neighbourhood purchasing precious stones. Without any hesitation, she slipped the necklace into her pocket and left the apartment. It was likely that the jewellery would end up in the ownership of some German woman, but she did not care. The price was not bad for the circumstances and the millions of drachmas she received would go a long way, even if their value had dropped between the time they were handed to her and the moment she paid for her ingredients. As long as she could return home with her battered shopping bag bulging with food, she was happy.

While they were eating, Themis had been thinking of her best friend. Fotini had not returned to school since the day she had collapsed. This was almost a week ago now. Had Fotini's mother moved them both back to Kavala? Her innocent thought was that Fotini had not had time to alert her.

On Monday, Themis disobeyed her grandmother's strict instructions that she should come directly home from school. Now that acts of resistance were becoming more common, the Germans were looking to make arrests. Girls and boys, women and men, faced detention if they were out after the curfew so Themis knew it was not just foolhardy to wander the streets alone in the semi-darkness, it was dangerous too. With Germans or Italians, whose reputation was even worse, patrolling the street, a solitary sixteen-year-old girl was vulnerable. In spite of all this, Themis walked briskly past the road that led to their square and towards Fotini's house.

She walked as fast as she could and arrived at a moment between afternoon and dusk when the light seemed reluctant to leave. It was mid-January and everything looked silver grey.

She knocked loudly on Fotini's familiar door but there was no reply so she knocked again and then a third time, even louder. Themis looked around her. Perhaps one of the neighbours might know something, but there was nobody to ask.

Two German soldiers stood at the end of the street. One of them seemed preoccupied, looking in the other direction, blowing smoke rings into the damp air. The other stared at her. She was wearing an old coat of her mother's but suddenly felt naked and pulled it tighter round her. Themis made one more futile attempt to rouse someone inside, but realised the house must be empty. It had only one room, after all.

When she looked up, the soldier who had been menacing her with his gaze was walking towards her. Without considering the impression it would give, Themis turned from the door and ran, taking a circuitous route that led her back to the main street. Only then did she pause to catch her breath, hiding in the entrance of a derelict shop in case the soldier was on her tail. The street was not lit and the space where she crouched was in shadow.

She put her hand out and realised there was a sandbag across the door. Perhaps she should sit there for a moment. As she touched the rough sacking to balance herself, she heard a noise. Like a squeak. Rat-like. Themis was terrified of rodents. The city had been overrun with them recently, all of them as hungry as its inhabitants. They were crafty and successful competition for any human being scavenging for food.

She let out an involuntary yelp and jumped away. Only then, as her eyes were becoming accustomed to the darkness, did she see that this was not a sandbag at all. It had a human shape and there was an area, the colour of an eggshell, that stood out from the rest.

The sound came again. It was a man's voice.

'Help me . . .'

With great trepidation, Themis bent down to take a closer look. The man repeated his plea.

'Help me,' he whispered through parched lips.

Themis had not met such need face to face. She knew that most people in this city were lacking food and felt some guilt that her own family was fortunate in having money coming in from America.

'I don't have anything with me,' she said breathlessly. 'I'm so sorry. I'll bring you something.'

Her grandmother would be getting anxious now so she must be home soon. She would return with some food later.

Themis hurried through the dark streets. Several groups of soldiers scrutinised her as she passed.

As she ran up to the apartment, the fragrance from her grandmother's cooking floated down the stairwell and when she pushed open the door, everyone was already seated round the table.

'*Yia sou, adelfí mou*,' said Panos sweetly. 'Hello, little sister.'

'She's late,' growled Margarita.

'Your grandmother has been beside herself with worry,' scolded Thanasis. 'Where have you been?'

Themis was flushed with exertion and for a moment could not speak. She helped herself to a glass of water and then drew breath.

'I met a man . . .'

'*Theé mou!*' Kyría Koralis cried out, her bread-knife held in mid-air. 'Oh my God!'

'I found him in a doorway. I need to take him something. Bread. Anything.'

'Who is he, this person?' asked Margarita.

'Why were you talking to him anyway?' demanded Thanasis. 'What were you doing out there? You are meant to come straight home after school. Don't you realise it's dangerous? Don't you know you are breaking all the rules? How stupid *are* you, Themis?'

Themis sipped her water but her mouth was dry.

'I just saw him there,' she said almost inaudibly.

'You're not going out into the street again at this time of night,' said her grandmother.

'And you're not taking food into the streets — now or at any time, for that matter,' Thanasis added emphatically.

'There are soup kitchens for those people,' said Margarita.

Dinner was served now and everyone sat with a full plate in front of them. It was the most filling recipe in their grandmother's repertoire and everyone's favourite: stuffed cabbage. The minced pork was so plentiful that it spilled out of the carefully rolled leaves to mingle with the lemon sauce poured over them.

Themis could not eat. She dug her fork into the cooked meat and sat there for a while staring at her plate. Everyone else continued. She was thinking of the man who was waiting for her to return. Then she thought of Fotini. The mystery was not solved. Her best friend's name still got a negative reaction from her family, even after all these years, so she did not mention her anxiety.

She played with the piece of bread next to her plate and, when nobody was looking, dropped it into her lap and then later into her skirt pocket.

There was no chance of getting out of the apartment again tonight without causing a fuss, but the following day she would leave early for school, retrace her steps to the empty shop and after that go to Fotini's again. Perhaps at that time of day she might catch someone in the street who had seen her.

She hardly slept that night. Anxiety about her friend and the sound of Margarita talking in her sleep did not help. She was out of the house before anyone stirred, checking that the lump of bread was still in her pocket and helping herself to the heel of the loaf left over after dinner. It was still on the table, wrapped in a cloth to keep it fresh.

There were many more people on the streets than the night

before. Greeks outnumbered soldiers at seven in the morning and nobody gave her a second glance. It was a bitterly cold day and snow had fallen. Her breath came out in a cloud as she walked. She remembered the location of the shop, even though one derelict business looked very much like the next. It had a worn red sign above it: '*Sidiropoleíon*, Ironmonger', and the windows were painted with the name of the owner, Vogiatzis, so she knew she had come to the right place. The doorway, however, was empty. Perhaps someone else had brought him something to eat.

With little further thought of the man, she continued on her route to Fotini's, gnawing on a piece of her crust. She attracted envious stares from one or two children that she passed, and remembering bread was rationed she quickly concealed it inside her coat.

Themis pushed her bare hands deep into her pockets to keep them warm.

Once at her friend's house, she knocked, timidly at first and then more loudly. There was the same silence from inside as before.

Tearfully, she made her way to school. It was no warmer there. The classroom was unheated and her fingers could scarcely grasp a pencil. At the end of the lesson she approached the teacher to see if she knew anything. Several other children had not turned up for some days now, but what could anyone do? There was a lot of sickness around that winter – from the common cold to tuberculosis. There were rumours of an epidemic of the latter.

When school ended that afternoon, she bumped into Giorgos Stavridis in the street. He was with Fotini's 'crush', Dimitris, who asked Themis where Fotini was. The girls were so rarely seen without each other.

Themis shook her head. 'I don't know,' she said with a lump in her throat. She missed her friend's voice, her clever answers to questions, their conversation. Everything about her.

The boys hurried off in separate directions. Everyone liked to be indoors by dark.

It was sadness that made Themis slow as she walked home that day rather than the deep snow. It was the first time she had experienced that just putting one foot in front of another could be an effort.

When she got back to Patissia, she looked up at the balcony and could see her grandmother sweeping. Dead leaves from her lemon trees fluttered down towards the street. She climbed the stairs and went out to tell her that she was home. Kyría Koralis pecked her on the cheek and they both stood for a moment looking out over the square. All the trees were bare now and the ground was blanketed in white. The sky was colourless too.

Then, even in the fading light, something caught Themis' eye. It was something so familiar, something that she knew so well, that it was almost part of her. It was a particular shade of red and against the snow it stood out.

'*Yiayiá!* Look! Over there. Do you see it? It looks exactly like Fotini's coat!'

Kyría Koralis' eyes followed the direction of Themis' finger.

'It does look as if someone's dropped a coat,' she agreed.

They both peered over.

'Well, you should go and get it just in case. Whether or not it belongs to your friend, you can't just drop a coat like that. So many people are without . . .'

'I'll go down,' said Themis.

She took the stairs two at a time and as she walked across the square, she saw that two men had paused by it and were picking it up. Two people to lift a piece of clothing?

She quickened her step and got there just as they had gathered what she now realised was more than just a coat. The temperature seemed to plummet even further.

'It's a girl,' said the man, who now carried the lifeless body in his arms.

His comment was addressed to Themis, who stood by, staring with complete disbelief. She caught a glimpse of Fotini's face. Her friend was almost unrecognisable with her cheekbones pushing through the skin and her eyes bulbous. She looked like a ninety-year-old woman, but there was no doubt in Themis' mind that this was her friend.

As the head had lolled to one side, Themis found Fotini's vacant eyes staring into hers. She had to look away.

'Never seen a corpse before?' said the other man, addressing Themis, who was sobbing now. He stepped forward to close her friend's eyelids.

'This is the tenth we've found this morning. Tragic.'

These workers were paid to walk the streets each day to gather corpses. Along with the black marketeers, they were among the few whose lot had improved since the start of the occupation.

Kyría Koralis watched from the balcony and saw her granddaughter plodding along behind a man who carried the red bundle. Panos had come in meanwhile and she called him outside.

'Panos. Can you go down and fetch your sister,' she said with urgency. 'I think she has found her friend . . .'

'Fotini?'

'I think she's died,' Kyría Koralis said quietly.

'*Theé kai Kýrie*, Lord God,' muttered Panos with a catch in his throat.

Like everyone else, he knew it was the coldest winter for years and the famine was killing thousands each week in Athens alone. Until this moment, though, it had not yet touched their family.

He left the flat and ran out into the square and towards his sister, who still followed the slow progression of her friend's body, sobbing uncontrollably.

'Themis,' he said, putting his arm around her and keeping pace. 'You can't go with her.' The majority of dead bodies, especially if they were not identified by family, were taken outside the city for burial.

His sister could not speak but she clutched on to Panos' hand. He could feel her shaking.

When the corpse carriers reached the edge of the square, Themis broke down and had to be supported by her brother. Fotini was being lifted on to a cart already occupied by several other bodies. For the first time, Themis noticed that her friend's feet were bare and blue. Someone must have stolen her shoes. This was death without dignity.

The two men began to pull the cart, slowly and jerkily across the broken surface of the street and a few minutes later they had trundled into the main road. Panos watched until they were out of sight, with Themis' head buried in his chest.

They stood there in the frozen twilight, grateful for each other's warmth.

Gently Panos led his sister home. Kyría Koralis boiled water and made her a hot infusion using her few remaining dried herbs. Then she tucked her, still fully clothed, into bed.

Themis was trembling so violently that she could not hold her drink but sipped it from time to time from her grandmother's steady hands. For now there was nothing to say. No words could lend comfort. Nothing justified Fotini Karanidis' death and any attempt to rationalise it would just be empty words.

The sight of her friend's lifeless body and crumpled coat would always haunt her.

Chapter Seven

THEMIS WAS CONVINCED that when Fotini had collapsed she must have been on her way to their apartment, perhaps even to ask for some food. It would have been the first time she had come to where they lived.

Two days later, when she had summoned the courage and the strength, she went back to Fotini's house. There was a possibility that her mother was looking for her daughter.

Panos accompanied her and it was he who knocked on the door. After a moment or two, a small crack appeared.

'Who is it?' asked a man's voice.

These days, when someone came to the door, there was always a chance that a German or Italian soldier might be on the other side.

'We're looking for Kyría Karanidis . . .' Panos spoke a little hesitantly into the darkness.

The door was opened a little wider and they found themselves face to face with a man. From the look of him he was clearly relieved to find two young Greeks standing there.

'Kyría Kara . . .? That's who was living here . . .?'

'Yes, she was,' said Themis. 'With her daughter.'

'Have you seen her?' enquired Panos.

A look of bewilderment passed across the man's face.

'I've seen no one. Look, do you want to come inside?'

Themis gripped tight on to her brother's arm as they entered. Fotini's books were still on the shelf. Even her school bag was there, sitting at the end of the bed. The same plates and the single metal pan were in their usual places.

Themis burst into tears.

'All her things are here,' she said quietly through her tears. 'Exactly as before.'

'My sister's friend died. A few days ago,' Panos explained to the stranger. 'This was her house.'

The three of them sat at the kitchen table. Themis was in the same seat as she had always taken.

The stranger looked nervous.

'Maybe I should explain why I am here,' he said. 'I'm a soldier, or maybe I should say "was". When our unit was disbanded, I got back to my home to find it had been taken over by German officers. What could I do? I was wandering the streets. Lots of us were. We had nothing.'

'I know,' said Panos. 'There are wounded soldiers everywhere and even they are living on the streets.'

'Eventually, I started looking for somewhere to sleep,' said the man. 'And people were saying that there were empty houses up in this area.'

He paused for a moment.

'I only realised the reason they were empty when I arrived a couple of days ago. But I needed a roof. It's cold. It's so bloody cold . . .'

Themis sat quietly, listening, weeping. It was left to Panos to respond.

'You don't have to justify what you've done,' he said.

'I'm Manolis, by the way,' the man said. He forced a smile.

'And I'm Panos and this is Themis. Themis' friend was called Fotini. You understand that she lived here . . .'

'Yes. I'm so sorry for your friend, Themis. These are terrible, terrible days.'

'We don't know if Fotini's mother will ever come back. We don't know what has happened to her. But if she does, will you say that Themis Koralis came to see her?'

'Of course. Though I don't know for how long I'll be here. I want to fight again,' he said. 'How else are we going to get rid of these bastards?'

There was a pause. Panos fished around inside his coat and produced some tobacco. Themis knew her brother smoked because she could smell it on him but where he had found the tobacco she could not imagine.

He rolled a cigarette and passed it to Manolis. The other man accepted it as though he had been offered a bag of gold.

Panos then made another for himself and leaned so close that his words were almost inaudible to his sister.

'There are a few things we can do,' he said. 'Behind the scenes, if you see what I mean.'

Themis realised Panos was putting his trust in this man. To admit that he took part in acts of espionage and resistance was a dangerous step, but instinct told him that Manolis was a kindred spirit. Manolis had fought in Albania almost to the death and had been rewarded with penury and a stranger's empty house. Anger and despair were etched on his face.

Themis followed the low-voiced conversation, glancing from one man to another but she was impatient to leave. It made her so sad to be in this house without her friend. While the men were making their plans she left the table and went across to the bed. Fotini's bag was lying there.

Kyría Karanidis might return even now, so it did not seem right to take it, but she wished very keenly to have something to remember Fotini by. Themis ran her hand over the smooth leather. Perhaps there was something inside, a keepsake that might not be missed if it was gone? Themis undid the buckle.

Inside there was a battered exercise book. Fotini's neat hand-writing on the front cover stating her name, her class and the name of their school, made Themis' heart lurch. Opening the front cover, she read some lines of poetry that Fotini must have copied out in defiance of her mother. They were from Ritsos' forbidden poem, 'Epitáfios'.

All Fotini's knowledge, hopes and emotions were gone now. Did they still exist but somewhere else? It was the first time in sixteen years that Themis had been struck by life's futility.

Themis tucked the exercise book inside her coat, next to her heart. She would not look at the rest now, but in subsequent days she would turn each page and read every word.

As she looked up, the men were standing up to shake hands, agreeing to meet again.

What she had not heard were the words that Manolis spoke to Panos behind his hand.

'The mother's body was found in the street last week,' he said discreetly. 'The neighbour told me.'

Panos knew that now was not the moment to break such news to Themis. There was a limit to the sadness that his sister should have to face. Themis did not need to know that proper burial was rare these days and that Fotini's mother had probably joined dozens of others in a mass grave. His only hope was that the bodies of mother and daughter were close to one another.

In Athens alone, almost fifty thousand had collapsed and died from malnutrition over these months. Freezing temperatures and food shortages were a lethal combination. There were children whose final hours were spent scavenging for food or lying, lice-ridden, in the street, too weak to move. They were such a common sight that people would simply step over them to go on their way. Every passer-by would have his agenda: to find food, visit a soup kitchen or even to call in on a seamstress who might be fashioning a new coat from an old one. Nobody had time to linger. Survival was the only concern.

Themis would not get out of bed for many days and her grand-mother had to coax her to eat.

'Just a little, sweetheart, just a spoonful. Just for me.'

It infuriated Margarita to hear their grandmother talking to Themis as if she were a baby. The older girl was as jealous of her younger sister now as she had been when she arrived and could not understand why Themis felt so much grief for what Margarita called 'her refugee friend'.

'Let her be,' she said to her grandmother. 'She's just doing it to be the centre of attention. If she eats, she eats.'

Even putting the differences in their political sympathies to one side, Margarita found Themis irritating in all ways. One day, she saw her younger sister curled up in the foetal position on their bed and was reminded of their mother's behaviour all those years before. Shame and anger filled her.

Although Themis was eating very little, the boys had voracious appetites. Piece by piece, Kyría Koralis had sold the jewellery to buy food and the box was empty but for one final item.

One late spring day she rolled the ruby earrings round in her hand and then, with neither guilt nor regret, set off across the square to sell them. Each piece she sold diminished the assets of her daughter-in-law, but improved the children's chances of survival. As she accepted another packet stuffed with notes, she told herself that her son would have approved.

For several months, Margarita had not had the opportunity to pry in her grandmother's cupboard. And in past weeks, it had been even trickier because Themis rarely left the apartment. That day, with her grandmother out and her sister asleep in the next room, Margarita took her chance.

She could feel immediately that something was wrong. The small chest that had once overflowed with treasure was light. Empty. Margarita, almost overcome with nausea, rummaged frantically through her mother's clothes. Had the jewels somehow tumbled out and got lost in the folds of silk and wool? In a state of frenzy, she scattered blouses, skirts and scarves across the room, tossing them into the air so that if anything was concealed, it would fall out.

Just as she shook out the last garment, she heard the sound of a key in the lock.

It was Kyría Koralis, letting herself in, her arms filled with provisions. She had gone straight from selling the earrings to a place where she could purchase meat and potatoes. A delay of even a few hours could send the price of such things even higher and she needed to use the drachmas before their value plummeted further.

Her granddaughter burst out of the bedroom into the hallway holding the wooden chest, its lid wide open. Dismay was etched deep into her face, accusations ready to fly from her lips.

Kyría Koralis was prepared with a story.

'They are all in the bank, *paidí mou*,' she said. 'When the Germans leave I'll get them back again. You can't be too careful.'

'But weren't they safe here?'

'With the Germans on every street? And Italians? They're even worse.'

'But . . .'

Kyría Koralis bombarded Margarita with reasons and excuses.

'And you know they sometimes go and live in people's homes? So do you imagine they would think twice about taking our valuables?'

'I know about that, *Yiayiá*. But they haven't yet bothered us—'

'And the streets!' Kyría Koralis added. 'You know how dangerous the streets are, *agápi mou*! Even if it's just a few desperate people you can't take the risk.'

Although she was lying about the jewels, it was true that not only the German and Italian soldiers were guilty of theft. There were also crimes of violence and opportunism carried out by Greeks against one another. Stories abounded of watches being ripped from wrists, and pendants from necks. Hunger drove people to desperate behaviour. What choice did a man have if he saw his wife vainly attempting to breastfeed their baby? If both mother and child were malnourished, he could not stand by while both of them starved to death. The rich were still rich and potentially the source of a meal.

Kyría Koralis succeeded in pacifying her granddaughter and allowed her to preserve the dream of being reunited with the jewellery. Margarita promised herself that as soon as the Axis troops left, a new and glamorous life would begin. Diamonds, silks, stockings and visits to Zonars. Nowadays, she was more determined than ever to have these.

She had recently found work as an assistant in an expensive dress shop in Kolonaki and had higher than ever aspirations. Even during these days of desperation, there seemed to be women who had enough for beautiful clothes, or German officers who wanted to send something home for their wives.

Meanwhile, she had already learnt that the occasional kiss with a foreigner could translate to a pair of nylons or even a lipstick. There was a particular smile she had learnt in front of the mirror that seemed to invite some kind of exchange, and after studying a few old magazines she had practised to make it perfect. The jewellery, when she got it back, could only increase the opportunities she dreamed of.

As the months went by, though, there was no sign that occupation would ever end. Most members of the Koralis family became frustrated that neither the government in Athens nor the government in exile did anything to bring freedom closer. As Kyría Koralis had feared, Panos, along with many others, had joined the National Liberation Front, EAM, an organised resistance created to take action against the occupying forces. Her younger grandson was constantly in a state of fury that, from every angle, the country was being made to suffer and at least this group might do something.

'First they occupy us, then they steal everything there is to eat,' Panos ranted at his brother. They were sitting at the table and Panos pointed down at the meagre dinner in front of him. Thanasis had recently been accepted for police training and was sometimes given a meal at college, so he was not hungry that night. The girls carried on eating in silence, almost oblivious to the soundtrack of fraternal argument. Panos had more to say.

'And then on top of that the Germans make the Greek government give them money. And you say these people are our friends!'

Whatever his brother said, Thanasis was steadfast in his beliefs. Even the preposterous 'loans' to cover the cost of occupation demanded by the Germans from Greece did not change his mind.

He continued to support the collaborationist government without questioning their actions and believed that one day even Panos would come to terms with German influence in his country.

'You would make life easier for yourself and everyone around you if you accepted things as they are.'

'But even Tsolakoglou wants a reduction in the payments!' retorted Panos.

It was true that the Prime Minister was reaching the limit of his tolerance and demanding greater leniency from the Germans.

Themis did not join in the debate. Everything Panos described was so obviously an injustice. Fotini was one of many thousands who had died from starvation in Athens that winter. Greece was at breaking point.

Chapter Eight

A FTER FOTINI'S DEATH, Themis lost interest in school. Perhaps she would return to her studies when life went back to normal, but no one could imagine what normality was any more and had no idea when it might return. The absence of the brightest spark in the class had left a space in the front row, but there were more than a dozen empty seats now. When she heard that learning German and Italian was now compulsory at school she had no regrets about not being there.

Instead of attending her *gymnásio*, Themis went each day to help at one of the city's soup kitchens. A long line stretched down the road even before the place opened and people stood patiently in the cold and the rain for the next hour or more while she and the team of other female volunteers chopped vegetables and boiled up cauldrons of water. By ten in the morning, a thin soup was ready to serve.

Every day Themis looked for the face of Fotini's mother in the queue. Surely if she was in need, she would come here? She scrutinised the crowd. Many looked less than human: there were people with the bodies of children but the expressions of the old, men with eyes that bulged from their skulls, women with furry chins and limbs, this pelt being the body's natural reaction to starvation and cold. Many were barefoot. Occasionally there was someone so weak that they struggled to hold a mug of soup.

Each day, she came home with the same question on her lips.

'Do you think this will go on for ever?' she would ask, looking for reassurance from her brother. The collaborationist government gave the ordinary Greek people little reassurance that it had any plans to improve the situation. It was obliged to meet the occupiers' demands, so living conditions were next to impossible for all except those who exploited the black market.

'Whenever you can,' Panos told her, 'scrawl something on a wall, but make sure you're not seen. Every little word will help demoralise the bastards.'

Drawing graffiti seemed a little futile to Themis, but suddenly Panos seemed more optimistic and promised her that they would soon rid themselves of the Germans.

'The government may not be doing anything,' he told Themis, 'but other people are.'

'What do you mean?' she asked excitedly. 'Is something going to happen?'

Of late there had been a rumour of German withdrawal, but it turned out to be just that. The only benefit of the rumour had been that those who hoarded their goods had released more on to the market and prices had temporarily fallen.

'Something is already happening, Themis.'

He spoke to her quietly, even though there was no one else at home.

'What?' she whispered excitedly.

'Something is happening every hour, every day,' he explained.

'But *what*?' she asked, with urgency. 'Tell me! Tell me!'

In spite of Panos' desire to protect his sister's innocence, he wanted her on his side. There might be moments when he needed her to cover for him and this could happen any time soon.

'I'm helping someone,' he said rapidly. 'A woman who lives close by. She sometimes shelters British soldiers. You would never imagine it looking at her, but she is the bravest woman I have ever met.'

'But what do you have to do?'

'Well, you know I'm working in a *kafeneío*? It's opposite her house so I can keep an eye, create a distraction if it's hard for the people she is helping to leave. It's close to here, in another street near to Patission Avenue. I do other small things, like finding spare clothes.'

'Is it dangerous?'

'Yes. You mustn't tell *Yiayiá*. Or the others. I am exactly the kind of person that Thanasis would arrest.'

'Of course I won't tell them. I swear.'

Panos knew that she was as good as her word.

'Can I do something too?' asked Themis eagerly. 'I want to help. Tell me what I can do!'

'Nothing for now,' replied Panos. 'But I'll tell Lela . . .'

'Lela?'

'That's her name, Lela. Lela Karagiannis. I'll tell her that you are "with" us. And if we need something . . .'

'I'll do anything to help,' Themis promised.

'You know not to mention anything to the others. And I mean anything. This is life and death, Themis. You understand that.'

Panos knew that in the game of resistance and subterfuge, a teenage innocent such as Themis, who still looked so much younger than her years, could be invaluable. The occupying soldiers invariably picked on the most obvious young men as their suspects when the real perpetrator, an innocent girl or an old lady, might be right under their noses.

Themis was happy, first that Panos had confided in her, but even more so because she might be allowed to take some action herself. Anything would be better than simply accepting the status quo. As soon as possible, she hoped to be called on to do something that could make a real difference.

Warmer temperatures were coming and fewer corpses were seen on the street but inflation and shortage of all commodities continued to put adequate food way beyond the reach of most people. The government seemed powerless to improve their situation, and at the end of 1942, only Thanasis was optimistic when the Prime Minister, Georgios Tsolakoglou, resigned. He was replaced by Constantine Logothetopoulos, who had studied medicine in Germany and was married to the niece of a German field marshall.

'I am sure he'll do a better job,' said Thanasis cheerfully when he came home from the station. Being in the police force more than satisfied his desire for order, discipline and a uniform, and the family had never known him happier.

He was smiling and eager to bait Panos with the news.

'He is a Germanophile,' he said triumphantly, 'so he'll be able to get more favourable terms from them. That's good for everyone, isn't it?'

With every comment he made, Thanasis drove a dagger deeper into his brother's beliefs.

'He's just another bloody puppet!' Panos exclaimed. The new prime minister had congratulated the German ambassador for his country's success and everyone knew it.

'I don't even believe we're really brothers,' Panos continued. 'You seem to have *Nazi* blood.'

'Panos!' interrupted Kyría Koralis. 'Stop. You offend all of us by saying such things. Think of your mother and your father!'

She was standing at the stove stirring a pot that contained little more than hot water and lentils. Now that the jewellery had all been sold, even Kyría Koralis felt the full impact of austerity in the kitchen. When the bread was cut she swept every last crumb into a jar for later use, substituted grated aubergines for meat and boiled raisins to create a syrup.

The children all stared at her. Several months had gone by without any mention of their parents. Eleftheria had become little more than a ghost in Themis' imagination. Sometimes she saw her in a dream, an ethereal figure in white robes in a ghostly space.

A letter had recently arrived, addressed to their father but opened by Kyría Koralis. It had taken three months to travel across occupied Greece and was the brief annual report giving Eleftheria's condition. Themis' image was not so far from reality. Her mother never wore anything other than a pastel-coloured hospital gown these days and she was regularly confined in a white room, but it was a padded cell rather than the almost paradisiacal situation her daughter imagined. Kyría Koralis had hidden the letter away so that none of the children would have any idea of their mother's situation.

Themis, trying to contain the spark that had been ignited between her brothers, suddenly suggested that they should try to bring their mother back to Athens. The idea was met with little enthusiasm from her three siblings and blank refusal from their grandmother.

'After all this time, she is better off where she is,' said Kyría Koralis categorically, careful not to reveal what she knew about her daughter-in-law. 'There is no chance of travelling there. And the Nazis have no sympathy for anyone who isn't . . .'

'Isn't what?' enquired Themis innocently.

'Normal,' said Margarita, finishing her grandmother's sentence.

'What do you mean?'

'You know she isn't normal,' taunted Margarita. 'Don't pretend. And maybe it runs in the family, in any case.'

She leaned towards her younger sister, caterwauling like one of the Furies, her face pulled into a ghoulish grimace.

'Stop it!' commanded Panos. 'Behave.'

'Me? You can't tell me what to do!'

She launched at her brother, continuing to squeal like a harpy.

'You're heartless, Margarita. Utterly heartless.'

Without even waiting to eat the soup that had been set down in front of him, Panos grabbed a piece of bread and left the table.

Margarita stopped squawking, momentarily ashamed.

There was a temporary lull in the conversation. Their minds were on their father as well as their mother.

Kyría Koralis had been waiting for the right moment to tell the family that their father had stopped sending them money. Now that every last piece of jewellery was sold, she had to come up with a reason why their meals were increasingly frugal.

'He is sorry that he can't provide for you, but his situation in America is not very easy now.'

The explanation was so vague, so flimsy, that there was nothing they could say.

The only income now was Thanasis' police salary, Panos' tips from the *kafeneío* and some meagre earnings of Margarita's from her dress shop, more and more of whose customers, as time went by, were German officers buying for their mistresses.

Their meal finished, Thanasis and Margarita left the table. Themis continued to sit there, musing over the absence of her parents, who had never seemed more distant and uncaring than at this moment.

'Does it really make any difference who your parents are?' she mused out loud. 'And how come we are so different, us four, and yet we have the same mother and father?'

'It's a mystery to me too. I only had one child myself, but you four . . .' Kyría Koralis shook her head. 'It baffles me. I can see a resemblance between you and Panos – you're as similar as two drops of water – but the other two?'

'It's hard to see what we have in common.'

'I don't know, *agápi mou*, I really don't know,' Kyría Koralis said, reflecting on how little anxiety Themis gave her compared with Margarita.

Margarita's comings and goings were always a source of unease but more so was the presence of perfume and fine stockings in her bedroom. Kyría Koralis knew that there was a need for her granddaughter to dress smartly for the shop, but her ready access to luxury goods was unusual for an eighteen-year-old.

The turning of one year into another usually brought a moment of optimism, but the beginning of 1943 was not marked by the prospect of any change. The Koralis family was hungrier than ever now that their table was bereft of eggs, meat and oil. While all of them were slimmer than in the past, Kyría Koralis suddenly and dramatically lost weight. The three flights of stairs to the apartment almost defeated her and when a fever set in she could not leave her bed. Thanasis acted quickly, finding a specialist doctor to come and see her. As they all feared, the diagnosis was tuberculosis. There was an epidemic in the city and hospitals were overstretched, but he exploited every privilege he had now that he was in the police force and a bed was soon found for her in the Sotiria Hospital.

In the first weeks of her hospitalisation, Thanasis drew up a rota so that one of the children went each day to see their grandmother but the conditions were unhygienic and patients so densely packed that the chances of infection for visitors were high. They heeded her plea to stay away.

Without Kyría Koralis' influence, there was nobody to mediate, moderate, or ensure that there was any fairness at the table. Themis undertook to cook, but her attempts to produce a meal from a few shreds of offal or a piece of root vegetable failed miserably.

Now that Kyría Koralis was not there keeping a watchful eye, always questioning, always fussing, all four of her grandchildren had greater freedom to come and go as they pleased. It would have grieved her to know that Panos was out of the house most nights and she would have fretted even more if she knew that he was drawing Themis on to what she thought of as 'the wrong path'.

The success of ELAS, the military arm of EAM, had, during the previous year, encouraged more people to join them. They had combined forces with their non-communist counterparts, EDES, as well as the British, to sabotage German and Italian transports, and managed the spectacular and disruptive destruction of a bridge near Gorgopotamos in the north. This triumph was a huge boost to morale, and the confidence of many Athenians was further boosted by the growing realisation that the Germans were not unassailable.

Many thousands, including Themis, displayed a new boldness when Kostis Palamas, a poet whom she and Fotini had admired, died at the end of February. They saw his burial service as an opportunity not just to mourn but also to show that their love for their homeland was uncrushed.

When she saw Panos grab his coat and leave, Themis could not restrain herself from following. She felt guilty about abandoning her duties at the soup kitchen but the compulsion to bid farewell to Palamas was overwhelming. It was several kilometres to the First Cemetery where the poet was to be buried and they linked arms as they walked, heads down to avoid eye contact with any soldiers, police or other civilians. They trusted no one these days.

On their route, they avoided Syntagma and took a detour through Plaka. It was a long time since they had felt its ancient paving stones beneath their feet and Themis was happy to glimpse the Parthenon above her, gleaming brightly against a chilly blue sky. She had not seen it this close up for many months.

Thousands of people were walking in the same direction, past the Temple of Zeus and up the hill. There was a gentle, steady flow. People were mostly silent, all shabbily dressed.

A few soldiers stood at the cemetery gates, watching nervously.

As they arrived, all that Themis and Panos could see were the backs of people's heads. They moved into the dense mass and were soon immersed.

Themis was too small to see what was happening at the front but occasionally caught a note of the service. It was, for her, a farewell to Fotini too. Many times in the past weeks she had reread her friend's exercise book and now, beneath her breath, she muttered the lines of one of the many Palamas poems that her friend had copied out. They had never meant so much until this moment:

O young life, wiped out by the blow of death
As you were dreaming in the rosy dawn . . .

The funeral of one person was always a reminder of other deaths. Themis would never forget Fotini, nor the terrible injustice of her early demise.

Then somewhere in the great throng, one person began to hum a familiar tune. A second joined in and added the words. Within moments there were four, eight, sixteen, exponentially on and on and the sound spread like a wave through the crowd and swelled into a display of patriotism that the onlooking troops could not silence.

Everyone from the front to the back opened their lungs and sang at full volume. It was the National Anthem and the words, if only they had understood them, could not have expressed a stronger message to their German and Italian enemies. They recounted the misery of the Greeks under the Ottomans and their struggle to be free. At this moment all those singing yearned for similar liberation.

From the Greeks of old whose dying
Brought to life and spirit free,
Now with ancient valour rising
Let us hail you, Liberty!

As they came to the end, there was silence. The crowd seemed stunned by its own act of rebellion, conducted under watchful German eyes. Their spontaneous outpouring of grief had not just been for the great poet, but also for their wounded country and countless personal losses. Such emotion had long been repressed and for a few moments they remembered how freedom had felt. Many who were there that day began to dream of liberation. Like many others, Themis had the sense that this defiant act of collective singing had suddenly made everything seem possible. From that moment her own boldness grew.

★

Shortly after Palamas' funeral, Kyría Koralis' health improved.

'I'm not ready to leave this world yet. Not like Mr Palamas,' Kyría Koralis said to Themis, who had resumed her visits despite Margarita's histrionic protests that she would catch tuberculosis and pass it to her.

'You look much better this week, *Yiayiá*,' said Themis, encouragingly, observing the colour in her grandmother's cheeks.

'I hope they'll discharge me soon,' said Kyría Koralis.

Themis talked to the nurses, who confirmed that her grandmother would be able to leave within a few weeks.

At around the same time, the forced mobilisation of the Greek civilian population was announced. Famine and desperation had already caused several thousand Greeks to sign up for work in German labour camps, but now men between the ages of sixteen and forty-five were told they must fight for Germany. The descriptions that filtered back home of the cruel conditions in the labour camps meant that this threat of more general German conscription was greeted with fear and horror. Panos struggled to contain his rage and told Themis that he would do everything to avoid it.

Some days later Themis set off to visit her grandmother again. When she got to the city centre, she found her way blocked by a massive demonstration. Panos had warned her that this might happen. People were protesting against civil mobilisation. She tried to find another route but eventually gave up.

That night Thanasis was annoyed that Themis had been prevented from visiting their grandmother. He objected to such protests.

'Is it surprising that people object to the idea of being taken off to Germany?' Panos demanded of his brother.

Thanasis did not answer, but even his silence was calculated to provoke.

'You would go and work in Germany in a labour camp? You would be happy doing that?'

'I already have a decent job,' answered Thanasis smugly. 'Otherwise, why not? At least it's work.'

'You listen to all this propaganda and believe it. That's the problem.'

'Propaganda! You're the one that swallows the propaganda, you bloody communist.'

Panos did not immediately respond to his brother. He was proud of his beliefs and would not deny his communist leanings. Surely it was correct to support the poor and oppressed?

As Thanasis saw it, Panos was following the pernicious Soviet path.

'Why can't you see any benefits in the new order of things?' he shouted with frustration at Panos.

Themis shrank slightly into her chair. She was much looking forward to her grandmother's return, knowing that such violent outbursts between the brothers would be at least partially contained.

'Do you really want to know why?' Panos retorted. 'So that there are rights for everyone in this country. Not just for the rich. Not just for politicians and Nazi sympathisers. The poor have a right to eat and the left has a right to free speech. If you want to live under German occupation for ever, that's your choice. But unlike you, I'm not submitting to the Nazis.'

Thanasis lifted his arm to take a swing at his brother, but Panos was expecting it. He expertly dodged the fist as it came at his face and moved behind the back of a chair, picking it up to defend himself. Panos was lean and nimble. He would always lose in a physical fight with his brother, but always won the game of ducking out of one.

On 5 March there was a bigger anti-government rally, with

banners demanding a ban on mobilisation and attacking the Prime Minister. Seven thousand people gathered in the centre of the city, among them wounded veterans from the campaign in Albania, government workers and students. Shops were shut and businesses stayed closed. It was tantamount to a strike.

When the crowd was fired on by the police, seven people died and dozens more were wounded. Thanasis had been on duty that day elsewhere in the city, but some of his colleagues were responsible for the deaths.

The brothers did not speak for many days. The event had been a victory and a defeat for them both: the Prime Minister blamed the communists for stirring up trouble and provoking violence, but also announced that there would be no civil mobilisation after all. Greeks would not be sent to Germany to work.

When Kyría Koralis was finally discharged, she arrived back after months of absence to find a great and burdensome silence in the apartment. The old lady walked slowly from room to room. A few items of clothing lay around in the bedrooms and she glanced at the photos of her son and the various portraits of his children on the dresser. Only their images reassured her of their existence. Everything seemed to have changed.

This wretched war, she thought, as she made a feeble attempt to light the stove, it's taken everything away.

Thanasis was regularly required for overtime and Panos was away for long hours in the *kafeneío*. Margarita spent all her waking hours in the shop, and Themis now ran the soup kitchen. It was rare for them all to sit around the big mahogany table now. It was as if those past noisy years had never happened.

It was true that the conflict which held Greece in its grip had changed their lives, but the ravages of time had also played their part.

Within the next few days, the Prime Minister, Logothetopoulos, left office.

'I can't say I'm sorry,' commented Panos. 'He didn't do much to help us, did he?'

'I'm sure he did his best,' responded Kyría Koralis, attempting to pre-empt a reaction from Thanasis since, for once, the boys were both home.

'But he sympathised with the Germans, *Yiayiá*. Everyone says so,' chimed in Themis.

'Well, let's hope that the next person will help his *patrída* a little more,' responded the old lady. 'And bring us all the bread we need.' She was more preoccupied than ever with feeding her family.

'He might be able to get us food,' said Panos. 'But this new man, Rallis, used to be a friend of Metaxas, so we know where his loyalties lie.'

Thanasis, for once, kept his thoughts to himself. He knew that Ioannis Rallis had a specific objective: to bring the communists under control. By that summer there were thirty thousand active members of the ELAS resistance and the Germans no longer had the manpower to deal with them alone. To the horror of many, the Germans provided weapons to a security battalion specially created by Rallis. Greeks were now armed to fight Greeks.

A few weeks later, with the fight against the resistance now greatly intensified, Panos left to join the struggle. He had warned Themis that he might leave Athens with Manolis, whom they had met that day at Fotini's house, but they agreed that he should keep his destination a secret. It would be safer for them both. Margarita was very capable of pulling her sister's hair, hard. She had been practising for years.

Both Panos and Themis were confident that his empty bed

might not be noticed for a while. His hours were irregular and Thanasis often did night duty.

In fact, two days passed before anyone mentioned his absence and while no one knew precisely where he had gone, they all understood the reason for his departure.

Chapter Nine

For Thanasis it was dangerous to have a member of family fighting for the communists and he was keen to ensure that the rest of the family was on his side. His 'theatre' was, as ever, the big table around which they always sat, which was more marked and dented than ever by pieces of crockery and cutlery angrily banged down.

Every time he came in from work, he brought the latest news, naturally told from the government perspective. The communists were achieving great success and he described the situation with increasing disgust. ELAS was taking over whole areas in the north of Greece and one night he had heard something that particularly disturbed him.

'They've set up their own courts,' he protested. 'Even a new taxation system! And anyone who doesn't agree with their politics becomes the enemy.'

'That's not right, is it?' responded Kyría Koralis.

'And they're persuading women to join them. Did you know that?' he continued. This upset Thanasis more than anything.

Themis had been half-listening and now her interest was fully aroused.

'They're abandoning their families and using guns,' he added, with evident disgust. 'Women in trousers! With weapons!'

Margarita, who had loved parading about in her EON uniform (it still hung in her wardrobe), was sitting in the corner, sewing on shirt buttons for her brother. She still had a passion for dressing up, but these days it was *haute couture* she aspired to.

'Trousers!' she echoed. 'How unnatural.'

Themis daydreamed. What would trousers actually feel like? She imagined they must be very comfortable. If someone handed her a pair, she would put them on in an instant.

She had long since learnt that it was better to stay silent during Thanasis' diatribes and nowadays it was more important than ever. Themis had a book on the table and was pretending to read. It was her standard subterfuge and lately she had something to hide.

As she had promised Panos before he left, Themis had begun to help the woman who had inspired him with her bravery: Lela Karagiannis. At the same moment each morning, she walked down the nearby street where Karagiannis lived an ostensibly normal life with her husband and seven children. From time to time she was discreetly passed a message telling her where to be and when. The instruction would outline an assignation, usually an encounter with a stranger with whom Themis had to engage in a short, artificial conversation before moving on. Essentially she was acting as a decoy, but her actions were so subtle that she hardly understood them herself. She never even saw Lela Karagiannis, but it was enough to know that she might be playing a role in saving a life, aiding an escape or providing cover for some greater act of resistance. If it could make even the smallest dent in the Axis hold on her country, it was worth it. Every act of resistance helped to distract German troops.

As Themis idly flicked over the pages, Thanasis continued, 'The ELAS leader is a monster!'

'But didn't he work with the British to destroy that bridge?' interjected Kyría Koralis.

'That was more than a year ago,' snapped Thanasis. 'And it was the last time he co-operated with anyone. Now Velouchiotis just does *what* he wants, *how* he wants. And most Greeks hate him.'

'Why do Greeks hate him?' asked Margarita.

Thanasis always demonstrated unfailing patience when his sister was slow to understand. Margarita was one of the few for whom the occupation had brought great benefits. This was a war that she did not particularly want to end.

'Because he even attacks other resistance groups now. They say he's violent even to those on his own side. He is an animal!'

'Please. . . Thanasis,' interjected Kyría Koralis.

She felt that he had said enough. She simply hoped that her granddaughters would always be protected from the brutality now rumoured to be commonplace in communist-held areas outside Athens.

Themis was quietly scornful of her sister's detachment from the turmoil that enveloped their country. She observed how Margarita, wrapped up in her own thoughts and dreams, came and went from her work each day, immaculately dressed, always with a smile on her face. More and more often, she was not even at home for their evening meal, as was the case on the night of September 1943 when they heard the radio announcement that the Italians had surrendered to the Allies and would be withdrawing from Greece.

'It's good news, isn't it?' Themis said to her grandmother.

Thanasis was out too so they were eating alone.

'Let's hope so, *agápi mou*,' she said. 'I just want this war to end . . .'

Before leaving, Mussolini's troops sold guns, grenades and even motorbikes to ELAS, and the knowledge that the Italians' absence would put additional pressure on the Germans significantly boosted morale in Greece. It also intensified resistance activity against the Nazis. Suddenly ELAS had new stocks of ammunition, but violence between the communist resistance and the resistance on the right also broke out. Thanasis, like many others, began to suspect that the communists would try to take over the whole country if and when liberation from the Germans came.

'Who would you rather have on your side if the Germans go?' he demanded of his grandmother. 'Mr Stalin, the communist? Or Mr Churchill, who believes in democracy? Because that's the choice.'

'All I really want is for Panos to come home safely,' replied Kyría Koralis, trying to avoid the question.

'But fighting with the communists is never going to be safe,' he told her. 'Because they're bullies. Don't you know the stories about them, *Yiayiá*?'

'They can bully the Germans all they want, as far as I am concerned,' replied Kyría Koralis. 'We have to get rid of them.'

'But it's not just the Germans they cause harm to! You know what happens every time they kill even a single German?'

His grandmother shook her head.

'The Germans take revenge. *Dozens* of Greeks die. And I mean dozens.'

'But Panos wouldn't mean that to happen,' objected Kyría Koralis.

'Maybe not. But these lefties are doing more harm than good. And I wish my brother could see it that way.' Thanasis never missed a chance to aim some criticism at his brother, even in his absence. His was a lifelong campaign to ensure that his grandmother should continue to favour him over Panos.

He would never see things as you see them, Themis thought to herself. He never did.

These stories of retribution on the mainland and islands were legion and, one December evening, Themis and Kyría Koralis stood reading a newspaper that Thanasis had left on the table.

They reacted with equal horror, Kyría Koralis mopping tears with her apron as she took in what had happened, details of which had been given by an eyewitness.

During the previous month, in order to wear down the resistance that had developed in a mountainous area of the Peloponnese, German occupation forces had organised a military operation around the town of Kalavryta. Their mission was to eradicate Greek guerrillas and retrieve seventy-eight German soldiers who had been abducted. When the corpses of some of the captured soldiers were found, an order for reprisals was signed by General Karl von le Suire. Vehicles and troops then advanced towards Kalavryta, burning down several villages on the way.

When the Nazis arrived in Kalavryta itself, they pushed women and children into the school building, locked them in and set the rest of the village alight. Outside, almost five hundred men and boys over twelve years of age were then forced to march up to the hill overlooking the village. There they were lined up and methodically machine-gunned down. The witness, an old shepherd, who had been out in the fields with his livestock when the soldiers arrived, returned just as the killings began and said that the massacre of the male villagers took more than two hours. When the women and children escaped from the school every building in the village was ablaze. Over the following hours and days, numbed by shock, hunger and the cold, wives and mothers, sisters and grandmothers, began to bury their menfolk.

According to the witness, the hands on the church's clock tower stopped at thirty-four minutes past two. This, he said, was the time that the first man had fallen. After murdering the men and boys, the Germans had slaughtered thousands of animals and set fire to crops, leaving survivors with neither homes nor food.

Themis was in tears by the time she finished reading, imagining how the women must have felt as they buried their loved ones. She suspected that the living might have envied the dead.

For once, the Koralis family were in agreement. The killing spree in that small town and the nearby villages was an act of unjustifiable brutality and revenge. It had taken more than a thousand lives. They all expressed the hope that Panos had been far away from these horrors, but even so, Thanasis could not resist making a link to his brother, suspicious that he might have been involved.

It was the Nazis who had murdered without mercy, but he insisted on focusing blame on the communists.

'ELAS should have respected the wishes of the villagers in Kalavryta,' he said, 'and kept away.'

'But *nothing* justifies slaying all those innocent people,' cried Themis. 'Nothing!'

'I am telling you, Themis. ELAS should have known there would be reprisals for killing German soldiers!'

'But why do you have to blame someone apart from the Germans? Why are you blaming the Greeks?'

Themis could not keep her emotions in check. The barbarism of the massacre had shocked her, and now her brother seemed almost to be excusing it.

'Please!' said their grandmother in a conciliatory tone. 'It's a terrible thing that's happened. But it's not going to make anything better if you shout at each other.'

'I just want Themis to understand those poor people in Kalavryta paid the price for ELAS' pointless actions. And she should understand that this is what the leftists do. They put everyone in danger. Like Panos! He puts all of us in danger.'

'Enough, Thanasis,' Kyría Koralis said. 'Enough.'

'I can't listen to him anyway,' snapped Themis. It was the first time that she had stood up to her brother so openly.

Seething with anger, she stormed out of the apartment, leaving Thanasis lecturing their grandmother about the dangers of the communist rebels and the benefits of arming tens of thousands of Greek militias to defeat them.

'I know it looks as if they are siding with the Germans but isn't that better than having those leftist idiots taking over our motherland? Please think about it, *Yiayiá*. What kind of Greece do we really want?'

Kyría Koralis did not respond. She just wanted everything to be as it had been before the occupation, to have enough food on the table, to know that the lights were not suddenly going to go out, and to have some new leather soles for her shoes. She was still recuperating after her stay in hospital and these debates sapped her energy.

For the next few months in the Patissia apartment, uneasiness between Thanasis and Themis grew. The only family member who seemed happy was Margarita, who went about looking radiant.

'It's nice to see someone with a smile on their face,' said Kyría Koralis when they were alone one day.

Margarita hugged her grandmother.

'I am happy, *Yiayiá*,' she whispered into her ear. 'I'm in love.'

'In love?' Kyría Koralis cried out, with pleasure.

'Shh . . .' her granddaughter reprimanded. 'Nobody must know.'

'Why?' asked Kyría Koralis. 'Why is it a secret? Love is a wonderful thing.'

'Because . . .' she answered, lowering her voice to a whisper, '. . . it's with a German officer.'

Kyría Koralis did not know how to react but, before she had

time to say anything, Margarita had rolled up the edge of her sleeve to show her something.

'Look!'

On her wrist glittered a diamond watch of such delicacy and beauty that her grandmother gasped.

'Where . . . where did you get it?'

'He gave it to me!' she said conspiratorially. 'Isn't it beautiful?'

It was clearly not a brand-new watch and Kyría Koralis was reminded of all the jewellery she had been obliged to sell. It must have been owned by someone else who had suffered as they had, or perhaps even one of the departed Jewish families who, it was rumoured, had been obliged to leave all their possessions behind.

'He's given me lots of other things too!'

The old lady did not know what to say. She asked no more questions and promised to keep Margarita's secret to herself. She knew what Themis would say.

Themis, meanwhile, grew more suspicious. She even asked her grandmother how she thought Margarita always found silk stock-ings, when everyone else had thick pairs darned or criss-crossed with ladders. And why she imagined her hair was in the latest style, so well coiffed and stiff with lacquer.

Kyría Koralis shrugged, keen to prevent the storm that would result if she told the truth.

Eventually Themis confronted her sister directly.

'Where do you get all these things?' she asked, knowing that the answer could only be from a small number of sources. The black market? A German soldier?

Margarita justified her glamorous appearance with characteristic venom.

'We can't all go round looking like you,' she taunted her sister. 'Some of us like to try a little harder. Isn't that part of the war effort?'

It was true that Margarita had to be well dressed for the shop. Over the past eighteen months, she had adapted every item from the pile of her mother's old clothes still in her grandmother's wardrobe as well as altering other dresses she bought second-hand. She stood in front of the mirror for many hours at a time with a box of pins at her side and carefully tailored a garment around herself. It was a knack that she had developed and the resulting dresses, in vivid florals, crèpe de Chine, silk and velvet, perfectly fitted the contours of her body.

Nowadays it was common practice to recycle. Nothing was thrown away: from potato peelings to worn socks, there was a use for everything. Margarita had truly found her *métier* and the results of her work were miraculous. Poured into her glamorous outfits, Margarita's attempts to emulate the movie stars was helped by her full figure (rare in Athens during those times) and a pout that she had finally perfected.

Themis caught sight of her sister in the street one afternoon. She was with her friend Marina and the pair of them were chatting with two officers in Nazi uniform. The four of them were laughing and smiling and the familiarity between them all was evident. One of the soldiers touched her sister's arm and then the girls walked off in a separate direction from the men. Themis noticed the soldiers look over their shoulders to get a final glimpse of Margarita and Marina, who had now linked arms. Themis recognised that even their swaying, flirtatious walk was designed to hold male attention.

Unlike Margarita, Themis blended easily into the grey Athens background. For women from eight to eighty, dresses were cut to the same plain, mostly button-through style, and her dowdy, thread-bare clothes were typical. What Margarita and Themis considered 'part of the war effort' was very different.

The blandness of Themis' appearance was helping her continue to play a role in the quiet struggle against the occupying force. Sometimes she went to sit in the *kafeneío* where Panos had worked and eavesdropped on conversations that in turn she could pass on. She understood that the departure of the Italians had put great strain on the Germans, along with increased raids by British and Greek special forces on the islands. In addition, there was growing anxiety over the advancing Russian army. Each day, she felt a little more optimistic and proud that she might be part of a bigger campaign.

Large areas of mountain Greece were now under communist resistance control and the Germans began to rely increasingly on the Greek security battalions to fight them.

It was a blow to Themis and everyone with left leanings when, apparently determined to prevent Greece falling under the influence of the Russians, Britain lent its support to the right-wing resistance forces. She feared more and more for Panos and all those he was fighting with. They now effectively had German, British and Greek resources against them.

The Germans continued to perpetrate barbaric acts of revenge even as they were losing their hold. On 1 May 1944, the day that in peacetime would have been a joyous celebration of summer, two hundred communist prisoners were executed in Kaisariani, in retaliation for the killing of a single German major-general. Themis and Thanasis scarcely exchanged a word about this event, which occurred in a nearby suburb.

When Allied troops landed in France in June, the Germans were already struggling to keep control over Greece. Resistance activities were demoralising them, which gave Themis cause for optimism, but each day brought new calamity. Counterattacks seemed to be stronger than ever.

Another massacre aroused disgust and debate in the apartment. This time it was in the village of Distomo, one hundred and fifty kilometres west of Athens, and even Margarita was distressed to learn of it.

Information was sketchy at first because there were few eyewitnesses, but a handful of survivors reported that German soldiers went from house to house bayoneting everyone they could find: babies (born and unborn), men, women, children, even dogs and livestock. The priest was hanged and other bodies were found strung up in trees; people were cut down in the main street as they tried to flee. In one afternoon, the population was almost wiped out and most buildings razed to the ground.

'They say that hundreds were murdered,' Themis murmured.

'I'm sure that's an exaggeration,' said Kyría Koralis.

As usual, Thanasis used the news story as evidence of resistance fighters causing trouble for ordinary Greeks, but to Themis it sounded like another example of the Germans looking for an excuse to kill.

'Leftists had been firing on the Germans. That's what started it all. It happens time and time again!' he raged. 'The innocent pay the price.'

'Yes!' cried Margarita, her voice full of sentimentality. 'They say that even newborn babies died. So why don't the resistance just stay away?'

'But ELAS didn't kill them!' protested Themis. 'The *Germans* did!'

Themis could scarcely contain her frustration with her siblings. They were blind to the fact that the resistance was struggling to liberate her country. Every day at the soup kitchen she looked into the eyes of people who were hungry, homeless or afraid, and knew that it was the Germans who had reduced their lives to this, not ELAS. The period of extreme famine was over but there were still many who were destitute, with nothing but what they stood up in.

Added to this, many Jews were now in hiding around the city and in need of help. Tens of thousands had already been sent to Poland by the Germans, but some had ignored the summons to register, sensing that their lives were in danger. Themis often went home via one of a number of safe houses, casually leaving packages of food in a hallway. Those living in fear of the Germans and their spies were often saved by Lela Karagiannis' network, which spread across Athens. Themis never met these invisible victims of Nazi terror, but she knew that she was helping them survive.

Themis assiduously followed her routine, always carrying in her mind an image of Fotini. If she could save even one person, she was saving someone's child, someone's brother, someone's friend, and any risk was worth it. One July day, as she strolled nonchalantly down a street in the usual neighbourhood, the note that was slipped into her hand was not along the usual lines. There was no drop-off address for food. No instructions. It simply stated: *'Keep walking. Don't return.'*

Her hands shook as she read it and her legs only just carried her to the end of the road. She knew it was important to act as if nothing had happened, to keep going and then take a detour home.

The next day, Thanasis announced with something like glee that a local woman had been arrested by the Germans.

'For espionage and hiding subversives,' he said.

Themis knew immediately that he was referring to Lela Karagiannis. Somebody must have betrayed her. Perhaps even

Thanasis himself had informed on her. She struggled to dismiss the idea from her mind but day by day she was growing more and more mistrustful and isolated from her family.

As Thanasis was reporting this news, the door opened. Themis expected to see Margarita, flouncing in with her high heels and broad, scarlet smile. Instead, it was Panos who came towards them in the half-light.

It was more than a year since he had left and Themis' joy was as undisguised as Thanasis' displeasure.

'You survived, then?' asked Thanasis bluntly.

'I can't believe it. You're back!' said Themis simply, hugging her brother tightly.

Panos said nothing. Initially, Themis had not realised what a terrible condition he was in but as she held him close the truth became evident. It was almost uncomfortable to embrace him, so sharp were the bones that almost broke through his skin.

She noticed that his face and hands were covered with sores.

Thanasis recoiled.

'We must bathe these,' said Themis, leading him to a chair. She quickly put on a pan of water and reached for the jar of salt. 'Some of these look infected.'

Panos silently complied, taking off his shirt to reveal long, deep wheals across his back. He said very little for a while, occasionally wincing as his sister dabbed at his wounds.

'You were whipped?' asked Thanasis.

Panos glanced up at his brother. No answer was needed. Thanasis left the room.

Themis was full of questions, but knew that now was not the time.

'Thank God you're back,' she said quietly. 'Thank God.'

While she was still treating her brother, their grandmother came in from her errands.

'*Panagiá mou!*' the old lady cried out. 'Panos! Where have you been?'

She spoke to him as though he was late for a meal.

She suddenly noticed what Themis was doing and recoiled at the depth and severity of the lesions.

'*Agápi mou, agápi mou* . . .' she said tearfully. 'You poor boy . . .'

Over the course of the next few hours, they learnt more. Panos had been arrested in the mountains by a member of a security battalion and handed over to the Germans. For the past few months he had been locked inside the prison in Haidari, not far from where they were sitting now.

'We were beaten every day,' he muttered. 'Every few hours the door opened and they took one of us away. We never knew whose turn it would be.'

Panos' eyes were full of pain as he retold the events of past weeks. He had known many of those who had been executed at Kaisariani and even now experienced moments of guilt that he had not been among them.

Themis put her brother to bed but the cool, fresh sheets were soon marked with the blood that seeped through the dressings. Over the following days, she kept Panos company and he told her about his months engaged in acts of sabotage, his arrest and the sub-human conditions in the prison. In turn, Themis told Panos of her small rebellions against the occupier and they shared their sadness over the courageous Karagiannis.

Margarita kept her distance, squeamish about the way her brother looked.

Thanasis did not go near him either, and slept on the couch rather than share a room with him.

★

As Panos slowly regained his strength the Nazis gradually lost theirs. Over the following months, with defeat on the Eastern Front and invasion by the Russians, Germany was forced to capitulate. In October 1944 they withdrew from Athens but, as they made their way north, they went on a new campaign of destruction, wrecking roads, bridges and railways as they passed.

The family were as divided as ever in their reaction to the end of occupation.

Themis, who had longed for this moment, felt a huge sense of relief. On a warm, sunny day in mid-October she joined the throng of people who streamed down Akademias Street towards Syntagma, cheering and waving flags.

It was only as she retraced her steps through the dilapidated city to the apartment that she realised it would be some time before she could walk the streets unafraid. Lela Karagiannis had been executed in September, only days before news of the German withdrawal. Someone, perhaps even in her own street, had betrayed her. The foreign troops might have gone, but other enemies remained.

Themis was almost home and as she passed the little church of Agios Andreas, she noticed a posy of white flowers had been left on its threshold. Intrigued, she bent down to read the label attached to them.

'*Ellada. May you rest in peace.*'

Themis paused. The author of this note was right. There was peace now but the Greece she once knew had died. Peace and death. Death and peace. One did not cancel out another.

She stood up and surveyed this ancient building that had witnessed both Turkish and German occupation.

Themis knew that her grandmother sometimes went to church, but the darkness of these past years had led Themis further from, rather than closer to, belief. It was years since she had been inside.

She pushed open the door and was taken aback to find the cramped interior bright with the flames of a thousand candles. A lone female shrouded in black sat motionless in the front pew. Themis could see her bare, scrawny legs, the protruding veins visible even in the darkness.

The space was no bigger than the Koralis' living room, every inch of its walls covered with paintings of the saints. In the flickering light, Themis studied their faces. A religious education teacher had once tried to explain the notion of '*charmolýpi*' to her class and her lecture had been met with thirty blank faces. Now, Themis wholly understood it. Joy-Pain. It was eloquently traced into the expression worn by every saint that looked down at her. She studied the very particular look in their eyes and realised she had seen it so many times. After all these years, she understood what the hapless teacher had been trying to get across about iconography: it was discernible in the unfathomable depth of the eyes, in the set of the lips, in the firmness of the jaw, in the angle of the head. In biblical terms it was the Joy of Salvation achieved through the Grief of Sacrifice. Peace and death, hope and despair, co-existing simultaneously and inextricably.

For Themis, childhood had ended with a flash of red coat in the square. It was also when she had let go of any faith. Three years on, now eighteen years old, Themis still felt the sting of grief. She continued to grieve the pointless death of Fotini, but now her heart had been lifted by the return of her brother. She understood that the bitter and the sweet must always live side by side.

When she went home, she sat on Panos' bed and talked about what she had seen.

'Perhaps that's what adulthood is,' said her brother.

'To understand that happiness is always tainted?'

139

'I know no more than you,' he said gravely. 'But it seems to be true, doesn't it?'

They were alone in the apartment. Margarita and Thanasis were at work and Kyría Koralis had already gone out to find sugar in the local shop, optimistically imagining that rationing would have ended that day.

'We have achieved a victory and yet I cannot celebrate it,' continued Panos. 'Even if I felt strong enough to go out into the street, I wouldn't.'

Themis nodded with understanding.

'I saw men behaving like animals these past years. And some of them are out there, walking the streets,' said Panos.

There was an audible tremor in his voice. Since his return, Themis had noticed that it was not uncommon for Panos to lose control over his emotions. Tears ran down his cheeks.

He was still very frail but at least they might be able to feed and rebuild him, she reflected.

Thanasis was also uneasy about liberation, though for different reasons.

He believed that Greece could have benefited from a longer-term connection with Nazi Germany but accepted that the Fates had not decreed it. Now he was looking forward to the return of the government in exile, hoping they would put the communists in their place. It infuriated him that ELAS was now basking in glory, claiming the victory over the Germans for themselves.

Kyría Koralis was ambivalent, as always trying to sympathise with her grandchildren but failing to please any of them. What mattered to her most was that shops and markets might once again be well stocked with meat and oil and bread and all the other essentials of life that had been missing for so long.

Margarita's emotions were without ambiguity. Even '*lýpi*' –

sadness – did not describe it. Grief was closer. She sobbed and beat her pillow with her fists. Nothing her grandmother or anyone else could say would comfort her.

'He's gone . . . He's gone,' she wailed. '*Mein Geliebter*, my beloved, he's gone. *Mein Geliebter* . . .'

'Perhaps you should go to him, *agápi mou*. You might have a much better life in Germany. And he is so generous to you, this Heinz.'

It was first love, deep, strong and undying, and Margarita was inconsolable. When her words failed to comfort, Kyría Koralis tried another ploy.

'There will be someone else, my darling,' said the old lady, desperately. 'One day. I promise. There'll be someone else.'

Themis overheard her sister's lamentation and understood better what she had seen of Margarita and Marina with the two officers. The German language had become familiar in the street over the past two years, but nevertheless she was sickened to hear the sound of it in her own home.

'It does explain everything about these past months,' she whispered to Panos.

'She's a little traitor,' said Panos under his breath. 'And there are plenty more like her.'

'Plenty more collaborators, you mean?' asked Themis.

Panos nodded.

They both knew that the occupation was over, but the war was not.

As the last of the German soldiers left, tensions rose and antagonism between the brothers once again began. Panos' focus was on how those who had collaborated with the Germans should be dealt with. He had personally suffered at their hands.

'So what do you think should happen to anyone who supported the Nazis?' Panos challenged.

'That will be up to the new government, and they seem to have promised positions to some communist nominees so you should be pleased about that.'

Thanasis' sarcastic statement was designed to provoke but Kyría Koralis stood by, ready to be referee.

'Perhaps there are more important things to do than for Greeks to punish Greeks,' she said. 'Maybe we need to forgive.'

Panos and Themis exchanged glances.

'The most important thing is to put our country back together,' added Kyría Koralis.

'*Yiayiá* is right,' said Thanasis. 'Listen to her. We have to rebuild.'

She *was* right, of course. Thousands of villages had been left in a state of dereliction, tens of thousands of people had lost their homes and everything they owned, crops had been destroyed, churches damaged. An unknown number had died through famine and violence, some of it perpetrated by Greek against Greek.

Few who surveyed their devastated land were not touched by '*charmolýpi*' during those days, their joy at liberation tarnished by the sight of their country in ruins. For some, however, there was a less subtle feeling: a burning desire for justice.

Panos knew who had betrayed him and who had whipped him in the Haidari prison. They were men of his own nationality. Forgiveness was not uppermost in his mind these days.

Chapter Ten

'THEY'RE TOO WEAK . . .' Thanasis muttered as he read his newspaper one evening during the following week.

'Who?' asked Kyría Koralis.

'The government. If they don't demobilise the guerrillas, there'll be trouble.'

'You expect the communist resistance just to lay down their weapons?' exclaimed Panos. 'Why should they? Without any guarantees?'

'Guarantees of what?'

'A role, Thanasis! A role in the new government. Without ELAS, the Nazi flag would still be flying on the Acropolis.'

'You have no proof of that,' retorted Thanasis. 'The Germans didn't leave because of the communists. That's a ridiculous claim.'

'They played a big role in undermining them, Thanasis. You know that as well as I do.'

Thanasis did not contradict him, but as usual held fast to his position.

'Whatever your opinion, I don't know why the army doesn't use force to make them disarm.'

'I'm sure they know what they are doing,' insisted Kyría Koralis. 'We must be optimistic. At least we have food now . . .'

'More than we did, anyway,' said Themis, putting her arm around her grandmother. 'And you are so good at making the best of everything, *Yiayiá*.'

She was eating one of her grandmother's *gemistá* with obvious appreciation. Kyría Koralis could turn the most basic of ingredients, even rice and tomatoes, into food for the gods.

Unlike the others, who had put on kilos even in the first weeks after the Germans had departed, Margarita had grown thinner and more wan. Her breasts no longer pushed against the seams of her dress, and her belt was being drawn in notch by notch. At a moment when the city seemed to have regained its smile, she had lost hers. Even her beloved dress shop had closed down, now that the Germans had left. There was not enough custom.

Kyría Koralis thought she was the only one who knew the depth and the cause of the girl's sorrow. Themis and Panos were equally aware but offered no sympathy.

One evening when Themis wanted to defuse her brothers' argument about ELAS' role, she led Panos to the balcony where they sat down together in the last of the light.

'Try to ignore him, Panos,' she urged. 'He's just trying to provoke you. But you know the truth better than anyone.'

'It's obvious what's happening,' said Panos despairingly. 'But he refuses to see it. The government is back from exile with the Prime Minister, the government army brigades are on their way and thousands of British troops have arrived!'

'Panos, keep your voice down.'

'But, Themis, you know their aim. To crush us! To stop us having any power. And after all we've done to kick out the Germans . . .'

Themis well understood the situation. She put her hands on her brother's shaking shoulders and told him to be calm.

'There is nothing we can do at this moment,' she said.

The moon had come up and Themis noticed the glint of tears in her brother's eyes. She handed him her handkerchief.

Margarita went with her friend Marina to see the several thousand-strong government brigades march through the streets of the city.

'They were so handsome,' she whispered to her grandmother later. 'At least there is someone to keep us safe, in case the communists attack.'

'*Agápi mou*, don't speak like that. They won't attack us.'

'Don't be so sure, *Yiayiá*. Didn't you hear how they killed anyone who didn't support them? They're cruel, the communists. Worse than the Germans.'

'Keep your voice down, Margarita. Don't let Panos or Themis hear you say these things.'

'But it's true, *Yiayiá*. And I'm glad there are soldiers in Athens, whatever anyone says.'

Panos spent most of his days sitting at home. His sole outing each day was a short walk to buy the only newspaper he trusted, *Rizospastis*. He read it cover to cover and then left it on the kitchen table to provoke his brother. It never failed to infuriate Thanasis, who made a great show of putting it in the bin as soon as he returned home.

'Your problem is that you just sit around all day reading, thinking you know everything, when you know *nothing*,' he said scornfully. 'You should try and get out there a bit more.'

Panos was eager to do just this and, towards the end of October, as the hours of daylight decreased, his energy increased and from time to time he ventured out into the square. He looked at people and wondered. Even over the past months, he had never really known who were his friends. There was not always a uniform to make it clear.

Themis had time on her hands now that the soup kitchen had closed and went with Panos for slightly longer walks. One morning, not far from the centre, they both came to an abrupt halt. As they turned a corner they saw, just up ahead, a group of soldiers. They were not Greek.

'British,' said Panos under his breath. The khaki uniform was unmistakable.

'Everyone said they were coming,' said Themis.

As she said this, a convoy of trucks went by, in each of which were similarly uniformed men. They counted.

'Thirteen,' said Panos. 'Fifty in each.'

'Six hundred and fifty,' said Themis.

'Well done, little sister,' teased Panos.

'And I suppose that's not all,' she replied. 'There are rumours that Churchill is sending thousands.'

They kept walking and soon came level with the soldiers on the pavement.

One of them looked up and smiled at Themis and she immediately felt her brother bristle.

'Do you have a light?' asked an English voice.

Panos did not understand the words, but the gesture was clear enough. He got his treasured lighter from his pocket and the whole group leaned in to share the flame. The oldest of the men then produced a packet of cigarettes, an American brand, and offered one to Panos, who took it gratefully and with a smile.

He took the first puff while he was standing there with him. He had never tasted such sweet tobacco.

'*Efcharistó*,' he said. 'Thank you.'

'Ef-harry . . . stow,' one or two of them said, attempting their first Greek. 'Ef-harry . . . stow! Ef-harry-stow!'

Panos took his sister's arm and steered her round the laughing men. They took a long route home so that they would not pass them again.

'They seemed friendly enough,' Themis said.

'Don't be deceived,' said Panos. 'They're here because Churchill hates communists. And that's what they've come for. To help this government get rid of us.'

'How do you know that?' objected Themis.

'It's obvious, Themis. Churchill detests fascists but some say he loathes communists even more.'

With such a large military presence, normality had in no sense returned to the city, but over the next days Themis began to notice a few 'Position Vacant' signs in shop windows. She needed something to do so she began to stop and read them.

One day, on a stroll with Panos, she saw an advertisement in the window of a city-centre pharmacy and went inside to enquire. She had very sound knowledge of science and mathematics, and the owner, Kýrios Dimitriadis, could see that she was willing to work hard. In the first week of November she began.

From the moment she entered each morning, Themis walked into another world. The flawless symmetry of the rows of glass flasks, the neatly stacked boxes, the pattern of black and white floor tiles gave her a sense of calm. The pharmacy was spotless and the service meticulous.

One of her jobs was to keep the glass fronts of the big wooden cabinets free of fingerprints and to polish the dark mahogany frames. It was also her responsibility to take down the larger porcelain jars and refill them.

'They're almost as big as you,' smiled the pharmacist's son, who always seemed to be present when she had to climb the old wooden ladder to reach the higher shelves, sometimes holding her ankles 'to steady her', as he described it.

Themis felt very uncomfortable. His motive became even clearer when he trapped her in the shadowy storeroom and barred her exit, until she kissed him. She was angry and repulsed, not merely by the sweaty body pressed up against her, but by the abuse of power. He well knew how much she needed this job.

As essential drugs became more available over the following weeks and Themis learnt how to mix remedies for common illnesses, she also became expert at dealing with the Dimitriadis boy's unwanted attentions. Eventually he gave up his clumsy attempts at seduction and ignored her completely instead.

In exchange for her diligent work, the kindly father helped her to make ointments to calm Panos' scars and a mixture for her grandmother's persistent cough. Themis was almost sorry when the hour came each day to hang up her white coat behind the laboratory door. In the pharmacy everything was in its place, unlike in her home, where there was little harmony.

Thanasis was also working hard: his days at the station were long, his duties arduous and he and his colleagues were on constant alert. Towards the end of November, there was a rally attended by thousands to celebrate the anniversary of the founding of the Communist Party and he was assigned to attend. It sickened him to stand and listen to the speeches. If they were going to disband ELAS, insisted the speakers, then they should also demobilise the government army units.

Thanasis brought his fury home.

'We can't have these bloody communists making demands and wanting to take power. So the Prime Minister has to take control,' he said, banging the table.

'Thanasis!' said Kyría Koralis, wincing at the violence of his outburst. She was depressed. It was only weeks since the enemy troops had gone and already another conflict seemed to be brewing.

'Maybe it's not that simple,' said Themis. 'Not everyone agrees with his plans.'

Margarita sighed. 'Why don't you ever just accept things as they are, Themis?'

'Because, Margarita, some of us don't like it when things are unfair,' she said quietly. 'We put up a fight.'

Margarita pouted.

'I didn't notice you protesting,' she retorted.

'You were too busy making friends with Nazis to notice *anything*,' said Themis.

Margarita lunged at her sister and slapped her hard across the face.

'You little *bitch*! Take that back. *Now.*'

Themis was reeling from the blow, holding the side of her face.

Thanasis held Margarita's arms to restrain her.

'Thanasis, let me go! Let me go! How *dare* she?'

It was not the accusation that she objected to, but the fact that Themis seemed to be making light of her love affair.

'Calm down, Margarita. Please.'

'She's a little *bitch*. She doesn't understand. She'll *never* find love. Nobody will *ever* want to marry her.'

The hatred that poured out of Margarita shocked them all. Even Kyría Koralis. Thanasis led his sister to her bedroom and the murmurs of their voices could be heard for some time. Themis remained in the kitchen and held a cold cloth to her swelling face.

Not long after this, the Prime Minister, Georgios Papandreou, issued a deadline for the communist resistance forces to report for demobilisation. Twenty thousand of them outside Athens went on alert and refused to give up their weapons. The six ministers in the government who supported ELAS resigned in protest at Papandreou's order and called for a demonstration.

Thanasis' hours were increased in preparation. A protest was expected.

On 3 December, he did not return home at the expected time. A meal waited for him on the table. The others had started. Margarita sat there absent-mindedly stirring her soup round and round without lifting the spoon to her mouth.

'He'll be back soon,' she said. 'You told him you were making *kléftiko* and I'm sure he won't miss his favourite dish.'

Panos was almost silent. He was annoyed with himself for not having the energy to go down to the centre, but the weather had turned cold and his fever seemed to come and go. He still needed a stick to walk any distance. If there was any kind of demonstration, he wanted to be there, especially now he suspected that Thanasis was there witnessing it. A copy of *Rizospastis* lay on the kitchen table and its headline, summoning supporters on the left to join the planned demonstration, seemed to reproach him.

Although her conscience had urged her to show solidarity, Themis had chosen to spend the day at home with Panos. She knew how much he would hate not to be part of the action, and used the excuse that it was a Sunday.

'I've worked so hard this week,' she said. 'I just want to rest.'

Not long after they had begun to eat, they heard a great commotion in the street. Themis leapt up.

Panos pulled himself out of his chair too.

Themis ran to open the balcony doors. A group of people were talking excitedly in the square below. Then they all heard a familiar sound.

'Gunfire . . .' said Panos, quietly. 'It's a long way off. But I'm sure that's what it is.'

'Well, we don't know who is shooting who,' said Kyría Koralis. 'So we mustn't jump to any conclusions.'

As they stood looking over the balcony, a neighbour ran into the square. He spotted them looking over the railings.

'There's been a killing,' he shouted. 'In Syntagma. They've fired on the protesters! The police just shot at them. It's mayhem down there!'

The neighbour was a known leftist, but he looked keen to get home and away from the trouble.

The four of them on the balcony looked at each other, with expressions of fear, horror and confusion. Themis ran inside to turn on the radio, but music was playing as normal and it was not broadcasting any reports.

'I don't want *any* of you going down there, do you understand? You are all to stay at home.'

Their grandmother's uncharacteristic sternness left no room for argument. It seemed that the best course of action now was to wait for Thanasis. He would know everything.

Around ten that night, as pale as a ghost and almost as sound- less, Thanasis came through the door. He drew out a chair from the kitchen table and sat down.

As the others gathered all around him, Kyría Koralis served up a plate of *kléftiko* and put it down in front of him. Thanasis pushed it away.

He put his head in his hands for a moment, before looking up.

'Do you know what happened?' he asked his grandmother.

'We heard a few things. But you were there,' said Kyría Koralis. 'So tell us.'

Thanasis began hesitantly, reliving events he wished to forget. His words came breathlessly, sometimes incomprehensibly.

'We had shut off the streets to Syntagma. That was early on. But some of them got through . . . And gradually more and more . . . There were tens of thousands of them. Children and women . . . not just men. And we were supposed to keep them away. They were converging on the police station!'

'But what were they doing?'

'Shouting at us! Waving banners . . .' he said, looking down at his hands, which rested on the table, '. . . and screaming at us, as though we were the enemy. Then they started attacking us, thrashing at us with their banners, and lashing out with their fists. And more and more of them joined in. It was terrifying. So we fired a few blanks to dispel them.'

'You were terrified of women?' asked Themis with disbelief. 'And *children*?'

Thanasis continued as though he had not heard her.

'They had broken through the cordons and were pouring into the square—'

'But how did people get killed? Because that's what they're saying . . .' pressed Themis.

'Someone – I don't know who – someone replaced their blanks with live ammunition.'

'*Theé mou!*' exclaimed Kyría Koralis, repeatedly making the sign of the cross over her breast.

'People began to fall. Ten? Twenty? No one knows.'

'But it can't have been *one* person firing at them,' said Panos. 'It must have been several of you.'

'Not me, Panos, maybe several of them, but not me. Not me!'

Thanasis' words were defensive. He seemed determined to

separate himself from these deaths. For the first time he looked up from his own hands, and into his brother's face.

'I did *not* kill anyone.'

Several moments passed before anyone spoke.

'So was that the end of it?' Themis asked.

'No. A massive crowd surged into the square, more and more of them, and round the police station. We locked ourselves in. It was chaos. I could see from the top window . . . One of the officers was trapped outside and he was kicked to death. There was nothing we could do. They started trying to get in, screaming and shouting and throwing things at the windows.'

By now Thanasis was crying like a child in his grandmother's arms, his whole body shaking with shock. Kyría Koralis was stroking his hair, rocking him and muttering words of comfort.

Panos turned away, disgusted by his brother's complicity in these events. In Panos' view, Thanasis had always supported violence against honest people, but it appeared that he had never had to confront the reality. He looked at his brother with disdain.

What kind of coward was he, weeping as if the events had nothing to do with him? Had he not stood and let them happen?

They listened to the radio that night and heard Papandreou laying the blame squarely at the feet of ELAS, stating that they were leading the country to civil war, accusing them of 'stabbing their country in the heart'. Panos quietly withdrew to his room.

The others stayed up, trying to make sense of it. Even the official reports were confused. Nobody seemed to know what had happened, who had fired the shots, who was culpable, how many had died. Some reports said two dozen. Some only half a dozen. It was the same for the numbers of wounded. Nobody was sure.

Eventually everyone retired. There was nothing more to be said that night.

The magnitude of these events meant that the police were on high alert and Thanasis had been told to report for duty early the following morning. His eyelids were heavy, but each time he allowed them to close, he saw a crowd closing in on him. Even on this cold night, his sheets were ice-cold with sweat. He slept for no longer than an hour or two.

He rose before dawn, his fingers trembling as he buttoned his heavy grey jacket. Thanasis had always been so proud of this uniform but today was aware that it made him a target. With great trepidation he emerged into the dark of the day and set off in the direction of the city centre.

At five in the morning, the streets were silent save for the sound of his own metal-capped heels. At one point he heard a long, low, eerie howling and quickened his pace. He did not want to face some stranger's grief. When a black shape darted out in front of him, he realised his mistake. It was a cat on heat.

Halfway through his journey, a small delivery van slowed down as it passed. The driver had lowered his window and Thanasis felt the man's eyes on him. He turned his head to encounter a look of hate and accusation.

'Murderer!' shouted the driver, spitting out of the window before driving off.

Although the mood at the police station was sombre, he was relieved to arrive at his destination.

Thanasis was immediately dispatched to man a post on the other side of Syntagma. It was only a fifteen-minute walk but his legs shook with anxiety as he set off. He had never felt more vulnerable but kept his head high and his eyes straight ahead. Fear must never show on a policeman's face, he told himself.

Around mid-morning, in spite of their grandmother's protests, both Panos and Themis got ready to leave the apartment.

'You aren't well enough,' Kyría Koralis pleaded to Panos.

'I want to pay my respects to the dead,' he answered.

'It matters, *Yiayiá* . . .' Themis tried to explain.

'But you don't know the deceased,' insisted the old lady. 'You don't even know their names.'

Panos and Themis exchanged a glance. Any ELAS comrade, dead or alive, was their friend.

Linking arms, they set off down Patission Avenue towards Omonia Square. Their pace was slow, with Panos leaning heavily on his stick, and by the time they reached the city centre, they found themselves at the tail end of a long procession.

They could not see much, but reports of what was happening at the front circulated among the crowd. Apparently there were twenty-four coffins in the cortège.

'The police are telling people they're full of stones,' said a woman. 'But they're not.'

'Each one of them has a body,' said another. 'The body of an innocent.'

Flags and banners fluttered above the heads of the crowd. The dampness of the air had made them heavy but they still furled and unfurled in the wind. Many of them were stained with red: the blood of the previous day's victims.

'There are so many women here,' Themis commented to her brother.

They watched as a small group of women screamed in the face of a policeman who stood impassively on a street corner. He would not retaliate today. There was an atmosphere of hysteria as widows drunk on grief screamed and wailed.

The biggest banner of all read:

When the people are threatened with tyranny, they must choose either chains or guns.

Guns were standard issue for both police and gendarmes who were keeping an eye on the situation, but they were also in the hands of government troops who were now positioning themselves for a struggle. Even after the demonstration ended, the city remained on edge.

Themis and Panos walked slowly home, fearful of what might come next.

'Something will happen,' said Panos. 'I am sure of it. That procession won't be the end of it.'

Kyría Koralis was fretting.

'When do you think Thanasis will be back?' she asked. 'He'll tell us what's happening, won't he?'

Thanasis did not return at the usual time, but they got some news from the radio. ELAS troops had moved into the capital and begun attacking police stations and government buildings.

Clashes swiftly intensified and thousands of British troops joined with the government army to fight the communists.

'You see,' said Panos to Themis. 'This is what they were waiting for. The chance to wipe us out. Fucking British!'

Kyría Koralis darted a disapproving look at her grandson.

'Please, *agápi mou* . . .'

'Shh, Panos. We're trying to listen,' said Margarita.

Themis followed Panos out on to the balcony. He was standing there with a look of fury on his face, one hand gripping the balcony rail so hard that the whites of his knuckles showed, the other holding a cigarette. His frustration at not being out there taking part in the action was palpable.

'I know what you're thinking,' she comforted him.

'We've swapped one set of foreigners on our soil for another,' he said. 'Instead of a German general attacking us, there's a British one. I told you, Themis, that man Churchill only cares about one thing.'

Themis nodded. The British Prime Minister's views on the communists were well known.

Street fighting was fierce and this time, no one had blank ammunition.

As the battles raged, the radio reports said, British soldiers used tanks to fire on ELAS, who had seized many police stations in the city and appeared to have the upper hand. Violence intensified with men, women and children all dying in crossfire between the various factions. Even during the occupation there had been no such bloodshed in the streets. Normal life in the city now ceased completely. Stores, restaurants and hotels were all closed and supplies of electricity and water cut. Bursts of sniper fire deterred anyone from going outside.

After three days, Kyría Koralis was beside herself with anxiety. Thanasis had not returned to Patissia since the fighting began.

'My precious boy,' she muttered, weeping over a photograph of her favourite grandson. It showed him graduating at the police academy. 'My darling boy.'

Estimates for the number of those already killed in the fighting varied, but the number of dead police was known to be more than five hundred.

'I'll go to the hospital nearest his station, *Yiayiá*,' said Margarita comfortingly on the fourth morning. 'Maybe he's there. We'll find him. Don't you worry.'

'It's so dangerous, *agápi mou*.'

'Themis will come with me, won't you, Themis?'

Themis thought it was madness to walk through the streets and the only word she could hear inside her head was 'no'. But she did not say it. Thanasis was a member of the hated police force but he was still her brother.

The two of them made for the Evangelismos Hospital, zigzagging through the backstreets. Without a word, they surveyed the wreckage as they got closer to the centre. It was shocking to see the glass of shop fronts and cafés shattered, façades destroyed by shells, walls spattered with the spray of bullets.

Margarita wanted to blame ELAS, whilst Themis was certain that government forces and the British had been responsible. A hostile silence lay between them.

Halfway to their destination, they passed Themis' pharmacy. All shops had been closed since the fighting had begun but now that they came within a hundred metres she realised it would not reopen for a very long time. The only reason she knew it was the Dimitriadis' shop was that a section of porcelain jar had rolled out into the gutter. Next to it was a label with the familiar name, one that she had been so proud to work for.

Themis stepped on to the threshold, the shards of glass crunching beneath her thin soles. The black-and-white tessellated floor had survived but every glass phial on every shelf had been destroyed, as if used by a sniper for target practice.

'*Panagiá mou . . .!*' she gasped. 'My beautiful shop.'

'It's not *yours*, Themis. It never was.'

Margarita was standing on the pavement. She was not interested in the damage.

'Come on,' she said. 'You can't just stand there crying.'

Themis did not move.

'We need to get a move on,' Margarita nagged.

At that moment the crack of gunfire made them both leap with fear.

Themis pulled her sister into the shop doorway.

'Get down,' she ordered her.

For once, Margarita did what her sister asked her. They both crouched in the shadows on the carpet of glass. For a while they held on to each other, brought close by fear.

The sporadic sound of gunfire continued in the street for a long while and at one point they heard voices directly outside.

'That was English they were talking,' said Themis, when the men had walked on. 'British troops.'

From time to time, the gunfire intensified again and they cowered even lower, holding their hands over their ears. At last, night began to fall and it became too dark for a gun to be aimed with accuracy. Only then was there silence.

Margarita peered at her watch. She had told Themis that it was a gift from a loyal customer at the shop but her sister suspected that it was from her German lover.

'It's nine,' she whispered. 'We have to get home. It's too late to go to the hospital.'

Themis nodded. All she wanted was to be in the safety of their apartment. The sisters held hands and, with their heads down, ran the entire length of Patission Avenue until the familiar turning to their square.

'We couldn't get there,' said Margarita breathlessly to their grand-mother, who was standing waiting expectantly for news. 'It was too dangerous.'

Both were exhausted but their sleep was regularly broken by bad dreams that night.

The following morning, a colleague and school friend of Thanasis came round to see them. Giannis looked apprehensive when he appeared at the door. He clearly had something to tell them.

'I don't know exactly what happened,' he said nervously, 'but we were on duty yesterday and we came under fire.'

'*Theé mou, theé mou*,' Kyría Koralis kept on repeating, crossing herself over and over again.

'We had to take cover in a nearby building – and it was shelled. It caught fire and we got trapped. I managed to get out but . . .'

'What?' urged Margarita.

'. . . Thanasis wasn't behind me. He didn't come out . . .' Giannis' voice tailed off.

Kyría Koralis sank into a chair. Themis and Margarita grasped each other.

'But it's all right. I've found out that he's in the Grande Bretagne. They're using it as a hospital.'

Kyría Koralis began to cry.

'How badly wounded is he? Can't we bring him home?' asked Margarita.

Giannis hesitated for a moment. 'I think he is safer where he is,' he said. 'And the military doctors are the best. I'll bring you news when I get it.'

Themis wondered if he was telling them everything he knew, and her suspicion grew when he seemed to change the subject. He told them that ELAS were arresting people they suspected of collaboration and taking them to interrogation places. It could happen to anyone if there was the slightest suspicion.

'You've just got to say the slightest thing against them,' he said, 'and you're done for.' He mimed having a gun at his head.

Then Giannis said he must leave. He was on duty again but promised to return if he found out any more.

The family was left in a state of relief and fear. At least they knew Thanasis was alive.

During the following days, the news in general continued to be disturbing as fighting continued. They were all aghast when a mass grave was found in one of the suburbs and it proved to most that ELAS was terrorising the city. Panos said little. He was suddenly ashamed of what his comrades were doing.

People seemed to be losing their humanity. The schism that existed between left and right had been allowed to widen, the polarisation to deepen, and now the city was paying the consequences.

Day after day, there were new and shocking reports of brutality and execution.

Survival became the central preoccupation of day-to-day life. The water supply was often cut off and bread was once again hard to come by.

'It was better when the Germans were here,' moaned Margarita. 'Now we can't even go out into the street.'

Themis could not contradict her. It had always been relatively safe to go outside before, but now it was foolhardy.

They gradually learnt to negotiate the dangers of the street, but what they had never imagined was that terror would come inside the home itself.

Kyría Koralis was dozing one afternoon, trying to put her worries about Thanasis to the back of her mind. Panos and Themis were sitting with their ears close to the radio trying to hear a news broadcast. Margarita was flicking through a well-thumbed German magazine. Suddenly the main door flew open; a single kick from a boot had been enough.

The entry of four British soldiers was so unexpected that they all froze where they were sitting. None of them really understood what was being shouted at them but instinctively put their hands

in the air, even the old lady. They were waved into the corner of
the room. All they knew was that they should get down and away
from the windows.

Before the Koralis family could really take in what was happening,
two of the soldiers had swept the cloth off the mahogany table,
dragged the heavy piece of furniture across the room to the balcony
doors and pushed it on to its side. Now, crouched behind it, they
took turns to lean round the side to take aim. The glass from the
doors was shattered into a thousand pieces and shards were scattered
across the floor. One of the soldiers crawled on all fours to the
balcony itself and began to fire.

Kyría Koralis, Margarita and Panos had been cowering behind
two armchairs but now managed to make their way unscathed
into one of the bedrooms. Themis stayed where she was.

In answer to the British shots came a volley of machine-gun
fire, and the battle between the soldiers and whoever was down
in the square continued for more than half an hour without a
moment's pause. Themis could see dozens of spent bullets lying
on the rug and wondered what would happen when the ammunition ran out. The notion that the assailants in the square might
come up to their apartment to hunt down British soldiers made
her feel sick to the point of nausea. They had no escape route.

Suddenly, one of the soldiers took a direct hit in the head.
Themis almost vomited as she saw the man's brains spill out on
to the floor. His death must have been almost instant. It was
shocking to see a stranger's corpse in their living room and she
had to look away.

After some time, everything went silent. The soldier who had
been on the balcony crawled back into the room and sheltered
behind the table, even though several bullets had penetrated it.
The atmosphere was tense. For some time, the soldiers sat whis-

pering to one another. Two of them shared a cigarette. It was obvious that their comrade was dead so there was no sense of urgency about leaving and, eventually, when they were confident enough that the coast was clear they left, dragging the body with them. Themis felt herself almost stop breathing as they passed her hiding place. For the second time, she wanted to retch. The smell of their sweat and the dead man's blood nauseated her.

Once the Koralis family had recovered a little from the shock, they spent the evening sweeping up the glass and picking tiny splinters out of the furniture, scrubbing stains from the rug and collecting spent cartridges. The table was put back in position, and Kyría Koralis spent hours polishing it, trying to remove the shrapnel marks. Tomorrow they would get the glass doors boarded up.

The following day, they heard a loud explosion. They all rushed to the balcony and looked out across the square. Flames were licking out of an apartment.

It had been blown up.

'Perhaps the communists mistook it for our place,' said Margarita. 'They say that they attack anywhere that might have given shelter to their enemies. And we had British soldiers here.'

'I never imagined we would be on the front line,' said Kyría Koralis tearfully. 'I hope dear Thanasis is safe.'

For the next seventy-two hours, Athens continued to be a battlefield. Sudden bursts of gunfire and the regular thud of shells put their nerves on edge and, with stories that some of the streets had been mined, going out to find food was more perilous than ever. Panos could not move fast enough, so the girls both went.

'At least something has brought them together,' commented Kyría Koralis, trying to find something positive to say to Panos. 'It's nice to see them talking, not just bickering.'

Her grandson did not answer.

'Do you think they will be allowed to go and fetch Thanasis?' she said brightly.

They still had no real idea of the nature of his injuries, but Giannis had called in again to tell them he was in good hands.

'I think he still needs proper medical care, *Yiayiá*,' Panos responded, realising that his grandmother had not read between the lines.

The situation worsened as ELAS troops arrived in Athens in large numbers and continued the fight against the British forces. Conciliatory offers came from the Prime Minister, Papandreou, saying that he would compromise once the communists had agreed to disarm, but there was no trust between the two sides.

Panos, Kyría Koralis and the two girls spent many more days effectively trapped in the apartment. In the low December light, it was gloomier than ever with the balcony doors still boarded up. They spent most of their time gathered round the radio, which kept them informed of the dramatic events taking place close by.

Papandreou resigned and was replaced by the more fiercely anti-communist General Plastiras. The King, who had remained in exile since the occupation, agreed to delay his return until there had been a referendum on the monarchy. The growing sense of division in the country was already severe enough, without adding to it the presence of the royal family, whose very existence was resented by so many people.

Then came rumours of retreat by ELAS troops. These turned out to be true, as did the information that they were taking hostages with them as they went. They seized thousands and force-marched them into the mountains. Reports of their actions shocked everyone, whether they were on the left or right.

'It's barbaric!' cried Margarita. 'People are being dragged from their homes and forced to march barefoot. And they're having to sleep outside in this cold . . .'

'How can they do that, Panos? How could anyone do such things?' asked Themis.

'I don't know, Themis. There is no excuse. I don't know what's got into them.'

'Desperation?' suggested Margarita. 'They know they're losing.'

Neither Panos nor Themis could disagree, nor could they condone such barbarism. The terror the communists were perpetrating was turning many of their own supporters against them.

In February, a treaty was signed at Varkiza, requiring the communists to release hostages and give up their weapons. Parliamentary elections were also promised for that year. Finally, it seemed that a semblance of their old life might return to the Koralis family.

'We just need Thanasis home now and everything will be back to normal,' said Kyría Koralis forcing a smile.

None of them wanted to dent their grandmother's optimism, but they all knew that there was much to be done before any kind of normality could be re-established. They were expecting Thanasis to be discharged soon, but no one was sure what state he was in. When he might return for duty was also uncertain, but Giannis had told them that he would be entitled to an invalidity allowance.

Neither Kyría Koralis nor her three other grandchildren currently had an income and Panos reflected that the prospect of living off his brother was galling in the extreme. He kept this thought to himself, however, since there was nothing else to keep them all warm and fed.

None of them had been out of the building much in two months but Kyría Koralis had not been out even once. She had not seen at first-hand the terrible destruction that had been perpetrated in the city. Bullets, shells and mines had left indelible scars. Her granddaughters had not even mentioned that both their places of work had been reduced to rubble.

Thanasis was brought home one morning in early March. A police truck dropped him in the square below and painfully, stair by stair, he made the long climb to the third floor.

He had been given a new uniform to wear for his return, but he did not look ready for action. Half of his face was concealed by a dressing and his right arm was strapped up in a sling. He would never again fire a gun, now that two of his fingers were missing.

Kyría Koralis wept when she saw her grandson. He had told Giannis to conceal the extent of his injuries from his family.

'Oh, my poor boy,' she cried. 'What did they do to you?'

The old lady embraced him as if he were made of porcelain, then led him gently out on to the balcony. She sat him down on a chair, put a blanket over his legs and then went inside to make him some coffee. For the first time that year the balcony was touched by a shaft of sunshine. Perhaps this long and terrible winter was over at last. Down in the square too the trees were beginning to show signs of life.

Thanasis was happy to be at home. After the initial period in the Grande Bretagne, about which he remembered nothing, he had been transferred to the Evangelismos Hospital and his time there had been wretched. Regardless of their wounds, the police were seen by the communists as the enemy and even as he lay there, he had feared attack.

The brothers were obliged to co-exist and spent most of the day confined in the small apartment with little to do but read their respective politically biased newspapers. Soon they regained the strength to argue. Suspicion that the terms of the Varkiza agreement were not strictly adhered to by either side created immediate sparks between them.

'ELAS was meant to hand in its firearms,' said Thanasis.

'They did,' replied Panos firmly.

'But not their automatic weapons,' replied Thanasis, slapping his paper with his good hand to emphasise the point. 'According to this, they kept everything but the unusable ones.'

'Thanasis, are you just wanting to fight?' asked Panos wearily. 'Because neither of us is really in the right condition for that . . .'

Themis listened but did not join in. She looked at them both and felt a great sadness. The two of them were no longer the young warriors they had once perceived themselves to be and were as irreparably damaged as the city itself.

Thanasis did not reply.

'The government has violated terms too, in any case,' Panos continued. 'They've arrested hundreds of ELAS fighters and thrown them into prison camps.'

Thanasis came back at him straightaway. 'But what if they had committed criminal acts?'

'Demobilisation wasn't meant to mean imprisonment,' snapped Panos.

He knew, though, that many ELAS soldiers, still armed, had retreated to the north of Greece or escaped beyond the borders. Brutal right-wing retaliation for the hostage-taking had begun, and with political instability and new fears of inflation, there was no sense that the conflict had ended.

In the Koralis apartment, Thanasis was frustrated by his near inability to walk. As he confided to Margarita, it was his idea of hell to be trapped listening to the breath of a communist.

Spurred by a similarly strong desire to get away from his brother,

Panos started going out to meet the handful of old friends who remained in Athens, including Manolis, the soldier Themis had first encountered at Fotini's house. Many in their group had fled or been captured, but they now heard that Zachariadis, the General Secretary of the Communist Party, had announced his plan to form a new army.

'The fight isn't over until our comrades are freed,' said Manolis.

'And if Zachariadis does what he's promising, then we should all sign up,' said Panos.

In the smoky sidestreet *kafeneío*, there was rising enthusiasm.

'Unless we want this country to be ruled by people who collaborated with the Nazis, we have to do something about it!'

'Who's happy to pick up a gun again?'

There was a murmur of assent.

The *kafetzís* who kept an eye open for them suddenly sent a teaspoon clattering across the floor in their direction. It was the sign he always used to warn them if they should leave. Across the street, he had spotted a member of the security battalions who was crossing the road right now.

Panos and his friends slipped out through the back door.

Chapter Eleven

THE CITY WAS struggling to return to normality. Themis' pharmacy reopened in another building and she was soon back at work, putting the inventory in order, weighing, measuring and taking notes on everything that Kýrios Dimitriadis was teaching her.

In the Koralis apartment the routine of the old life no longer ticked with a regular beat. Thanasis was at home and in a state of profound grief. His disabilities were going to be lifelong and he was in constant pain for which the only relief could be morphine, which he refused to take. It was a daily struggle to deal with his new vulnerability. Painstakingly, he was teaching himself to write with his left hand but struggled to do other basic things like wash and dress himself. Kyría Koralis was always there to help him.

The old lady accepted that her three other grandchildren came and went to their own schedules and she always made sure there was a pot of something on the stove to which they could help themselves. Pulses or rice were once again the basis of their diet.

At around ten o'clock one October evening, they all realised that they had not seen Margarita that day. She had found a job with a dressmaker, often working long hours, but it was unusual for her not to be home by this time.

'She didn't say anything to me about being late,' said Thanasis, who spent more time with her than the others.

Midnight came and their concern grew.

The last time Themis had seen her was in the morning. Themis recalled that her sister was still sleeping when she left for work. She and her grandmother went into the bedroom. If her best dress was not hanging in the wardrobe, it might indicate that she had gone out for the evening, perhaps to a musical performance. Occasionally she was invited by a colleague or customer.

Everything was in place except, Themis noticed, for one thing. Her winter coat was not on the back of the door. The weather was still warm in Athens and it was not yet time to wear anything woollen. Themis said nothing to her grandmother, who was standing anxiously next to her.

Themis turned to look at her sister's side of the bed; Margarita's was lazily made, the counterpane still crumpled, the sheets untucked. Then she noticed something poking out from under the pillow.

It was a note, hastily written on the back of a bill. Margarita must have known that sooner or later it would be found.

Dear Family,
It is now a year since Heinz left, and I cannot live another day of my life without him. I have decided to try and reach Germany. I will let you know when I get there.
   Margarita

'*Theé mou,*' whispered Kyría Koralis. 'I knew she would do that one day.'

Both the boys came into the room to see if something had been found, and Themis passed them the letter to read.

While Panos and Thanasis comforted their grandmother, Themis slid open the top drawer of her sister's bedside cabinet. It was empty. She had sometimes seen Margarita slipping her earnings in there and now understood what she had been saving for. She also saw that the little German phrase book that used to sit on top of the cabinet was missing.

'But how will she get there? Who will she travel with? What if something happens to her?'

'I am sure she'll be all right, *Yiayiá*,' said Thanasis, comfortingly. 'She knows how to look after herself.'

It was hard to imagine such a journey, especially with the terrible state of both road and rail systems, but there were thousands of refugees all across Europe, and, with her stubbornness and charm, Themis was confident that Margarita would survive. More importantly, she hoped her sister would find what she was looking for.

For the next few months, they waited and hoped.

In January 1946, news came that the first elections in a decade were to be held. That same week, Themis came home from the pharmacy and saw a letter lying on the mat. Her legs were shaking as she ran up the stairs, two at a time, and burst into the apartment.

'It's from Margarita!' she called out, waving the battered envelope. 'It's from Germany!'

She handed it to her grandmother, who slit it open carefully with the knife she was using to chop vegetables. The letter was as brief as the one that had announced her departure.

Dear Everyone,
I finally tracked Heinz down. Berlin is in a worse state than Athens.
War destroys everything. I miss you and hope you are well. Take
care.

   Love, Margarita

The letter was non-committal and yet, in spite of its brevity, Themis read something unexpected between the lines. The 'miss you' and the 'love'. Were they perhaps real?

All those difficult years with her sister seemed to vanish as she began to picture her in Berlin. There had been photographs of its derelict streets in the newspapers, so she knew that this much was true. Themis realised how deeply her sister must love this foreigner to have left for somewhere so unknown and so austere. She had never experienced such a passion herself, and felt a momentary pang of envy.

Thanasis had taken the letter out of her hands to read it.

'Is there an address?' asked Kyría Koralis. 'Does it say where she is living?'

'Nothing here,' he said. 'Perhaps it's on the envelope?'

Panos picked up the discarded envelope from the kitchen table and held it up to the light. An address had been smudged, probably by snow or rain on its journey.

'Just the Berlin postmark. That's all.'

'We'll have to wait for another letter,' said Thanasis. 'Perhaps the next one will tell us more.'

Kyría Koralis' expression was one of despair.

'My poor little Margarita,' she said. 'It doesn't even say if they are to marry.'

'As long as she is safe, *Yiayiá*,' responded Panos. 'That's what really matters.'

The combined relief and disappointment aroused by the letter were soon overshadowed by the forthcoming elections. Although women did not have the right to vote, Themis was glad that they were taking place.

'At least it's a chance for fairness!' she said. 'Maybe it will be a new start for this country!'

'Let's hope so, *agápi mou*,' responded Kyría Koralis. 'I am sure everyone will vote sensibly.'

'What do you mean, *Yiayiá*?' challenged Panos.

'I hope that every man will vote for the good of the country. That's what I mean,' she said.

Thanasis interrupted, aggressively. 'And not for his own selfish ideas. Or to open the gates to Stalin.'

'Thanasis . . .' said Themis, trying to calm the atmosphere, but he carried on, determined to make his point.

'Make no mistake, Panos, if the communists have their way, this country will just become a Soviet satellite. And that is *not* what's best for this country.'

Panos got up and leaned over Thanasis, his fury ill concealed.

'You think these are proper elections? That they're democratic? When there are thousands of people still in prison? And hundreds of thousands being persecuted? The same people who resisted the Germans?' Thanasis ignored the questions. 'The left will abstain,' Panos continued bluntly. 'None of us will vote.'

'That's your choice, you stupid, fucking communist!' Thanasis shouted triumphantly to his brother's retreating back.

Since his return from hospital, Thanasis had displayed extremes of emotion. Themis had once got home from work to find him quietly weeping on the balcony. More plentiful than tears were the moments when he lost all self-control. Even with his grand-mother in the room, he showed no restraint in his language.

Themis sat quietly. Even if she was shocked by Thanasis' outburst, she did agree with him that there was something illogical about turning down the chance to decide who governed. Her grand-mother felt the same.

'It's madness,' muttered the old lady, shaking her head. 'It's their chance to have their say. And then they don't take it. What's the sense in that?'

When the elections came in late March 1946, the mass absten-tion inevitably opened the way for a right-wing government, and the monarchy returned from exile. Former ELAS resistance fighters had already retreated into the mountains to escape repression and now the situation became even more polarised. Soon the new government was accusing the communists of receiving arms from across the borders in Bulgaria and Yugoslavia.

Thanasis was still not mobile enough to return to work, but his mood improved following this election. As if to mark the moment, he decided to remove the bandages that had kept his face concealed for more than a year and a half.

When Themis came in that day, she only just managed to repress a gasp. The whole of the left side of her brother's face was hid-eously disfigured, a jagged scar ran from eye to chin.

Panos said nothing. He rarely looked at his brother in any case.

For the first few days Thanasis tried to maintain some dignity by continuing to shave, but could not confront himself in the mirror for more than a few moments. A beard began to grow on one side, but not a single hair emerged from anywhere close to the scar, merely accentuating the disfigurement. Only his grand-mother referred to it.

'You're still such a handsome boy,' she told him. 'And it will fade.'

Both of them knew she was lying.

★

174

By the end of the year, the scattered resistance groups led by the Communist Party leadership formed the Democratic Army of Greece, DAG, the new army they had planned. Panos and most of his friends decided to join up straightaway. Manolis was hesitant.

'I think I've had enough of fighting,' he said.

The rest of the group were scornful of his lack of commitment and an hour later, after listening to his friends' arguments, he was persuaded to change his mind. The whole group clinked glasses together.

'To the communist army of Greece!' they chorused. 'To DAG!'

Back at home, Themis was dismayed that Panos would be leaving again.

'I am well enough now,' Panos said to her. 'I can't sit here any longer, listening to the radio and reading the reports. I don't just want to *hear* about the struggle, I want to take part in it.'

'You'll be restless if you don't, Panos. But are you strong enough?'

'I'll soon find out,' he said, taking his sister's hand.

'Will you be saying goodbye to our grandmother . . .?'

'No. I would rather Thanasis didn't know, so . . .'

'I'll help you, like the last time. It gave you a bit more time to get away.'

For the next forty-eight hours, Themis tried to distract herself from the sadness of Panos' impending departure, doing practical things such as darning the holes in his spare socks and buying some extra bread for him, which she wrapped in a cloth and stuffed into his pocket.

He left early, creeping out so quietly that Thanasis, who was in the same room, was totally unaware.

Only Themis, who had lain awake all night, heard the discreet 'click' of the latch. She resisted the temptation to leap out of bed, run and embrace her brother. She must not alert the rest of the household. Thanasis would have no hesitation in handing Panos over to his former colleagues. In these past years, many on the left had been betrayed by members of their own families and the grey area between friend and foe no longer existed. As far as the policeman was concerned, Panos was the enemy.

Tears rolled down Themis' face and into her pillow. She was missing her brother even before he had crossed the square to be picked up by a truck to begin his journey to the mountains.

By the time Kyría Koralis and Thanasis realised that he had gone, he was already far away. Themis put on a show of dismay, though Thanasis was not fooled.

'It's no surprise to me that he's left,' said Thanasis almost smugly. 'But he won't find it easy up there in the north. The government army is ready to fight him.'

Weeks went by and they heard nothing from Panos himself but the news stories of what was happening far away on the borders did nothing to reassure them of his safety.

'He must be so hungry,' Kyría Koralis fretted, listening to a radio report about small units attacking villages merely to find food. 'He was thin enough before he went.'

'There are innocent people in those villages. And they're killing them,' said Thanasis. 'They've had to impose martial law up there to stop the communists doing anything they damn well please.'

Even though her heart was with Panos' cause, Themis could not defend his army's actions. There were many first-hand accounts of rape and abduction, and she hoped that her brother was not responsible for such atrocities.

The broadcast they were listening to also suggested that other countries were supplying aid to the communists.

'And if they start getting help from north of the border, then the government will *destroy* them,' said Thanasis. 'Because it makes them traitors. My brother is a bloody *traitor*.'

'Please, Thanasis,' pleaded his grandmother.

When he got angry, his scar reddened. The jagged trench glistened now as though the wound was new and blood was still rising to the surface. The surgeon's stitches had been swiftly but clumsily executed.

It upset his grandmother to see him like this. She wanted him to be as he once was: her favourite grandson, the handsome one, the one who was most like his father. He had changed so much since his accident, not just in his looks but in his personality too.

Themis watched Kyría Koralis play an ever more intensive role with her brother. Cutting up his food and doing up his buttons were merely the practical things. In addition, she had to soothe him, calm him and nod in agreement with his views. Themis understood that her grandmother was motivated by love, but was none the less sickened by it.

The more reports came in of the communists gaining ground, the more regular became Thanasis' outbursts of anger. Civil war had deepened and everything around him seemed to be collapsing. His own city was still in a state of disintegration, the government was falling apart and people averted their gaze when they saw him in the street.

Thanasis scarcely left the apartment, whereas Themis tried to be out as much as possible to avoid her brother's simmering fury. The gloom of their home, where the electricity often failed and their breath came out in icy plumes, was almost unremitting in those colourless January days.

In spring 1947, Thanasis became a little more cheerful when the bleak outlook for the Greek government was marginally alleviated by aid from America. He knew that this economic support was not destined merely for feeding and rebuilding. It would also be used to finance military action against the communists, a fact that he openly celebrated.

Themis had learnt not to react. Since Panos had left, she did not have anyone to express her fears to. It was impossible to know from looking at someone's face what they believed or which side they were on, and even reaction to rumour or news was not a reliable indication of political allegiance. Only the new girl who had joined the pharmacy to replace Kýrios Dimitriadis' son seemed to be a like-mind. The son had joined up with the government army to fight the communists and, on her first day, Eleni had muttered something critical under her breath.

The same month that American aid was announced, Themis felt a change in the air. She paused to look at the headlines of *Rizospastis* at the kiosk one evening. Hundreds of communists had been arrested in Athens and over the next few weeks executions began.

Thanasis was always happy to relay stories of success in eliminating communist bands. He believed what he wanted to believe and read the newspapers that raised morale among the right.

Themis, on the other hand, heard that some soldiers in the government army were poorly trained and that, as well as being undisciplined and underpaid, many of them were deserting. Stories were also circulating that the communist army was increasing in manpower as a result, and the left-wing press implied there could soon be an independent communist state within Greece.

Battles were being fought over cities in the north and *Rizospastis* printed a map in late July that showed extensive areas under communist control. Themis daydreamed of Panos, victorious, on the front line of every battle. To these she added another dream: of escaping from Athens to join him.

★

The battles of the civil war were being fought elsewhere, but the hardship spread to Athens just as it did to every other city and village. Food shortages were now as they had been during the occupation and hundreds of thousands had fled the villages, fearful of communist brutality. The lack of food affected everyone, left and right, as did the arrival of these internal refugees on the streets of Athens.

'None of this misery would be happening if the communists weren't trying to take over the country!' Thanasis exclaimed.

Themis quietly tolerated her brother. Sometimes an event took place that put a smile on his crooked face and then she realised that his complaints were preferable to his gloating. The arrest of thousands more communists in July 1947 was a source of great satisfaction to him, and he was positively gleeful when he found out that staff from *Rizospastis* had been arrested.

'Soon Panos' precious communist newspaper won't be able to print any of its lies,' Thanasis said with satisfaction.

It was rare now for Thanasis to mention Panos' name and Themis flinched. His tone of voice reminded her of the hatred that existed between her brothers.

'It shows who is on the right side of the law,' continued Thanasis, adamantly. 'And who is not.'

None of Thanasis' statements needed a response, but occasionally Themis reacted without thinking.

'If you make up your own laws, then anyone can be on the wrong side of them,' she answered back, immediately feeling a pang of regret.

Even within her own house, she was anxious about expressing criticism of the authorities. In the street, there might be people who shared her views but in the apartment she was alone.

On her way to the pharmacy, which remained open despite

dwindling stocks, she always took a glance at the newspaper head-lines. She knew by now that some kiosk owners were making an extra living out of informing so she was careful to peruse the headlines of both the left- and right-wing press without buying either of them.

The facts encouraged her. In spite of the government's success with arrests and executions, the communists continued to take towns and villages, and support from their neighbours, Bulgaria, Yugoslavia and Albania, helped them maintain the upper hand.

Thanasis had bragged that everything would change once more American aid arrived and he was right. When it began to flow in, communist grip in many areas began to wane and the govern-ment army, with more weaponry and manpower, began to achieve greater success.

In December 1947, the Communist Party established its own Provisional Democratic Government and attacked Konitsa, a city in the north-west, to make it their capital, their own Athens. There were great losses on both sides but, with the help of the govern-ment army, the people of the city successfully defended their town.

In Patissia, all three members of the Koralis family followed events ever more closely. To hear of a leftist incarceration or death gave Thanasis huge pleasure, and he was thrilled by the government win and the new law that officially outlawed the Communist Party.

'Those bandits will get what they deserve,' he said. He never dignified communist fighters with the name 'soldiers' and not once did he express any anxiety over his brother's safety.

As the left came under increasing pressure, Themis began to feel that she should take an active part in this conflict. Every day it weighed more heavily on her mind that she could no longer be a mere bystander.

There was nothing specific to keep her in Athens. Life in the apartment was tense, with Kyría Koralis constantly trying to placate Thanasis. Themis had concluded that her grandmother must share his right-wing views and found it abhorrent to listen to them both. On top of this, her job was about to finish. A few days earlier, the pharmacist had apologised that he would not be able to pay her at the end of the month. Stocks, as well as customers with enough money to purchase them, had run out.

The final impetus for her was an image in Thanasis' newspaper. The face of the new King's wife, Frederika, beamed from the front page. She had been photographed in Konitsa where she had gone to raise morale among government troops. Themis had always shared Panos' dislike of the monarchy but with Queen Frederika, it was more than that. She was German, the granddaughter of the Kaiser, and her brothers were known to have been in the SS. Many believed her to be a Nazi and now she was openly supporting the soldiers who were hell-bent on destroying the communists.

Sometimes the thought of Fotini still guided Themis. What would her friend have done? Surely she would have fought for justice and democracy?

The photograph taken in Konitsa reminded Themis that the communists needed all the help they could get. As soon as she could, she would join them.

Chapter Twelve

THEMIS HAD TOLD no one that she was losing her job and one day in late January 1948 she left, as usual, early in the morning. She had hurriedly scribbled a note and wedged it under a book by her bed, knowing that her grandmother would not go into her room until later in the day. She took her normal route but, a few hundred metres before the pharmacy, stopped to greet a young woman, a contact of Eleni's, her former colleague. They linked arms, turned into a sidestreet and strolled along as if they had not a care in the world. Eirini (Themis did not even know her family name) had a network of contacts, and by mid-morning Themis was in a truck taking her out of Athens.

Their 'story' for the next few days was quickly explained to Themis. The four girls and a boy were children of the farmer, who was driving, and they were on their way back to the country-side, having brought in produce from their smallholding. The young people quickly introduced themselves and established each other's ages. It was just about credible for them to be siblings. Katerina, the oldest, was a dramatic redhead. Then came Despina, who had long black hair. Themis was next in age order and Maria was the youngest, only just eighteen. She was even smaller than Themis and very fragile-looking, with light brown wavy hair and very blue eyes. The only boy, Thomas, was their big brother.

Many times along the road to the north they were stopped at checkpoints and, though their story was credible enough, Thomas, the 'son', was twice taken from the truck and interrogated. Every policeman and gendarme was determined to make arrests and a single departure from the script could betray them all.

On one occasion Themis found herself scrutinising the face of a young policeman. He reminded her of Thanasis before he was injured: proud and handsome, his moustache perfectly clipped and his hair neat from a weekly visit to the barber. A wave of sadness swept over her as she thought of her brother's shattered leg, his mutilated hand and a face made ugly by bitterness and scars.

Soon the battered vehicle was being waved on and the engine choked into life once again.

'Don't stare at them like that,' grunted Thomas. 'It takes nothing for them to pick on someone. And with a pretty face like yours, you could be the first to leave our little party.'

'Sorry,' mumbled Themis.

They drove on for many kilometres before having a short break.

'How often have you been on this road?' she asked the 'farmer'.

'More times than I can count,' he answered. 'And it's a miracle they don't notice I have a different family each time!'

Themis smiled.

'Though I always have a son and four daughters,' he added, chuckling. 'So the soldiers feel sorry for me. Who wants four daughters?'

'Probably nobody, when they're farming people,' said Katerina.

'You'll all turn into men soon,' he said more seriously. 'You'll have no choice.'

'What do you mean?' asked Maria innocently.

Thomas enlightened her.

'Trousers, for a start,' he said.

'Trousers,' repeated Despina. 'I *always* wanted to wear trousers.'

Themis listened, excited.

'And you'll be taught how to hold a gun.'

Maria was aghast.

'A gun?'

'Why do you think you are on this journey?' asked Thomas with scorn. 'To play with dolls?'

'I can do first aid,' Maria answered helpfully.

The other two girls, Despina and Katerina, were giggling. Unlike Maria, they knew what to expect.

'There is some need for nurses,' said Thomas kindly, 'but the real urgency is for fighters.'

Maria looked crestfallen.

'It's not easy up there, Maria. You need to realise that.'

The five young people climbed up into the back of the truck again, and the farmer set off. Conversation continued.

'Have you been before?' asked Themis.

'My brother was there with the government army,' answered the boy. 'He changed sides but came back to Athens when he was injured. He told me how tough it is, whatever side you are on. It's bloody. And brutal.'

All four girls were silent for a while. Maria turned away so that her face could not be seen, but when she glanced round, Themis noticed that her face was streaked with tears.

Thomas told them tales of success and failure by communist bands and the girls listened sometimes with excitement, sometimes with horror. Even for him, the stories were second-hand, but there were many hours to fill on this journey. He made them laugh as well as cry and even taught them some of the comrades' songs.

Along the journey, the five young people learnt about each other's lives. All of them had members of family on both left and right.

'I don't want Greece to be governed by collaborators,' said Katerina. 'That's why I am on this truck.'

'I was a teacher but I lost my job because my father was arrested,' said Despina. 'The whole family is branded now. No one is even allowed to *believe* in communist principles under this government.'

Their 'father' played his role well at checkpoints. Thomas took over the driving at night, so they only took occasional stops and slept on the move. After a few days they came to communist-held territory.

'Do you know much about where we are going?' Themis asked the farmer one night.

'I've never been there,' he answered cagily. 'I won't be taking you right to the end of the journey.'

When they reached the border with Yugoslavia he stopped his truck. Another, bigger vehicle was waiting for them. Six or seven young men were already sitting in the back when Thomas and the girls climbed in.

For many hours it rattled along the rutted roads, stopping once for a puncture to be mended. They had each been handed a flask of water and a slab of bread.

'How far is it now?' Themis whispered to Thomas, who was next to her.

'I heard the driver saying that we should be there before dark.'

One of the other men in the truck joined their conversation.

'I've heard good things about Bulkes,' he said. 'We'll be well trained and they say there's plenty of food.'

It was not the first time Themis had heard the name. She felt a mixture of excitement and trepidation. According to the right, Bulkes was an indoctrination camp, full of Greek children kidnapped by the communists. According to the left, it was a place of hope and equality, where partisans were trained to fight for a better world.

Around six in the evening, they drove through the gates. Themis was wide-eyed. There were rows of accommodation huts and everyone was in uniform. There were children as well as men and women, and most were smiling.

Themis and the other girls were dropped off first and the men continued on their way. After registration, they were each handed a uniform and shown into one of the huts. There were rows of low camp beds, each with little more than a few centimetres between them, and they hurriedly changed clothes and tucked their dresses under their beds.

Themis looked down at the unfamiliar sight of her legs in thick, tobacco-coloured fabric. She had never felt more excited. Trousers. She felt both more naked and more fully clothed than before.

At the door, where the young woman chaperoning them gave them each a felt hat, there was a ragged pile of unpaired boots. They were in all sizes, their laces tangled, some with flapping soles, others with holes in the toe. Themis began to rummage.

'You'll be doing a lot of walking,' said the woman brusquely. 'So make sure they fit. And don't take too long. I need to show you round.'

Eventually, with each other's help, they all found pairs. The leather of the boots that Themis chose was stiff, but at least they would last, she thought. Maria's were softer, but the laces threadbare.

'Do you think nurses are given different clothes?' Maria asked Themis from behind her hand.

'Let's just wait and see,' she answered. 'We have to do what we're told for now.'

They followed the young woman, who did not give them her name, on a tour of the camp and she monotonously rattled off information. A section of Bulkes seemed to be a refugee camp, where people who had fled from the government army were allowed to live in safety.

'In many ways it's just like an ordinary town,' said the young woman.

This was clearly true but the facilities were infinitely superior to those that now existed in most of Greece. Themis was impressed.

'There's a hospital over there,' she continued. 'And we also have an orphanage.'

She lifted the flap of a huge tent in which children were sitting in rows, silently reading.

'It looks very disciplined,' said Despina, recalling her own class-room back in Athens.

The young woman did not react to her comment.

'Some of the books are even printed here,' she said, continuing the tour. 'And there is a monthly magazine for the children.'

The four of them were impressed. Maria gasped with excitement when they were shown the theatre.

'So are there musical evenings? Plays?'

'Sometimes,' answered their guide.

They stepped to one side of the unsurfaced road to let a small truck pass. It was loaded up with potatoes.

'We try to grow our own food,' she said. 'Many hectares surrounding Bulkes are under cultivation. And there's livestock too.'

The young woman then handed something to Katerina.

'Share it,' she instructed. It was years since any of them had tasted the bitter-sweetness of chocolate. Within seconds it was gone.

From what Themis could see, this was a place where people lived in safety, and children were fed and educated. She knew that Greece had once been such a country but it was a distant memory.

It was dark now and they followed their guide along the unlit road to a big wooden building. It was time to eat. Each one of its three thousand inhabitants was allocated a number that dictated what time he or she could have a meal, and much else in connection with the daily timetable.

The stew was good.

'Meat . . .' said Maria with amazement. 'It's actually meat.'

They noisily scraped every last trace of sauce from the enamel bowls and then wiped them clean with warm bread. Themis looked around for Thomas but a sea of new faces stretched into the distance.

'Everyone looks the same in uniform, don't they?' commented Despina.

That night they became even less distinguishable one from the other. One of the captains stood at the flap of their tent with a large pair of scissors.

'Use these if you wish,' he barked. 'They're sharp.'

Despina took them from him and immediately began to hack off her hair. Within an hour, a great pile of hair, black, brown and gold, lay in a heap.

When Katerina was handed the scissors she passed them straight to Themis.

'You're not going to use them?'

'I can't,' answered Katerina. 'I can't do it. I could more easily cut off my arm.'

Themis had never seen more dramatic auburn hair and could see why Katerina was reluctant to part with it.

'You should keep it anyway! It's the perfect colour for the cause!' said Despina.

Themis hesitated. She was sentimental about her own reddish-brown plait that had been part of her for as long as she could remember. Nevertheless, before giving herself time to change her mind, she grabbed it with her left hand, hacked it off and threw the skein of hair on to the pile.

'Will you tidy it up a bit around my ears?' she asked Katerina, trying to hold back her tears.

Silently, Katerina did as she was asked and then stood back.

'It suits you,' she said, smiling. 'You look a bit like a boy, though.'

Themis was not the only one to have cast aside her femininity. All of those who had chopped off their hair looked more masculine now, more like soldiers.

'My hat fits much better,' said Themis, planting her cap firmly back on her head. 'It won't fall off now.'

There was no mirror so she could not see herself. Vanity was not encouraged in this camp and she noticed that night that the dress under her bed was gone.

At five thirty the following morning, they were woken by a siren. Themis leapt out of bed. It was still dark.

Two hundred women dressed mechanically. It had been bitterly cold the night before so Themis had not taken off her uniform. January in Yugoslavia was the coldest month. Even the biting winter when Fotini died had been nothing like this.

Everyone filed outside, and Themis, Despina, Katerina and Maria followed the group of other new recruits. There were fifty or so, slightly more men than women, and they immediately formed two lines and marched in step for five kilometres until the 'town' was no longer in sight.

Themis was glad of the solidity of her boots, but by the time they reached the training ground, the unforgiving leather had left her with blisters on both heels. The recruits were instructed to queue outside a hut and she felt a mixture of fear and excitement when she glimpsed the neat stacks of rifles inside.

Once given hers, she followed the example of those in front and passed it across her shoulder. She was surprised by its weight and could not imagine lifting it to her shoulder and being steady enough to aim. The dark grey metal was so very cold and the mechanism looked complicated. Themis suddenly felt out of her depth.

In the next hut, she was handed an ammunition belt. There were fifty bullets in all and she clipped it proudly round her middle. What would Margarita make of how she looked? Themis imagined her horror and scorn.

All that day they were trained in how to clean, load and fire their weapons, but Themis was not a natural. When she pulled the trigger, the rifle butt ricocheted against her and bruised her bony shoulder.

She concentrated hard, but was not unaware that one of the soldiers training them seemed to spend more time helping her than the others.

'Like *this*,' he said, showing her with his own rifle, and then seizing her weapon from behind and holding it up to her shoulder in the correct position.

'You will *never* succeed unless you do it properly, and do so right from the start.'

His manner was firm but patient and Themis found herself wanting to please him.

All that day and the following ones, he was always somewhere close by. There were hundreds of other soldiers but he was the only one she would recognise in a crowd, as if all other faces were out of focus except for his. The most striking thing about him were his profuse dark curls (he had more hair than Themis). His eyes were dark and his face chiselled, and when he bent in towards her to demonstrate something there was a sweetness about the way he smelled. They did not exchange either first or family names. It was neither relevant nor permitted.

She said nothing to her friends. Maria had her own concerns to deal with. She could scarcely lift her gun and punctuated the day with bouts of crying that she was obliged to hide from the soldiers who were teaching them.

When the four women lay in their beds that night, her quiet sobs were audible above the gentle snoring around them. Themis could not sleep. She felt protective towards the younger girl, who had clearly not expected these harsh conditions.

'I am sure it all gets easier,' she said comfortingly. 'Most things are difficult at the start.'

'But I wanted to be a nurse,' Maria whimpered.

'I think we have to train with a gun first. Then you must ask them. I am sure they need nurses too.'

'Or I could help look after the children here,' continued Maria.

Themis fell asleep to the sounds of Maria's snivels. The day had been exhausting and it would not be long until they had to get up again. Her night was filled with dreams. Margarita, dressed glamorously, had returned from Berlin and was in the Patissia apartment. Thanasis and Kyría Koralis and her sister were all sitting at the table, at the centre of which there was a revolver. Evidently they were waiting for someone. Margarita was radiant, her hair lustrous. She was back to her old self, in a mustard-yellow dress that showed off her cleavage and at her neck was a diamond and pearl choker. Her hand rested on the gun. It was she, Themis, whom they were expecting.

Unlike the previous night when she had shivered with cold, Themis woke bathed in sweat. The dream had been so real, somehow so close to possibility.

She tried to find a comfortable position. How could one family have been split in this way? Fragmented, torn. Where was her mother now? Her father? Without doubt, he had forgotten them all. Panos? His whereabouts were unknown, but she hoped that he might be somewhere close to her in the north of Greece. Margarita, who had gone to Berlin, was a stranger now.

As she tried to settle back to sleep, she heard a girl's voice.

'You had a bad dream?'

The words gave Themis a start.

'Yes. I did. I'm so sorry if I woke you,' she replied.

It was the girl in the bed to her right. Until now she had avoided eye contact with Themis, and her pale expressionless face never changed. They were in the same training group and Themis was puzzled by her very evident unhappiness. Most of the women there were excited to be acquiring new skills hitherto thought to be the preserve of men. Some of the boys, many of them not much more than sixteen years old, struggled just as much as the women to master the weaponry but everyone took what they were doing seriously, and most smiled from time to time.

Tonight it seemed that she wanted to talk.

'I try not to go to sleep at all,' she said. 'Because if I do, I have nightmares like you.'

Themis could tell from her nasal tone that the girl had been crying.

'You should try and think of something nice before you go to sleep,' she advised her.

'But there is nothing nice.'

'There must be something . . .' said Themis brightly.

'There isn't,' the girl replied. 'There was nothing left.'

She was muttering almost incoherently now and Themis had to lean towards her so that she could hear.

'They came to our village in the mountains. They hanged my father. I saw it. In front of my eyes they hanged him.'

A few moments passed before she continued, 'I tried to find my mother. I was with the other kids from our village and we were told to wait in the square. Then they set fire to all the houses and made us walk away from the village. I thought it was to keep us safe from the flames. But we didn't stop walking. We walked for days. I wasn't wearing my coat when they came and they wouldn't let me go back for it. And then I started bleeding. I didn't know what it was . . .'

The girl was sobbing. Now Themis understood why this girl looked so haunted. She could not think what to say, but she instinctively rested her hand on the girl's head to comfort her and stroked her hair.

They both lay awake until daybreak, exchanging names and then their stories to pass the hours. As they dressed, Frosso asked Themis a question. There were no tears in her eyes now.

'Do you understand now, Themis? I was forced to come here. And they expect me to fight next to the people who murdered my family!'

Her voice became steadily louder as she spoke and once again she was close to tears.

Now that she knew her story, Themis appreciated why this skeletal girl looked so sullen. It also explained the blank expressions of some other faces in this camp. Themis was here because she wanted to fight for a cause, but there were many for whom it had not been a choice.

'I am a prisoner here,' Frosso whispered in her ear. 'And one day I will turn my gun on these people.'

Only Themis heard her, but the words chilled the air around them.

A siren was going off and most of the women had already filed out into the chilly air. Themis' neighbour fixed her eyes straight ahead. Her face was expressionless, as usual, but now Themis knew what lay behind it: grief for her losses and fury against the perpetrators.

Before going out through the door, they reached up to take a rifle from the row of hooks.

That day, they were training on different equipment and Themis found herself watching Frosso. She noticed her fierce concentration. Nothing would betray what thoughts lay behind her expression but Themis did not doubt that at some moment in the future she would take revenge.

They were out on the hillside for several days and then for one day practised manoeuvres in the forest. Women were treated exactly as men and no concessions were made for any differential in their strength. In the second week they were put into groups and taught how to use a field gun. The soldier with the curls was there again, in charge of Themis' small group. She scolded herself for doing her best only in order to impress him, embarrassed at the impurity of her motivation. He did not seem to treat her any differently from the others, but she looked up once or twice and found him staring at her.

Over the next few weeks she caught herself looking out for him again. On some days she did not see him at all. On others she would catch sight of him in the distance, perhaps queuing for food or marching at the head of a column of new recruits being taken for training. She told herself to stop thinking about this stranger because there was no purpose in it, but she could not keep him out of her dreams.

In the final week of training, the recruits were shown how to lay a mine. Themis' hands shook with fear. If she did not kill someone, she might be killed herself. When her courage failed her, she thought of Fotini and how uncomplaining and brave her friend had been about the hardships she had endured. It helped Themis to overcome her anxiety.

Finally, Themis and her group were taught the hit-and-run tactics that the communist army were using against the government army. This strategy was allowing them to stage attacks on villages with great success and to keep ahead of an army whose main problem was a lack of mobility.

Soon they had grasped the basic principles of guerrilla warfare and before long they would have to use their skills not just in practice manoeuvres but against their enemy.

On their last night, the hundreds of recruits who had trained together in the past weeks were gathered in the camp's theatre. They were addressed by a visiting general who exhorted them to go forward with courage and optimism. They would be fighting for the noblest cause, for freedom, for justice, for equality. They should hold nothing back! Their country depended on them! The shadow of fascism should be banished for ever! The speech was rousing and Themis, appointed to be a flag bearer, waved it with enthusiasm, entirely caught up in the euphoria that had infected the crowd.

When she looked around, she caught the eye of the soldier who had trained her. He was smiling at her but she did her best to pretend she had not noticed and turned away. As she did so, her attention was drawn to someone else. Across the sea of heads, she saw that a lone figure had climbed on to a chair. It took Themis only a second to recognise the distinctively gaunt figure of Frosso.

Before anyone had time to pull her down, she screamed out at the general who was making the speech. 'Bastard! Murderer!' Then there was the glint of a handgun as she lifted it to fire in his direction.

There was an immediate commotion when those that were closest wrestled her to the ground. Then came the crack of gunshots and it was unclear from where they came.

Proceedings came to a temporary halt and Themis tried to see what had happened to Frosso. Everyone else was trying to do the same and Themis was not tall enough to get a decent view. Within ten minutes, they were all instructed to be seated again as the speech must be continued. A body had been taken from the tent.

The general cleared his throat and recommenced proceedings, announcing first of all that a comrade had betrayed them, and had therefore suffered the severest consequences of her actions. Themis remembered her first conversation with Frosso and shuddered. She was shocked by what had happened. Brutality had bred brutality. Now the life of this frail-looking young woman was gone. It was an inevitable end to her act of revenge and the ceremony moved forward without further pause. Themis had to put aside any emotion.

In groups of ten, they now stood before the general to swear the communist army oath.

Many of the words matched beliefs that had been hers since childhood. With body and soul, Themis wished to rid Greece of fascism and to defend democracy and honour. She spoke the words with conviction.

I promise:

To fight with gun in hand, to shed my blood, and even to die in order to rid my country of the last foreign occupier.

To banish fascism. To secure the independence and integrity of my motherland.

To defend the democracy, honour and progress of my people.

To be a brave and disciplined soldier, to obey orders, to observe regulations, and keep the secrets of the Democratic Army of Greece.

To be a good example, to encourage unity and reconciliation, and to avoid any action that dishonours me.

My goal is a free and strong democratic Greece and the progress and prosperity of the people. And in the pursuit of this goal, I offer my gun and my life.

Themis was bursting with pride as she read but when she reached the final clause, she hesitated. It seemed to her full of venom.

If I ever break my oath, may the vengeful hand of the nation and the hate and scorn of the people fall upon me without mercy.

The phrase was full of cruelty and spite, and she found herself lowering her voice. She remembered how she and Fotini would mime words at EON meetings if they did not believe in them, and she did a similar thing now.

Once her turn for this public declaration was over and she had returned to her seat, she wondered how those who had been forcibly recruited, such as Frosso, could pledge everlasting loyalty. Evidently some of them did, simply to stay alive.

Themis was sitting with Despina and Katerina. She asked herself if her two friends shared these doubts about the malevolence of these words. If only Panos was somewhere close, she could ask him if he had believed each and every line of the oath. Perhaps during the next weeks or months, their destinies might bring them closer. Then she began to wonder about the views of the soldier who was sitting a few rows behind, whose eyes, even now, she could feel on her back. It was time to file out and Themis' group went directly to the meal tent.

Maria was absent. After two days of high fever, she had needed medical attention.

'She always wanted to be in the hospital,' said Despina, with a hint of sarcasm.

The schoolteacher had never been sympathetic to Maria's constant complaints and tears.

'She should never have come here. A woman like that is a liability,' chipped in one of the boys in their group. 'Think what she'd be like up in the mountains. She'd be dead in a day.'

There were murmurs of agreement from some other men.

'I can't see the point of having women with us,' muttered another.

The two men who had spoken were overheard by one of the captains and reprimanded. The rules were simple. There was to be no discrimination, either with words or actions.

Another inviolable rule was that there should be no relations between men and women. This would undermine morale, endanger fellow soldiers' lives and create tensions within the groups. Any individual found deviating from this would be punished or expelled. Communist leaders could behave as brutally with their own soldiers as with anyone they fought against.

In the communist army, women were given the same chances as the men, but they had to prove themselves. During the months since she had left Athens, Themis felt that she had become a different person. Physically she had gained in strength. Beneath her trousers, her calf muscles bulged and the weight of the rifle no longer bothered her. The only discomfort she had suffered were the blisters on her feet but, thanks to Eleni, who had insisted she take a pot of beeswax ointment with her, the lesions on her feet were already healed and her skin was hardening. She felt strong, purposeful, excited, ready.

Their group of fifty had been divided and subdivided. There were no concessions made for any friendships that might have formed. The terrain they had instructions to capture was extensive and they were being sent off to different parts of it. Despina was going to the Peloponnese with a well-established unit and Maria had been promised a job in the camp orphanage. She had shown herself incapable of aiming a rifle.

Themis was happy to discover that she and Katerina would be staying together, but it was with feelings of turmoil and confusion that she overheard a conversation between one of the officers and the soldier who haunted her waking hours and dream-filled nights. She heard the name, Makris, for the first time and understood that he had been appointed second in command of their unit.

Chapter Thirteen

I N THE WARM spring sunshine, thirty of them bumped along in an open lorry: ten women and twenty men whose uniforms were the same. Already Themis could not imagine wearing anything but trousers. Generous patch pockets at the front and sides had space for almost everything she possessed, and she loved how freely they allowed her to move.

As they travelled south towards Greece, she sat next to a man whose face was almost entirely hidden by a copious brown beard. With his long, straggly hair he resembled a wild animal, perhaps one of the bears that were reputed to roam the mountain range that lay ahead. He seemed to have no inhibitions as he laughed and chatted to her, leaning in if she could not hear something above the noise of the engine.

At one point he rolled a cigarette and held it out to her. Although she declined he insisted on her taking a puff.

'I don't think it's for me,' said Themis, spluttering.

'You'll soon get used to it,' he joked, indicating all the other women around them who were happily smoking.

When one of the men on the truck leaned over to speak to

him, Themis realised that the man she had been talking to was the captain of their unit.

'I hadn't realised . . .'

'No reason to apologise,' he told her. 'We're communists here.'

'But . . .'

Seeing that she was flustered, the captain tried to reassure her. 'There's a hierarchy, but no formality,' he said firmly.

The constant revving and droning of the engine as it struggled to negotiate the broken road, and the other soldiers' shouting and occasional bursts of singing, did not make it easy to hold a conversation. Themis answered a few questions about her background and wanted to ask the same ones of the man she now knew to be Captain Solomonidis. In the end she only had the courage to ask if he knew where they were going.

'Yes,' he said. 'Of course I know. And you'll find out soon enough.'

It was hard to tell if the evasive answer was lack of trust or policy.

As they talked, they both watched the ruggedly mountainous landscape that they were approaching. Themis did not turn her head to look at the captain but she was aware that the curly-haired soldier, Makris, was opposite, watching them. From time to time she was also aware of a hostile glance from another woman.

The journey passed quickly. Every so often, the lorry would stop for them to stretch their legs and coffee would be brewed on a makeshift stove. It was more like a school outing or a day out in the country, and memories of long-past pleasures returned.

In one village, a woman emerged from her stone cottage with a wreath of fresh flowers. She approached Themis and placed it round her neck, the sweet scent of the colourful, wild sprigs filling the air around her.

Themis realised it must be May Day, but it was not the arrival of summer they were celebrating now.

'It's the day for workers' rights!' shouted the captain. 'Dance!'

Whatever was in their minds, they all linked arms and formed a circle. For the first time in years, as the sap seemed to rise from the earth, Themis forgot the sadness that burdened her. Her worries about Panos, the unease about Margarita and her sadness for the crippled Thanasis, all vanished for a few seconds. Not since childhood had she felt a moment of such carefree pleasure.

Then the man whom she could not get out of her mind came across and very deliberately put his arm through hers. Soon they would be marching together, disciplined and in time, but for now their feet moved to a gentler, steady beat as they paced the movements of the dance, a traditional rhythm familiar to them all. It took their minds away from the impending fight.

This is the harmony I want to restore to our country, Themis thought.

The sweetness of the cake brought out to them by the same kind woman who had given Themis the flowers revived all their spirits. Honey dripped from their fingertips as they hungrily devoured every last crumb. Never had any *glykó* tasted as good.

The captain had a bottle of *tsípouro*, which he passed round in the dusk, and each soldier took a sip before clambering back on to the lorry, warmed by the dancing and the alcohol. The light was fading and temperatures were dropping as the vehicle began its climb into the mountains.

Themis was at the back of the truck now and once again felt the glare of the woman. She kept her eyes down, not wanting to meet her hostile stare, but was aware, if she looked in the other direction, that Makris was watching her.

To distract herself, Themis talked to Katerina, who was sitting next to her. An hour or so later, her head lolled on to her friend's shoulder and she fell into a profound and dream-filled sleep.

Woken by the crunch of the lorry's handbrake and sudden silence from the engine, she sat up and rubbed her eyes.

The back of the lorry was being opened from the outside and one by one the soldiers jumped down, their kitbags thrown down to them by the last person.

The landscape was unfamiliar but as the sun came up she could read the sign. They were just outside a village and Themis was reassured by the sight of the familiar alphabet reminding her that they were back in Greece, the motherland for which they were now trained to fight and liberate.

The plan for the next few days was explained to the unit. The main concern for the present was to secure supplies for the following weeks. The only source was the villagers themselves and not all of them were generous with what they were prepared to give. If they did not hand over enough willingly, then they had to be 'encouraged'.

Themis knew that this was a euphemism for force but she had to obey orders. This was what she had sworn in the oath and there could be no deviation from the single set of beliefs that now united them.

That night, as she lay under the stars, she remembered how much her family used to argue and debate. There was never a mealtime without altercation, and while she recalled how exasperated her grandmother had often been, she realised now how precious that freedom had been too. They had all been allowed their differences of view.

Beneath her thin blanket, she could feel the sharp edge of every stone. It was the most uncomfortable night she had ever spent. The captain had repeatedly told them that everything was going to get much tougher.

'This is a holiday compared to what's coming up,' he said. 'There will be a moment when we have to be battle-ready. You will know when that moment comes.'

They marched for the next two nights and then camped again. The following day Themis received instructions about her first mission: the key stages were to raid, to seize supplies and to recruit additional people into the army. Three of them spent the evening clandestinely scouting a nearby village, making estimates of the number of inhabitants, what resources they had, and if there were likely to be any firearms to seize. They reported back that the men of the village appeared to have left and from what they could see the oldest boys there seemed to be around thirteen.

Their unit was up before dawn to surround the village. None of the women and children who lived there had any idea what was happening when they heard the first gunshots that day. It was a rude awakening.

The strategy was to raid as many houses as possible as quickly as possible to instil maximum fear, and then, with a megaphone, instruct the remaining inhabitants to reveal themselves voluntarily (the first group effectively acting as hostages). In general, villagers did not risk jeopardising the lives of the others, so this was a technique that invariably worked, especially when the men had already left the village.

Themis watched the group of fifty or so women and children standing in a huddle by the fountain in the main square, terror written on their faces. The soldiers stood round them in a circle. There were many more villagers than soldiers, but it was a question of who held the power.

The captain took the arm of one of the younger women, pulled her out of the group and interrogated her.

Themis was shocked at his manner. If the girl had personally betrayed him and his country, he could not have been more brutal. When had the men of this village left? And where had they gone?

The girl mumbled a response. This village supported the communists, she claimed, but the fear on her face conveyed the truth.

'Your mouth says one thing, your eyes another,' he said. 'You're a lying bitch.'

The captain, whom Themis had likened to a kindly bear, struck the girl hard across the face before barking an order to his deputy.

'Take the old ones into the woods. The kids we'll leave here. The fit and healthy will come with us. Get them to bring out every last crust before we go. I want to be out of here before noon.'

Instructions were parcelled out to each soldier. Themis was in charge of escorting five of the younger village women from house to house to make them empty cupboards of everything they contained. One of them held her baby at her breast as they walked. None of them spoke. All the while, Themis held her rifle by her side. Anyone who tried to escape must be shot, without exception.

Pulses, bread, potatoes, fruit – one by one the items were dropped on to blankets that had been laid out in the village square. Once the process was complete, three blankets were piled high with provisions. They also took the largest pots they could find. There was no point in gathering food without something to cook it in.

A separate group was dispatched to hunt for arms and, in several houses, rifles were found. Some of them had been buried under a dirt floor, others were hidden inside a child's cot. Little ammunition was found, which might explain why the village had not been able to defend itself when their unit had arrived.

No one spoke. The only sound that broke the silence was the

wail of the baby whose desperate cries began to grate on Themis' nerves.

'Why don't you go and sit with the children and . . .'

'Thank you,' the mother said gratefully.

She walked away towards the children who stood together in a tight circle under a plane tree, watched over by Katerina. Even the children who were naturally so boisterous simply stared down at the dirt.

Themis' job was almost complete. Each house that they emptied had a cross scratched on the door. All forty were now marked in this way and she shepherded the women back to the village square.

The rest of the unit had reappeared. Only three out of a dozen of the older women were with them.

The blankets with food were tied up into bundles and strapped to a pair of mules that had been found.

'Leave the old ones here. And the one with the baby. She'll hold us up,' ordered Makris.

'What about the children?' Katerina asked. 'What's going to happen to them?'

Makris looked at her with disdain but not just because she had spoken out of turn. Everyone else seemed to know what awaited the children.

'Four of you will march these children north,' he said.

There was a murmur among the soldiers. They had just come from the north.

Makris quickly selected the four who would be undertaking this journey.

'Where are they being taken?' whispered Themis to Katerina who was standing next to her.

Her friend shook her head. They surmised, soon enough, that

the children were going to Bulgaria and would be taught how to be good communists.

'The older ones will come with us,' Makris continued. 'They'll soon learn to fight.'

The captain scrutinised the group of children for one final time. There was a boy of about thirteen, solid, with square shoulders. Themis calculated that he was heavier than most of the women.

'You!' barked Solomonidis. 'On your feet. You'll come with us.'

The young women, all of them mothers, were penned in at gunpoint twenty metres away and many of the children were crying now as they realised what was going to happen.

They were not allowed to say goodbye to their mothers.

'The sooner we get out of here the better,' said Katerina under her breath. 'I can't stand all their noise.'

What had begun as a few whimpers from one or two children had turned into wailing from them all and their distress spread to their mothers. One of them tried to break free. She was the one closest to Themis.

Themis found herself with a gun pressed hard into the woman's chest. She was shrieking now, hysterical. Nothing was going to come between her and her child.

'Dimitri!' she screamed.

Her fury gave her the strength to push Themis aside and Themis found herself on the ground as the woman broke free and ran towards her child.

The captain acted quickly and raised his weapon, firing a single shot into her back.

The *crack* of the bullet silenced everyone. The sight of a mother collapsing lifeless in front of her son shocked them all. For a moment no one moved.

The still body was a reminder to them all, both captives and soldiers, that they must obey orders. Themis was aware that she had let the group down by allowing the woman to break free and instantly began to fear the repercussions. Almost immediately afterwards, she felt guilty that this was her first thought rather than sorrow that an innocent woman had been executed, and she realised that her way of thinking was already changing. This was a war and she was a fighter now.

Within a few moments, there was a flurry of renewed activity. It was a matter of urgency to leave now. The village women had to form a line and the soldiers started dividing them into groups. Some began to sob once again.

The official story was that the older women were to be left guarded for an hour and the soldiers that were keeping them in check would then make a swift exit from the village to catch up with the rest of the unit.

Themis was among the first group to leave, but she heard the instructions given by the captain to the two soldiers being left to guard the women. Before leaving, he told them, they should bury the *yéroi*, the old ones, in the wood.

Themis was familiar with the idea of people being punished for the sins of their fathers, but these mothers were going to pay for the sins of sons. Even being related to a member of the government army had made them suspects. The realisation that some of these simple village women would be slaughtered by her fellow soldiers sickened Themis, but she had sworn the oath now and was committed to act as instructed.

Looking at the ground, she cast everything out of her mind except for the order she had been given: to start marching the youngest among the women away from their village. Like them, she must put one foot in front of the other and perhaps, after a while, the hypnotic rhythm would cut out feeling and thought.

Although nothing had yet been said, she knew that she had made a foolish error and would be under scrutiny now.

The operation on the village had taken less than four hours. It was one o'clock and the target for the remainder of the day was to march approximately thirty kilometres south. If the terrain had been flat this might have been easily achieved, but they were in the mountains and many of the village women were poorly shod. They walked for six hours, stopping for only five minutes at a time, once to take some water (sourced at a communist-friendly village en route) and once to eat some bread and fruit. Both soldiers and captives ate the same amount on the journey. The captives would soon become soldiers too and needed decent nourishment.

Themis' legs moved mechanically and her stomach was hollow. It was difficult to concentrate. If any one of the women in her charge had the will or energy to escape, she would succeed. Themis did not have the strength even to lift her gun.

For the last few hours of daylight, they were trekking through dense forest. Sunlight barely penetrated the canopy of leaves high above them and it was hard to make out the path ahead. It was the captain who led the march and who made the decision to stop. They had reached a clearing and there was a stream running nearby and space for them all to sleep for the night.

Themis was relieved of her duty of guarding a group of captives but her work was not done. She was assigned the job of wood gathering with Katerina and two of the men. Within twenty minutes, a fire was blazing and the team who was preparing ingredients from the provisions that had been gathered earlier that day was ready to start cooking. Thirty of them soon began to eat and the bean stew disappeared fast. Each of them had a tin bowl and a cup. Once the soldiers had eaten, the bowls were washed in the stream and the new 'recruits' were handed their rations. There was no sound except for the urgent *ting-ting* of spoons on metal.

Themis could not help watching and wondering as the women ate. In spite of their state of mourning and loss, hunger was still a powerful urge. They ate to stay alive. Already the events of the morning seemed many days ago.

Once the food was finished and the fire had died down, every last flake of ash was buried so that they left no trace.

Before being allocated their place to sleep for the night, they must listen to the captain. First, he addressed the grieving women.

'You have joined the rightful heirs to the future of Greece. This army is leading us towards a new Greece, free of tyranny, free of the influence of the Nazis. Your menfolk have left you to fight for the government, for the forces of fascism and evil. Think of this: they left you. *We* give you the chance to fight. To fight like men. To be treated as *equals*.'

Moonlight shone into the clearing and illuminated the pale faces and blank eyes of the village women. One or two of them wept. Themis could not help thinking of Frosso and the brutality that she must have witnessed. Would any of these women be driven to commit the same acts?

Solomonidis then addressed the rest of the unit.

'Tomorrow brings us closer to our goal. To establish a new Greece. A free Greece. Today we have a bigger army. Every day we are expanding our numbers and soon the whole of Greece will be ours.'

His deputy then stepped forward.

'Tonight we must rest. There is another long march tomorrow. But as usual we must have you all doing your part to keep watch.'

Makris began to read out names and even while he was doing so, Themis felt her eyelids closing. Her whole body longed for sleep.

'*Koralis!*'

It was her punishment for what had happened earlier in the day. She was to be on night watch. Her name was one of ten. Five were assigned the task of keeping guard over the new recruits and five were positioned at various distances around the camp. Guerrilla groups were always vulnerable. They were expert at surprise attack but there was always the possibility that the government army might start practising the same technique.

Themis was sent to the furthest point. Three hundred strides south. That was the instruction. And she followed it precisely.

Well out of earshot of the main camp, Themis found herself almost drowning in the darkness. She had rarely experienced such silence and it weighed heavily on her, like loneliness. All she could hear was her own breath.

She sat on the ground, with her back against a tree, looking away from the direction of the camp. Occasionally she imagined a rustle of leaves, perhaps a rabbit or mouse, and heard the flapping of wings beneath the treetops. Themis had spent so little time out of Athens during her life that she was unfamiliar with the noises of the forest and her ears were sensitised to even the smallest sounds.

The only way she would know that four hours had gone was when someone came to relieve her of her duties. Meanwhile, she tried to judge the passage of time by observing the moon.

For a while Themis hummed: nursery rhymes from childhood, songs she used to sing with Fotini, a favourite tune of Vamvakaris. When she ran out of music, she began to reflect. Random memories came back to her and with the benefit of geographical distance and time, she saw events of her life in new ways. She thought about the collapse of the childhood home, and the fall that had left Panos with a scar and remembered that he had always been

the one to feel the wrong side of their father's slipper. Her recollection of a thwack on bare skin coincided with the sharp snap of
a twig and she sprang to her feet, her heart pounding. It was too
soon for the end of her shift, she thought, but there must be
somebody nearby.

Themis was right. The dark outline of a figure was coming
towards her through the trees. It was a silhouette she recognised
immediately. The emotion this sight aroused was not one with
which she was familiar. She had felt anger many times but it had
always passed. The same with grief and loss. This sense of yearning,
however, was different. It lingered, like an ache.

Makris looked as if he was simply out for a stroll, hunting for
game, perhaps, with his gun slung casually over his shoulder.
There was a confidence about him that she had not noticed
before. He did not look that much older than she did, but he
had an enviable ease as though the situation they found themselves
in was entirely normal. They were standing in a mountain forest,
a long way from home, armed, on alert, hungry and yet he
seemed contented.

She was nervous, anxious about saying the wrong thing or giving
a bad impression, so she waited until he spoke. His voice was
familiar, but the tone was different. It was softer than she had
heard it before and for the first time gave the impression of a good
education.

'I came to check that you were in the right place. Most soldiers
can't walk in a straight line.'

'That's something I can do very easily,' she said, encouraged by
his tone into risking a little humour. 'From my home, down
Patission Avenue towards the Acropolis is a direct route.'

'I grew up climbing hills,' he replied. 'I was born under
Lycabettus, in Kolonaki.'

He could read surprise on Themis' face when he mentioned the wealthiest area in Athens.

'I know. You think it's full of right-wingers and royalists . . . Well, it probably was among my parents' generation. But among mine, it was almost the fashion to support the communists. So here I am. And I believe in the cause more than ever.'

Themis was spellbound by his idealism. Each word charmed her and she was reminded of Panos, who had the same fire burning within him. Everything that had taken place that day was for a greater goal, the ultimate good. She must keep telling herself this.

To her amazement Makris put his hands on her shoulders.

'Look,' he said. 'You need to learn something. When we raid these villages the inhabitants have nothing to lose. There will always be someone who tries to escape or to attack. They are the enemy until we bring them round to our way of thinking. And even then they're under suspicion.'

His voice was soothing but then it suddenly changed, from kind to cruel. Themis was shocked. He began to criticise her, harshly and mercilessly.

'If you don't take more care during a raid, you will endanger the whole unit. *Think*, Koralis. Do *nothing* without thinking,' he hectored. 'You made a mistake today and it could have cost lives. You have to stay in charge in such situations.'

By the end of his short speech, Themis' eyes were stinging with tears. Then, as surprisingly as it had vanished, the gentle voice returned.

They were standing face to face and Makris took Themis by the elbows this time. It was a gesture of reassurance, both comforting and gentle. The sweetness that returned to the distinctly cultivated voice was such a relief that her shaking knees could scarcely hold her up.

'You will learn,' he said. 'And you will learn faster than anyone. I guarantee it.'

'I promise to do my best,' she replied. Themis wanted to please him perhaps more than she had ever wanted to please anyone.

'Tomorrow there will be new opportunities to show what you can do,' he said, continuing to hold her. 'You will show me how good you are.'

'I will,' she replied.

He held on to Themis for a moment longer than necessary. He was close enough for her to smell the tobacco on his breath.

Then he consulted his watch.

'I'll keep you company for a while,' he said. 'Time goes slowly when you're alone.'

Themis did not know how to react so she said nothing. They sat leaning against the tree and Makris lit a cigarette for himself. Rings of smoke drifted up into the sky.

'Tell me something about yourself,' he said. 'You don't have to be shy.'

'I was born in Athens. I'm twenty-two . . .'

She was embarrassed. There was nothing much more to tell him.

'How long have you been with the army?' she asked. It seemed a formal enough question to be inoffensive.

'I've been a communist for more than ten years now,' he answered. 'My uncle was arrested during the Metaxas dictatorship and sent to an island prison.'

'Why?' asked Themis.

'He simply disagreed with the regime and said so in his newspaper.'

'How long was he in prison?'

'He died there after two years.'

Themis wondered if a cloud had passed in front of the moon because the darkness seemed to intensify.

'He printed the truth. And he died for it.'

'My brother Panos used to talk about dying for the truth too,' said Themis, feeling more relaxed now. 'But my other brother had a different idea about what truth was, so there was always a lot of arguing.'

'The freedom to print the truth matters beyond all else,' he said. 'And the truth is that the communists should be given their role in this country.'

For a moment Themis was confused. Makris clearly believed that some kinds of freedom were sacrosanct but the women being force-marched came to her mind. The thought was a fleeting one and she quickly slipped once again under the spell of his words.

Soon enough, Makris got to his feet. Themis got up too.

'See you at dawn.'

Themis watched his back retreating through the trees. She had heard that he had the nickname *liondári*, the lion, and as he padded off noiselessly into the woods it was obvious why. He was as silent as a big cat and his halo of curls very like a mane. Themis wondered if she had ever felt happier. She was fighting for the winning side, her army was at the height of its powers, and she was in love.

Every day she saw Makris and often they marched side by side. She told herself it was probably accidental, but he always seemed to brush against her, electrifying every hair on her body.

A few weeks later, once again on guard duty, Makris came to keep her company. This time there was no moon and in the darkness he took her completely by surprise.

They sat and talked for a while about tactics for raiding a nearby village the following day. Then Makris took Themis' hand and began to play with her fingers, weaving them between his own.

His skin was rough but his touch was gentle and she did not pull away. Only once before had she been the object of any male attention, when the son of the pharmacy owner had pursued her. This was a different situation. She craved this man's every glance.

The rule that there should be no relationships between men and women in the communist army was rigorously enforced. Since her infatuation with Makris had begun she questioned herself many times: did emotion alone constitute a liaison? Her naïvety did not help her to find the answer and she could not confide in anyone.

As Makris stroked the surface of her skin, she succumbed to the sensation, and the questions faded from her mind. She felt an involuntary physical reaction that did not seem to be contained in one part of her. A current seemed to run from the palm of her hand, on which he now traced small circles, to every extremity in her body, even to the tips of the hair.

Though it was dark, Makris must be able to see how she was responding and when she closed her eyes, the sensation only grew more intense. She felt her temperature rise as his fingers moved to her neck and then traced a line towards the buttons, which he carefully undid. There were two conflicting voices, both appealing to Themis with equal volume. One of them told her to pull this stranger's hands away. The other told her that she must submit to his seduction. In the end, the silent power of desire overruled all else.

As her shirt fell open to the waist, his lips travelled from her neck to her mouth and then down to her breasts. She savoured the taste of tobacco that lingered on her tongue as she instinctively moved her hands to touch his head and to run her fingers through the curls that she had first noticed and admired so long ago. He gently slid her clothes away from her body and her uniform now protected them both from the dampness of the forest floor. She had seen a few romantic films but her knowledge of sex was non-existent. It had certainly not occurred to her that making love would be painful.

An owl shrieked. Perhaps it covered the sound of her cry. Themis did not know. He held her close for a few seconds and then rolled away and got up.

'I must get back to the camp,' he said. 'Someone else will be here soon to take over.'

Themis dressed quickly, suddenly feeling cold and vulnerable, despite the balminess of the night.

Over the following weeks and months, the pattern with Makris continued. He would post Themis to a far corner of the territory that needed to be watched and come to see her in the middle of the night. Privately, he began to call her 'little fox' because of the slightly ginger tone of her hair and she continued to be spellbound. He allowed her to call him by his real name, Tasos, when they were alone, which made her feel even closer to him. During the day they did not speak, but she knew he watched her and she watched him. Her feelings for this man were all-dominating, obscuring the pain of her aching limbs and the hunger in her stomach.

In the same month that Themis lost her virginity, there was another significant event in her life. The unit arrived close to a small hamlet, and a recce had revealed that the half-dozen or so houses had been evacuated by its population. Themis was sent in with two other soldiers to gather anything useful that had been left there. She was about fifty metres behind the others with her gun loosely slung over her shoulder. As they sauntered down the main street, a slight figure suddenly and noiselessly appeared from a doorway. He was behind her comrades but in front of her. He shot them both expertly at point-blank range in the back. One bullet per man. Themis was unsure whether he had seen her or not but she could not take the risk.

It seemed that the next moments were in slow motion and yet in reality it took less than two seconds for her to aim her rifle and fire. The months of training had been for this. It was kill or be killed, and she acted fast, letting off a whole magazine into the body to be sure of success. The sound of ammunition ricocheting off the walls around her was deafening. She stared at the still shape in front of her. She had stolen a life. She was a murderer, a thief. If she had strangled this man with her bare hands she could not have been more sickened by her action and, from the dark windows of the empty homes around her, she imagined that many pairs of eyes had watched.

Curiosity made her go closer and it was then that she realised how young her victim had been. He had only the faintest hint of down above his top lip.

'*Theé mou*,' she whispered to herself, only now realising that she had tears rolling down her cheeks. He had not even taken his first shave.

She backed away and walked across to the lifeless bodies that had once been her friends. This made her feel less remorse for the boy she had killed. It was impossible for her to move them so she ran back to the camp and soon returned with some others to help dig their graves. Themis could not bear to look as the corpse of the boy was also taken for burial in a nearby olive grove.

The experience left her in a state of shock and remorse for several days, but with each subsequent killing, the impact on her progressively lessened. As time went by, and her technical skills improved, her ability to distance her emotions also got better. In spite of her unpromising start, she had become an accurate shot and was soon known as one of the soldiers who never wasted a bullet. Every time she killed, Themis' first thought was whether Makris would praise her. His sparing words of encouragement were more than enough to satisfy her.

The unit had many successes but some failures too, and Themis became as adept at tending wounds and even preparing a body for burial as at killing. Generally, though, theirs was a nimble team, narrowly missing capture many times and surviving a harsh winter and a wet spring that left them in damp uniform for days on end. Most of the captured women were still with them, though some of them had died en route, physically incapable of surviving the hardship.

When the summer of 1949 came it brought extreme heat, giving them burnt faces and cracked lips.

Circumstances had changed for the communist army during that year. In 1948 it had been at the height of its powers but now the border with Yugoslavia was closed and the government army was preparing a major offensive against them in the north-east. This was not far from where Themis' unit was hiding out. Meanwhile the communists had begun to act more like a conventional army.

The affair between Themis and Makris had continued throughout the changing seasons.

Sometimes she allowed herself to wonder what would happen if and when the war was over. Would they return to Athens together? Where would they live? Themis even imagined introducing him to her grandmother and was certain that she would be won over by this handsome, educated man.

'I think the captain suspects,' Makris said, one hot night. 'We have to be careful, little fox.'

Themis was happy when he used the *nom de guerre* that he had given her, and nodded. Everyone knew that Solomonidis had been having a relationship with the same partisan for years now, but that did not mean he would show leniency to others.

'We will have to be more cautious from now on,' he said, pecking her on the forehead as he left. For the first time during their romance, their meeting had not ended with a passionate kiss. Themis was left with a feeling of emptiness. It nagged at her all night.

Her guard duty seemed to go on for an eternity but eventually she heard the sound of approaching steps accompanied by cheerful humming. She immediately recognised the owner of the voice as Philipakis, a soldier who was always smiling and telling jokes to the women.

'Here, that's for you,' he said, handing her a lump of bread he had saved from dinner. 'I could do with eating less. Look at me!'

She forced a smile. Even with the great distances they covered each day, Philipakis' waistline seemed to expand. It was uncommon for anyone to give away their food and she gratefully nibbled on it as she returned to the camp.

Back in the clearing, she realised she was shivering and put her blanket down next to Katerina. She lay close to her friend, desperate for any warmth.

She slept deeply for the three hours that remained until dawn and was woken by the sound of her friend's voice, low but urgent in her ear.

'Come on,' urged Katerina. 'We're leaving.'

She handed Themis a sip of coffee and hauled her to her feet.

Themis rolled up her blanket and fell in behind the column of soldiers, looking around her for Makris.

The march was shambolic today. Some of the women they had recently captured were refusing to co-operate, which made the pace slow. Most of them were at the front of the column and several of them were being prodded with rifle butts to make them walk.

Today they must cover many kilometres. Tomorrow they would be aiming to take another village.

All through the day, Themis looked for her lover but all around saw only a sea of grubby and unfamiliar faces. They had now joined with several other units and most of these soldiers were strangers.

Several days went by and there was no sign of the man she loved. Fear and obsession made her reckless. She *had* to know what had happened to him. During a short pause in the trek to their destination, Themis strode up to the captain. She had a story ready.

'Makris lent me some tobacco from his ration,' she said, as casually as she could manage. 'I can pay him back now but do you know where I'll find him?'

'Makris?'

The captain looked at her, slightly puzzled.

'A few of the units west of us were decimated,' he said. 'He's been promoted to captain in one of them.'

Almost sick with shock, Themis turned away so that Solomonidis could not see her expression.

'*Efcharistó*,' she muttered. 'Thank you.'

She found her place next to Katerina again and, against all rules, the older woman linked her arm through hers.

Tears streamed unchecked down Themis' face. She stumbled along blindly, reliant on her friend to guide her. Every member of the unit plodded up the hill with their eyes downcast, so no one else noticed the wretchedness of her expression.

An hour or two into the march, Katerina spoke to her.

'Whatever has made you cry,' she said, using words that had always worked with her younger siblings, 'it will seem better tomorrow.'

The passage of time lent no comfort to Themis, though, and the ensuing days only brought a greater sense of desolation. She told herself many things. Perhaps Tasos had wanted to save them both from a painful farewell, or maybe he had not been given advance warning of his own relocation.

Themis' mind went back to Margarita's anguish the day the love of her life had left and very belatedly felt sympathy for her sister. Only now did she appreciate what such loss and bereavement felt like. She discovered that the symptoms of a broken heart made her physically sick, but did not allow her to shirk responsibilities. For a few days she could not eat, but Katerina forced her to drink. In this heat, dehydration was becoming a problem and two sick women had already been left behind. Themis did not want to be left to die and steeled herself to swallow small amounts of food.

As the war continued, it was more important than ever to keep up the momentum of the struggle. They had all been told to prepare for a fresh onslaught from the government army, who were newly bolstered by American supplies.

'It's for the cause, Themis,' Katerina reminded her. 'You must remember the promises we made.'

Themis nodded. Love for her country still motivated her, but the hope of seeing Tasos again gave her the will to live.

Chapter Fourteen

THE AUGUST HEAT was making them all lethargic. Even during daytime marches, Themis felt that she was sleepwalking and on most nights her head hardly touched her blanket before weariness overcame her.

It was ten days since Makris had left and there was a plan to raid a small village. As usual they spent the night several kilometres from where the following day's action would take place.

'There are just a few old people there. It looks like the younger generation has already left,' Captain Solomonidis briefed them, smiling. Using this information, he had devised the strategy for the attack.

'We can look forward to a good dinner tonight,' boomed out his deep voice. 'The elderly don't consume much, so it usually means plenty of supplies.'

There were many similar villages from which the inhabitants, terror-struck by the advancing communists, had already fled. They sought the relative safety of towns and cities, fearing enforced recruitment, the abduction of their children and the reputation for barbarism held by many of the communist fighters.

As the unit advanced into the village, full of confidence and anticipating an easy takeover, the sixty-strong group was met with a barrage of machine-gun fire. Several dozen partisans were immediately mown down.

They had entered the village as usual from different directions but the gunfire was stronger on one front than the others. Themis was among the rear guard and had a split second to realise what was happening. As soldiers around her were being hit, she threw herself to the ground. For a few minutes, bullets whistled past her and then someone fell heavily across her legs. Whoever this person was, the weight of them told her they were dead. She shut her eyes tight.

The ambush had been perfectly laid. For more than a day her unit had been followed, unwittingly, by soldiers of the government army. Their own survey of the village had been superficial and those instructed to do it had only seen what they expected to see.

After thirty seconds, there was a stillness followed by the occasional *pop* of a gun. Not a single member of Themis' unit had had a chance to lift a weapon. Not one shot was fired in return.

Themis lay still, knowing that the slightest movement might invite a bullet. She could feel a dampness seeping into the fabric of her trousers. It must be blood. There were shouts, and the thunder of footsteps reverberated around her as soldiers poured into the village.

Government army soldiers had not only been concealed in the houses, there had also been reinforcements waiting in the surrounding area.

For a moment Themis found herself staring at the well-polished toes of a man's boots. They were a centimetre from her face and she could even see a distorted reflection of herself in the sheen.

'Before you do anything else, check for any papers and bring them to me. Leave the dead where they are. Bring the wounded to the square.'

She listened to instructions being barked and heard occasional cries of pain as soldiers began to sort the living from the dead. Soon it was her turn to be prodded with the sharp end of a rifle.

The still-warm corpse was pulled away from her. Then she opened her eyes and found a rifle pointed in her face.

'Get up.'

Themis struggled to her feet. She reached up to touch her face and could feel it was badly grazed from when she had fallen. Apart from that she was unharmed.

There seemed to be very few members of the unit still alive. Bodies were strewn everywhere she looked and her legs shook so violently that she could scarcely walk the two hundred metres to the centre of the village.

Those who had been shot in the stomach had fallen backwards and in spite of herself she looked at their faces and saw their expressions frozen in anguish. The sight of her dead captain was shocking: it seemed impossible that such a giant of a man could be felled by a single piece of metal. His arms were splayed wide and his thick, dark hair was matted with blood. A government soldier was leaning over him, going through his pockets and there was a look of triumph on his face as he called out to the soldier chaperoning Themis.

'Here's our prize!'

The old ladies of the village cowered in doorways. They had been forewarned of the terror that was to come, and several of them had agreed to act as decoys when the unit had entered.

Themis would not look at them as she passed. She held them responsible for the deaths of her compatriots and friends. Collaborators, every one of them.

It was then that she saw Katerina. The distinctive mane of flame-red hair that she had always refused to cut had spilled from her cap and now tumbled over her face. She must have been shot in the back and had attempted to break her fall. Her arms were splayed and both wrists lay at strange angles, clearly fractured.

Themis could not hide the horror she felt at seeing her lifeless friend, and an involuntary sob escaped from her throat as she stumbled forwards to touch her cold face.

'Get up, now!' barked the soldier. 'Hands in the air!'

Poor, beautiful Katerina is dead, Themis thought to herself. There was nothing she could do now apart from try to save herself and she quickly stood up again, swallowing the salty tears that ran down her face.

She was ordered to join the group of unwounded survivors and they huddled together under a mighty plane tree that gave shade to the whole square. One by one, their hands were bound behind their backs.

Twenty metres away lay a dozen of the badly injured. Two government army officers were walking down the row, pausing at the feet of each one and making a note on a clipboard.

Suddenly Themis and the other survivors who could still walk were being pushed against a building, their backs to the square. The same soldier who had pulled tight the ropes that now chafed their wrists blindfolded them. One of the women began to whimper.

'Shut up!' commanded the soldier. 'We don't want your noise.'

The man next to her was quietly praying.

Themis bowed her head. Terror gave way to a sense of overwhelming sadness. Was life to end like this? In darkness and defeat? Beneath the dirty strip of cotton that covered her eyes, she could feel her tears. It filled her with grief to realise that life was to end when she felt it had only just begun.

Then the shots began. She counted. One . . . Two . . . Three . . . Four . . . They were as regular as the ticking of a clock but not as loud as she had expected. It was almost time.

Five . . . Six . . . Seven . . . Eight . . . Nine . . .

She could still hear the mutterings of her neighbour's prayers. Nobody next to her had fallen. She would have heard that. But still the gunshots continued.

Ten . . . Eleven . . . Twelve . . .

Then there was nothing. The sound of some soldiers' voices a short distance away broke the silence. Sweat poured down Themis' face and neck. She was saturated with fear, with relief, with despair, with the relentless August sun.

Five or ten minutes passed before she felt fingers fumbling to remove her blindfold. She and the other survivors were free to look around them. Themis blinked in the brightness and slowly turned to see what had taken place. The wounded were no longer there. They had disappeared. All that remained were some patches of blood in the dust. She realised that their eyes had been covered to prevent them from witnessing their cold-blooded murder.

Terrified-looking villagers were being herded into the square. They had endured their own ordeal.

Along with the other ten or so, Themis was bundled roughly into the back of a truck. A government soldier loitering nearby approached them and very deliberately spat in Themis' face. She could feel his saliva running down her cheek.

With her hands bound, there was nothing she could do. It was the ultimate humiliation. As they crouched down in the truck, stripped of identity and dignity, Themis had to fight back the tears.

She looked down and focused on the stitches of her trouser hem. It was important to maintain control.

'Koralis . . .'

She heard her name spoken in a whisper. The woman they all knew to have been the captain's lover was leaning towards her.

'Use my sleeve,' she whispered.

In an act of kindness that Themis would never forget, she leaned towards her and allowed Themis to wipe the drying spittle from her face.

When Themis looked up again, she saw her silently weeping, her normally expressionless face swollen with grief.

Poor woman, thought Themis. At least there was a chance that Tasos was still alive.

Themis lost track of time as they bumped over the rutted roads. There were nights and there were days but she counted neither. Nothing mattered. The motion of the vehicle, the heat and the lack of food induced such intense nausea that she could neither speak, nor sleep. One of the captives became so ill that the truck stopped. Even before any of them had time to realise what was happening, the driver had moved off.

'With a cough like that, he won't have long to suffer,' he shouted over his shoulder. 'You can stay there with him if you like.'

The others were too weak to protest and they watched helplessly as the pale face gradually disappeared in the distance. Had he inadvertently regained his freedom, wondered Themis.

The hours of passivity and sense of defeat took away all motivation even to talk. Suddenly Themis realised that the driver had slowed right down and the sound of other vehicles could be heard. Despite her almost catatonic lethargy, she sat up and peered through the slats of the truck.

There was traffic coming from all directions. They were in a city and passing familiar buildings. All the others were awake now and looking about them, exclaiming at the sight of landmarks that they knew so well. The Parthenon. The Temple of Zeus. Syntagma Square.

Athens. Themis was so close to home. She wanted to jump from the truck, run the length of Patission Avenue and fly into the safety of her grandmother's arms. She imagined there might be a meal waiting on the table. It was months since she had eaten any good food and her whole body craved decent nutrition. Back in Patissia, she would live in secret, grow her hair again. Panos would protect her, if he got back, and her grandmother would hide her. Surely even Thanasis would not betray his youngest sister?

The driver did not appear to be stopping, though, and her sense of disappointment grew as she felt the engine accelerate.

A short while later, however, he did slow down. They were still not so far from the centre of the city and the passengers on the truck all looked at each other. One of them realised where they were. He had even been there before. It was a place synonymous with terror.

'It's Averoff,' he muttered. They had been brought to the notorious prison, where both men and women were tortured into submission and 'repentance'.

They were all told to get down and the soldier roughly divided the group. The selection process appeared to be random.

'Not you lot,' said the soldier who had come to supervise the handover. 'Just you, you, you and you.'

Four prisoners were shepherded towards the dark, forbidding gates. One of them nodded a farewell to the others standing outside. Neither side understood the basis for the separation.

'Get back in!' said the soldier, giving Themis and each of the others an unnecessary shove in the back to push them back into the truck.

The engine started up again.

When they reached the outskirts of a small town south-west of Athens and were unloaded once again, they realised they were being delivered to a local prison.

'You'll soon be waving the flag for our Queen,' the driver said as he unbolted the back of the vehicle. This was enough to strengthen Themis' passionate commitment to her beliefs. Frederika still invoked a visceral hatred in her.

During the next few weeks Themis was moved from jail to jail, humiliated, sick and numbed by a sense of defeat. Pale and underfed, she imagined herself invisible, just as she had done as a child to avoid provoking Margarita's spite. The talent she had developed then for avoiding attention she used to full advantage now.

The time passed in a haze of occasional abuse, usually delivered in kicks and beatings. There was constant travel and she lost count of the number of times she was loaded into a truck and pushed into a new but similarly comfortless small-town prison cell. It seemed that jails were so full now that there was no space even when inmates were crowded on top of each other, often twenty in a cell made for eight.

Conversation focused on the other prisons that the women had visited. Themis soon appreciated that she had been lucky to be spared Averoff, where the screams of the tortured kept everyone awake night after night and the guards competed with each other to conjure up new and sadistic punishments. Some women had done a spell on the island of Chios. From what they described, although conditions were cramped and filthy, they had something to do to pass the time. They did their own shopping and cooking, organised the camp and were comparatively free. Others had been on Trikeri. It was full of scorpions and rats but, from what Themis gathered, they could hear the sea and the sound of birdsong, glimpse the clouds and sometimes feel the sensation of rain on their skin. Anywhere without this constant stench and suffocating claustrophobia would be paradise.

She thought of the sweetness of the air she had breathed in those months of action on the mountains, the sound of night birds and the breaths of cooling breeze on her face. She remembered how she used to lie awake on clear nights looking up at the bright stars, astonished by the immensity of the galaxy. Space and the open air were what she longed for, as well as Tasos' embrace.

Conditions in the urban prisons were universally squalid but every so often, when new prisoners arrived, some of the existing ones would be moved out and taken elsewhere. Themis was always happy to be transferred. It at least allowed the hope of something better.

Sometimes during the journey, one of the younger ones would attempt to escape. This meant a jump from the moving vehicle. Invariably the truck would screech to a halt and the escapee would be carelessly thrown back among the other prisoners, an arm or leg usually broken in the fall. Only rarely was an escape successful and when the guards were quizzed at the next jail they just shrugged their shoulders. If someone had got away it was better just to amend the figures. One missing? What did it matter? There were tens of thousands of these people, as hard to quantify as rats, and as unwanted. One unaccounted for made no difference to the guards.

Themis had lost track of time, and even of where she was, when some new prisoners were thrown into her cell one day. Those such as herself who had been there a while were desperate for word of the outside world, but this time the newcomers brought bad news.

The communists had survived their various defeats for more than a year but even as Themis had been suffocating in yet another stifling cell, the final battles of the civil war had been fought on the mountains of Grammos and Vitsi. Losses for the communist army had been heavy and most survivors had fled to Albania.

There was a stunned silence among the dozen women hearing this news for the first time.

'It's finished,' said one of them bitterly, after a pause, and there were murmurs of agreement from other women.

'But it's not the *end*,' protested Themis with despair. 'It can't be . . .'

For a while, the women with whom Themis shared her filthy rat-infested space were divided between defeatism and determination to rejoin the fight. A few weeks later, in mid-October, the guards gleefully gave them the news that their leader, Zachariadis, had announced a ceasefire. The conflict was officially over. Thereafter, every news bulletin was exploited as an excuse to further mistreat the captives, to taunt them with the statistics of the dead and to gloat over their humiliation.

Some of the women to whom Themis was shackled openly grieved the death of their country but Themis refused to accept that the fight was done. Her sick, exhausted body felt defeated but her mind was still free. The number of prisoners increased markedly and, always optimistic, this increased Themis' hopes of seeing both her lover and her brother.

The war had effectively come to an end but their period of captivity had not. Towards the end of the year, she was on yet another journey with hands bound. As usual, the destination mattered little. Themis' head had dropped on to her neighbour's shoulder and for several hours she slept.

When she woke, it was to a new scent. The wafts of diesel that they had all been inhaling had been replaced by the smell of the sea.

The truck had stopped and they were being ordered to get down. Themis saw a ragged group of soldiers at the water's edge and, although their uniforms were dark with grime, Themis recognised them as members of the communist army. Her group was being herded towards them.

Relieved to be stretching her legs, Themis approached unsteadily. The soldiers' hands were tied too and they were all skeletal with malnutrition. She had not seen a mirror for many months, but imagined she looked just as they did.

Across the water, a boat was approaching the nearby jetty. It was a simple fishing skiff but more than thirty lined up to embark. Themis was the last of the first group to board and was roughly pulled in by the helmsman. They all sat with thighs touching in a craft made for half a dozen, water lapping over its sides.

Themis could see a barren stretch of land ahead but it was impossible to tell how far away it lay. Half an hour passed as the boat struggled across the waves. Neither she nor her siblings had ever learnt to swim and, moreover, none of them would have a chance even if the boat sank close to the shore.

As they lurched up and down and side to side, lower and lower in the water, she was overpowered by nausea. Several others were already vomiting over the side.

The man sitting next to her could see Themis' face turning green.

'Keep looking at the horizon,' he muttered. 'Don't take your eye off it. We're almost there.'

'Where . . .?'

The boat was being pulled into a pier and tied up by several uniformed men.

Suddenly Themis saw the flash of a blade in the sunlight and her state of numbness turned to fear. A knife was passed down to the helmsman and, rocking the boat almost to the point of capsize, he reached out to the closest of his 'passengers' and cut through the rope that bound his hands. One by one, as their arms were freed, the sodden prisoners disembarked.

Themis turned to look at the landscape that lay in front of them. There were words marked out on the hills in huge white stones.

ZITO O VASILIAS
LONG LIVE THE KING

Her head was clearing. She had seen photographs of this place. Everyone knew of its reputation. It was the most notoriously brutal of all the island prisons. Makronisos.

Chapter Fifteen

A RRIVAL IN THIS barren place seemed just another test of endurance and Themis told herself that she would survive.

'Long Live the King'. Even the tone of the message on the hillside seemed comparatively mild, compared with slogans that had been hurled at her in past months: accusations of bandit, slut and whore.

Men and women were divided and soldiers barked out instructions. The men were the first to march beneath a giant archway. Themis took in the words written above their heads:

I MAKRONISOS SAS KALOSORIZEI
MAKRONISOS WELCOMES YOU

She had heard many stories about Makronisos. All of them were second-hand and she now wondered if they had been exaggerated. After more than a year living rough as a soldier, followed by the horrors of prison, the sight of ordered rows of tents enough to accommodate tens of thousands was almost welcome. They rose up the hillsides in every direction, fanning out into the distance as far as the eye could see. In her state of weariness, her only thought was that perhaps there might even be something other than hard ground to lie on.

Many years before, on one of the few occasions their father had taken them out of Athens, she and her siblings had gone to Cape Sounion. She recalled looking across the sea towards the barren, colourless island in front of them. 'Uninhabitable and uninhabited' was how her father had described it and she could hear his almost dismissive words even now.

Nowadays it clearly was inhabited and, as she soon learnt, new legislation had been passed, allowing the island to take in women as well as men for 'correction'.

The place teemed mostly with young government soldiers, smartly dressed in pale uniforms, well shaved, hair neatly clipped. It looked like a well-organised army camp, not the bare, empty island she had always imagined. It was full of noise: music, announcements, shouts, the chanting of priests.

Themis searched the crowd for the two faces she longed to see. With such a sizeable population, perhaps Tasos or even Panos might be here, and if they were not here yet, there was a possibility that they might arrive. Even now as she looked out to sea, there was another small boat making its way across the choppy waters and her spirits rose a little.

A nudge in the ribs broke her reverie.

'Come on,' her neighbour urged. 'Our turn.'

It was time for their group to make an official entrance. As they passed beneath the archway, a blast of military brass fanfared them. Her stomach still churning from the roughness of the sea and her eyes dazzled by the low sun, Themis struggled to make sense of what was going on around her.

On the other side of the archway, everything seemed to change. She stumbled across the stony ground, the wind whipping dust and grit into her eyes, nose and mouth. Announcements were being broadcast through a loudspeaker but they were incomprehensible and clashed with the sound of brass and drums.

Narrowing her eyes and keeping her face to the ground, Themis followed the feet in front of her. At one point she looked up to see one woman being mercilessly whipped by another. A group of male soldiers was observing and laughing. It seemed to be purely for their entertainment.

'You are nothing! Do you hear me?'

The victim was cowering from the blows, neither screaming nor crying. Her silence only made her seem more vulnerable.

'*Eísai ethnomíasma!* You are a germ! A germ that will destroy our nation.'

Themis looked away, feeling vicarious shame for the unknown woman. She did not want to add her own stares to those of the people jeering and hurling abuse.

'*Symmorítissa!*' some of them shrieked at her. 'Bandit!'

'Bulgarian!' shouted some others.

Themis noticed the joshing between the assailant and one of the men, whose trousers were falling down around his ankles.

'And you're a *thief* too,' he cackled. 'Give me back my belt!'

The whipping stopped as the woman doing the beating returned his belt to him.

Everyone in the group held their sides with laughter.

Themis turned away and continued to trudge. Ten or fifteen minutes passed before she looked up again. As she did, she noticed the cold eyes of the men who passed in the opposite direction. Their lack of expression was chilling.

When they finally came to a halt, Themis' group of twenty was lined up before a figure who was waiting to address them. With the sun setting behind him, all they could see was a silhouette.

'Welcome,' he said before a dramatic pause. 'Alas, each one of you has stepped from the natural ways of womankind.'

The voice was deep and disarmingly gentle.

'But you are the lucky ones. Here on this island, we can help bring you back to the right path. You will acknowledge the errors you have made and repent of your ways. Don't think of this place as a prison but as a place for correction.'

There was not a single murmur of dissent. His tone was kind, contrasting dramatically with the cruelty and abuse that was all they had heard in past weeks and months. Themis listened to the words carefully.

The speech continued but the tone changed to one of exhortation.

'There is only one path home, only one route to reunion with your family. It is very simple.'

Then they heard a new word. From now on they would hear it so often that it would be like a breath or a noise.

'You will all sign a *dílosi*. And when you do, you will go home to where you belong. Your families will be waiting with open arms.'

Dílosi metanoías. A declaration of repentance. *Dílosi, dílosi, dílosi* . . . The word would ring in their ears.

Themis found it ridiculous. She would *never* repent of fighting for her rights, against a regime where so many had collaborated with the Nazis.

Pointing towards Cape Sounion, the speaker came to the climax of his speech.

'Imagine yourselves back on the mainland. Your consciences clear. Women once again. Fully Greek. Fully alive.'

He paused for a moment, almost as if he expected applause, then turned away and marched back towards the sea.

His pseudo concern was soon replaced by the overt cruelty of their female guards.

Marched to a tent that would be shared by fifty of them, they were given thin cotton dresses and Themis found herself struggling to do up the buttons, her fingers were so frozen by the cold. She did not ask anyone for help. This time she would try to limit the possibilities of pain and loss. There would be no Katerina.

Their tatty communist army uniforms were left in a pile outside the tent and later that day Themis watched as the trousers of which she had been so proud were put in a pile with others, set on fire and reduced to ash.

At first, some of the women assigned to guard their tent were kind enough and Themis soon realised that they were prisoners who had already signed a *dílosi*. Their mission was to encourage their charges to do the same.

The majority of the women in Themis' tent were stubborn, and none would easily turn her back on her beliefs. Many of them had recently been transferred to Makronisos from Trikeri and they regarded themselves as the hardest to crack. They even looked different, their lined faces deeply scored by sun and wind.

Themis had experienced the brutality of a policeman's whip and a soldier's boot but now she and the others were subjected to periods of pointless and gruelling labour. Day after day, they were forced to carry rocks from one location to another.

When the sun started to go down, physical work ended and indoctrination began, including the obligatory singing of patriotic songs and marching. It was a daily requirement to sit for hours on end in the huge concrete stadium. Unprotected from the fierce wind that constantly battered this barren rock and unpredictable showers of hail and heavy rain, they listened to the droning voices of their captors. What Themis hated most of all were the haranguing speeches they were subjected to, but she had long ago developed a way of shutting down her senses, appearing to concentrate while not really hearing. At least these hours gave them some repose and Themis obligingly stood when necessary to sing, separating thought from action as she had practised with Fotini.

The women in the tent reinforced each other's resolve. 'Never, never, never,' they said under their breath so that the others could hear. And at night the whisper went up and down the tent: '*Never, never, never*'. Never would they turn their backs on their comrades. Never would they turn their backs on their communist ideals. Never would they sign the *dílosi*.

Within a few days, Themis had grasped the layout of Makronisos. There were separate zones, one for those who had not repented, one for those who were on their way to 'rehabilitation' and a third for those who had signed the *dílosi*.

Alpha, Beta, Gamma were the names of the zones. A, B, C. One, two, three. They were told that these were also the simple steps they must take to cleanse themselves, to be reborn.

In a state of weariness, Themis followed the flow of the day. Along with the thousands of other prisoners everything was done in timed shifts including the daily visits to the cold, charmless cathedral, which had been quickly built out of concrete in the centre of the island.

'They expect us to *pray*?' muttered one of Themis' group. 'I will pray for the death of our guards. That's all I will pray for.'

She was overheard by one of the guards and Themis never saw her again.

A subtler form of torture was the relentless noise. Not only were there constant announcements over the Tannoy, orders barked in their faces and the screams of the tortured, but on some days music blared from the loudspeakers without interruption. Nationalist songs, military bands and snatches of orchestral music were played over and over again.

One of the women who slept close to Themis was taken one night and buried up to her neck in the sand outside. The following morning they all had to file past her. It was a form of torture designed to terrorise them all.

After that the woman lost her sanity. All the humiliation and physical abuse to which she had been subjected did not seem to have affected her as much as the relentless blast of music. She stood up one night and began to scream, her hands clamped over her ears.

'Stop! Stop! *Stop!*'

Her shrieks attracted the guards who came into the tent and pulled her out. Such a protest gave them the perfect excuse to punish her again.

For the first time, Themis realised that all music needed silence to have meaning. Without pause it was simply noise.

A few days later, for no apparent reason, the music stopped. The unpredictability of the decision was almost equally nerve-racking, giving no reassurance that this particular torment might not recommence any time.

Every so often, the prisoners were handed a copy of the island's magazine, celebrating the signing of repentances, reporting on government army activities and showing photographs of Queen Frederika on a tour of the children's homes she had opened. Her sunny, well-fed demeanour beamed out from the page, making Themis' temperature rise in spite of the cold. The woman seemed well-meaning, but Themis could not forgive her for so blatantly supporting the right.

Sometimes, when their guards and torturers wanted time off for themselves, the women were encouraged to do some needlework.

'*Womanly handicrafts*, that's what we do while they take a break,' muttered one of the longer-term 'inmates' sarcastically to Themis.

Sewing had been a passion of her sister's but Themis had always been averse to it and everything it seemed to represent. Reluctantly, she selected a square of the discoloured linen from a pile, threaded her needle with cotton and sat down on the stony ground outside the tent. She chose red.

Nobody was shouting, no one was bullying, there was just the noise of the wind as it rattled the branches in some twisted trees.

Fifty women sat in silence. The woman next to Themis had a cloth spread across her lap. It was edged with a pleasing symmetrical pattern like a row of zigzags.

'Look,' whispered its owner, orienting the cloth so that Themis could see it from another angle.

Themis was impressed. Now she could see that the pattern comprised an acronym repeated all the way round the outside. ELASELASELASELAS.

'And in the middle, I will also sew the name of our motherland, *ELLAS*. But I'll spell it wrong there too . . .'

The girl, who was much younger than Themis, smiled mischievously.

Embroidering the initials of the communist resistance army, ELAS, for whom the girl's three brothers had died, was one of the many small rebellions taking place around her. In the guise of traditional island patterns, Themis saw birds in flight and ships in full sail. 'They represent our freedom,' explained one woman. Such acts of subversion achieved little but kept their spirits from dying.

Themis sat for some time, staring at the white square on her lap. In theory the subject for their embroidery must be something that celebrated the motherland. She loved her *patrída* as vehemently as the guards who kept her here and she was determined to show it.

Having knotted the thread, she pierced the fabric from the underside, and to her great satisfaction saw the point of the needle appear right at the very centre, exactly where she wanted it. From here, she began to embroider the outline of a heart. She could say it represented her love for Greece and for her family but with every stitch she would think of Tasos. She had felt so complete in the mountains with him and wondered if that's what Plato had meant when he talked of the Other Half. She certainly felt she had been cut in two. Her dream of being reunited with the man she loved at least gave her hope for something, and each time the point of the needle pierced the cloth and she pulled the scarlet thread through, she imagined herself pulling him closer.

For the first time, she understood the pleasure of sewing. The concentration took her mind away from her situation, and the small size of her hands, which had sometimes been a disadvantage when handling a gun, was now a benefit.

As the months passed, the days grew longer and hotter. Themis was becoming progressively more exhausted by the days of hard labour and was often beaten for slacking. Needlework was the only activity for which she had energy. One of the women was lamenting that her periods had ceased, making it only two of the fifty women in the tent who still menstruated. Some were relieved to find themselves spared the monthly curse, but others feared that it would never return. Themis remembered how Fotini's periods had stopped and malnutrition had long since done the same to her.

All day, she felt the sun beating down on her neck and at night lay on her bed in a delirium of nausea and discomfort. She could not sleep. It was then that she heard screams. They were not the screams of a woman, but of a man. A high-pitched squeal such as a wounded animal might make. Torture on the island had intensified. The government authorities were not satisfied by the number of *dílosis* being signed on Makronisos and had demanded an improvement in results.

One night, without warning, three guards came into their tent and dragged one of the women away. They did not take her far. The guards wanted the others to hear everything so that they could imagine what was being done to their victim.

Her screams traumatised Themis and when, an hour later, the woman was roughly pushed back into the tent, she was almost too nervous to look.

Whimpering, the woman fell to the ground and for a moment lay still, naked and curled into a foetal position. Three others quickly gathered around her and one began tearing up a sheet getting ready to bathe her wounds.

'*Theé kai kýrie!* Look at her feet!' Themis heard one of them saying. 'They've destroyed them.'

That day the woman lay motionless on her thin mat, a reminder to all the others of their potential fate. The following night there was another victim and on each subsequent night another. Rape was common, but some returned without fingernails and others were beaten with socks full of stones or had cigarette burns on their breasts. Each one was evidence of what happened if you refused to sign the *dílosi*.

No one could ever predict the precise time when the flap of the tent would be flung open and the next victim randomly chosen. Themis remembered how she used to feign sleep to try to make herself invisible to Margarita and the night that the sound of heavy army boots stopped next to her bed, she squeezed her eyes tight shut, hoping, praying, willing it not to be her turn.

Resistance to violence of any kind was pointless. She slipped her feet into her boots and walked calmly between the two guards, trying to breathe, telling herself to be brave. So often she had rehearsed how she would react when her time came. She would try to think of the sweetest things she knew, of Tasos, of his lips, of her unfinished heart.

A few metres from the exit, one of the soldiers put his hands on her shoulders. He spoke quietly, his face so close to hers that their lips could almost have touched. It was intimate. She felt violated even before anything had taken place.

'You can save yourself,' he said. The soldier was not much older than her, but his teeth were rotten and black and his breath smelled like excrement. She almost gagged with revulsion.

'If you want, you can save yourself,' he murmured again.

Themis said nothing. Clearly her silence annoyed him.

'Tell me that you don't wish to die. Tell me that you will sign,' he said, so quietly but so close she could feel his hot breath on her lips.

'Say that you will sign!' screamed the second guard, leaning in to intimidate her further. 'Just sign! Then our work is done.'

Themis contemplated the idea just for a moment. It would mean a return in shame to Athens, to face Thanasis (perhaps even Margarita, who knew?). It would be a denial of all her beliefs, a betrayal of so many people she had fought with. There would be the reading out of her '*dílosi metanoías*', the statement of repentance, in the same church where she had understood *charmolýpi* for the first time. The public humiliation of the pointing finger, the scornful glance, the gloating of neighbours whom she knew to have been collaborators. No, it was a form of suicide, the abnegation of her 'self'. How would she ever face Tasos or Panos when she saw them again?

All of this filled her with greater fear than the soldiers who intimidated her now. She must stay strong. The nicotine on the soldier's breath filled her mouth and bile rose up from the pit of her belly. Suddenly she was heaving and vomiting, and the two soldiers were turning away in disgust. She crouched down on the ground and wretched until her stomach was dry.

'Get the bitch up,' one soldier ordered the other.

Themis was pulled to her feet and whipped several times across her back. Before roughly pushing her back into the tent, one of the soldiers sadistically twisted her arms behind her back until she thought they would come out of their sockets.

Guiltily she watched as they pulled another woman from her bed and then listened in terror to the screams that came from outside. The woman was being raped, and Themis knew it could have been her.

Eventually Themis' 'substitute' was dragged back, unconscious, and dropped unceremoniously on to her bed. Several of the other women tended to her as she came round, screaming in pain from the cigarette burns that covered her face and neck. They dabbed gently but uselessly at the wounds but when morning came it was clear that the scars would disfigure her for ever.

The soldiers were finding the strength of the female will to be greater than their determination to make them sign and their frustration only made them crueller.

For several weeks, no one in Themis' tent had signed. It gave them a reputation, and the soldiers adopted new tactics. Punishment was no longer a terror saved for the night and they were often subjected to daytime beatings. Themis' skin was sun-darkened but there were many patches further blackened by bruising. To try to break them, the guards picked people out for solitary confinement. Themis was one such victim and she endured three days and nights shut in a damp and lightless cave. Bread was thrown in once a day but with no way of calculating the passage of time, she often ate it too quickly and then had nothing. These were the hours of her deepest misery and despair.

One day, when it seemed only moments since they had gone to bed, they were woken by shouts.

'Get up, you stubborn whores. Outside. Now.'

The sun had not risen and the stars were still visible as they stumbled into the early morning. Though it was April, there was still a chill in the early morning and their thin clothes were no protection against the elements.

This was something new. They were used to sudden awakening and bullying at all times of day, but now they were being marched at speed towards an unfamiliar part of the island, far from the tented areas to a place where no one would hear or see what they were subjected to.

After a forty-minute hike, they reached an area of scrubland. The sun had risen and Themis looked around her and up at the blue sky. Nothing had yet happened.

They were all standing in a huddle and the soldier in charge directed them to stand apart.

'Like this!' he said, demonstrating what he wanted them to do. 'Arms out!'

When the women did not respond, he shouted: 'Aeroplane!'

They were all obliged to stand in the same ludicrous position. They were being tortured for their beliefs on an invisible cross.

After a while, numbness set in and Themis experienced a temporary loss of pain. Other women had fallen to the ground, fainting from the unseasonal heat and exhaustion. When they came round, they had to resume the position. A few of them sobbed, but their crying was without weeping. Dehydration had robbed them of their tears. Nothing moistened their eyes or their throats.

They stood like this, with the sun soaring higher and higher into the sky and, when most of the women had dropped to the ground, the verbal bullying began once again. The soldier screamed to be heard above the buzzing of a thousand flies that swarmed over the carcass of an animal rotting nearby.

'You can stand, each day, for a week, a month, a year, like this,' he said, smirking. 'We don't mind. We're happy for you to expand our air force.'

He paused for a moment to acknowledge the titters of appreciation from other soldiers standing around and, pleased with his attempt at humour, he was encouraged to continue.

'The Americans have given us a helping hand but we could always do with some reinforcements.'

All the soldiers were laughing and jeering now.

The position the women were obliged to adopt was calculated to make them look ridiculous, but it was to their bodies and spirits that the real damage had been done. Several lay still in the dust and those who had any strength helped the fallen. Very slowly, when they were allowed, they all staggered back to the camp. There was no natural water supply on Makronisos and when one of the women noticed a trough left for the goats, she ran towards it, dropped to her knees, and plunged her face into the fetid, tepid water. Themis followed and drank thirstily, scooping the water into her mouth as if it was the sweetest wine. All the others waited patiently for their turn and the soldiers did not intervene. They stood at a distance, smoking and chatting to each other as if their job was done.

Even now, no one in the group had signed the *dílosi* and the guards took it as a personal failing that the women continued to resist. It would be a triumph if even one of them gave in. The guards' strategy was simple. That night and for several days they were not fed.

Everyone in the tent was now sick. Many had dysentery, four were taken from the island with suspected tuberculosis and several had developed sepsis from untreated sores. The soldiers were sadistic but they did not want to risk their own health and for a while left the women to die or to recover.

Themis was in a state of delirium for several days following the hours of intense humiliation in the sun. Nevertheless, she was forced outside and pushed with a rifle between her shoulder blades to the daily parade.

'If you can walk, you can attend,' said the soldier, jabbing his gun into her spine.

She almost fainted on the path to the theatre but was held up by two solicitous women, one on either side. It was only with their kindness that she got there and once they had gently lowered her into one of the stone seats they moved away. Such kind deeds could be punished.

The dust was stirred up that evening by a strong wind and Themis looked downwards to prevent it from going into her eyes. Even so, the grit seemed to burrow its way beneath her lashes.

She heard the beat of soldiers' feet on the stony ground and, peering through half-open eyes, she saw the dim outline of men filing past. These were the soldiers who the previous day had signed the *dílosi*. It was a triumph for those in charge of them. Ten all at once.

God knows what they were subjected to, thought Themis. They were being fêted with almost religious fervour.

A priest stood with a line of officers. He was chanting.

'It's like a baptism,' said one of the other women under her breath.

'They're being rebaptised,' said another. 'Reborn. Purified.'

Themis closed her eyes. It disturbed her to imagine how these good communist soldiers had compromised themselves, but worse still was to witness the gloating of those who had bullied them into it. These soldiers, who had signed *dílosis* themselves, now led the celebration for the latest 'conversions'. Their leader was preparing to speak.

'Think what they'll get back home,' said her neighbour.

'A good meal,' replied her other neighbour, talking across Themis, 'and a warm shower, and a comfortable bed, and clean clothes and . . .'

'That's not what I meant,' said the first firmly. 'They'll find scorn. Derision.'

It was true that the repenters would face humiliation from those on both sides when their declarations were made public. Nevertheless, Themis suddenly felt a pang of envy that they would soon be home and away from this hell. For a moment she was lost in reverie.

Then she heard a voice. Just four words were enough for her to recognise the cultured intonation.

'You have saved yourselves.'

She knew the timbre of that educated accent so well, the way certain words were emphasised.

'You have changed your path,' he continued. 'You are redeemed, to live once again as full citizens of Greece.'

Tasos? Was it really him? She had heard that heat stroke could give you delusions and, with the setting sun behind him, Themis could see only a silhouette. She desperately wanted to be wrong.

The sun went down rapidly now and as it did his image became clearer. She blinked with disbelief. It really was Tasos, standing there with a mocking smile. It was many months since she had seen him and although, in that time, many of the women around her had changed beyond recognition, he seemed not to have altered by even one curl.

Themis' heart was beating hard, the shock all the greater given that he must have been the chief protagonist in obtaining *dílosis* from the men that stood before him.

Drowning in a confusion of passion and rationality, she called out his name.

'Tasos . . . Tasos!'

Nobody, including Makris, responded. On Makronisos everyone knew him as Makris and the new 'converts' and all the guards turned to look at her. It was audacious behaviour to draw attention to yourself in this way.

The women on either side of Themis urged her to be quiet.

Everyone was looking at her, except for the man she loved. He carried on with his speech, apparently oblivious.

'And now, before you leave this place, it is your duty to make your fellow Greeks see the light, as you have done. Your mission now is to save as you have been saved.'

There were murmurs of discontent. These men had been expecting immediate liberation but this was not to be.

Makris spoke with quasi-religious zeal but his audience was now distracted by Themis, who had called out again. As soon as he finished, the guards marshalled the new converts and got them out of the theatre, to vacate it for the next part of the parade. Only then did Makris have a clear line of sight towards Themis. He turned his gaze on her.

Themis met his eyes with her own and saw nothing but a vacuum of non-recognition. The face was the same but there was nothing in his expression to suggest that she was anything other than a stranger.

The same fathomless eyes that she had loved so much now filled her with fear. They were as dark as hell, as cold and empty as the cave where she had been sent for solitary confinement. She could do nothing but watch with disillusion and grief as the man she loved turned away. Something had been stripped out of him and, as she stared at his retreating back, she felt something had been torn from her too.

Everyone was looking at her now. A few of the guards were laughing and pointing. The women around Themis looked embarrassed for her, but angry too. This loss of control would undoubtedly have repercussions, possibly for all of them.

Chapter Sixteen

Back in the tent, Themis was oblivious to everything and everyone. She lay on her mat, her eyes closed to the world. She did not even weep. Her ideals were one thing, but she realised that hope of a joyous reunion with Tasos had been what really sustained her. Now this was gone.

The rest were outside to collect their evening ration of bread but an overwhelming nausea had killed her appetite. She was sick with sadness and sunstroke.

Suddenly a commotion disturbed her reverie. The authorities on Makronisos liked to have an excuse for both mass as well as individual punishment and had seized on Themis' undisciplined behaviour with vindictive enthusiasm.

The women were all coming back into the tent now, talking in high voices, some of them shouting and protesting. She opened her eyes and realised they had all gathered around her bed. Feebly, she tried to sit up.

'You!' one of the toughest women in their group said, leaning down and jabbing her finger towards Themis. 'You! This is all because of *you*!'

'Yes, it's your fault. Entirely your fault.'

'There's no food. Not a crust between us.'

'And it's because of *you*.'

All the camaraderie and the mutual support between the women had evaporated. They would happily have found a way of physically punishing her if they could but their sharp tongues were enough for now.

In the moment when Themis had been vainly calling out Tasos' name, they had swiftly drawn the conclusion that the two had been lovers. It was common knowledge that this was against all the rules of the party, a sin against the beliefs and practices of the army.

Several of the women, hungry and angry, began to taunt her.

'So he's forgotten you, has he?'

'Shame! Shame on you, you little slut.'

The abuse continued until the women got bored and went to lie down on their own mats. Hunger kept most of them awake. It was a terrible night for them all.

As the days passed, Themis realised that many of the women no longer spoke to her and that even the most sympathetic had become enemies.

The memory of Tasos' blank stare haunted her and she told herself that he must have been brutalised to have gone through such a transformation. As tears began to soak her blanket she thought of the times they had made love. This was the image she would try to keep in her mind.

In the following days the prisoners were assigned to what was described as a special building project. The regime on Makronisos had decided that they should construct a model of the Parthenon. It was the true symbol of their *patrída* and, by building it, the wayward detainees of the island would recognise where their loyalties lay. The carrying of heavy stones from one end of the island to the other would remind them of their duty.

The midday temperatures of late April were intense and sweat poured down Themis' back as she trekked up and down with her burden. Like several others, she had found a spare piece of cloth from the embroidery box to cover her head but was told to remove it.

The same day on which she placed her first stone on this parody of the Parthenon, Themis suddenly found herself doubled up with pain. Incapable of walking, she clutched her stomach in agony.

One of the few women who still spoke to Themis was permitted to help her back to the tent.

There were always several women in the tent who had been allowed to remain there in the day, either because they were disabled from a severe beating or were feverish and suffering from an as yet undiagnosed disease.

Like all the other women, Themis' bones protruded from her shoulders, hips and knees. There were no mirrors but her 'reflection' was provided by her fellow captives and she imagined herself the same emaciated shape. Sometimes she ran her hands across her joints feeling them become progressively sharper.

That night she lay on her back clutching her abdomen. Perhaps if she put some pressure on it, it might give some relief. As she pressed the epicentre of discomfort, she noticed it was more rounded than normal and she remembered from the famine of 1941 that starvation could cause a stomach to bloat.

Then she felt something else. Through her cramps, she could feel something strange and unfamiliar. She lay there keeping her hand in the same position. It happened again a few moments later, the same stirring from inside her. Surely, it could not be. There it was again, the unfamiliar movement from within her belly. With a mixture of shock and pleasure, she knew that what she was experiencing was new life.

Charmolýpi, she thought, doubling up with pain but simultaneously feeling an intensity of joy that had been absent for so long.

After an hour or so, the cramps seemed to lessen and the thrill of her discovery to increase. Lying there, afraid that if she moved the pain would return, she tapped her fingers against her thigh and tried to count. How many months had passed since Tasos had made love to her. Seven? Eight? She had long since lost track of days and weeks. There had been nothing to measure them against, nothing to count them for.

She could tell no one of her suspicion. This most precious secret must be kept to herself. Only a few days ago, she had watched as a woman was stripped of her newborn because she would not sign a *dílosi.* The baby had arrived on Makronisos along with its mother and the scene of anguish haunted Themis deeply. She recalled with profound guilt that she had once separated mothers from their children and such acts weighed more heavily on her conscience than ever. Even as the grief-stricken woman was given a final chance to keep her daughter, she had not signed. She had placed her commitment to her beliefs above all maternal instinct.

Becoming a parent was something Themis had never imagined. It seemed impossible that another life was growing within her after all the hardship that her body had been subjected to in past months. Another human being had been sharing and enduring it all.

For the next few days she went about as if her head was in one place and her body in another. She was light-headed. There was no longer any pain. Conversation with her unborn baby was continuous. Her own and the child's became the only voices in her head. They drowned out the strident voices of the soldiers and silenced the wailings and tears of her fellow captives. One night when she was pulled from her bed, stripped and beaten, she turned her back on her assailants, taking the blows on shoulders and spine to protect her stomach.

She was constantly looking out for Makris. Every day when they marched towards the place where they collected stones for the new Parthenon she searched for his face among the guards. Even more than before, she wanted to attract his attention, to shout out to him. Before it had been purely to tell him that she was there. Now she had something to say to him: 'I am carrying our child.' Putting their differences to one side, surely he would want to know this? Her memory of his cold, expressionless stare was not one she could erase from her mind, but nevertheless she wanted to tell him the news.

One evening when she went down to the sea with a group of others to wash her clothes, she saw some men along the shore and could not avert her eyes. So disabled were they that their broken, pathetic bodies made her weep. If one of them had been Panos, she might not even have recognised him. Perhaps Makris himself had been responsible.

The days passed. She felt her stomach stretching, even though it was still imperceptible to anyone but her. Some of the other women had protruding stomachs that accentuated their skinny legs and arms, and breasts that were still generous from a child-rearing past. Themis observed how female bodies never lost the vestiges of pregnancy and birth, even if a state of near starvation reduced the rest.

Once or twice, a sense of fear and uncertainty swept over her but this passed. She must remain strong. Not just for herself now.

Almost instinctively several other women knew that she was no longer suffering in the same way as they and were suspicious.

'She's going to *sign*,' she heard one of them saying. 'I'm sure of it.'

Themis had seen for herself that a state of almost peaceful

257

resignation often came before a woman's decision to renounce her beliefs. You could see it in someone's eyes. Everyone could see that there was a change in Themis' demeanour but their interpretation was wrong.

Largely ignored by most of the women, Themis often found her hand resting on her belly. It was still unnoticeable to others. Her once-small breasts had swelled, but the dresses they wore were shapeless enough to conceal it.

As the days passed, the sun went down later so there was more time for needlework before the light faded. Themis still worked on the heart but nowadays she had other thoughts in her mind: love for the unborn child, who kept her company day and night, gently moving and prodding from within to remind her of its existence. The first heart was almost finished. The dense, satinwork stitches had padded it out to a pleasing fullness and now, to continue the pretence that she was creating a religious piece, she began to sew the words: '*Mitéra Theoú*', Mother of God. She planned to stop when it read: '*Mitéra The*— and enjoy her private understanding of its meaning. In the opposite corner of the cloth, she had begun a second, smaller heart. When the time came for them to fold up their work, she tucked it into her pocket.

One morning, they were woken early. It seemed only an hour or so since they had gone to bed and it was a rude awakening. Five soldiers came in and walked up and down the rows of sleeping women, whacking them with a stick. Within minutes the women were outside, each holding her rolled-up blanket under one arm as instructed.

Bleary eyed, they stood shivering in the darkness, confused and disorientated. Twenty minutes later they were told to start walking down towards the sea.

Moonlight glistened on the water, illuminating the familiar signs laid out on the hillside in white stones. Then they saw two small boats moored at the quay and Themis felt her hopes rise. They were saying goodbye to Makronisos. They were not being liberated, but perhaps they were going somewhere that was less of a hell.

Twenty-five women and four guards squeezed into each small skiff. Some of the women began to ask questions, but they were ignored. Perhaps the guards themselves did not even know the answers.

The water between the island and the mainland was unusually flat that day and, even with their inadequate engines, the boats got them across to Lavrio within half an hour.

There was a group of soldiers waiting for them and soon they were packed on to a truck. There was so little room that some of them had to stand.

Themis felt a sense of resignation. Whatever her destiny, her only preoccupation was with protecting her unborn child. She put her blanket between herself and the side of the truck and thought of the foetus in its ever-diminishing space. She hoped the child was oblivious to everything taking place only a few centimetres away, and yet she hoped it might be familiar with her voice.

As they were driven along and the sun climbed high, someone began to sing a gentle traditional song. It was a song that they all knew from childhood and soon most of them joined in, Themis loudest of all, hoping that her baby could hear. The soldiers up front were oblivious to the sound of the choir.

Many hours into the journey, the woman next to Themis peered through the slats of the cattle truck and suddenly gasped: 'It's my town! We're in my town!'

The women closest to her craned their necks to see.

'We're in Volos! We just passed the end of my street.'

Seeing her birthplace from a different perspective was less of a comfort than a source of grief and the woman wept inconsolably. To be so near and yet so far from home was a double blow.

They trundled eastwards, away from the sun that was now slowly setting. Most women were dozing, the singing had stopped and there was time to think on this seemingly endless journey. Themis began to think of her family and for each member there was a question. Her grandmother. Was she still strong enough to be taking care of the home? Thanasis. Had he regained his strength? Margarita. Was she still in Germany, another broken country where thousands wandered, searching for lost family and food? Panos. Was he captive like her or had he escaped across the border? Her mother. How would psychiatric patients have been cared for during the occupation? The Nazi regime had not been known for its sympathy to anyone but the strong and able-bodied.

Her father. Had he been the only one to survive the chaos that had engulfed the rest of his family? America played a crucial role in Europe now but was itself unscathed. Now that she was to become a mother she questioned, for the first time, his decision to abandon his children. She closed her eyes and thought of a paper boat her father had once made when they went to the seaside. Perhaps it was on the same day that he had taken them to Sounion. For a while it had floated, as stable as if it were made of wood, but suddenly it disappeared and she knew it had sunk, pulled down by its own, brine-saturated weight. She had not been able to understand why her father had tried to persuade her it was out there sailing on the ocean towards its destination. It was clearly a lie.

The truck stopped for a few moments so that the drivers could swap over and the women had time to relieve themselves where they could. They were then given a single flask of water to share between all two dozen of them. The first one began gulping it back.

'You greedy cow!' said the woman next to her, snatching it out of her hand.

Her action caused the first woman to spill several drops in the dust and there were shouts of fury from those still waiting to drink. They were ready to fight each other over a few drops of water. By the time Themis was handed the flask there was only a mouthful left and it made her even thirstier than before.

The truck trundled on for a few hours and, much to the relief of all the women, who were plagued by cramp, it broke down for a few hours, giving them welcome respite. Eventually, around dawn the following morning, there was a crunch of brakes and Themis was thrown against the woman next to her.

When the back of the truck was let down, the extraordinary beauty of the Pelion landscape was revealed. There were olive trees in their immediate surroundings and beyond, pines covered the folds and curves of the hills and mountains that stretched as far as the eye could see. It was a landscape created by the gods and unravaged by man. Themis stood still for a moment and stared. The colourlessness of these past months only increased her appreciation of the sweep of emerald and azure that stretched out before her.

A sharp voice cut into her brief moment of reverie.

'Get into order,' one of their guards bellowed. 'And make your way down to the boat.'

The women formed themselves into a ragged line, their legs barely functioning after the hours of inactivity, and stumbled towards a boat that bobbed in the shallows.

They were obliged to wade into the sea and their clothes were heavy with seawater even before they clambered in.

For the first time, Themis' pregnant belly made her feel cumbersome and her damp dress clung to her, dragging her down. Two of the women had to help her on to the boat and, as she sat there shivering, she noticed that they were staring at her. The wet fabric had moulded itself around her middle. Then their attention was drawn to the approaching shoreline.

'It's Trikeri,' grumbled the woman next to Themis. 'I was there before.'

There were disgruntled murmurs from a few others. Themis did not understand their dismay. There was one soldier chaperoning them and only one on the land to bring in the boat. It was evident that they did not expect them to escape.

'At least this island has trees,' mused Themis as she surveyed the outline of the land they were fast approaching. 'And surely nowhere could be worse than Makronisos.'

Chapter Seventeen

THE WOMEN WHO had lived on Trikeri before complained bitterly about their return. It seemed a backward step, rather than a move closer to freedom. Themis was in a different mood. Her first impressions were of trees in blossom and the gentle sound of waves lapping on the shore. Perhaps the baby's heartbeat might synchronise with their rhythm.

As they stood in small groups waiting for someone to tell them what to do, Themis heard the whisper of leaves in the breeze. On Makronisos, any such sound would have been lost in the noise of soldiers shouting and bullying.

Themis held the arm of another woman as they climbed the steep hill away from the shore. Her belly suddenly seemed much more swollen than at the beginning of this journey.

On their way, Themis noticed a monastery. Though she had lost faith in the idea of spiritual protection, she nevertheless wondered if its walls might offer some refuge and hoped that she might be one of those chosen to live inside.

The woman, who had been there before, warned her against it.

'It's always dark in there and it's full of damp. For pity's sake, don't get yourself picked. You're better off in the open air.'

Themis had to believe her but when they were led into a barbed-wire enclosure on the hillside and told to construct their own tents she wondered how anything could be worse. Over the next few days, the women put together makeshift accommodation with stones and lengths of canvas, but it was easy to imagine that even the slightest wind could bring everything down. At night, she thought she could hear the sound of children crying in the distance.

Kindness seemed more common on Trikeri than on Makronisos, though. There were only women prisoners here and they soon called each other *adelfi*, sister, and acted as though the struggle to hold on to their ideals was a collective rather than a personal one.

Themis' condition was obvious now and the other women would not allow her to lift even one stone but took on her duties for her. Some of them even gave her part of their own food rations and though the foul stews of beans and dry bread often made her gag, this generosity touched her beyond words. Of course, their concern came with curiosity. Who was the father? Was she married? What would she name the baby? How did it feel to be with child? She avoided answering any of these.

Most of the women were total strangers to Themis and yet it appeared that they would make sacrifices for an innocent, unborn child. As she became less mobile in the last days, Themis realised she had something to offer in return. The women from the villages were often the most physically robust but the least literate. Themis found that she was a natural teacher and, using poems and songs that they already knew by heart, she slowly began teaching them to read and write.

The deep creases of concentration, the joy of satisfaction on their lined faces as they scratched the shapes of the letters for the first time – MI, ALPHA, RO, IOTA, ALPHA – ('Maria!' said one), touched her deeply. These same women, when her time came, would be by her side, sharing knowledge that could not be written.

After a week or so, when their clothes were clean, an official photographer arrived. Each woman was to appear in a group shot and they must all smile. It did not matter how many attempts were needed, each photo had to feature a row of contented faces. They were intended to prove to the outside world that these women were healthy, fit and being detained for their own benefit.

When Themis was handed her copy to be sent with a letter home she did not recognise her own face. It was the first time she had seen herself for almost two years and the image that she stared at was not the person she knew. Her hair just touched her ears (though its manly shape had long since grown out) and her face was rounder than she remembered, and lined in a way that made her look ten years older than her twenty-four. She was in the back row of three so it was impossible to see the shape of her body. Perhaps it was just as well as it concealed her pregnancy.

She was handed paper and pencil.

'*Dear Yiayiá,*' she wrote. '*I am on Trikeri island now. There is a nice convent to stay in and plenty of trees to give us shade. The soldiers here hope I will be released soon, but I am not so sure.*'

The letter was returned to her the following morning with the last phrase crudely deleted.

'Write it again,' ordered the guard. 'I'll watch you.'

There was nothing untruthful in the finished version, but it did not give a single clue to her own feelings. Her letter left on a boat that night and would arrive in Patissia some time later. Themis pictured Kyría Koralis slitting open the envelope and wetting the contents with her tears. She imagined Thanasis scrutinising the photograph and expressing his hopes that she would sign a *dílosi*.

On one of these long days, when she was immobile with

exhaustion, Themis found herself watching one of the women draw. She knew her name was Aliki, but nothing more.

'Those awful photographs told such lies,' observed Themis. 'But your drawings show the truth!'

'And yet the photographs are what the world sees of us,' commented Aliki, who was capturing the image of one of the older women. Her tools were a piece of charcoal she had rescued from a fire and a piece of paper she had stolen when they were writing their letters.

'Were you taught?'

'Not really,' answered Aliki. 'I've always liked drawing. I never did well in maths or science. But I could always create likenesses. The teachers didn't like it much when they found them. It's strange how threatened people can feel when they see someone else's version of themselves.'

The marks Aliki made on the paper traced the lines of suffering left by the years of persecution that her subject had endured. The events of past years had not, however, destroyed her beauty and the portrait showed the strength of the woman's character, her huge almond-shaped eyes as bright as an eagle's. Aliki had caught the glint of determination and pride.

Themis was sitting watching the image emerge from the page.

'Kyría Alatzas,' she proclaimed, 'you will love what Aliki is doing. She is making you so . . . real!'

The old lady beamed with pleasure, opening her mouth into a wide smile that showed her absence of teeth. It was a gesture that aged her by half a century.

When it was finished, Aliki passed the drawing across to her to admire.

'You can keep it,' she said. 'Or we can hide it in the usual place. The guards will only destroy it if they can.'

The old lady handed it back. She wanted it to be safe.

Themis admired Aliki for the risk she took to give pleasure to her fellow prisoners. For a while they sat and chatted, sharing their stories of what had brought them to Trikeri.

Aliki's calm and gentle demeanour changed when she described the stages of her journey.

'I'm from Distomo,' she said.

Themis scarcely needed to know more. No one had forgotten the horrific crimes perpetrated there by the Nazis.

'I lost everything. Parents, brothers, sisters, aunts, uncles. And my home. I was able to hide, but I have sometimes wondered if it would have been better for them to find me too.'

Themis was silent. She felt her baby stir within her.

'Afterwards I managed to get to Athens and find my aunt who was living there. I did nothing for a while. I just stayed in her house. In front of the tribunal, the monster in charge, Lautenbach was his name, stuck to his story that he was trying to protect his men. I saw his face, Themis, and from where I was hiding, I saw him giving instructions. They bayoneted my family, my friend's child whom I had just baptised, my neighbours . . . I even saw them beheading a priest.'

'It must have been so terrible . . .' said Themis quietly.

'I won't describe the details to you. They even posed for photographs when they were in the village – while the houses still burned. There's evidence, Themis. There are photographs of them smiling . . .'

Themis shook her head. It was obvious how much Aliki had suffered.

'The words of witnesses were ignored and all those in charge were cleared,' she continued. 'There has been no justice for those murders, Themis. More than two hundred of them.'

There was neither anger nor bitterness in her voice, which puzzled Themis but, as Aliki talked, she began to understand.

'Nothing will *ever* extinguish my fury,' she said. 'No one was punished for those deaths, Themis. And people who collaborated with the Nazis still walk the streets of Greece. But I found a way, Themis.'

In answer to Themis' quizzical look, she continued, 'I joined the fight. I signed up to the communist army so that I could take revenge. And that is exactly what I have done. It was the only way I could get any justice for my loved ones. For each one of my family members, I have taken the life of someone on the right.'

The communists had a reputation for brutality, which she had witnessed herself, but Aliki had not seemed like someone capable of ruthlessness.

'An eye for an eye,' Aliki muttered, preoccupied now with the lines she was tracing on a fresh sheet of paper.

Themis silently counted. Aliki must have killed at least eight people. She knew she had at least as much blood on her own hands, but this woman's actions had been very well calculated.

A few minutes passed before Themis broke the silence.

'What are you drawing?' she asked.

'You,' smiled Aliki. 'You look so . . . fecund, so full, so beautiful.'

Themis felt herself flush at Aliki's words. Beauty had never bothered her. Margarita was 'the beautiful one', not her. She had always been 'the clever one'.

Aliki worked quickly as the light faded. The charcoal made soft sounds and Themis smiled as Aliki continually glanced from the paper to her face and back again. Her head was slightly tilted to one side and her brow was furrowed with concentration. Within ten minutes she had finished her task and held it at arm's length to compare the likeness.

Themis could tell that she was pleased.

'You'll remember this moment,' said Aliki. 'It won't come again.'

Themis reached out to take the portrait, wondering what she had meant. She almost gasped when she saw the expression that Aliki had captured. It was a look of profound contentment and peace. For the past few minutes this was exactly what she had felt.

It was not long before she understood the ephemerality that Aliki had referred to and wanted to capture.

The sense of stillness came to an end later that night. At around two in the morning and without warning, Themis' waters broke, soaking her clothes and her straw mattress. Nothing had prepared her for the pains of labour that immediately followed. No woman had warned her that they would make her wish for the relief of death.

Nothing to which she had been subjected in these past months could compare. She had been beaten on the soles of her feet, had her back shredded with a whip and soldiers had stubbed their cigarettes out on her breasts – but this was different. This was relentless. For hours she screamed. Throughout the night, two women held her hands, one on each side, and a third mopped her brow. Others sat close to comfort her. From time to time she was aware of Aliki's voice and then it faded. All she could hear at times were her own deep, primeval groans.

The guards kept well away. They had seen and heard a woman in the throes of childbirth before and it repulsed them to listen. They went far enough away to be out of earshot. For them it was a night off. They would go down to the seashore to drink *tsípouro* and later on would raid a tent in a different part of the island.

As it was getting light, the pains increased and one of the women told Themis to push. As her body was being rent in two, she screamed one last time. Everything in the tent went still. How could such agony bring life into being?

Then suddenly there was a breath of silence before the breath of life and the scream of the newly born.

Themis lay still. Two women efficiently busied themselves with the afterbirth, another cleaned the baby and, within moments, Themis cradled him in her arms.

The pains came back from time to time, but she was anaesthetised by the outpouring of love she felt for the tiny human being.

Aliki was by her side, showing her how to breastfeed, stroking her head, offering words of encouragement, bringing her an infusion made with oregano that she had gathered that day.

'It's almost biblical,' smiled Aliki, looking at the queue of women wanting to see the baby. 'Though a stable would have been cleaner.'

The arrival of new life was rare on Trikeri. Some who still retained their religious faith stood by and crossed themselves, muttering prayers and giving the baby a blessing from God. Others just wanted to get close, to see something small and perfect, who against all odds had come into the world. One woman had found a tiny fragment of smooth blue glass on the beach that day and had saved it. It was the closest thing anyone might find to a *matóchandro*, the blue-eye bead protecting newborns from the evil eye. She pressed it into Themis' hand.

Themis was already fretting about his arrival in this cruel world. Until now, he had not heard or seen or felt anything except for a warm dark sea but from this moment he would have to face it all. Themis looked at his perfect hands, his long fingers and his tiny feet and marvelled at the fully formed nails. Gingerly she touched his head, feeling the pulsating softness at the top of his skull, and was filled with terror as she contemplated his vulnerability. She had understood the notion of dying for a cause (the possibility of it had been ever-present for years now) but this seemed nothing now. To protect this baby, she would lay down her life a thousand times.

She fed him, laid him on her chest and then slept for an hour. Later on that morning, some of the women who had their own small children brought them to see the baby. One of them reached out and touched him with a timid forefinger, uncertain what to do but aware that the arrival of another small creature was something good. None of them remembered anything but this life in captivity, a place where smiles were rare and hunger constant. Themis was touched by their interest and the way in which their expressions seemed to brighten when they saw her child.

These children were innocent, their 'crimes' non-existent and they had no sense of what their mothers were keeping them from. With the signing of her name, a woman would gain not just her own but her child's liberty too. As Themis knew, the ramifications of such an act were many.

A less welcome visitor was one of the guards who came to note down that a child had been born and to whom.

One of the accusations hurled by the guards was that they were not natural women. They were an aberration, sacrificing their offspring for their own misguided beliefs, making political prisoners out of their progeny. This singled them out for particularly harsh treatment. The children themselves were not always spared. They were beaten by the guards if they misbehaved.

'You are not worthy of any kindness,' the mothers were told by a visiting official, not long after Themis' labour. 'And if you want to be treated like men, we will punish you like men.'

To instil the greatest possible fear into all of the women, they sometimes randomly picked on one of them and hanged her. One morning the mother of a child was taken to the gallows. By evening, seven women had signed a *dílosi* and the following day they left on a small boat: seven women and eight children, the eighth being the child of the executed, who would be taken to one of Queen Frederika's camps.

Aliki stayed by Themis' side, holding the baby whenever Themis needed her to. Most of the time, the little one was strapped to her chest so she could more easily gather firewood, pick *hórta* and carry supplies from the seashore, all of which were duties she was still expected to perform. Sometimes the pair of them would sit in the olive grove, hiding for as long as they could just in order to rest.

Within his first two weeks, the baby had been exposed to enough dirt and bacteria to endanger the health of a grown man. He had been a normal weight when he was born, with his little stomach as round as a ball, and a good layer of fat on his thighs. Now all this had gone. And however much time he spent on the breast, he did not gain any weight.

'Do you think he's ill?' Themis asked Aliki tearfully. 'I don't think he's growing.'

It was obvious that the child was losing many grams a day and his crying was almost constant.

Aliki knew that something had to be done.

'Perhaps it's your milk,' she replied, her words almost drowned by the baby's lusty cries. 'Sometimes it's hard to produce enough. This terrible diet, the salty air, lack of water. All of those things together . . .'

After a short while at Themis' breast, the child slept. He was exhausted by his own protests, the frustrations that he could not articulate, the hunger that he could not satisfy. His energy was spent for now.

Aliki was compelled to tell Themis something that she had not intended to share. The baby's cries had stirred a visceral response in her.

'Themis . . . I think I could help feed your baby.'

'But . . . how?'

'I've helped several women in this way. I had a baby too, you see . . .'

'Aliki,' breathed Themis. 'What happened?'

Themis could read the pain in her friend's expression but had to wait until she was composed enough to answer.

'He was born here. I would say that I went through much less to bring my baby into the world than you did with yours,' she said, trying to smile.

'I am so sorry,' said Themis, who assumed that the baby must have died.

Realising what she was thinking, Aliki corrected her.

'No, no! It's not what you think. He was healthy and strong. There were dozens of babies and small children here then but the guards used them mercilessly, even more so than now. Every day, they threatened to take them away if we didn't sign.'

Aliki paused for a moment. The baby was waking up again. Both women knew that he would soon be demanding nourishment that Themis could not provide.

'One day they actually took two little girls away from their mother. You can't imagine how terrible it was. The poor woman found a way to take her own life.'

Themis listened, rocking her baby as she did so.

'After that the rest of us were given a final warning and many began to sign. I wanted to hold out, though, because I was still sure that we were going to win. Zachariadis hadn't announced the ceasefire then.'

'You've seen how determined and cruel these people are, Themis. They started threatening to take children away and put them in one of the Queen's camps. Then one of the women here, a prisoner, started talking about Frederika. She told us that she was good-hearted and that the children would be safe and well educated. Lots of others believed it because they wanted to. It meant that they could hold on to their principles and have their children safe at the same time.'

'But, Aliki!' exclaimed Themis. 'That woman! Why would anyone want *her* to bring up their child? She's a fascist!'

'I know that, Themis. A child would be safe in body, but not in mind. And I was not the only one who thought like this. There was a mother, Anna, who confided in me that she would sign the *dílosi* to liberate herself and her little girl, but then she would try to escape to Albania. She said she would take my baby too. Both of us wanted our children to grow up as communists so we agreed that this would be the best plan. And when we were all liberated, I would find her.'

Themis could see that Aliki's eyes were welling up and put an arm around her. A few moments later she continued.

'So four of the women, including Anna, signed, and just as the guards had said, they were allowed to leave the following morning. Four women and five children. Of course they have no way of communicating with us, so I don't know what's happened to my child. I just hope he is safely out of Greece. It's nearly eight months ago but already it feels like years. I don't even know exactly how he would look now. Babies change so quickly . . .'

Themis watched helplessly as the face of this strong, self-assured woman crumpled like a leaf. It was Aliki's turn to weep.

There was a moment of strained silence that was soon broken by the baby's crying.

Themis tried to put him to her breast but he moved his head to one side and continued to scream. Instinctively she held him out to Aliki, who lifted her shirt to let him suckle. The effect was instant. Suddenly the baby was calm, satisfied by the milk that flowed from the other woman's breast.

The women smiled at each other.

'Thank you,' whispered Themis. 'I could feel his desperation.'

'I'm sure you will be able to feed him again soon. But at least I can help for now. The others I've fed were soon back at their mother's breast.'

Aliki closed her eyes. Themis knew what might be going through her mind.

'Perhaps someone else is feeding my son now. Who knows?'

The days went by and the women stayed close to each other, Themis with the now fast-growing baby strapped to her and Aliki by her side, always ready to suckle him when he was hungry.

One evening, Aliki showed Themis a drawing of her own child. She must have done it while he was sleeping.

'He's so handsome,' exclaimed Themis. 'Look at his dark curls.'

The child had a mass of curly hair with long lashes, full cheeks and dimples.

'He's eight months there. I did it some while before he left.'

Themis could see that the words were almost too hard for her to say.

'We all think our own children are the most beautiful on this earth,' replied Aliki. 'To me, he was a little god.'

Themis handed back the drawing, Aliki refolded it and slid it beneath her mattress.

The cruel life of Trikeri continued. The food was foul, the punishments were relentless, the beatings continued in hidden places. There were still thousands on the island and hundreds of children, but with no rations allocated for offspring, there was a constant shortage of food. Small boys especially whined with hunger.

'The little one manages now,' said Themis. 'But things will change when he is old enough for solid food.'

'Perhaps you will both be gone by then,' replied Aliki sadly. She had made the ultimate sacrifice herself, letting her child go, but she did not blame those who chose to sign. She admitted, if only to herself, that she had moments of great regret.

'I will *never* sign,' said Themis flatly. 'And I will *never* allow them to take away my child either.'

Aliki, wanting to change the subject, raised a new question.

'We call him "*to mikró*", "the little one",' she said. 'But he will need a name soon, won't he? He's growing so fast now!'

'You're right,' said Themis. 'I suppose it should be his grand-father's, but I don't know what that is, at least on his father's side.'

Aliki looked mildly surprised. Themis had not yet been ready to share her own story.

'And on your side?'

'My father is Pavlos. I can't use that because of the King. What was . . . is the name of your son?'

'Nikos. After my father. I didn't know the name of his paternal grandfather either.'

'Oh,' responded Themis without surprise. 'Who was his father?'

'He was in my unit,' replied Aliki. 'We served together. Not for long, but for long enough.'

'Was he killed?'

'I don't know. Perhaps he was. Or maybe he is still alive. He left our unit unexpectedly.'

For a moment there was an awkward silence before Aliki, gazing into the distance, spoke again.

'I don't think I will ever love again.'

'This little one's father left without saying goodbye too. But I saw him on Makronisos. He had joined the other side. He was torturing people on our side.'

'*Theé mou*,' said Aliki. 'Are you sure?'

'I'm certain,' Themis replied.

'But at least you know he is alive!'

'Is that such a good thing?' asked Themis, trying not to sound bitter.

'I still dream of finding Tasos,' said Aliki.

'Tasos . . .?'

'Yes. I would be so happy for Nikos to meet him. But my heart tells me he is dead. He would have been one of the last men standing on Grammos.'

Themis sat there, deep in thought, rocking her baby who slept in her arms.

Tasos was not an uncommon name. She had known several at school and even had a distant cousin with the name. She tried to dismiss the idea, but the possibility that both children had been fathered by the same man hung in the air.

Another blow then fell like an axe, putting all doubt aside.

'He would have died with a sword in his hand,' said Aliki, her voice full of love and admiration. 'Some people knew him as *liondári*, the lion, not just because of his courage but his hair too. It was like a lion's mane, but black.'

Themis felt as if all her blood drained from her. For a moment, she could not speak, but the baby was stirring and she busied herself with rocking him and humming to him, hoping that Aliki did not notice how violently she was shaking.

Now that she was certain that the father of their sons was one and the same, she wondered if it explained why Aliki had bonded so easily with her child. Did he remind her of her own? Themis' little one had only a hint of dark pelt over his scalp but little curls had begun to sprout like pea-shoots around the nape of his neck. Perhaps in time it would become more obvious.

It took Themis less than a second to make her decision. She would say nothing. Why destroy Aliki's image of her lover-hero and replace it with something more bitter? As soon as she had composed herself, she spoke.

'What do you think of the name Angelos?'

'It's perfect,' responded Aliki, immediately. 'He is an angel. It suits him.'

'So let's call him Angelos, then,' said Themis.

From that moment this name, plucked from heaven rather than either side of the family, was given to the baby. Themis felt no need to go to the priest of the island. Angelos already had the little *máti* sewn to the inside of his trousers and that would be enough to protect him from the devil.

There was an informal school for the children and with Aliki feeding her child, Themis was free to teach small groups how to read and write. For the alphabet, she used sticks to make marks in the sand, and taught them to count with small stones. Storytelling passed plenty of time too. Recognising that children caused less trouble if they were occupied, the guards did not obstruct these activities.

The temperature soared in late July and throughout August. Flies swarmed around the camp and hovered in clouds over food and latrines. Some of the women had dysentery, malaria and even typhus, and almost all had coughs and skin lesions. There were several qualified doctors and nurses among the detainees, but they had no medicines at their disposal and all they could do was attempt to diagnose and offer advice.

On this desperate filthy island, nothing was ever clean. Skin, clothes, bedding, cooking utensils were constantly grimy and it was a miracle that bacteria did not annihilate them all. At night they took turns to guard for scorpions and snakes, and even if tales of rats coming to chew their toes at night were anecdotal, they still kept some of them awake and watchful.

In those sweltering summer months, the heat induced lethargy in the guards as well as the women and for several hours a day the captives could follow their own pursuits. The soldiers continued to harass them to sign *dílosis* but even their bullying was sometimes half-hearted in the heat. Occasionally someone relented and for a few days the guards left the other women alone.

The older village women, even if they could not read, had skills that had been passed on from a previous generation. They gathered dry grasses, separated them into different shades and deftly wove them to create hats with varying sizes of brim and crown. Now they had something with which to protect their heads from the burning midday sun, but the hats were also things of beauty too. With the shorter pieces, they made fans so that women could cool themselves at night when the air was still.

A group of younger ones found a fallen olive tree, hacked off small pieces and began to carve them: spoons and dishes for daily use, as well as small sculpted human figures, which would be lovingly fashioned before being carefully hidden.

Others made dyes from the flowers that grew on the hillsides and with fine tips of wild grass they painted on flat grey pebbles that were found in abundance on the beaches of Trikeri. They reproduced in miniature Arcadian landscapes, birds in flight, sometimes even cartoons. Like the needlework on Makronisos, each artistic creation was an act of subversion, but as the weeks went by and liberation seemed ever more remote, each woman needed a way to keep her spirits from sinking. Aliki, when not feeding Angelos, had her charcoal constantly in hand. She worked quickly, the accuracy of her likenesses achieved with extraordinary speed, and slipped the finished result inside her dress as soon as it was done.

While they were engaged in these activities, they often sang quietly: songs of revolution, mostly, and an often repeated verse composed by one of the captive women:

On this harsh island where we strive,
The sun beats down, our souls survive.
They crush our hands and make us blind,
And steal our lives, but not our minds.

Themis had resumed her sewing. She had finished her hearts and began a new project. Making use of scraps of rag, sometimes from the discarded clothes of the executed, she made puppets to entertain the children.

'I used to hate sewing!' Themis joked to Aliki.

'That's hard to believe,' Aliki smiled. 'You look like a professional seamstress.'

Together, the two friends constructed a little wooden theatre and the children crowded round. The innocence of their expressions and the delight on their faces brought light to Trikeri.

Intellectual pursuits gave them strength too. Very discreetly, the more educated gave lectures on such subjects as the Greek philosophers and the principles of Marxism. They all needed to refresh their minds on what exactly it was that had brought them to this place and why they were prepared to suffer for their beliefs. Sometimes they forgot.

Tranquil times could suddenly be interrupted by the announcement of a trial or an execution. The terror of these always hung in the background, never allowing the prisoners to be complacent or to have nights that were undisturbed by nightmares.

Themis watched Aliki breastfeeding her baby and knew he would not have survived without her. Her reliance on her friend became even greater when she was paralysed by stomach pains. Suspected of typhus, Themis was isolated and, during the many days of fever, she sometimes hallucinated that she was once again in solitary confinement on Makronisos, living in a twilight between life and death, senses unstimulated by sound or light.

When she recovered, Angelos was pink-cheeked, giving his first smiles and with a tooth in bud. Aliki smiled when Themis took him in her arms for the first time in many days and exclaimed at how heavy he was. Their love for this child was shared.

Though he had not been baptised, women and other children made a fuss of Angelos when his first Saint's Day came in November. There were no gifts but they sang and played games, and it helped to allay the otherwise overwhelming sense of futility that lay over them like dust.

One cold December morning, when life seemed to have settled into a routine, albeit a harsh one, everything changed. Themis was the first to emerge from the tent, with Angelos in her arms. The ground all around was white and her immediate thought was that the first snow had fallen. Soon she realised her error. Dozens of pieces of paper had been spread out on the ground, and taking a closer look she realised they were Aliki's drawings. She turned round to warn her friend but Aliki was right behind her. Both of them were being scrutinised by the two guards standing either side of the tent flaps.

For many months, Aliki had kept her stash of sketches hidden between two rocks but they had been discovered. The forty or so women, including Themis, whose portraits she had drawn were easy to identify.

Ushering everyone into a huddle with the butt of his rifle, one of the guards issued the warning that unless the artist came forward to identify herself, all those whose likenesses now fluttered on the ground would be executed.

Their breath came out in white clouds in the icy air and Themis, holding Angelos so tightly he began to cry, shivered with fear rather than cold.

Without a moment's hesitation, Aliki stepped forward. She understood what they accused her of. She had shown the reality of the torment endured by these women and her drawings clearly criticised the violation of their rights. Highlighting such abuse was a crime in the eyes of the authorities.

'*You* are the criminal,' announced the guard. 'Not the State. And to imply otherwise is punishable by death.'

Aliki was allowed one last day and night. Neither she nor Themis slept, even for a moment, passing the hours sorrowfully in whispered conversation.

Themis promised her friend that she would do everything she could to find her child and, when she did, she would bring him up as her own and love him as Aliki had loved Angelos.

Holding back her fear and grief, Aliki handed Themis a piece of folded paper. The drawing of her own son was the only one that had escaped the guards' vandalism.

'There is a lock of his hair inside too,' said Aliki. 'I hope he still has his curls.'

At five o'clock that morning, a female guard appeared at the entrance of the tent and Aliki stood up. Themis also got up from her filthy mattress, holding the sleeping Angelos in her arms.

Aliki planted a kiss on the baby's head, breathing in the sweetness of his skin for the last time. The two women then briefly touched hands, before Aliki turned towards the guard and walked slowly from the tent.

Moments later, as Themis stood looking out towards the trees, she heard the dull and distant sound of a single gunshot. At close range, the guard did not need to waste more than one bullet.

Themis closed her eyes but tears pushed through her lashes and rolled down her face and on to Angelos' cheeks. When she finally stopped weeping, there was a new question in her mind. For Aliki's sake, and for both their sons, should she now sign the *dílosi*?

Chapter Eighteen

Feeling the absence of the woman whose scent he knew so well, Angelos would not be pacified during the following days. The figure whose arms had reached out to him so many times was missing and he cried inconsolably.

Themis could do nothing except weep with him and retreated into the olive grove to hide from her fellow captives as well as to avoid the guards.

After that, Themis lay awake for many nights with the question going round and round in her mind. She knew that the signing of the *dílosi* was the ultimate failure, but could she deny her own son his right to a proper life? His own bed? A chance to meet his family? To eat her grandmother's food?

Winter now settled in, with longer nights and several centimetres of rainfall most days. The colder climate brought different diseases from those that had afflicted them in the summer.

Threats that Angelos would be taken from her were now a daily occurrence. One morning she was raking a piece of stony ground, which the prisoners had been told they could cultivate in the spring, and had the child dandled on her hip. He was teething again and whinging a little. Themis tried to suckle him a little, but even this was not enough to soothe him and the sound of his crying was getting on the nerves of a nearby guard.

'There are plenty of women who can look after him. *Real* women,' spat one of the guards contemptuously. 'We'll be putting him in better hands soon, just you wait.'

The realisation that Makris had betrayed not just her, but another woman, haunted Themis more now that Aliki had gone. The man whom she had worshipped as a hero, a warrior against the forces of the right, had proved himself a traitor.

Makris' duplicity was not the only reason that her idealism waivered. When the guards recounted to them a thousand crimes committed by the communists, she knew that she could not disregard every fact and figure. Some of the atrocities were irrefutable. The conflict in which she had fought had seen cruel and shameful acts on both sides.

A few months after Aliki's execution, Angelos became ill. It was then that Themis truly questioned her own judgement. Could the communists retain her loyalty at the expense of the life of an innocent child? Many women had developed coughs and several had been diagnosed with tuberculosis. When Angelos became feverish one night and woke with eyes and nose running, Themis knew that she could no longer procrastinate. She agonised over the decision but with Angelos' temperature rising, she realised there could be no further vacillation.

It was time. She would sign. In doing so, she would not only save his life, but she would fulfil her promise to Aliki too and begin her search for Nikos.

Two sheets of flimsy, lined paper were shoved into her hands.

'Write!' ordered the guard, giving her a pencil.

Angelos played in the dirt next to her as she sat on the ground with the guard standing, looking over her shoulder.

'And get on with it,' he barked, prodding her in the back with the butt of his rifle. 'I haven't got all day and nor have you.'

Themis had submitted to cruel treatment, endured such pain, eaten bread that was crawling with grubs, scorched her skin in fire and sun. All of it would end if she filled these pages with sentiments of regret and repentance and promised allegiance to the government.

She rested the paper on her knee and began, well aware of the expected tone and format. With some detachment, she watched her hand gripping the writing implement and guiding it fluently left to right.

It was a familiar sensation, having to express something that she did not believe. She had been doing it since the EON days. Knowing that it was a means to an end and, this time, the key to her freedom, she effortlessly faked contrition, submission and apology.

The tone had to be oleaginous and exaggeratedly subservient towards the authorities and she found herself wondering how anyone would be convinced by such a document. It seemed ridiculous, knowing as she did her inner beliefs and commitment.

Themis felt the eyes of the soldier on her back, but also imagined the distant and approving gaze of both Fotini and Aliki, urging her to take this chance for herself and two other lives.

Within ten minutes, she had covered four sides of paper with self-flagellation, with promises, with assurances, impressing herself with the expressions of false sincerity and humility that she had conjured up.

She read it through again for spelling errors and took a last glance over the lines, knowing that sooner or later it might be read out in public somewhere close to Patissia. Shakily, she added her signature, saving herself and hating herself all at once.

The guard stubbed out a cigarette underfoot, snatched the sheets from her and cast his eyes over the text.

'You and your brat can get ready to leave,' he snapped and walked off.

Themis got up and took Angelos into her arms.

The little one playfully pulled on one of her ears and she smiled and kissed his cheeks. He deserved this sacrifice of hers and she felt light, as if her whole body was floating. All her regrets vanished.

Three other women had signed a *dílosi* that day. For the first time since she had arrived on Trikeri, several of the guards smiled at Themis. She did not return the gesture. In an hour's time the boat was coming to take them to the mainland.

She hurried back to the tent. Several of the women who had been her friends turned their backs on her. They regarded her as a traitor to the cause and one of them spat at the ground near her feet.

Another gave her a look of sympathy.

'Take care of the little one,' she said. 'May he always be blessed by such love.'

Then one of the youngest whispered into her ear: 'Don't forget us, Themis. God is on our side.'

Themis held back her tears. She was grateful for forgiveness, even if it was only from these two women. To sign a *dílosi* was a betrayal and an abandonment of her fellow prisoners. She could not deny it to herself.

She must gather her few possessions. From beneath her mattress she drew out her embroidery. It represented a past love but also a present one. Then there was the small line-drawing of Nikos, along with the single, dark curl of his hair, wrapped within it. She had sewn it into the hem of her blanket for safety and now quickly undid the stitches, pulled it out and stuffed it into her pocket.

Then she took Angelos and hurried down to the quay where a boat was waiting. She ignored the resentful stares of the other women who looked up as she passed. Word travelled fast around Trikeri.

Themis could not suppress her sense of excitement. She had no idea what life was going to bring but as she stepped gingerly on to the boat she wanted to shout out with joy.

It was a fine spring day, the sun was reluctantly giving out its first warmth and the breeze was sweet. As the boat chugged across the water, the two guards smoked and chatted as if they were on a pleasure cruise. The three other women on the boat played a clapping game with Angelos as he sat on his mother's lap and moments later they reached the mainland.

Near a decrepit army truck, a few soldiers stood waiting for them, cheerful, sardonic, perhaps, in their offers of congratulations to the women. One of them put out his grubby hand to pinch Angelos' cheek, the gesture implying that both he and Themis were now his kin. Themis drew away, disgusted. Her signing of a *dílosi* had given him no such right in her eyes.

For Themis, life had altered beyond measure since she had travelled this road all those months earlier to reach Trikeri. Between the slats in the side of the vehicle she noticed all the changes in the landscape that had been made by the civil war. Not only had many hillsides been denuded of trees, but every town and village they passed through bore the scars. Buildings had been destroyed, and whole communities lay deserted. Many people had fled from their villages to seek safety in the towns, often simply to avoid being caught up into the communist army.

She looked away and began humming the lullaby that had

so often soothed Angelos to sleep but the swaying of the vehicle had already worked its magic, simulating the rocking of the cradle he had never known. For many hours he slept soundly on her chest and as temperatures fell, she could feel his warmth and the easy rhythm of his breathing. His cough had not developed and his pink cheeks indicated good health rather than fever. He stirred in her arms, his eyelids fluttering as if he dreamed.

On this dark road, looking out into the blank space of the night, she felt the pure and deep ache of love for her child.

At one point, Themis lay Angelos on the seat beside her and dozed off, resting her hand on his back to make sure he was safe. Her otherwise unfriendly companion did the same. The child drew affection even from strangers.

Many hours into the journey, the driver stopped and one of the other soldiers took over. One of the women Themis had shared the journey with got out. They were close to her home town and she would walk from here. Her farewell to Themis was without emotion. Throughout the journey they had hardly spoken a word and Themis' attempts at conversation had been met with no response. The woman seemed empty and broken with a blankness in her eyes.

At dawn they had reached the edge of a city. As if by instinct, Themis woke. Green mountains had long since been replaced by grey buildings, and trees by lamp-posts. They were in Athens.

Themis was fully awake and alert now. Her throat was dry, not just through lack of water but with anxiety. She was excited and at the same time full of trepidation about seeing her family. Who knew what the reaction to her might be? To Angelos? Had her grandmother suffered because of her imprisonment and her politics? Had Panos returned? Margarita? How would Thanasis treat them? These past months she had given little thought to any of these questions and suddenly she must confront them.

On the corner of Syntagma Square with Stadiou Street, the truck stopped. A moment later she was standing on the pavement. She had no memories of such crowds, except during demonstrations. People passed her without a glance, all of them purposeful, perhaps hurrying to work or a rendezvous. It was as if life had carried on as normal and the country had never been at war, either with another country or with itself.

A woman with a child collided with them as if she and Angelos were invisible, and then, judging from her scowl, said something rude that was drowned by the noise of traffic. Themis looked down at her simple clothes, perhaps worn by several people even before her, and realised that she looked like a farmer's wife, and a dirty one at that. Angelos was grubby too.

She glanced up at the Grande Bretagne Hotel. It gleamed as it always had done. A woman in a fur coat was emerging from a chauffeur-driven car and being greeted by the doorman. The rich were still rich, she thought. The world really had not changed.

Themis turned up Stadiou and walked slowly northwards. Angelos was getting heavy and her shoes were so worn that she could have been barefoot for all the difference it would make to her comfort. The cold of the paving stones penetrated her bones.

She soon passed the café that her sister had loved so much. Zonars. It had opened just before the Germans invaded and attracted the 'best' of Athens society. It seemed that it still did. Without shame she stared through the plate-glass windows. Perhaps feeling her gaze, one of a table of women drinking coffee inside looked up. Themis saw her put her coffee cup down and a moment later the woman had appeared next to her, so close that Themis was almost overwhelmed by her perfume. It was many years since she had smelled such a heavy fragrance and she was immediately reminded of Margarita.

'My dear,' said the woman, pressing several notes into Themis' hands. 'Please take this.'

Themis noticed that the woman had not even paused to put on her coat before running out on to the street. She stood there for a moment in her emerald-green silk dress, with rows of pearls at her neck and diamonds at her ears, then turned and quickly strode away.

Meanwhile, two of the woman's friends were standing right up against the window, waving the backs of their hands. Themis easily read their lips: 'Shoo, shoo!' they were crying, as if she was a pigeon stealing a farmer's newly sown seed.

Feeling her cheeks redden with shame and humiliation, she stuffed the money into her pocket and hurried away. Angelos bounced against her as she walked and she realised that the money she had just been given was all that stood between them and destitution. Anxiety now took hold of her. Supposing she got to Patissia and her family were no longer there? This was not beyond possibility and, if it were the case, they might both starve. Themis hurried on, her eyes cast down, not wishing to meet any curious gazes, contempt or pity, all of which she had felt in the first moments of her so-called freedom.

The streets were almost the same as she remembered, with some buildings still showing damage from shells and bullets. Many of the shops remained closed and she noticed that her pharmacy had been turned into a cheese shop.

Perhaps forty-five minutes later she reached Kerou Street. Her heart was beating from exertion and nervousness. The trees in the square were just as they had been and the small gate that led into their apartment building was the same, just slightly rustier and creakier than before.

Angelos gurgled. She stroked his head, running her fingers through the curls that had grown profusely in the past few months. She reassured him that everything was going to be all right. What did he know? Since the moment of his birth he had been loved and protected. Weeks of deprivation were forgotten and the days when her milk had not flowed were erased from memory. Even recollection of Aliki may already have vanished.

The main door to the building was ajar so she went in and began to climb the stairs. Familiar smells of cooking enveloped her: Kyría Danalis on the first floor, her dishes always heavy with garlic, Kyría Papadimitriou on the second, who always seemed to have burned something. One more floor. Her legs trembled. She was weak with excitement, with yearning, with fear. It was impossible to identify her overriding emotion. Like her grandmother's cakes, a dozen ingredients were mixed so smoothly together it was impossible to extract one from another. Her grandmother's perfect, sweet cakes . . . Yes, they were in her mind as a distinctive aroma wafted towards her. Vanilla. Cinnamon. Apple? She had reached the third floor.

Angelos was waving his arms. Perhaps he could smell the fragrance and recognised something desirable, even though the sweetest thing he had ever tasted was a drop of honey from the end of her finger.

She knocked on the door, gingerly at first. Then a little louder, when nothing happened. A moment later it was opened by a few centimetres.

Kyría Koralis peered through the crack and saw a vagrant on her threshold. It was common on the street to see such gypsies with their babies, but people rarely came right to the door to beg.

She had a kind heart, though, and more than enough food, since she still cooked as though her home was full.

'I'll get you something,' she said loudly enough for the beggar to hear. Then she shut the door, returning a moment later with some bread wrapped in brown paper.

'*Yiayiá*,' the beggar said quickly, 'it's me. It's Themis.'

Kyría Koralis peered out into the darkness.

'Themis?'

She threw open the door and a small amount of light from the open windows in the apartment flooded the hallway.

'*Panagiá mou*. No. You can't be Themis.'

She stood back in an attempt to focus on this woman with her worn-out clothes and ragged hair. She scarcely noticed the small child in her arms.

'You're not Themis,' she said very definitely.

Themis heard footsteps coming slowly up the stairs behind her.

'Is this person bothering you, *Yiayiá*?' said a male voice.

'She says she is Themis,' Kyría Koralis answered.

'Themis is dead,' Thanasis said sharply. He had told other people this on previous occasions and, not having heard from her in a year, believed it to be true.

Themis turned round to face her brother.

Like his grandmother, Thanasis did not immediately recognise her.

'What are you doing coming to our door?' he said.

'It's my door too,' said Themis boldly. 'I used to live here.'

Her brother was dressed in police uniform, and she noticed that he leaned heavily on a stick. A ray of light fell across his face, illuminating his scarred cheek. She had forgotten the extent of his wounds.

'So who . . .?' asked Thanasis, pointing at Angelos.

'This is my child,' said Themis.

Thanasis stepped around her and stood in the doorway next to Kyría Koralis. Both of them scrutinised her.

'You had better come in,' muttered Thanasis.

'It is your granddaughter, *Yiayiá*,' he confirmed, as if Themis had been presented to them in an identity parade.

Kyría Koralis shook her head in disbelief.

'*Panagiá mou*,' she said. 'Themis? *Mátia mou* . . . Is it really you?'

Tears were now streaming down her lined face and she was crossing herself over and over again.

Finally, Themis was allowed over the threshold. Angelos was being obligingly quiet and she held him tightly to her.

Once she had stopped weeping and exclaiming, Kyría Koralis began fussing. Surely Themis needed to eat? To drink? The baby? A blanket? Warm milk? Milk and honey?

Themis sat down at the familiar table and looked around her. Nothing had changed.

'Perhaps you should explain yourself,' barked Thanasis. His manner was of a police officer about to begin an interrogation.

Angelos was curious about what was happening around him and turned to look at his great-grandmother. The effect on her was immediate.

'*Agápi mou! Moró mou!* My darling baby!'

Angelos smiled and clapped his hands together.

'This is my *yiayiá*, Angelos,' said Themis.

With the instinctive urge that a woman cannot resist, Kyría Koralis put out her arms to him. Angelos did not turn back towards his mother but rotated himself towards the old lady. Themis happily passed him over, relieved to be free of his weight for a while.

In that instant a bond between child and great-grandmother was formed. He sat contentedly on her lap and then she rested him on her hip as she cut a new-baked apple cake into pieces and handed it round. Kyría Koralis was just eighty now but still strong, and proved that the power to carry a small child never wanes with age.

Themis helped herself to a glass of water. She knew she had to give a plausible account of the past two years, but first she wanted to know about Panos and Margarita.

'The good news is that Margarita is settled in Berlin. It suits her,' said Thanasis. 'You can read the letters if you want. She writes every so often. She didn't marry the officer, but things worked out in a different way. There was plenty of work there right from the beginning. Clearing the rubble in the streets of Berlin was largely done by women. Did you know that? The volume of debris, the damage done by the Allies was immense, and it had to be moved before any rebuilding could be done. Margarita helped move the stones and the broken bricks and shattered plaster, piece by piece . . .'

Themis found it hard to imagine her sister doing such manual labour but was glad that Margarita had found a new life. She was not sorry that she had stayed away. It was her beloved brother who was more on her mind in any case. Thanasis had given her more than enough information on Margarita for now.

'Panos?' she interrupted.

Thanasis hesitated for a moment, exchanging a look with their grandmother.

'He's dead.'

They were the words Themis had dreaded. She gripped the glass in her hand, her head bowed, and focused on the pattern on the tablecloth. It was a struggle to contain her anguish.

Thanasis continued without emotion.

'He was killed at the very end of the war. On Grammos. We

had a visit about a year ago from someone called Manolis, who had fought with him. All we know is that it was in the final assault. They should have given up. Admitted defeat. But they went on to the bitter end. The communists just wouldn't accept defeat.'

Themis could not speak. Even though it was news that she half expected, it did not alleviate her grief. Thanasis used even the announcement of Panos' death as an opportunity to vent his political views. He obviously had not changed during the time she had been away.

Kyría Koralis had taken Angelos to the balcony and was showing him her plants, telling him their names, pointing out things in the square below and attempting to teach him words: 'bicycle', 'children', '*kafeneío*', 'lorry'. She did not want to listen to her grandson describing what had happened to Panos. Even now she could not bear to be reminded of the animosity that had raged between the brothers. To hold the little one in her arms gave her unadulterated joy and she did not want this moment to be tarnished. The new life in her arms seemed a miracle after all the death and destruction.

Thanasis, however, did not regard the child as something wondrous. For him, the appearance of a baby added to the shame of Themis' return. Not only had his sister fought for the wrong side but she had returned with a bastard child. As if this family was not tainted enough already by stigma.

Kyría Koralis came back inside with Angelos, who was happily playing with the gold cross that she wore round her neck. She sat down again, close to her granddaughter, and handed Angelos back to her.

Thanasis had limped from the room. He had no wish to see his sister's tears.

'I'm sorry it's such terrible news, *agápi mou*,' Kyría Koralis said to her granddaughter. 'I am sure he died bravely, fighting for what you both believed in.'

Kyría Koralis' words were well meant but she already worried that the civil war would be rekindled in Kerou Street.

There was other news to share with Themis. Like Thanasis, she delivered the good news first.

'Your father is still in America. He is remarried and has another child. You have a half-sister! A few months old.'

'But . . .? What about our mother?'

'Sadly your mother died two years ago. That's why he was able to remarry.'

Themis could not think of any 'right' response. There was so much to absorb and she was still taking in the death of her brother. Eleftheria Koralis seemed like a figure from another life. It was two decades since she had seen her mother and the information stirred almost no feeling.

'Oh,' she said. 'I see.'

Themis felt numb with it all.

'You look tired, my dear.'

The word was inadequate for Themis' state of exhaustion.

Kyría Koralis quickly made up the bed that Themis had slept in as a child and then held Angelos while she undressed.

It was two years since Themis had enjoyed the scent of soap and she slowly ran a sponge over every centimetre of her body before drying herself and climbing into a nightdress. It was borrowed from her grandmother, since her own clothes had been discarded. When the letter Themis had written from Trikeri had arrived, Thanasis had hidden it, believing it would be better not to raise any hopes in his grandmother of seeing Themis again.

Angelos had not felt warm water on his skin before and splashed about with delight as they bathed him in the sink. He cried when they took him out of the water but he was soon happily gurgling again.

Before long, mother and child lay beneath fresh linen sheets and a soft counterpane. Inhaling the smell of lavender, Angelos fell asleep almost immediately and Themis did soon after. It was years since she had slept on a proper mattress, with four walls around her, and the knowledge that there was no threat of being dragged from her bed, no chance of screaming or gunfire or sirens, allowed her a night of dreamless sleep with Angelos nestled in the crook of her arm.

Travelling from Trikeri had drained her of all energy but, the following morning, she woke with one thought only. A new journey must begin.

The smell of her grandmother's coffee woke Themis and it took her a second to remember where she was. Angelos was just stirring.

How well he lives up to his name, she thought, lifting him as she rose from her bed and kissing him on the forehead.

Kyría Koralis had already stewed some fruit and had it ready to spoon into the mouth of the hungry child. Her enthusiasm for her great-grandchild was uncontainable.

'*Moró mou*, my little one,' she exclaimed, throwing her hands up with delight when he appeared at the door. 'I have made something delicious for you!'

She chatted to him as though he had been there from the moment of his birth and Angelos accepted his great-grandmother too, happily being taken from his mother's arms to be fed and played with by the old lady. Life in the camp had made him sociable. There had rarely been a moment when there were not other adoring women and noisy children around to hold him, play with him and sing him songs, and there had always been Aliki, of course.

Thanasis appeared briefly before departing for his shift at the police station. With each step he struck his stick hard on the tiled floor. It was nearly seven years now since his injuries. Ever since then he had been semi-retired on full pay, but was nevertheless obliged to present himself each day, to guarantee his pension.

A coffee, made a few moments earlier by Kyría Koralis, was sitting on the kitchen table: double, very sweet. As every day, he tipped it into his mouth without a word and crashed the cup back on to the saucer.

In the morning light, Themis could see his asymmetrical face more clearly. In all these years, the blemishes had not faded. On one side, the scars still looked as fresh as new wounds, the skin had never closed over the line of bulging flesh beneath. The perfect, right side was only a reminder of what he had lost and further emphasised the hideous damage.

Angelos looked up from the spoon that was being lifted to his mouth and caught sight of his uncle. He began to scream.

'I'm so sorry. I'm so sorry,' said Themis, struck with embarrassment and shame. 'I think it's your uniform. He has seen so many soldiers. And most of them were shouting.'

It was a semi-plausible excuse for Angelos' reaction. The highly polished buttons on the jacket, these days done up with so much difficulty, the cap, the stiff navy-blue trousers were all reminiscent of the authorities on Trikeri and almost every man the baby had ever seen in his life was similarly dressed. None of them had spoken a kind word.

There was nothing they could do to stop him crying.

Without a word, Thanasis turned from the table and left the apartment.

As soon as he had gone, the child's cries subsided.

'Oh, Yiayiá, I am so sorry.'

299

'Even adults sometimes react badly when they see him. But what can we do? Little Angelos can't be expected to understand.'

'It's terrible. I thought . . .'

'What? That his scars might have healed?' said Kyría Koralis quietly. 'Unfortunately not. And he lives with these reactions every day.'

'He seems so angry with everything. Maybe it's understandable.'

'Thanasis was always angry, my dear. You know that. For a while he hasn't really shown it, but I am afraid . . .'

'What of? That I will provoke it?'

Kyría Koralis nodded.

'After you and Panos left, he was always calm.'

Now that she was older, Themis understood how hard it must have been for her grandmother during those years when all four of her grandchildren were bickering and squabbling under her feet.

'While he isn't here,' she said, referring obliquely to Thanasis, 'you must tell me about the little one. Tell me about his father.'

Themis took a deep breath. The version of Angelos' life story that she told now would be the one that was repeated over and over again. She could tell of her broken heart, the shock of discovering the truth about Makris, the chance meeting with Aliki, but, even before she began, she decided to reshape the past years, omitting much and adding a little.

She began with the excitement of training in Bulkes, the friends she had made there and what she had learnt. She described in detail the place where she had acquired new skills and felt so purposeful about the future they had wanted to achieve, where all would be equal and everyone would have enough. With conviction, Themis told her grandmother that she had no second thoughts about what she had been part of, and described the periods of fighting and travelling, though not how many times she had raised a gun to her shoulder.

Of ambush, capture and periods in the filthy prisons on the mainland and then on Makronisos and Trikeri, she spared Kyría Koralis all but the minimum details.

'And the baby? Where was he born?'

'Trikeri. He was born on Trikeri. His father was a soldier. One of our unit.'

She knew that her grandmother would be wondering if the child was the product of rape by a guard. There were many babies who were the result of this, but she was anxious to reassure Kyría Koralis that Angelos was a child born out of love.

'His father was killed.'

She heard the words as if someone else had spoken them. And then the same words echoed by her grandmother.

'His father was killed?'

'Yes,' said Themis, swallowing the words. 'Fighting for our cause.'

Angelos filled the otherwise uncomfortable silence with his contented gurgles.

'Well, the child is a joy and a blessing,' said the old lady warmly, touching the baby's head.

With his unruly mass of dark curls and cherubic smile, he would have won even the hardest of hearts. The apartment in Patissia had been lacking in life and joy for so long, and overnight it had returned.

'He is a gift to us, Themis.'

'That's how I see him too, *Yiayiá.*'

'And something good has to come out of the mess we've lived through. We have to get on with things now, *agápi mou.* Whatever the rights and wrongs of anything that's happened, the little one is innocent.'

Themis described to her grandmother the devastation she had seen on her journey south from Trikeri. Kyría Koralis had heard all about it on the radio, but Themis had seen the reality of it with her own eyes.

'The whole country seems to be in ruins,' reflected Themis sadly.

'It can be rebuilt,' said Kyría Koralis. 'It's gone through bad times before.'

Themis feared this would take decades but did not say it.

Kyría Koralis handed Angelos back to his mother and began chopping ingredients for their midday meal. It took her all morning nowadays and she carried on talking as she worked, with Themis sitting on the rug close by, playing with the baby.

The past years had been so lonely for her and there was so much to share. Some aspects of normal life had carried on in the neighbourhood, with marriages and deaths, children and grand-children, accidents as well as good fortune. Businesses had been opened, closed, and some had even thrived. Kyría Koralis shared every last detail with her granddaughter and the morning passed by easily. Ever since her bout of tuberculosis almost a decade before, she had enjoyed robust health, outliving most of her friends. She was overjoyed to have someone to talk to.

'We'll find you a hairdresser,' she said at last. 'It looks as if you have been cutting it yourself!'

'I have,' said Themis, laughing. 'Does it look that bad?'

Kyría Koralis smiled, before adding: 'And the baby's? Do you think we should cut his too? Or not before his baptism?'

'Yes, we should wait until then,' said Themis, realising that she had inadvertently agreed to have her child baptised, something she had not intended to do.

Themis did not want to upset her grandmother and steered

away from anything but light conversation. She would raise the subject of Nikos in the next few days.

The food was simmering on the stove now and Kyría Koralis made coffee for them both and sat down for a moment.

'And what about Margarita?' asked Themis. 'How does she sound in her letters?'

'I think she is homesick in her way. She has been in Germany for over five years now. Would you imagine how fast time flies by . . .?'

'And where does she live?'

'Somewhere on the edge of Berlin, I think. She got married but not to the man she met in Athens. When she got there she discovered that he already had a wife.'

'But is she happy?'

'I don't know about being happy,' answered her grandmother. 'The first few years she was there, she was clearing the city, picking up stones. It's what a lot of women did.'

'Thanasis mentioned it, but did our Margarita *really* do that?' asked Themis incredulously.

'It was the only way to survive.'

'And she didn't want to come back?'

'She was too proud. But then she met Friedrich. That's his name. And he sounds kind. He's a bank clerk.'

'And children?'

'I'm afraid not. It's a great sadness to her. In her last letter she asked if there was anything I could send her that might help. Some kind of remedy. From how she describes the diet there, it's not surprising she hasn't conceived. But she won't come home. She's afraid.'

'She should be,' said Themis bluntly. 'She married a German, *Yiayiá*.'

'She's your sister, child.'

There was silence for a few moments.

'Well, she shouldn't give up,' said Themis, just for something to say. 'I am sure it will happen.'

'And then there's Thanasis. I doubt that he will ever be a father. Girls never look at him. You can imagine.'

Themis could.

At that moment, she heard a key in the lock and her brother reappeared. She sat there, tense.

'I've made your favourite,' said Kyría Koralis cheerfully to him. '*Gemistá!*'

Thanasis did not answer. He sat down in his uniform and waited to be served.

With some trepidation, Themis picked up Angelos and brought him over to the table, hoping that he would not cry. She handed him a spoon to keep him occupied and he immediately started to bang it on the table.

'So,' said Thanasis to his sister above the noise. 'You're back here to live?'

'Yes,' she replied.

'You have nowhere else to go, I suppose?'

Themis looked blank. Even though she knew what her brother was implying, she wanted to make him say it out loud.

'The father's family?' he added. 'I assume he was a leftie?'

'Angelos' father is dead,' she said. 'So I can't go there.'

Thanasis, who was served first, began to eat. Themis could see that he was chewing thoughtfully and waited to see what he would say next. She could sense that he was forming a strategy, and braced herself for the next blow.

Kyría Koralis tried to make light conversation. This poisonous atmosphere was so familiar from those past times but she had forgotten how heavy the air could suddenly become, and how tension took away her appetite.

'Shall I mash a little for the baby?' she asked nervously.

'Don't worry, *Yiayiá*. I'll feed him later.'

'So I suppose you could go and find our father? Live in America maybe?' persisted Thanasis. 'I am sure he would be happy to see you.'

Themis was aghast.

'But this is my homeland!' she exclaimed.

'But you fought for the wrong side, Themis. Perhaps Greece isn't really your *patrída* now?'

Thanasis could not resist reminding her that the communists had lost. His tone was sardonic.

'Thanasis, I really don't think your sister wants to go on a long journey now. Specially with the baby,' said Kyría Koralis.

'I am thinking of all of us, *Yiayiá*,' he said. 'Not just Themis and this . . . child.'

'His name is *Angelos*!' Themis exclaimed, affronted by the way Thanasis dismissively waved his hand towards her baby.

'I know what his name is, Themis. What I don't know is his family name.'

Thanasis' scornful tone was more than Themis could tolerate. She had always been able to contain her emotions and to brush off insult (Margarita had provided good training) but now she made a new discovery about herself. When an insult was directed against her child, she lost all control.

'How dare you, Thanasis? How *dare* you?'

Themis stood up from her seat, with Angelos in her arms.

At the sound of his mother's raised voice, the child had begun to cry.

'He's a bastard, isn't he?' Thanasis responded, undeterred by his sister's fury.

'Thanasis, please,' Kyría Koralis interjected weakly.

Themis had borne so much grief and pain over past years, with neither self-pity nor complaint. Nevertheless, they simmered within her and, with this statement, Thanasis had poured oil on a flame. She felt as though her whole body was on fire. The knife next to the bread, her grandmother's copper pan, even her own chair – all of them were potential weapons.

Instead, wearing her grandmother's old and shapeless dress, she held the protesting Angelos close and stormed out of the apartment. She heard her grandmother's voice protesting weakly.

'Themis! Don't go, Themis . . . Please!'

It was a damp April day and Themis immediately felt the drizzle on her face as she walked into the square. She tightened the shawl around Angelos to protect him and sat down on the bench next to the path. Every part of her was shaking with anger.

One of their neighbours passed by and looked at her quizzically, but not with recognition. She was a friend of Kyría Koralis and recognised the pattern of the borrowed dress. It was this that made her pause. Nothing more. The sight of people like Themis was a common one.

Themis looked up into the tree that sheltered her and saw that it was in bud, some of the leaves seemed almost to unfurl as she watched. The rain had stopped and patches of blue appeared between the clouds.

She watched her grandmother's friend disappearing across the square. The woman was carrying a basket of groceries and briefly stopped to greet a couple. Nothing seemed to have changed here, Themis reflected. Her own world had altered beyond recognition but in this square it was as though everything had stood still. The trees grew loftily as before, the shops were under the same ownership, the benches themselves were the ones she had clambered on as a child, just a little more bleached by the sun.

On her route from the square she passed the baker that the family had always used. Remembering she had transferred to this dress pocket the money from the kind woman in Zonars, Themis went in to buy a small loaf to nibble on. Kyría Sotiriou was a little taken aback to see her but managed very quietly to say, 'I'm so sorry about Panos,' as she counted out her change. Themis merely nodded in acknowledgement. It was too early for conversation or to answer any questions, and she wanted to give her grandmother the chance to sprinkle the seeds of her story.

Then she passed the kiosk and paused to read the headlines, several of which announced that Nikos Belogiannis, one of the leaders of the communist army, would face trial within a few months. Even now, the persecution continued, thought Themis.

Other names in the headlines were completely unknown to her. As she walked down Patission Avenue, she realised it was not just political figures that were unrecognisable. Fashion had altered too. She stopped outside a dress shop. Unlike Margarita, Themis had never cared too much about her appearance but she knew that she looked out of place in Athens in her grandmother's winter frock and hair that had been cut with a knife. In the next few days she would spend a few of her drachmas on a visit to the hairdresser.

Angelos was getting heavy and her back had begun to ache. Now that she was feeling calmer, perhaps she should go home. Both Thanasis and her grandmother might be having an afternoon sleep.

As she approached the main entrance, she saw her grandmother hurrying towards her. She was wearing a smile, but it was put there with some effort.

'*Paidí mou*,' she said breathlessly. 'My child. I am so sorry. What do I say? You see how angry he gets. It bubbles up so quickly. And it's worse now than it was all those years ago.'

'I was angry too, *Yiayiá*. I'm sorry, but I had to get away from him . . .'

'He's sleeping now. But I thought we could go somewhere together. You didn't eat even a mouthful.'

'I'm not really hungry now.'

'But we need to give the little one something to eat.'

'He's being so good. Especially when he doesn't really know what's happening,' agreed Themis.

'He is such a good baby,' said Kyría Koralis, gently tweaking his cheek. 'There is a small taverna down that little sidestreet. They'll have something cooked and ready. And I will insist you eat something, otherwise the little one will suffer.'

For a woman in her eighties, Kyría Koralis' gait was strong and steady. She did not need a stick and Themis marvelled at her pace.

The little taverna was full of people eating a midday meal, mostly men dining alone. Several looked up at the two women who walked in but most went back to their plates of stewed mutton, the dish of the day, almost immediately. They did not notice Angelos, who was asleep in Themis' arms.

The waiter brought them some bread and Themis flinched when his arm accidentally brushed hers.

A moment later he brought two plates of stew, and when he noticed the baby he returned with a smaller bowl and a teaspoon. It was the first act of male kindness that Themis had experienced for so many months.

'*Efcharistó polý,*' she said, with almost exaggerated enthusiasm. 'Thank you. That's so very kind.'

The waiter smiled back.

'*Hará mou,*' he said. 'That's a pleasure.'

The three of them began eating their meal. It was Angelos' first taste of meat. Even though he was given the smallest mouthfuls, his enthusiasm made it clear that he wanted more. Of the fatty sauce and the salty potatoes, he could not get enough.

'Look at him, *Yiayiá!*'

'I have never seen a happier child,' replied Kyría Koralis.

'I want him to remember this as the beginning!' said Themis.

'A nice rich stew and some potatoes?' laughed the old lady.

'Yes,' she cried out. 'And my grandmother's smile.'

When their plates were empty and wiped clean with bread, the women sat there for a few more minutes. Themis was in no hurry to go home.

Kyría Koralis read her mind.

'Thanasis will soon get used to you being there,' she said, reassuringly. 'And then he will leave you alone.'

'His politics won't change, though, will they?'

'Nobody's politics ever really change, *agápi mou.*'

'We just have to tolerate each other, I suppose,' said Themis. 'Perhaps that's all I can hope for.'

'And the baby!' Kyría Koralis reminded her granddaughter.

'Well, I know already what his political views will be!' said Themis.

'Don't be so sure,' said Kyría Koralis. 'You and your father would be an example of that. Politics don't necessarily run in the blood. Think of you four children.'

Themis felt her eyes pricking with tears. There had been so much to absorb in these past days and the confirmation that Panos was dead came back to her with force.

Kyría Koralis saw her reaction and put her hand on Themis' arm.

'I wish we could do without politics altogether,' she said.

Themis tried to smile. A world without politics was hard to imagine, even if Kyría Koralis had always tried to steer a way around them.

'Politics have destroyed this country,' said Kyría Koralis. She was right. The country had been torn apart by politicians on both sides.

'Maybe the Greeks are just ungovernable,' reflected Themis.

They had both been enjoying the warm and steamy restaurant, savouring the aromas that drifted from the kitchen as the trays of cooked food were lifted from the oven. The atmosphere changed with a reference to the conflict.

The waiter had cleared the plates and the owner would close up for an hour or so before the evening customers came.

'Now, we need to buy Angelos some new things and a dress or two for you,' said Kyría Koralis, cheerily. 'I've got enough this month from what Thanasis gives me. The State is quite generous, you know, and this is what we should spend it on.'

Themis eagerly accepted.

'Do you have enough for shoes too?' she asked.

'Of course,' replied her grandmother.

Themis had a feeling that in the next few months she would need stout footwear. She anticipated a good deal of walking and, in due course, would tell her grandmother why.

They spent the next hour shopping.

Angelos charmed the assistants by crawling around on the floor and happily playing with shoe boxes and tissue paper. At all times, Themis tried to avoid looking at herself in the mirror. Perhaps a haircut would help.

By the end of the afternoon, she felt less out of place in the

Athenian streets. She did not win looks of admiration (Themis remembered how Margarita used constantly to turn people's heads) but nor did she attract looks of pity or curiosity. She felt neutral, invisible, which was how she liked it, whereas Angelos was the centre of attention wherever they went. Strangers felt the need to touch his dark, glossy curls and exclaim.

'*Thávma!*' they all said. 'Miraculous!'

Themis smiled every time. She silently agreed. He was indeed a miraculous child. Purely and simply, he spread joy to others.

On the corner of the square, they bumped into two of Kyría Koralis' neighbours. The women had all known each other for many years.

'Who have we here?' one of them exclaimed.

The other woman was already weaving her fingers into Angelos' hair.

'Look at him! *Moró mou! Koukli mou!*' she cried. 'My baby! What a doll!'

Kyría Koralis answered, 'You remember Themis, my grand-daughter? This is her boy, little Angelos.'

As if synchronised, both women tipped their heads to one side to take another look at Themis. They had not recognised her.

'Of course! Themis!'

Kyría Koralis continued, 'Unfortunately, the baby's father was killed, so they're both living with me!'

Themis gave a slight nod to affirm what her grandmother had said.

They both muttered something about being sorry and went on their way. Kyría Koralis knew that by giving few details, few questions could be asked.

'They can assume what they like,' she said firmly. 'I refuse to talk about politics with anyone. Whether Angelos' father was in the government army or the communist army – what has it got to do with them?'

'Oh, *Yiayiá*, I do hope I haven't brought shame on you,' said Themis tearfully. 'I would never have wanted to do that.'

'You haven't, my dear. It's only Thanasis we have to worry about now.'

When they returned to the apartment it was silent except for the ticking of a clock. Thanasis usually left his stick by the front door but it was not there. Nevertheless, Kyría Koralis crept towards his bedroom and listened at the door. She wanted to double-check that he was not still inside sleeping.

'We're alone,' she confirmed, looking round as Angelos began to babble. It would be impossible to suppress the new sounds he was exploring each day.

'But you mustn't worry, Themis,' she continued. 'Your brother will get used to the new domestic situation!'

Themis took a deep breath.

'*Yiayiá*, there is something I need to tell you,' she said, with trepidation.

'What is it, *agápi mou*?'

Kyría Koralis had gone very pale.

'It's nothing bad, *Yiayiá*,' Themis said quickly. 'But I think I have to go away again for a while.'

'But you've only just come back! *Paidí mou*, you can't leave again!'

'*Yiayiá*, I have to,' she said.

The old lady sank into her armchair. Kyría Koralis, who had experienced such moments of happiness in the past day, did not hold back her tears.

'Why?' she asked quietly. 'Tell me why . . .'

Themis told her about Aliki, about the bond of friendship they had formed on Trikeri and how she had saved Angelos.

'Angelos wouldn't have survived without Aliki's help,' said Themis.

'But what does this have to do with you leaving again?'

Themis then explained about Aliki's son and her execution.

'*Theé mou* . . .' breathed Kyría Koralis. 'Why did they do that?'

'Because she drew portraits of us. And they showed the truth. They punished her for it.'

'So . . .'

'And I promised to find her son and to bring him up . . .'

Themis did not breathe a word about the man who had fathered both their children. Kyría Koralis would probably assume that Aliki's child was fatherless, just like hers.

Kyría Koralis had looked pale before. Now she was ashen-faced. 'But . . .'

'He'll be a brother to Angelos,' Themis said firmly.

She knew that it was a daunting task and had asked herself a hundred questions. Where would she find him? Where would she begin to look? All she had was the name of the woman to whom Aliki had given her child: Anna Kouzelis. There might be a hundred women with such a name in Athens alone.

'If I can find her, then . . .'

Ever pragmatic, Kyría Koralis cited all the obstacles at once.

'*Agápi mou*, are you sure it's a good idea? She might have got married or gone to live in another country. And the child might not even be with her.'

'I made a promise, *Yiayiá*. And I must do my best.'

Kyría Koralis got up to make some coffee. She was thoughtful as she stirred the *bríki* and Themis could see that her grandmother's hands were shaking.

'Let me help you, *Yiayiá*,' she said.

313

Themis poured the boiling liquid into two small cups and carried them to the table.

Her grandmother now sat deep in thought. The sight of Thanasis' jacket on the back of the door reminded her that one of the epaulettes needed to be stitched but also gave her an idea.

'You know who might be able to help?' she said.

'Who?' said Themis eagerly.

'Your brother.'

Themis looked puzzled.

'But why would he help me?'

'Because you're his sister,' Kyría Koralis replied.

It was well known that the authorities had files with the names and activities of all known or even suspected subversives. Themis knew that hers would be held somewhere with notes on her 'crimes'. It was unlikely that Anna Kouzelis' was not there too since the signing of a *dílosi* did not mean that a name was removed. Imprisonment and exile would never be erased from your personal records.

Themis took Angelos to sleep and lay down next to him on the bed. They were both still exhausted after the gruelling journey they had taken from Trikeri and neither of them woke until the early hours of the following day.

In the evening, Kyría Koralis broached the subject of police files with Thanasis. She was the only person who could have a calm conversation with him on any subject, specially one as sensitive as this.

'Themis wants to find one of her friends,' she said simply. 'One of the women she met while she was on Trike—'

'Don't say that word!' he interrupted her. 'Please *never* mention that place again. Not when I am here.'

'Sorry, *agápi mou*,' Kyría Koralis muttered.

'And not in front of anyone else, for that matter! I can do without the stigma of this . . . this . . . this red sister.'

'Shh,' coaxed Kyría Koralis. 'They're sleeping next door.'

Thanasis continued, undeterred, 'It will stick to us! Stigma always sticks! Like shit on a shoe!'

'Don't worry, Thanasis. Stay calm, my dear. I promise I won't say anything. Not to anyone.'

She could see Thanasis shaking and poured a little *tsípouro* into a glass to calm him down. He knocked it back in one gulp and banged his glass down on the table, empty. It was his way of asking for more.

Kyría Koralis obliged.

'So she wants to find out what happened to her friend?'

He sat for a moment, sipping the second measure.

'And suppose she meets up with this friend again? Wouldn't it be better if those women were kept separate?'

'I think she just wants to know where she ended up . . . She is curious, that's all.'

'I suppose it's harmless enough,' said Thanasis, grumpily.

In his mind there was something else too. Perhaps he could also find Themis' records. If there was any chance of modifying them to minimise the chance of anyone connecting him with a communist then he would do so.

'I'll see what I can do,' he said, finally. 'But I'm not promising anything.'

Kyría Koralis smiled. It was so rare for Thanasis to be obliging, even in a small way.

The next day, Themis wrote the woman's name on a piece of paper and gave it to her grandmother, who found the right moment to pass it to Thanasis.

Themis noticed him slip it into his top pocket before leaving for work. If she had believed that prayer would work then she would have gone to church, but instead she lit a small candle and put it on the window ledge.

Chapter Nineteen

For several weeks, the subject of Anna Kouzelis was not mentioned by Thanasis, although Themis asked her grandmother almost every day: 'Any news?'

Kyría Koralis knew she would get an angry reaction if she raised it with her grandson.

'We have to wait until he has some information,' she told Themis. 'We mustn't irritate him.'

Themis could scarcely contain her impatience. With each day she pictured the unknown child growing up, moving further away and becoming harder to find.

All the possibilities circled in her mind.

Aliki had wanted her child brought up as a communist so Anna might have made sure that he had been taken to one of the communist children's camps beyond Greece. She knew that many had gone not just to Albania, but also to Yugoslavia, Romania, Czechoslovakia, Poland, Hungary and Bulgaria.

'He might even have ended up in Tashkent,' she said to her grandmother.

'*Agápi mou*, until Thanasis has some news for us, you must try not to fret. And if he is there then you must accept it. Do you even know where such places are? How far away Tash . . . or whatever it's called, is?'

'No. I couldn't even put a finger on the map. But they say that some of the children live in terrible conditions there in abandoned hotels or like gypsies on the street . . .'

'That's certainly what your brother would say,' said her grandmother. 'But you mustn't believe everything. You know, they even had a day of national mourning for the children when you were . . . away.'

Kyría Koralis never referred directly to Themis' period of imprisonment.

'What do you mean? Mourning?'

'Queen Frederika made a speech about how we should rescue the twenty-eight thousand children—'

The mention of the Queen's name as usual provoked a reaction in Themis. The woman's face still regularly smiled out from the front page of the newspaper that Thanasis would leave on the kitchen table, a broadsheet that happily displayed its triumphalist right-wing politics.

'But they're not dead!' exclaimed Themis. 'And I am sure some of them are being well looked after.'

'I'm sure they are, *agápi mou*. It's so hard to know who to believe, isn't it? But look at this. It's in the newspaper today.'

She passed it across to Themis. It was a letter supposedly written by a child in an Albanian children's institution.

'Read it, *agápi mou.*'

'*Dear Aunt, Months go by and life gets better every day. It's paradise here.*'

She looked down at Angelos, who was sitting playing on the floor.

'It doesn't ring true, does it?' she said, concurring with her grandmother. 'I'm so lucky to have my child here with me, *Yiayiá*,' she said. 'Whatever his future, at least we are together.'

For almost every report on the communist children's camps stating that the children there were underfed and uneducated, there was one on the *paidopóleis,* the Queen's homes. In Thanasis' newspaper, these stories were always illustrated with photographs of smiling children, boys with uniformly trimmed hair and girls with neat plaits happily congregated outside white concrete buildings. Themis always scrutinised the faces of the boys doing keep fit, tilling a field or even being instructed in basket weaving. Might one of them be Nikos? One day there was a photo of a small boy on a swing, and she convinced herself that he was Aliki's son.

Every lunchtime, when she heard a key in the door, Themis hoped that this would be the day that news came. Six months passed and her disappointment grew.

The only positive development was that Thanasis had begun to talk with more warmth to his nephew.

'*Yia sou, Ángelé mou,*' he would say almost cheerily when he came in from work. 'Hello, Angelos. How's the little man today?'

Sometimes he would even play a game of peek-a-boo with him, picking up one of the embroidered cloths that lay on the table and hiding his face.

Angelos chuckled with laughter, almost making Thanasis' lopsided face break into a smile. The child was no longer afraid of his uncle and, in a way that was mysterious to both mother and great-grandmother, the pair formed a bond.

Thanasis and Themis barely spoke to each other. Thanasis harboured a great anger against his sister, even more so since he had been obliged to pay the local priest a hefty bribe not to read Themis' *dílosi*. That autumn the trial of Nikos Belogiannis was exciting international protest. For Thanasis, the communist leader was a traitor, accused of sending information to Moscow. For Themis, he was a true patriot who had exposed that many Nazi collaborators had been rewarded, rather than punished. It was an explosive subject and they had to avoid discussing it.

Almost at the end of the year, when the trees in the square were bare and the days were short, they were eating lunch. It was a Tuesday. Themis would always remember that her grandmother had made spinach rice that day and Thanasis was bent over his plate as usual, shovelling food hungrily into his mouth. His plate was almost empty and suddenly he looked up.

'By the way,' he said, his mouth still full, 'that friend of yours was rearrested and sent to jail.'

Themis dropped her fork.

'So you found her! Where is she?'

She managed to stop herself asking about the boy, but before she could get in another word, Thanasis answered.

'Anna Kouzelis is dead,' he said bluntly. 'And so is her child.'

Kyría Koralis saw her granddaughter's crestfallen face and immediately reached out a hand to comfort her.

Thanasis continued, 'But her papers say that there was another child.'

'Oh!' said Themis, eagerly leaning forward. 'What else did they say? Was there anything else? Tell me, Thanasis. Did they say anything about him?'

Themis had risen from her seat, unable to hide her agitation.

'Please tell me, Thanasis! Please!'

'Why is it so important to you?' he asked, very deliberately tantalising her.

'Just because . . . it *is*,' she cried out in frustration.

'Please, Thanasis. Please don't tease your sister!' interceded their grandmother.

'It didn't say anything specific. All I can tell you is that the children of these prisoners usually get taken away and looked after in a *paidópoli*. Queen Frederika—'

'Yes, Thanasis, I know about her children's homes,' snapped Themis with impatience.

'And in this case, it's almost certainly what happened,' continued Thanasis, ignoring his sister's interruption. 'The prisoner died. So what else would they have done?'

With a twinge of guilt, Themis felt a sense of relief. The continuing rumours about what happened to the children taken out of Greece had filled her with trepidation and, deep down, she had known that to go on a search outside her own country would have presented insurmountable challenges.

'At least if your friend's brat is in a Queen's home, he won't have trouble remembering he's Greek.'

Themis told herself to remain calm.

'And he'll know the real heroes of his country. He won't be *brainwashed*!'

A recent newspaper article had reported that Greek children growing up in the communist bloc were being taught a new version of history: that the true hero of Greece was not Kapodistrias, the leader of the revolution against the Turks, but Zachariadis, the infamous leader of the communist army.

Thanasis had not quite reached the end of his tirade.

'Because we won't do that to our little man, will we?' he said, plucking Angelos' cheek. 'We'll know our history, won't we, *moró mou*?'

He turned his attention fully to Angelos now. He was not going to tell his sister that the reason it had taken so long to bring news of Anna Kouzelis was that he had been looking for her records too. In this pursuit he had been unsuccessful. He continued to play with his nephew.

Themis did not rise to her brother's provocation.

Once Angelos was old enough to understand everything that was said, Themis would have to protect him from Thanasis' views, but for now the child gurgled and smiled, oblivious to the meaning of his uncle's words.

Themis was in turmoil. It was a relief to have information that might lead her to Nikos, but she did not know its implications. To occupy herself, she got up to wash the dishes. At least with her back turned to Thanasis, she could think.

Aliki was dead. Anna was dead. These women had wanted the best for their country but their lives had been cut short. Themis was almost overwhelmed by a sense of her own good fortune. She was alive and healthy with her beloved son close by.

As she carefully set the dishes to drain, she ruminated on what Thanasis had said. It was more than likely that Aliki's son was in one of the homes set up by the Queen. For the first time, she felt grateful for their existence. At least there was a possibility of finding him. At one time there had been eighteen thousand children accommodated in fifty or more *paidopóleis* scattered throughout Greece, from Kavala to Crete. In the past few years, only a few thousand children remained in a dozen or so homes, the majority having been returned to their families. It was a very different situation for the children who had left Greece. Tens of thousands were unaccounted for and almost impossible to trace.

Thanasis went for his afternoon sleep. Themis and her grandmother talked of what must be done. Even now, they could not tell her brother of the plan.

'It's always the same with Thanasis,' Kyría Koralis said. 'I don't give him something to worry about before it happens.'

'You talk about him as though he is a child,' protested Themis. 'Why do you protect him all the time?'

'You know why, *agápi mou*. I know he seems so tough. But underneath . . .'

Even Themis knew now that there was a gentler side to her brother, one that her son seemed to have drawn out.

Themis spent the night tossing and turning in bed and the following day, as soon as Thanasis went out for his shift, she began to compose the letter that she would send to each and every *paidópoli*.

It was a long time since she had held a pen in her hand and she needed to practise her handwriting before beginning the painstaking process of copying the letter a dozen times. She enjoyed the sensation of watching the pen move across the page and tried to overcome her tendency to scrawl. Even now she recalled the enviable neatness of Fotini's writing.

Once she was happy with the draft she began. The letters were written to the principal of each home, enquiring whether they had any children with the surname Kouzelis.

In these letters, Themis adopted the same name. She believed it was the only way to get her request taken seriously and would have a story ready if this was challenged.

I understand that a member of my family, Anna Kouzelis, has died and that her son has been placed in your care. I wish for him to be reunited with his grandmother and other close members of family including myself, his aunt, etc., etc.

Yours faithfully . . .

It was a shameless lie but she would do anything to be allowed to take Nikos into their family. At the end of the second day she meticulously addressed each envelope, went to the post office and posted them all off.

'Please,' she whispered, holding the letters to her mouth. 'Please bring back good news.'

Many weeks passed and there were no replies. It was even more agonising than the period when she was waiting for Thanasis to find news of Anna. Luckily, Angelos provided plenty of distraction, learning to walk, saying new words and eagerly experiencing new tastes.

Day after day, Themis watched from the balcony, following the postman's progress as he went round the square. When he reached their building, she would run down to the ground floor two stairs at a time to see if there was anything for her and often there were several letters lying scattered on the floor. They were always for the other apartments and, swallowing her disappointment, she put them in the appropriate pigeon-holes before ascending the stairs once again.

Every day, her grandmother tried to encourage her: 'I'm sure there will be news soon.'

Eventually, there was. The first letter came after a month or so.

'We regret to inform you that we have no one with that name staying with us.'

It was a very dark day for her, and became more so when she heard that Belogiannis had just been executed.

Over the following months, other similar letters followed. With each one Themis' spirits sank a little.

★

As the leaves began to turn, Themis realised that it was a year since Thanasis had given her the news of Anna's death. In those twelve months, Angelos had changed from baby to toddler and she tried to imagine what Nikos would be like now and how their first meeting might be. He would be capable of expressing his views and saying what he wanted.

Her mind was jumping ahead. First she had to find him and still there was no positive response from any of the homes.

One fine late autumn afternoon, she took Angelos out for a walk. The latest negative response from one of the children's homes had landed on the mat earlier that day and only three possibilities remained. Themis needed to distract herself and she took Angelos to Fokionos Negri, where he liked to run up and down the square. He was two and a half now and there were always plenty of other children there for him to play with, and even the statue of a dog, which he loved to go and pet.

While Themis waited on a bench, scrutinising him closely as he played with the other children, she was aware that a man was watching her from a café on the other side of some trees. He was alone, drinking coffee, and she noticed that he regularly glanced up from his newspaper and, almost without shame, stared at her. She began to feel uncomfortable.

'Angelos,' she called out. 'Angelos. Come, darling. It's time to go home.'

The little one was enjoying himself and made his mother chase after him, squealing with delight as he repeatedly ducked to evade her grasp.

Themis was agitated. The man's eyes seemed to burn her back and his scrutiny to pierce her like a blade. Stories were circulating that people who had previously been imprisoned on an island were being taken in again by the authorities. The signing of the *dílosi*

325

may have won her release from Trikeri, but true peace of mind would never be hers: the stigma of being a convicted leftist would always be there.

It was rumoured that all those who had signed were still watched. She had never believed it before but now she changed her view.

With sweat pouring down her back and her heart almost bursting through her chest, she grabbed Angelos firmly by the arm and pulled him away from his new playmates.

'Come on, Angelos, we're going. *Now*,' she said firmly.

It was the first time that the boy had heard such a tone in his mother's voice and the shock of it made him cry.

'*Óchi! Óchi!* No!' he wailed, aggrieved by this sudden change in her and the firmness of her grip on his chubby arm.

His crying only made Themis more agitated and drew the attention of the man, who had now put his paper to one side and was openly staring at them. With a mixture of embarrassment and fear, she picked up her child and hastened, as fast as she possibly could with the struggling weight in her arms, back to Patission Avenue and towards home.

'Please, Angelos. Please!' she pleaded to the now squalling child. Only as they climbed the stairs to the apartment did his crying subside.

Kyría Koralis had seen them approaching from the balcony and was standing at the open door.

'*Agápi mou*,' she asked. 'What on earth has happened?'

She set Angelos down and he stood holding the edge of his great-grandmother's skirt, looking up with some bemusement at the two women. Kyría Koralis was now holding Themis in her arms, comforting her as she sobbed.

'What has happened? Tell me, *mátia mou*. You're safe now. You're home and safe,' she said gently.

The little boy had wandered off to the corner and was finding something to play with in his toy box. After a few minutes, Themis managed to control her emotions.

'Sorry, *Yiayiá*. I'm sorry,' she said tearfully. 'Come here, darling. I'm so sorry, little one.'

Angelos approached her cautiously and when he was close enough, he allowed himself to be drawn into her embrace. His mother ruffled his curls and he snuggled into her, happy that they were friends once again.

Later on, when Angelos was asleep, Themis explained to her grandmother the reason she had behaved with such uncharacteristic roughness towards her child.

'I panicked, *Yiayiá*,' she said. 'For all I know, this man, whoever he is, might have been watching me for months. And these people need no excuse if they want to arrest you.'

'But you have done nothing, my darling,' responded the old lady gently.

Thanasis had already come in and was in his bedroom. Their voices were loud enough for him to overhear.

'You were on the losing side, Themis,' he reminded her, as he came out into the living room. 'And you are right to wonder who is watching you.'

'Thanasis! That's such a cruel thing to say to your sister.'

'It's true, *Yiayiá*,' he said. 'And my sister should be aware of that.'

He spoke almost as though he was doing Themis a favour in giving her the information. She was still worried and afraid, but her greatest fear was not even for herself: it was that they might take Angelos from her.

When Thanasis had gone out, she confided in her grandmother.

'If they take him, *Yiayiá*, I don't know what I will do.'

'They won't take him, *glykiá mou*. They can't.'

327

Themis was not convinced and for a few days she did not leave the house and kept Angelos inside with her too.

The furthest she went from the apartment was downstairs to the hallway in order to check on the postman's latest delivery. The sense of time passing only grew more intense with her growing disappointment and anxiety.

Kyría Koralis tried to persuade her to leave the apartment.

'It's not good for you,' she said firmly. 'And it's not good for Angelos.'

'I feel we're safer here,' Themis said. 'For the moment.'

She was stubborn and for the whole winter remained within the walls of the apartment building. Angelos was taken out each day for a walk by his grandmother.

Then one morning, spring suddenly announced itself. For the first time, the rays of the sun touched the square, and trees that had looked lifeless suddenly had a haze of green over them. Kyría Koralis persuaded her granddaughter to take a stroll.

All three of them put their coats on and went out, but Themis kept glancing behind them.

'Try not to worry,' said Kyría Koralis. 'I think we all deserve a little treat, don't you, Angelos?'

Reluctantly, Themis agreed that they should go to a café in Fokionos Negri. She had been past it a few times and noticed the pastries and, after a decade when even a gram of sugar had been hard to come by, it was still a novelty to see such things. The unexpected early burst of sunshine had brought everyone out that day and the streets were busy. Angelos held on tightly to his mother's hand on one side and his grandmother's on the other as they approached the café and went in.

The three of them sipped their drinks and Themis looked out of the window. For the first time in his life, Angelos experienced the taste of ice cream.

Suddenly Themis almost dropped her cup.

'There he *is*!' she whispered to her grandmother.

Kyría Koralis turned her old head round to see.

'Don't stare, *Yiayiá*!'

'You mean the one in the grey jacket? With the blue shirt?'

The café was busy but Kyría Koralis had immediately spotted the person that Themis was staring at. Most of the clientele was female.

'Yes, but please don't let him see we are talking about him. What am I going to do?'

'Nothing, *agápi mou*. He seems not to be taking the slightest interest in you, or anything else for that matter, apart from his newspaper.'

Themis, who had a clearer view, knew that her grandmother was wrong. He was staring at her just as he had done the previous time.

'*Theé kai kýrie*, he is coming over here. *Yiayiá*, I think we should leave. Now.'

Themis was flustered. She struggled desperately to get Angelos' arms into the sleeves of his coat.

'Angelos! Just do what you are told!' she entreated.

The child began protesting loudly. The small bowl of chocolate ice cream that his great-grandmother had been carefully spooning into his open mouth had been snatched away and he began to make a scene. The effect of the sugar itself and also having it taken from him was beyond endurance and his flailing arms made him uncontrollable. One of his hands caught the edge of the bowl and it smashed on to the floor, spreading dark brown sludge over the tiles.

'Angelos! *Se parakaló*! Please!'

The child's tantrum had brought the café to a standstill. The eyes of everyone in the room were on them and all conversations had stopped.

'Themis,' said a man's voice. 'Themis Koralis?'

Themis was frozen with fear, her mouth so dry that she could not answer. She stopped struggling with Angelos and he stopped crying. They both looked up at the man.

'You *are* Themis Koralis? Or am I . . . m–m–mistaken?'

The man suddenly seemed covered in embarrassment.

'R–r–really, I shouldn't have bothered you. I'm so sorry. I must have made a mistake. I thought you were s–s–someone I knew. My mistake, my m–m–mistake.'

He turned to walk away.

The man's awkwardness was endearing and Themis now realised that it was she who had made the mistake.

Hearing his voice, she suddenly realised who he was. She had been at elementary school with him and had sometimes bumped into him when she was a teenager. He had the same dark brown eyes she remembered from over a decade before, but, apart from the voice, the rest of him had changed beyond recognition.

'Giorgos . . .!' she said, without hesitation. 'You're Giorgos! Giorgos Stavridis!'

He turned round immediately and smiled.

'I'm so sorry,' said Themis. 'You must have thought we were so rude.'

Both of them soon overcame their embarrassment.

'Can I . . .?' asked Giorgos.

'Yes! Sit down. Sit down with us!' Themis replied as they began to converse.

'I'm so s–s–sorry that I didn't say hello before, but you were always hurrying away.'

'I'm sorry too, Giorgos. I didn't realise it was you. It's so long . . .'

'Yes. I don't know why you w-w-would recognise me.'

Themis laughed.

'Or the other way round!'

Themis touched her hair, still self-conscious about its length. Shorter styles had become the fashion, but she was suddenly nostalgic for her long plait. The last time Giorgos saw her it would still have been running down her back.

The waiter had taken more orders for coffee. None of them was in a hurry to leave now.

'I think you look just the same,' he said.

'Maybe,' she said. 'But I think you're being kind.'

'And Angelos? How old is the little man?'

He knew the child's name, as did everyone in the vicinity. It had been shouted out by his mother so many times just a few minutes before.

Angelos was sitting on his great-grandmother's lap and had calmed down now. He was watching the floor around them being cleaned by the waiter.

Giorgos smiled at the child, who was enjoying another small scoop of ice cream. Everything was peaceful again.

Conversation was friendly but superficial. Both Themis and Giorgos knew that there were many invisible lines and neither knew where they were drawn. She remembered that Giorgos' father had been a schoolteacher, but this was not enough to tell her what his politics were and even then it would not necessarily indicate what his son believed.

She glanced at his newspaper to see if it gave a clue to his political leanings but it was tightly folded in his pocket so she could not be sure.

The two of them stayed on safe ground and reminisced about school days and the people they had known. Occasionally they shared some snippet of information ('Ah, yes, Petros Glentakis, he went off to America' or, 'Vasso Koveos became a teacher and now has two children').

Themis remembered Giorgos as the most studious boy in the class. Most boys had been rebellious and noisy, but he had been a keen student, almost unnoticeable. Sometimes she and Fotini had walked home with him when the day ended, knowing that he would be spending even more hours studying than they.

Giorgos mentioned Fotini. It was so long since Themis had talked to someone who remembered her best friend and it led them, of course, into talking about the occupation.

'T-t-terrible days,' said Giorgos. 'Terrible days.'

No Greek would ever deny this.

'It changed all our lives, didn't it?' said Themis, to provoke another comment.

'And r-r-ruined them in some cases,' said Giorgos.

Even now, she did not know how to interpret what he said.

She stared at his well-trimmed fingernails and took in his neatly trimmed hair and oiled moustache. He was smartly dressed, his jacket perfectly pressed and his shoes polished. A civil servant, a lawyer, a doctor? He was so clean and scrubbed, without a hint of unpredictability or violence in his manner. She thought of various men in her life in these past years: her father, Thanasis, Makris, the men on Makronisos and on Trikeri. From every one of them, there had been something to fear.

Having exhausted talk of long-past school days, she hesitated to ask him what happened in the period that followed. It did seem natural, however, to ask him about the present. Knowing what he did might give her a clue as to whether he was on her side, or if he had avoided taking any side?

Finally, she plucked up the courage. His answer was immediate and unashamed.

'I work for the tax office.'

'Oh,' she said.

The fact that he was a government employee did not surprise her and confirmed that he probably did not sympathise with the left.

'That's a nice steady job to have,' said her grandmother.

'My f-f-father got me the job,' he said, almost apologetically, glancing at Themis.

Angelos had finished his ice cream and the sugar had taken its effect once again. His grandmother was having trouble keeping him in his seat.

Giorgos then talked for a few minutes with Kyría Koralis, who remembered his parents, while Themis took Angelos on to her lap.

'We must go,' she said after a while. 'Angelos needs a sleep.'

The three adults rose simultaneously. Giorgos was already paying the bill.

'Even for the ice creams?' exclaimed Themis.

'I insist,' said Giorgos, smiling.

As they stood on the pavement there was a moment of hesitation.

Angelos was tugging at his mother's hand and Themis held out the other to Giorgos.

'It was so nice to see you,' he said, taking it. 'P-p-perhaps we can meet again . . .?'

Themis smiled. 'Yes,' she mumbled. 'We must go now. But thanks for the coffee – and the ice cream.'

Giorgos headed in one direction and Themis, Kyría Koralis and Angelos in the other. After a moment or two, Themis could not resist glancing over her shoulder. To her disappointment Giorgos had already disappeared.

Her grandmother was chatting idly.

'He seemed nice enough,' she said.

'Yes, *Yiayiá*,' she responded. 'Just like he was when we were at school.'

'Perhaps you'll see him again?'

'Perhaps . . .'

For a few days, Themis found herself looking for Giorgos' face every time she left the house. More than once, she took Angelos for a walk past what she had assumed was his regular café, but there was no sign of him.

'No,' she said to Angelos firmly each time. 'There's no ice cream today.'

Themis was thinking of Giorgos one day the following week when she saw some letters lying fanned out across the hallway floor. She had begun to hope that he might put a note through their door. It was decades since their occasional walks from school but might he have a dim memory of her address?

She went to pick up the envelopes. One caught her eye. It was an official-looking letter, with a Thessaloniki postmark and the name *Kyría Kouzelis* typed on the outside.

It was so long since she had written under this pseudonym, and several months since she had received the latest reply from one of the *paidópoleis*. There were only two homes that had not yet responded and she had begun to resign herself to the idea that Nikos could be elsewhere and a new search might have to begin.

Themis took the letter, along with one for her grandmother with a German postmark, and climbed the stairs.

Angelos was cheerfully playing with Kyría Koralis. Small wooden bricks were laid out on the floor and they were building shapes together. Thanasis was yet to come home from work, so the scene was peaceful. When his uncle arrived, Angelos would want to play more boisterous games.

'We both have letters,' said Themis, putting them on the kitchen table.

Kyría Koralis had appeared at her side and was already eagerly slitting open the letter from Margarita.

Themis left hers on the table and went across to continue playing with Angelos. He was already protesting at being abandoned and, besides, she was in no hurry. She expected disappointment.

'Poor girl,' Kyría Koralis muttered. 'Poor child. Still no sign of a baby. Even after everything I sent her. What can she do? And the husband is impatient. Oh dear, oh dear . . .'

'That must be difficult.'

Themis tried to sound sympathetic but found it hard to feel very much for her sister.

'Perhaps I should suggest she comes back to Athens?'

Themis shot a glance at her grandmother but kept quiet. There was nothing she could imagine that would make their lives more difficult than an embittered Margarita living in their midst, her aspirations and hopes entirely dashed. An unexpected equilibrium had been achieved between herself and Thanasis, and if Margarita returned she was certain the fragile balance would be lost.

Kyría Koralis started preparing lunch and Themis absent-mindedly slit open her letter. It would say the same as the others: '*Many thanks for your letter. We are sorry to inform you . . .*'

She was still thinking about Margarita when her eyes began to scan the lines.

'*Yiayiá!*' she shrieked. 'I've found him! I've *found* him!'

She stood up and waved the letter triumphantly in the air.

'He's in Thessaloniki! I've found him. I've found Nikos!'

Themis was beside herself with joy. She picked Angelos up and danced with him, burying her face in his curls.

'Your brother is coming,' she exclaimed. 'Your big brother . . .'

She kissed Angelos on both cheeks before putting him down on the floor.

Kneeling down to be at his level, Themis took her son's hands in hers.

'Say *Nikos*, darling,' she said, almost beside herself with excitement. 'Say *Nikos!*'

The little boy, who was at a stage where he would parrot any word he heard and liked, dutifully responded.

'Niko,' he said dutifully. 'Niko.'

'Bravo, *agápi mou*. Bravo!'

Thanasis had come in quietly during the commotion.

'So,' he asked. 'What's all the fuss about?'

Themis hastily got up from the floor, straightened her skirt and passed her hand over her hair, knowing that she must look dishevelled. She was emboldened by excitement.

'You remember you found me the record of Anna Kouzelis? Well, I have found her son. And she asked me to take care of him if anything ever happened to her.'

Even now she was adding another layer of untruth but it would make no difference to Thanasis' reaction.

'Take care of him?' said Thanasis, aghast. 'What exactly do you mean, "take care of him"?'

'I mean just that. Bring him up as my own.'

Thanasis began to splutter. His indignation prevented him from speaking but his face said it all. His scar had reddened and his eyes bulged with fury.

'Try and stay calm, my dear,' said Kyría Koralis. 'And listen to your sister. Hear what she has to say.'

Kyría Koralis turned off her pan of boiling water and began to play with Angelos again.

Themis was shaking. Thanasis stared at her.

'Very well. I am waiting,' he said impatiently.

Themis had long prepared for this moment, rehearsing what she would say to her brother and anticipating his reaction.

'This boy. This little boy. He has spent these past years in one of the Queen's homes. He will be disciplined and well-behaved. They are taught good manners and patriotism and how to behave in church. Apparently they're model children, schooled just as Queen Frederika wishes.'

The words stuck in her throat like gristle from old meat but they were words that her brother would want to hear.

'But why should we have him *here*, Themis?'

'Because I promised, Thanasis. And don't you think it's better to give a child a normal life?' she appealed to him. 'And let Angelos grow up with a brother?'

'He'll be a nice, decent child, Thanasis,' said Kyría Koralis weakly. 'Those *paidópoleis* are very disciplined and the children are all nice and clean . . .'

'I have told them that I am his aunt,' added Themis. 'But to him, I will be his mother and Angelos and he will be brothers.'

Thanasis did nothing to hide his disgust and Themis could see the sweat of agitation dripping from his brow.

He came up with one objection after another.

'There isn't enough space,' he said.

'I don't mind sharing my room with two boys,' said Themis quickly. 'And besides, we might all move out one day.'

She harboured a dream of finding someone who might love her enough to adopt her children. The woman who had been a soldier and survived great hardship admitted to herself, with just a modicum of shame, that life in this society would be much easier with a husband.

'And how exactly do you think that will happen? Who's going to take on not one but two little bastards?'

'Thanasis, please!' pleaded his grandmother.

In spite of his affection for Angelos, Thanasis could still be cruel. Themis kept calm.

'Who knows? But I *promise*, Thanasis, that I will do everything to make sure that he fits in and becomes part of our family.'

The whole plan relied on her brother's compliance. If he really wanted to prevent it, he would succeed.

'I need time to consider,' he said firmly.

The conversation was over and Themis left the room with Angelos. Kyría Koralis returned to the stove and carried on making lunch. The subject of Nikos was not raised again that day.

In the interim, Themis made plans.

She decided not to wait for Thanasis' response. What did she care for it? She had no doubt in her mind what she must do, reminding herself of all the risks she had taken in the past, hiding, fighting, surviving hunger, torture and pain. She would not be afraid of her brother.

The *paidópoli* of Agios Dimitrios was situated close to Thessaloniki. In a few days' time, she would take the train from Athens.

Chapter Twenty

THEMIS PACKED A small tapestry bag of her grandmother's with two clean blouses, some underclothes and a knitted cardigan.

'It's a long way north,' warned her grandmother. 'And it might be chilly at night.'

Themis did not like to remind her that she had slept outside on the mountains of northern Greece.

Kyría Koralis tucked some dried fruit and bread into the side of the bag, gave her some money and waved her off. Angelos was still sleeping and Themis did not wake him, preferring to avoid a tearful farewell. She knew her grandmother would care for him well. Thanasis had already left for work.

Themis had never travelled by train, and the noise and confusion of the station was overwhelming. After a long wait, she found herself at the front of the ticket queue and bought a one-way ticket to Thessaloniki that would take her via Lamia and Larissa and arrive in the early hours of the following day.

'You're not planning to return?' asked the man behind the counter officiously.

It was too complicated to explain that she would not be coming back alone, and in any case did not know exactly when that might be.

By the time she found the correct platform her train was about to leave. In the chaos of passengers and porters shouting and giving orders, she narrowly avoided collision with two men carrying a trunk. Even as doors were still being slammed shut, the train began to pull out. For a moment she panicked that she was heading in the wrong direction but other passengers soon reassured her.

She found a seat by the window and stared out, her bag held close to her chest. She carried nothing of value except the letter from Agios Dimitrios and a book that she had brought with her, the recently published *Freedom and Death* by Kazantzakis. It was so long since she had had this many hours to herself, and she eagerly began to read. With the late-morning warmth coming through the window, she soon fell asleep, not waking until the afternoon when the landscape had flattened and they were passing through farmland near Lamia. Athens was already far behind.

She ran her hand along the spine of the book and her fingers traced the author's name. Nikos. Themis was missing her own son, but she was on her way to find Aliki's. A tingling sensation ran up and down her spine.

The whole day the train trundled through Greece. The windows were dirty so it was hard to see much of what lay outside, but they passed entire villages of burnt-out houses. For an hour or more she saw scarcely a single figure in the landscape. Only as they stopped at various small towns did there seem to be a population of any kind.

The whole country seemed submerged beneath dereliction. Themis had got used to the dilapidated state of Athens. It was the normality since the occupation and civil war, but this journey showed her parts of Greece that she had not seen before. It seemed that most of it was in a similar or even worse state of disrepair and she felt a twinge of guilt for the role she had played.

A young woman climbed aboard at Lamia and sat next to Themis. She was about the same age and on her way to live with her sister in Thessaloniki.

'Maria has found me a job as a seamstress,' she said, proudly. 'It's in a fashion house. *Haute couture.*'

'That sounds nice,' said Themis.

'It's a new start anyway,' said the other girl. 'And we all need a new start, don't we?'

Themis did not answer, even though she agreed.

Themis had enough food to share and the other girl gratefully took some. All day, she slept fitfully on and off, sometimes dipping into her book, at other times listening to the idle chit-chat of her travelling companion.

That night, both women agreed to keep an eye on each other's things while the other one slept, so Themis enjoyed a few hours of relatively comfortable sleep.

'You can't really trust anyone these days,' said the trainee seamstress.

In the early hours of the following morning, the train rattled into its final destination. The women wished each other well and went their separate ways.

Themis would never forget her first sight of the city of Thessaloniki. Mist was rising over the sea and she wandered away from the station and found herself on a wide esplanade that curved along the edge of the water towards a fortified tower in one direction, and towards dockyards in the other. Parts of the city seemed very grand to her, others were more industrial and some of the streets reminded her of Patissia.

Her grandmother had been generous with what she had put in her wallet and she felt no anxiety about sitting down in one of the pastry shops in her drab clothes and ordering a coffee and a sweet *bougatsa*, its creamy custard bursting into her mouth as she sank her teeth into the light pastry parcel. The waitress giggled and brought her another paper napkin. Themis' impression was that people were friendlier here, less anxious than they were in Athens.

For half an hour or more, Themis sat and watched people coming and going. It was coming up to eight in the morning, the time of day when people were at their most purposeful, the day was still new and everyone hopeful for what they would achieve. Themis looked at two or three young women hurrying along and wondered what their work might be. Shop assistants? Office workers? If the events of the past five years had not intervened she might still be working in the pharmacy and even be a qualified pharmacist by now.

She stirred her coffee absent-mindedly. She wanted to delay a little more before setting off, but eventually was ready to pay. Like the women who passed by, she too had a specific mission today. As she counted out some coins, she asked the waitress if she knew how to find a place called Oraiokastro. It was the suburb where the *paidópoli* was situated.

The young girl called her colleague over.

'Zoe, you live there, don't you?' she said. 'Oraiokastro? What's the best way to get there?'

The other girl drew a map on the napkin showing how to find the bus station, the number of the bus she should get, how much it would cost and how long it would take. Themis was touched by her kindness.

'What takes you to my town?' she asked.

'I have to visit the *paidópoli*,' Themis answered innocently. 'My nephew is there.'

The woman, Zoe, seemed surprised that anyone would ever want to visit such a place.

Moments later, Themis was walking along Aristotelous Street, disconcerted by the waitress' reaction but full of anticipation for the next stage of her journey.

Themis had enjoyed her brief time in Thessaloniki and reluctantly left the city behind. She took a seat at the back of the bus and when she glanced behind her caught a glimpse of a sparkling sea.

Oraiokastro was closer to Thessaloniki than she had imagined, and also the terminus of the route. When she got off the bus it was about mid-morning and a single enquiry got her to her destination. Five minutes later she was at the *paidópoli*.

A pair of iron gates towered above her and through the bars she could see a vast building stretching away into the distance, a huge Greek flag fluttering over its entrance.

She had not allowed herself to imagine this moment, and now felt daunted by what was ahead.

For so long she had been on the inside of bars wanting to get out; now she was on the outside hoping for admission. In the yard in front of the main building dozens of boys were playing. Some of them were kicking a ball, others stood around talking. One or two of them loitered shyly on the edge of the group.

The children were all wearing identical blue shorts and shirts, an outfit that reminded her of her own hated EON uniform.

Themis scanned the faces of the boys. What would Nikos look like now? She had a line drawing of him as a small child but that had been done four years ago. He would look very different now and there were at least fifty boys in the yard, *en masse* their faces all so similar: dark hair (identically cropped), dark skin, dark eyes. Suddenly a whistle was blown and they immediately fell into a single line and marched like soldiers into the building. It was silent again.

A moment or two passed before it occurred to Themis to push the gates. To her surprise, they moved easily and a moment later she was at the main door, nervously putting her finger on the polished bell.

Themis took a deep breath.

'Have courage,' she told herself. 'Stay strong. Think of Aliki.'

'*Kaliméra*. Good morning. Can I help you?'

The door had been opened almost immediately by a young woman, probably Themis' own age. She was neither friendly nor hostile.

Themis had rehearsed what she was going to say and the words tumbled out easily.

'I have come to enquire about a child,' she said. 'Nikos Kouzelis. I am his aunt.'

'Ah, yes,' the woman replied, as though she had been expecting her. 'Come in.'

Soon Themis was sitting in the director's office. On the wall hung a huge portrait of Queen Frederika, whose eyes met hers. Themis had not changed her views about the German even though she had successfully promoted herself as the mother and saviour of Greek children.

The director came in and she stood to greet him. As soon as they were both seated, he began to speak.

'So my secretary tells me that you wish to take Nikos Kouzelis from us.'

'Yes . . . I wrote to you.'

'I have the letter here,' he said curtly, looking down at it. 'Before releasing him, I need to inform you of a few things.'

The terminology reminded Themis of prison.

'First of all . . .'

Themis felt her heart thumping. The moment he demanded proof of her identity all might be lost, but she was ready with the excuse that all her personal papers had been lost in a fire during the events of December 1944.

'I need to tell you that he is a very rebellious boy,' continued the director. 'In spite of our efforts he does not really . . . conform, shall we say.'

'Oh . . .' Themis said, trying to sound disapproving. 'I'm sorry about that.'

'He does not really embrace the ideology of this institution,' continued the director strictly. 'So when he leaves, we will rely on you to continue with his education in that respect.'

'Of course,' said Themis, enthusiastically. 'My brother will happily undertake that.'

Referring to Thanasis made the conversation feel more authentic.

'The very least he must do is learn the words of our national anthem,' continued the director. 'And he must continue to say his prayers.'

An outsider might have imagined that he was talking about a youth, rather than a five-year-old child.

Themis continued to nod.

'Well, that completes the process, I think,' said the director. 'I just need your signature here.'

Themis hastily signed the paper he passed to her. It summarised the various things he had already outlined and her signature was her undertaking to fulfil them. Essentially, she must ensure that Nikos became a good citizen.

Yes, thought Themis as she picked up the pen. I will happily bring him up to be a good citizen: to love his motherland and his fellow Greeks.

She had no objection to these principles, even if her definitions were at odds with those of the austere figure who sat in front of her.

The director took a cursory look to ensure that the signature matched the one on her original letter but before the ink was even dry, he stood up and led Themis to the door. He politely opened it to let her through and thanked her for coming.

'My secretary will deal with the rest of the business,' he said.

Themis got the impression that it was a relief for him to reduce the population of the *paidópoli*, even by one. The process had been astonishingly simple.

Before she even had the opportunity to thank him, the door had shut behind her.

The young woman was standing there, waiting.

Finally, she was to meet Aliki's son.

Themis could scarcely keep up with the secretary as she marched down a series of long corridors. They passed a huge refectory where the children were eating, a series of classrooms and a laundry before reaching the dormitory. Here, Themis saw rows of closely packed bunk beds with a grey blanket neatly folded at the end of each mattress. There were neither curtains nor blinds. It was unwelcoming, uncomfortable, and reminiscent of the camp at Bulkes. It lacked even the subtlest hint that it was a place for children to sleep. Her mind travelled to the colourful quilted counterpane and the toys that lived on top of Angelos' little cot.

What Themis had not noticed when she walked in was a small figure in the shadows beneath a bed.

'Nikos!' said the secretary, in a tone that combined kindness with threat. 'There's someone here to see you.'

The boy cowered further, hiding his face in the crook of his arm.

'Come on, Nikos,' the woman said more sternly. 'That's enough. Come out now!'

She bent down to pull the child out, dragging first one skinny leg and then another, slapping his thigh hard when he resisted.

'You're leaving!' she said with a note of triumph.

With these words, he immediately stopped struggling. It seemed to Themis that this news suited both the child and the staff.

As he was dragged into the light, Themis found herself looking into two dark pools of the deepest brown. She suppressed a gasp of recognition. The lack of hair somehow accentuated the magnitude of his eyes. They were his father's and her reaction to them was visceral. He reminded her of Makris but, more importantly, his features strongly resembled Angelos'.

To Nikos, she was a total stranger, but to Themis, Nikos seemed like someone she had always known.

She had to resist the urge to take him in her arms and instead got down on one knee so that they could look each other in the eye.

Nikos stared at her with a boldness she had not expected. It was somewhere between defiance, insolence and curiosity.

'We're going to live in a new city together,' she said, resisting the temptation to introduce herself as his aunt. 'I'm taking you to live in a nice place with your great-grandmother and uncle too.'

She did not want to tell lies, but a little fabrication was essential.

The child did not speak.

'Collect your things,' said the secretary.

'I haven't *got* any things,' he said sullenly.

'Your clothes, then,' the woman snapped back, casting a friendly smile at Themis in case she might be giving the wrong impression of herself.

Nikos reached under the bed, pulled out a small metal box and opened it. There was a woollen pullover inside which he took out and tied round his waist. It was obvious that he had been disciplined to do this. To Themis, it made him seem very grown up.

Themis asked him if there was anyone to whom he wished to say goodbye but he shook his head. It appeared that he had no friends and no affection for the staff.

To her relief, the child willingly left this place that had been his home for several years. Without emotion and without hesitation, he took Themis' hand and walked with her along the marble corridors, to the main entrance and out through the gates. As they left, the director gave them a cheerful wave through his window. He then drew the curtains to protect his furniture from the sun.

Themis had already checked on the bus times back to Thessaloniki and they had an hour or two to kill, so she took Nikos for something to eat.

The child was quiet. She had not expected him to be otherwise but all that mattered to her now was that he held tightly on to her hand, full of trust, full of confidence that she was taking him to a better place. His willingness gratified her and soothed her anxieties.

They sat in a small restaurant where he hungrily devoured some stuffed vegetables, his face bent over his plate as if someone might snatch it away.

Themis chatted to him and for the first time mentioned that he would soon be meeting his little brother.

Nikos did not react to anything she said and it was hard to tell if he was even listening. Occasionally, the large brown eyes looked up at her but seemed to register very little. Soon he had finished eating and they got on the bus towards Thessaloniki.

Between their arrival back in the city and the departure of their train to Athens, they had another hour and Themis spotted a department store close to the station. She wanted to get him out of his baggy *paidópoli* uniform and into his own clothes.

The child became more talkative once they were in the shop.

'These aren't really mine,' he said, tugging at his pullover. 'Every week they leave something clean on the bed. Sometimes my clothes are tight, sometimes they're too big.'

Themis had noticed that he had to keep hitching up his shorts. They were obviously made for a much bigger boy.

'Well, let's get you something that's meant for you,' she said. 'Do you have a favourite colour?'

The little boy shrugged. There was not a huge amount of choice, but they found some trousers that he could roll up for now and a few shirts in different colours that fitted him. On the way out of the shop, Themis discreetly left the old clothes in a bin.

For the first time that day, Nikos looked afraid when they reached the station.

'It's a monster,' he said, clinging to Themis with fear. The train was belching out huge clouds of steam.

After some persuasion, he believed Themis' promise that he would be safe with her and allowed her to lift him up on to the step. They quickly settled in their seats and moments later they were on their way. It was early evening and almost immediately Nikos fell asleep.

Themis studied his face. With his long lashes touching his cheek, he reminded her so much of Angelos. The main difference was his hair. It was closely shaved, just as the heads of all the boys back in the *paidópoli*. She could not resist stroking the soft pelt and the child did not stir. For many hours he remained curled up beside her, like a contented cat, with her hand resting on his back. Little Nikos.

When it got light, Nikos spent much of the time looking out of the window. He seemed interested in everything they saw: horses, cows and even goats were creatures that he had only seen in books until now.

When the moment seemed right to Themis, she brought up once again the notion that he was going to have a brother. He looked at her almost blankly. Perhaps until they reached Patissia this was beyond his comprehension so she decided to let the matter rest and reached into her bag. Before leaving home, Themis had found some of her favourite fairy stories from childhood and now read and then reread them at Nikos' request. He was eager and excited about being told a story and after a while, she began to make them up, so hungry was he for more tales of gods and goddesses and mysterious creatures of the deep. By the time he fell asleep again, she was beginning to get to know this strange and beautiful little boy.

It was very late at night when the train drew into Larisis Station in Athens. Nikos woke up disorientated, as if disturbed from a bad dream, and began to cry inconsolably.

'Where am I? Where am I?' he screamed, thrashing his arms against Themis. 'I don't know who you are! Take me home! Now! Take me home!'

He shrieked as if he had been kidnapped and other passengers on the train began to look at Themis, some with suspicion.

'Nikos, calm down, *agápi mou*,' she said gently, fending off his flailing arms. 'I'm Themis, remember?'

The boy's tears subsided a little.

'And we're going home to meet your little brother. We're nearly there, in Athens.'

The child sniffed loudly, wiping his tears on the sleeve of his new shirt and catching his breath again as his sobs subsided.

'Do you remember? We left the *paidópoli*, and now we're going home . . .?'

Themis held her breath for a moment. One couple in particular was glaring at her. The spectre of child-snatching was not uncommon, especially after the twin controversies of some children being taken into communist countries and others being unwillingly put into the *paidopóleis*. Themis well knew that this was on their minds.

Nikos seemed to recall the situation now and let Themis put a protective arm around him. It was time to get off and Themis threw their bags down on to the platform, stepped down herself and then held out her hands to help him jump.

'Bravo, *agápi mou*,' she smiled. 'Not far to go now.'

The last bus across the city had left and there was a single taxi waiting outside the station, which she hailed. It was a first for her, as well as for Nikos.

Nikos pressed his nose right against the window and then turned to Themis, amused at the way the glass had steamed up. At last, she thought, he is smiling.

The fare finished every last drachma that Kyría Koralis had put in Themis' purse and, in the early hours, she put her key in the lock. She and Nikos were 'home'.

She noticed him looking around almost with suspicion and realised that the apartment must seem small and dark after the large, high-ceilinged spaces of the *paidópoli*.

Not wanting to wake anyone, she sat Nikos down on one of the armchairs and warmed up some milk. She tucked a rug around the child as he sipped from a cup. Within the next few hours, there were new encounters for him to face and she had real anxieties about them all.

Angelos was sleeping with her grandmother and she did not want to disturb them so she and Nikos went to sleep on the couch.

At around six in the morning, a door banged and Nikos immediately sat up.

Thanasis limped into the room. Without his stick, his gait was even more lopsided and, in the half-light, with his twisted body and misshapen face, he instilled terror into Nikos.

The child's scream woke Themis.

'I'm so sorry, Thanasis,' she said sleepily. 'I didn't expect you to be up so early.'

'What difference does it make?'

He walked over to the stove and clumsily began making himself coffee, feigning indifference to the strange child sobbing in his sister's lap. As he poured the foaming liquid into a cup, he turned round and spoke to Themis again.

'So you found him?'

The question did not require an answer but Themis wanted to introduce Nikos properly.

'Yes,' she said. 'Come on, Nikos. Let's say good morning to your Uncle Thanasis.'

The past few years in the *paidópoli* had given Nikos the experience to recognise modulations in the adult voice. It was in his interest to do what he was told when he heard certain tones, so he put aside his reluctance and faced the man who had terrified him just a moment ago.

Thanasis stared at the child with undisguised disgust. Nikos was a wisp of a child, pale and almost bald.

'So you're the new one?' he said with contempt. 'Let's see how Angelos takes to you, shall we?'

Themis clung to the hope that Nikos might not understand the implication behind her brother's words. He addressed the little boy as though he was a stray dog, a mongrel, a '*bastardaki*'. She managed to contain her rage and held tightly on to the boy's hand.

'We'll be meeting Angelos as soon as he wakes up,' she said cheerily to the child. 'It won't be long now.'

She cast a look of scorn at her brother, who was slowly stirring his coffee.

'I'm sure they'll get on well,' she said to Thanasis, adding under her breath, 'Better than some siblings, anyway.'

Kyría Koralis came in a moment later and the tension was immediately defused.

'So this is little Nikos!' she said with enthusiasm, scurrying over to take a closer look at him. 'I'm so happy we found you!'

Nikos smiled, sensing her genuine kindness, and the two women formed a protective wall around him, as if to keep him safe.

Thanasis left for work soon afterwards and Kyría Koralis went to wake Angelos.

Holding Nikos' left hand and Angelos' right, Themis put them face to face.

'Angelos, this is your brother, Nikos. Nikos, your brother, Angelos.'

Nikos understood the idea of brothers and sisters. There had been several boys in the *paidópoli* who had them and this special connection was something he had envied.

Angelos, on the other hand, did not really understand what his mother meant, but he sensed that the arrival of another boy was going to change his life.

The boys looked at each other silently and suspiciously.

Angelos tried to hide behind his mother and for a few days his constant chatter stopped. He did not want to eat.

'What am I going to do?' Themis asked her grandmother despairingly.

The change came when Nikos created a game. When Thanasis was out of the house, the women gave the older boy the freedom to play how he wished, remembering that he was accustomed to the expanses of the *paidópoli*. One day he created a game with a secret hideaway. It was constructed with a rug and a sheet and both boys disappeared into the camp with Angelos' toy cars. Their muffled chatter and laughter continued long into the afternoon. Kyría Koralis delivered a small picnic to what Nikos called their 'cave' and both women were delighted when the game continued the next day and the one after, and the camp became a semi-permanent structure in the living room.

From that moment, the boys were firm friends.

Even Thanasis begrudgingly admitted that Nikos was a welcome addition to the family. 'He keeps the little one entertained, doesn't he?'

Early one evening, Themis was drying the dishes. She watched with near disbelief as Thanasis settled the boys on either side of him on the arms of his chair. Both of them were giggling and excited. Within a few weeks of leaving the *paidópoli*, Nikos' hair had grown and corkscrew curls had begun to emerge. The two little boys had never looked more like brothers than at this moment.

Thanasis began to read to them. Filled with something close to joy, Themis left the room and watched through a crack in the door.

Chapter Twenty-One

T HE FOLLOWING YEAR, Nikos began school and they all walked together, there and back each day. It was the same institution that all the Koralis children had attended, but over the years it had become even scruffier than before.

On the way home, each morning Themis took a route through Fokionos Negri so that she could go to the *laikí agorá*, the vegetable market where produce was sold by the farmers coming in from the countryside. One day, she saw a familiar figure: Giorgos Stavridis. With the arrival of Nikos, he had slipped to the back of her mind but now that she saw him again, she recalled the warmth of their last meeting more than a year before.

Giorgos was sitting at a table outside the same café where they had drunk coffee together that time and, suddenly feeling bold, she approached him.

Angelos trotted behind.

'Themis!' Giorgos cried out with pleasure and surprise. 'And little Angelos! H–h–how he's grown!'

'Can we sit for a moment?' asked Themis.

'Of course, of c–c–course! And what can I get you? I know what the young man would like!'

'But it's . . .'

Themis was about to say that it was too early for ice cream, but Giorgos had already ordered. The coffee was on its way too.

'So h–h–how are you?' asked Giorgos, leaning forward. 'Themis, tell me h–h–how you are.'

Themis felt slightly uncomfortable beneath the intensity of his gaze. The way he asked was not in the style of someone simply passing the time of day.

'I . . . we . . . we are all well, thank you,' she answered. 'And how are you? It's been so long.'

Giorgos did not hide his pleasure at seeing her.

'I have been h–h–hoping to see you. Ever s–s–since that last time. I h–h–hoped I would see you again.'

Themis was flustered and felt the need to make an excuse.

'We haven't been taking many walks,' she said. 'And even now, we're just walking through on our way home from school.'

'But your little f–f–fellow is too young for school, isn't he?'

Themis had not intended to introduce the subject of Nikos, but now she would have to. In any case, she found herself questioning the idea of keeping any information back. The kindly Giorgos seemed genuinely interested in the answers to his questions.

She sent Angelos off to pat the stone dog and from where they were sitting she could keep an eye on him as he ran about with another small boy. Themis told Giorgos of the latest development in her life, but followed the same story that both Nikos and Angelos would be told: that Nikos had been taken from her some time before his younger brother had been born. Themis could see that Giorgos made no judgement of her.

As soon as the ice cream was served, she called Angelos back to the table and told him to eat it as fast as he could. She had realised that she was going to be late home. She must get to the market, go back to the apartment, do some chores and return to collect Nikos from school. The time had flown.

'Themis,' said Giorgos with a hint of urgency in his voice, 'I r-r-really must meet you again.'

The timid child had grown into a shy man and Themis could see that it had cost him a lot to express this. She realised that she wanted to see him again too, and this time she gave him her address.

'Goodbye, Giorgos,' she said, hastily putting on her coat. 'Thank you again for the coffee. And for the ice cream, of course.'

They shook hands rather formally and, as everyone did, Giorgos patted Angelos on the head. Nobody could resist the urge to touch his profuse and bouncy curls.

A week went by before a handwritten note addressed to Themis appeared in the Koralis pigeon-hole. It was from Giorgos suggesting that they go to the cinema. His proposal was a film starring a newly popular actress, Aliki Vougiouklaki. There was an early-evening showing, which meant that they would have time for a coffee afterwards.

For many months Themis had done little but play with the boys and do domestic chores, so she accepted with alacrity.

When the day arrived she got ready with great excitement, admitting to herself that it was more than just the change of routine that she was looking forward to. She brushed her hair carefully and Kyría Koralis came into her room with an old powder compact and some rouge of Margarita's that she had kept. Very cautiously, Themis applied it to her cheeks before leaving to meet Giorgos.

★

The film lived up to both their expectations. The light-hearted plot and the freshness of the delightful, bubbly actress, who was already the talk of the town, took Themis' mind away from everything but the present. When they parted company that evening, they agreed that it would be lovely to meet again soon.

A few months went by and they met several times, often going to the cinema or theatre. They enjoyed each other's company but never allowed conversation to reach too far beneath the surface. One day, Giorgos suggested that they meet for dinner in a central Athens restaurant. It was April, and the excuse he used was that it was his Saint's Day.

Themis had no hesitation in accepting but as soon as she got home, she fretted.

'*Yiayiá*, I have nothing to wear!' she said. She realised that she wanted something special.

The shops were beginning to fill with summer dresses and, the following day, with some drachmas pressed into her hand by her grandmother, Themis went to a local shop and bought a sapphire-blue dress. The colour of the fabric with the reddish hue of her hair was a striking combination. The sales assistant assured her it suited her, but she was not the only one that thought so.

When Giorgos saw Themis arrive for dinner a few days later, he almost gasped at the sight of her. On the other occasions when he had seen her, including several when she had not even been aware of it, she had been dressed in worn, dowdy clothes that might even have been her grandmother's.

The blue dress transformed her but it was not just what she was wearing that captivated him. It was the smile she gave him as she approached.

Once the greetings were over and they had chosen what they were going to eat, Themis accepted the offer of a glass of wine. She hoped it would calm her nerves.

It was the first time that they had several hours to talk face to face and Themis had decided that she had to trust this man and tell him more about her past few years.

She did not conceal from Giorgos that she had fought in the communist army and was open about her period of imprisonment. She even found herself explaining her beliefs, proud of what she had done for her cause. If this man disapproved then their friendship would have no future in any case.

She was pleased that he listened with rapt interest to everything she told him and accepted without comment that Themis was bringing her two boys up alone.

The waiter came and went and, each time he approached, Themis was careful to lower her voice. There was still a great deal of stigma attached to 'people like her' (as Thanasis so often pointed out). Her record was held somewhere on file, just as Anna Kouzelis' had been.

'There m-m-might be things in my past that you won't like, Themis,' said Giorgos, just after the waiter had cleared their plates.

Themis was aware that Giorgos' family had not supported the left (how else would they all be civil servants?) and leaned forwards. It was her turn to listen now.

'I was c-c-conscripted into the government army,' he said, hesitantly. 'And I fought on Grammos.'

It was hard to imagine Giorgos, this mild, gentle person, fighting in the vicious final battle. Thousands of leftists had died in the course of it, among them her own brother Panos.

There was a moment's pause.

'We all have a past,' Themis said eventually, for want of something else to say. 'And it can't be changed.'

Themis' hand lay on the table and Giorgos reached out to cover it with his own.

'It's true,' he said. 'We can't change history but we can try to move f-f-forward.'

'That's easier for some people than others,' said Themis, avoiding Giorgos' gaze. 'I feel I lost so much.'

'Yes!' he said enthusiastically. 'But look what you g-g-gained!'

She knew immediately what he meant. Life without the two boys would be unimaginable now. Without the events of these past years they would not even be sitting in this restaurant, at this moment, with the cheerful chatter around them, the clatter of crockery, the chink of glasses. Nothing would be as this.

Giorgos, perhaps never bolder than at this moment, grasped Themis' hand so tightly that she almost winced.

With resolution, his stammer momentarily gone, he spoke even more earnestly than usual.

'Themis, I must say something to you. It cannot wait . . . *I* cannot wait.'

Giorgos hesitated for a fraction of a second before continuing with ever greater haste, his words spilling out more fluently than Themis could ever have imagined.

'I want you to be my wife,' he said. 'Will you be my wife? Will you m-m-marry me?'

Themis was dumbfounded. The proposal was so unexpected that she could not for a moment even speak. She had already admitted to herself that she liked this man a great deal, but she had not dared to hope for reciprocal feelings on his side. Why would a man from such a family wish to connect himself so publicly with someone like her? Marriage had seemed an unlikely prospect, but to such a kind man, impossible.

As soon as she had regained her composure, she said the first thing that came into her mind.

'But you haven't even met Nikos!'

As soon as she said it, she realised that this was a minor obstacle and immediately qualified her words.

'But we can meet you after school tomorrow. Or whenever is convenient for you.'

Giorgos smiled. Themis had acknowledged, without even being conscious of it, that she had accepted the proposal.

As they left the restaurant, Themis took Giorgos' arm. It felt nice to lean on someone, albeit subtly, and beneath her fingers she was aware of the fine wool fabric of his suit.

A few days later, when Giorgos could arrange to have some hours off work, Themis walked through Fokionos Negri with Nikos on their route back from school. Without telling her why, she had asked Kyría Koralis if she could leave Angelos with her. The old lady had her suspicions but said nothing.

Themis and Nikos stopped at what they already called their 'usual' café. Giorgos was waiting for them.

Nikos was sullen. He did not like a departure from the usual routine of walking straight home for lunch and would not grant Giorgos even a cursory greeting.

'I'm so sorry,' Themis mimed to Giorgos, embarrassed by the child's surly behaviour.

'D-d-don't worry . . .' said Giorgos, before turning to the child. 'N-N-Nikos, d-d-do you like numbers or letters best?'

'Numbers,' answered the child sulkily.

'That's good,' he said. 'S-s-so do I.'

Once they had ordered something to drink, Giorgos produced

from his pocket a pack of playing cards and laid a few out on the table. Nikos began to take more interest.

'Now p-p-pick a card,' said Giorgos, fanning out a dozen of them, face down.

Nikos slid one out and studied it before returning it to Giorgos as instructed.

'Remember that c-c-card, won't you?'

Nikos nodded.

The card was duly replaced in the main body of the pack and Giorgos splayed them all out again, this time face up.

'C-c-can you see it?'

Nikos shook his head, glancing up at Themis.

'I wonder where it is,' she responded, joining in with the conspiracy.

Nikos shrugged.

'Take a look in my p-p-pocket.'

Nikos leaned towards Giorgos and there in his breast pocket he spotted the Jack of Diamonds. Giorgos pulled it out.

'That's my card!' said Nikos, totally bemused.

Giorgos performed several more tricks after that, impressing Themis as much as the child. She was immensely touched, knowing that he must have brought the cards specially to entertain the boy. He had, of course, brought them to woo her too.

Nikos was enthralled. This man in a smart suit, whom he had never met before, was a magician and he was performing just for him, every sleight of hand more extraordinary than the one before.

Within half an hour, the child was jumping up and down with excitement, squealing with delight each time there was a 'reveal'.

'More! More!' he cried, when Giorgos paused to drink his coffee.

'I c-c-can do one more,' he said. 'But we must ask your mother first.'

'Just one more,' said Themis, smiling. 'But after that, we must go home.'

'Why?' he protested.

'Because Angelos will be waiting for us, *agápi mou.*'

Giorgos performed a final trick and Nikos was allowed to keep the Queen of Hearts. She had been the key card.

'You l-l-look after her,' said Giorgos. 'And let me have her b-b-back the next time we meet.'

Themis looked across at Giorgos and realised he was smiling at her.

When they got home, Nikos reported with excitement what had happened and showed Kyría Koralis the card. Then, as they often did, the four of them sat round the radio and listened to a story from 'Aunt Lena'. As always, the popular broadcaster read with a blend of magic and innocence and lulled the children to sleepiness, one boy wrapped in the embrace of his great-grandmother, the other curled up against Themis. It was the most peaceful hour of the day.

That evening, when the boys had gone to bed, Themis told her grandmother that she was going to get married.

'*Mátia mou*, this is wonderful news. To that lovely man Giorgos? I am so happy for you,' she said, her eyes brimming with tears.

'Thank you, *Yiayiá*,' replied Themis. 'He will make such a good father to these boys. He was so kind with Nikos today . . .'

'I gathered,' smiled the old lady. 'He talked of nothing but Kýrios Stavridis today.'

There was a small pause before Kyría Koralis added: 'Perhaps one day you'll have a child together?'

'Perhaps,' said Themis. 'At this moment it seems a miracle to have found someone to love the ones I have.'

They had not heard Thanasis come in. He was usually home

before the boys went to bed but tonight an excess of paperwork had kept him there late.

'Your sister is getting married!' Kyría Koralis blurted out with excitement, before Themis had the chance to restrain her. 'To a very nice man, I must tell you!'

Thanasis, for so long starved of such love and deprived even of its shadow, had to congratulate his sister. As he did so, his true thoughts and fears came spilling out.

'The boys . . .' he said, with undisguised sorrow. 'Will I lose the boys?'

Themis suddenly felt unutterable sadness for her brother, a man who was unlikely ever to have children of his own.

'Of course you won't lose them,' she reassured him. 'I don't even want to move from here . . .'

'I will miss them if you do,' he said almost pleadingly.

Themis was surprised that her brother articulated such a thought. It was so unlike him to express any emotion other than anger, though even that was less frequent these days. As she lay awake that night contemplating the future, she realised that Angelos and Nikos accepted their uncle in a way that no one else did. Only on first sight had they reacted to his scars and wounds, but now to them he was simply Uncle Thanasis. Her brother's political views annoyed her as much as ever, but his affection for the children had done much to reconcile her to him.

Themis was adamant that she and the boys should stay in the square. She did not want to leave her grandmother and Thanasis. A solution was easily found. An apartment on the floor below, next to Kyría Papadimitriou, had been empty for several years. The owner had five adult children and none of them wanted it. The boys could each have his own room there.

Giorgos needed no persuading that this should be their home.

His sole desire was to please the woman he loved. With minimum redecoration, they made it their own and in no time the apartment on the second floor was almost indistinguishable from the one on the third, with similar solid, dark furniture, lace table-coverings and traditional rugs. Kyría Koralis insisted that they take the big mahogany table as she and Thanasis would not really need anything so large, now that there were just the two of them. Everything was made ready so that they would be able to move in as soon as they were married.

There was no reason to delay the wedding, apart from a few more introductions to members of Giorgos' family: firstly his widowed father and then his sisters. Themis knew that they did not approve of their brother marrying someone who already had children, but Giorgos dismissed their questions about the boys' father, which was easy, given how little he knew himself.

'Themis is a widow,' he told them. 'And once we are married they will become my children.'

Within a month of Giorgos' proposal, the date for the marriage was set. As she prepared for it, she felt very lucky that she had met such a man and that her sons would have a father to bring them up – not just any man, but a kind and loving one. The boys adored him and she could see that he would be the perfect father. Of course, she loved Giorgos too – and appreciated the affection and security that he offered to them all.

It was October and a fine, sunny morning when they set off to the nearby church. Themis wore a teal-blue silk dress with three-quarter-length sleeves and a crown of white roses in her hair. Giorgos had a dark suit. The boys, both with unruly mops of dark curls now, wore silver-grey suits and white shirts. Nikos refused to wear the jacket except when the photographs were being taken.

Kyría Koralis told everyone that it was the happiest day of her life and wore a turquoise dress to celebrate it. She remembered the day of her only son's wedding and how he had come to her on the morning and sobbed in her arms. He knew that he was doing the wrong thing. He did not love Eleftheria. It was too late to stop the wedding and she assured him that in time he would love her and that such financial security was not to be thrown away. As she looked at her granddaughter now, glowing with happiness, and the smart groom who stood next to her, she knew that this was a very different kind of couple.

Thanasis was the *koumbáros*, the best man, a gesture that touched Themis very deeply, and her brother carried out his duties with immense diligence and pride. Giorgos' father, Andreas, was a little stiff at first, but enjoyed talking to Thanasis and eventually relaxed, as did his Uncle Spiros. Both his sisters and their families came (the children were told, under no circumstances, to stare at Thanasis) and a few of his colleagues from the tax office. They also invited Kyría Papadimitriou and she attended with her sister. There was no reply to the invitation sent to Margarita, and Themis assumed it had never reached her. After the formalities were done with, they walked to a taverna in Fokionos Negri. One of Giorgos' brothers-in-law was from Crete and played the lyra, so at midnight there was singing and other people in the taverna joined in with some dancing.

Immediately after the wedding, the four of them moved into their new apartment. The balcony was directly below Kyría Koralis' so they even knew when she tended her plants, as the water dripped down on to theirs. They would call up to tease her and then the conversation would continue. The boys still had free rein to go in and out of their former home to play with Uncle Thanasis and spent plenty of time running up and down the stairs.

Giorgos began the process of officially adopting the boys as his own. His father had been in the civil service so he was able to expedite this through former colleagues and he asked Themis no further questions about the father, regarding his ignorance as a benefit.

Once paperwork was in order, then anything could become fact, and history could be rewritten. In some situations, Themis would have disapproved of this, but where her sons were concerned, she was grateful for it.

On one of their first evenings together in the new home, when the boys were both asleep, Themis and Giorgos were eating at the old table. Conversation turned to the past in a way that they had avoided before.

Giorgos admitted that he had hated fighting next to men who boasted of their former collaboration with the Germans.

'We were r-r-resting one night after a long march and this old veteran showed me something that made me retch. On the inside of his uniform he had p-p-pinned a Nazi badge. He said he had traded it with a German officer for some *tsípouro* towards the end of the occupation. He was p-p-proud of it, Themis, but I tell you, the s-s-sight of that swastika so close up, and on a man I was fighting with, was a shock. But what c-c-could I do?'

'We all have things in the past that make us ashamed,' Themis reassured him, putting her hand on his. 'I try not to think of the first time I killed . . . how young he was . . . whether I could have avoided it . . .'

Giorgos could hear the catch in his wife's throat. It was not the last time they would quietly share such things.

Chapter Twenty-Two

O<small>N THE EVENING</small> of their first wedding anniversary, Giorgos pushed a small package across the table towards Themis. He watched as she released the red satin bow, and removed the paper and carefully opened the jeweller's box. It was a watch, the first she had ever owned, and Giorgos wound it for her and then put it on her wrist.

Giorgos told Themis that at the moment when he spotted her after so many years in Fokionos Negri he had felt that time stood still.

'I was certain even then that I was meant to marry you and look after you.'

Themis kissed him.

'Thank you,' she said. 'It's absolutely beautiful.'

This man was her *plátanos*, her plane tree, and she felt lucky to have such protection and shade. Sometimes when she looked at the wedding photograph that stood on the dresser, it seemed that a miracle had happened.

She had something she wanted to tell him too. It was the news that she was expecting their first child.

'That's the best gift you could ever give me,' said Giorgos, taking Themis into his arms.

Anna was born in the summer of 1957 just as the school term was ending. Angelos had completed his first year and was a bright and eager pupil. Nikos, on the other hand, was being very rebellious and refusing to do his homework.

The boys were growing more physically alike than ever and were often mistaken for twins. In ways other than physical similarity, the differences between them became ever more exaggerated.

The teachers knew that Nikos was capable of doing everything he was asked, but he chose not to. He preferred to sit and draw. When all the other children were writing or doing science or mathematics, he was covering the pages of his textbooks with doodles. He was equally unco-operative with his classmates and deliberately picked fights with them. If Angelos saw a scrap going on in the school-yard, he knew that his brother would be at the centre of it.

As time went on, far from growing out of it, Nikos became more disobedient. By the time he was twelve, Themis was regularly being called in to see his teacher.

Kyría Koralis often came downstairs to help out with the children and was there one day when Themis came back from such a meeting with Nikos' teacher.

'He's a rebel,' she said. 'I don't think we'll ever change that.'

'You say that proudly,' observed Kyría Koralis. 'But a child needs to fit in . . .'

'Perhaps that's the problem, *Yiayiá*,' she responded. 'He doesn't *want* to fit in. He spent so much time when he was very small being disciplined and he is reacting against it now.'

'So you blame the *paidópoli*?'

'He was forced into a uniform when he was tiny.'

'And that's why he still hates doing what he is told now?'

'He detests anything regimented.'

Thanasis was in the apartment too, setting up a game of soldiers with the boys in their room. He overheard the conversation, appeared at the door and limped over to sit down with them.

'You need to persevere with him,' he whispered. 'Otherwise he'll end up like Panos or his father, whoever he was.'

'Thanasis! Don't say that! For pity's sake! *Don't* say that!' Themis said, terrified that the boy would hear.

Kyría Koralis, calm as ever, scolded her grandson.

'Thanasis, Giorgos is the boys' father now, so please don't refer to those things,' she continued.

'*Those things*'. This was how Kyría Koralis always referred to long swathes of the past: the years of her daughter-in-law's decline, the departure of her son, the occupation, the civil war, the loss of Panos, Themis' imprisonment. All of them were '*those things*' and she did not like them brought into conversation.

'Don't worry, *Yiayiá*,' said Thanasis, patting his grandmother on the arm. 'It's a secret between us three and it's in no one's interest that anyone should know more than he needs. It was just my private thought that there might be a bad streak in him. From his father.'

'Thanasis!'

Themis so rarely raised her voice, but Thanasis still had the ability to provoke her.

'*Agápi mou*,' urged Kyría Koralis. 'You'll wake the little ones!'

Three-year-old Anna and a newborn, Andreas, were sleeping in the next room.

★

Themis understood that with his body progressively weakened and wasted, her brother sometimes felt the need to exert his power with words. It was the only effective faculty he still possessed, but he could use it viciously. She knew he was speaking the truth when he admitted that it was 'in no one's interest' for anyone to know of her past. The stigma would affect his reputation too.

Themis could not help wondering if Thanasis was right about Nikos having a wayward streak, but she thought it probably came from his mother. In some ways his father was the conformist. It was Aliki who had had a streak of audacity that had led her almost fearlessly to execution and a stubbornness that stopped her signing the *dílosi*.

'Perhaps it was his time in the *paidópoli*,' Kyría Koralis said firmly. 'Disciplining a very young child, putting them to sleep fifty in a room, without the love of a mother . . .'

'Well, there's no telling what really lies behind his behaviour,' said Themis.

'And you will probably never know,' the old lady answered. 'Perhaps he's just jealous of his new brother?'

'I don't know. But what matters now is to get him through school.'

Themis and Giorgos continued to do their best with Nikos. He behaved well at home, played happily with Angelos and even got on the floor to entertain his little sister, pretending to be a sleeping lion that would unpredictably roar and send her shrieking into a corner. He was still enthralled by Giorgos' card tricks and began to learn how to do some simple ones himself. It created a bond between father and son. For hours each day, he practised the sharp moves that were invisible to the average eye.

One day Giorgos struggled up the stairs with a new record player. Themis had her doubts about this cumbersome new piece

371

of 'furniture', as she described it, but when he brought in a dozen or more long-playing records the following day, her attitude changed. Along with some light music and songs, he had bought 'Epitáfios' set to music by Mikis Theodorakis. Nana Mouskouri was singing and Themis could hardly wait to listen.

'Wasn't he sent into exile?' said Nikos, who knew nothing of the composer except for this. Themis said nothing. She knew that Nikos had no idea what this really meant. He just liked the word.

Themis often thought of Makronisos. She had not seen Theodorakis when she was there but wondered if Tasos Makris had ever crossed paths with him. Perhaps he had even been his torturer. Each time she thought of the boys' father her mood darkened. Recollections of tender moments when they had slept under the stars had long since evaporated. What lived in her mind was the image of the expressionless eyes that had stared into hers at that last meeting.

The obsessive repetition required for learning card tricks occupied Nikos' restless energy and seemed to calm him. Whenever he was ready to perform a new one for the first time, he went upstairs and showed Thanasis. His uncle always expressed genuine appreciation of the boy's skills.

The rapport that existed between the two of them was a mystery to everyone. Themis knew already that things could defy logic and comprehension, but the friendship between the son of a communist and a man whose life had been devoted to persecuting the left reaffirmed it. It was always Nikos who cut up Thanasis' food for him, who picked up his stick if he dropped it or went to buy his newspaper if he had forgotten it.

It was undeniable that they shared one particular quality: anger. Perhaps they recognised it in each other.

★

As he moved into teenage years Nikos became increasingly argu-
mentative at school. When he was still fifteen, Nikos and his
headmaster said a polite farewell. The pleasure was mutual, especially after the discovery that Nikos' parting gift to the school was
a series of life-sized caricatures of the teachers he disliked most
on the walls of the urinal.

For his sixteenth birthday, which was not many days later, there
was a family dinner. Kyría Koralis and Thanasis both came down
to join them at the old dented table.

When she finally sat down to eat, Themis cast a glance around
at her family. They seemed a homogenous enough entity. No
one knew of the complexity beneath and there were enough
likenesses to dispel any thoughts that father and mother were not
the same for each child. Nikos, who had grown even more
handsome with adolescence, was sitting at the head of the table
and Uncle Thanasis was next to him as usual. Angelos still looked
like Nikos but was much thicker-set and sat between Anna, who
was arrestingly pretty with fair hair and full lips, and Andreas,
who had the biggest brown eyes of them all. Kyría Koralis, who
was ninety-three, sat with the youngest member of the family in
her lap. Spiros had been born a few weeks earlier. The old lady
had made Nikos' favourite apple cake but Themis had prepared
all the rest.

In spite of their different interests and school results, Nikos and
Angelos got on well and joshed with each other throughout the
dinner. Themis marvelled that the evening was noisy but harmo-
nious, a combination that would have been impossible at this table
when she was sixteen.

Nikos himself did not seem very ambitious and Themis and Giorgos
worried about what he was going to do now that he had left

school. He spent most of the time in his room, drawing, and he told his parents that he wanted to be an artist.

'That's not a proper job,' Giorgos muttered to Themis.

'Let's at least give him some time,' she said.

Not long after, as if to accentuate the contrast between them, Angelos announced his desire to go to university. The way he studied reminded Themis of herself when she and Fotini had spent every afternoon together diligently writing their essays after school. Everyone said that Angelos had his father's brains, which both amused and annoyed her.

Giorgos had been promoted and was running a department in the central tax office, his quiet brilliance with figures being more than enough to outweigh his social awkwardness. The children were well fed and clothed and the family lacked for nothing.

In the fifteen years since her release, Themis had tried to take less interest in what went on in parliament. She made sure that she was never in the centre of the city when there was a demonstration, only occasionally read a newspaper and avoided the news on the radio. By contrast, she made a point of seeing every film featuring Aliki Vougiouklaki as soon as it came out, leaving the little ones with her grandmother and going to the nearby cinema. She was greatly enamoured of the exuberant, independent character of the actress, and then of course there was her name, an appealing echo of her old friend's.

Giorgos maintained a similarly neutral position. He had not had great political conviction even as a younger man (his time on the 'front' had only come about because of conscription) and, once his father had died, he was no longer obliged to murmur anti-communist views to please him.

If a political theme crept into the conversation at mealtimes, Themis skilfully diverted it towards a neutral subject. She did this with such cunning that no one even noticed. Memories of the fury that so often raged round the table all those years before easily returned. It was like standing in the path of a galloping horse and she had to avert the blows of its hooves, at any cost. She could not risk a repetition of the fighting that used to take place with the previous generation: the bang of a fist, the splintering of a glass overzealously put down, raised voices. Such gestures had translated into real violence, brother against brother, which had destroyed not just her immediate family but the whole country.

Regardless of Themis' fears and desires, politics were still a focus of constant debate in the country and there had been five elections in less than a decade. She had been excited when women were allowed to go to the polls back in 1956, but the frequency of elections since then was an indication of instability. Going to vote had become a routine that caused her anxiety rather than pleasure, and even now it seemed that the system did not offer either fairness or the results that she had hoped for.

The children, from Nikos down to little Spiros, had no notion that their mother cared for anything other than their wellbeing. This was mostly manifested in her desire to feed them and keep them looking neat and tidy for school. At different times, they had all been teased for having such highly polished shoes. None of them questioned if she had ever harboured any other ambitions or had any other role in life. These days she cared for the nonagenarian Kyría Koralis too and also cooked for Thanasis. The *gemistá* and *spanakórizo* now came from Themis' kitchen.

In the eyes of all their children, Themis and Giorgos were kind parents. They all had friends whose fathers often used a strap to beat them, or mothers who constantly nagged and scolded, and were secretly proud that this never happened in their own family. None of the three younger ones had the distinctive curly hair of the eldest two and they imagined that the now-balding Giorgos may have had such curls when he was a child. Little Anna looked exactly like Margarita and it was with feelings of *charmolýpi* that Themis watched Andreas grow up to look increasingly like Panos. Spiros was a carbon copy of Giorgos.

It was the spring of 1967, and yet more parliamentary elections were due in May. As ever, Themis was hoping to keep politics away from the dinner table, but was secretly excited when she heard that a more radically left-wing party might get into power. Conversation was drifting towards a discussion about the new party and Nikos and Angelos were beginning to bicker. Nikos was eighteen now and much more in favour of the left than Angelos. When Nikos mentioned the Nazis, stating that he hated all Germans and that their country owed Greece a huge debt, Themis suddenly thought it was time to remind them that their aunt had lived there for many years now. She wanted them to understand that they should not be prejudiced against every inhabitant of any country.

'Margarita? Who is she?' asked Andreas, intrigued by this new name.

Themis rummaged for an old photograph of herself and her three siblings to show them all. Even Angelos and Nikos only had a vague idea about her childhood, and when she told them that Panos had 'died during the war' they all assumed she meant during the occupation and did not ask any more questions. The longest conversation was about their Uncle Thanasis. They could not believe that the startlingly handsome teenager in the picture was him, and were shocked by the story of what had happened, having always assumed that his disfigurement was caused by an accident. They had heard people talking of the December 1944 events but had not realised how directly they had affected their family. There was a wedding photograph of Themis' parents too, and she took the chance to explain that her mother had died many years before and that her father had gone to live in America, since when they had lost touch.

After dinner, Themis and Giorgos went out to sit on the balcony. It was a warm April evening just before Holy Week and the trees were all coming into leaf. They could both feel the sweetness in the air. Washing took less time to dry and Themis had not needed her winter coat that day. The older boys went out and the three younger children were upstairs with their uncle. He had a television now and as long as they had finished their homework, she did not object to them watching a film with him.

The two of them sat quietly, listening to the occasional bursts of music and laughter from the floor above. They both felt that many things in their lives had resolved and exchanged a wordless look of contentment.

By the following morning, everything had changed.

Giorgos always listened to a transistor radio while he was shaving and knew immediately that something was wrong that day. Instead of music, there were continual announcements. Just after midnight, when most of the city was sleeping, a group of army colonels had staged a coup.

They were all shocked. There had been no warning signs of such a dramatic event. In a bloodless action, Greece had been taken over by the army and lines of communication with the rest of the world had been cut.

For most of the day all seven sat anxiously by the radio, waiting for the breaks in the relentless martial music when more announcements were made. Everything had been perpetrated with ruthless efficiency, and they listened to reports of how events had unfolded. Tanks had cordoned off the palace and government ministries, and a new prime minister had been sworn in. Roads were blocked so there was no point in going out. Schools and universities were closed and money could not be withdrawn from the banks.

'And there were elections coming next month,' protested Nikos, who was still too young to vote, but knew which party he wanted to govern. 'That's why they've done this,' he continued furiously. 'They were worried that the left was going to get in.'

'What about the King?' asked Andreas. 'Won't he save us?'

'They say he is at Tatoi, *mátia mou*,' replied Giorgos gently. 'I am sure he will help sort things out.'

King Constantine and his family, including his mother, Queen Frederika, were said to be at their country retreat outside Athens. The monarchy played a largely symbolic role, but many wanted to get rid of this anachronistic institution.

Themis raised her eyebrows and gave her husband a disapproving look.

'He's probably at the centre of it,' she muttered.

'Themis!' scolded her husband. 'You d–d–don't know that.'

Their views on the monarchy were very different. Themis still detested the 'German woman' and suspected that her family would be very happy to support a military dictatorship. Certainly, the King appeared to be supporting the colonels. Or at least he was not voicing any dissent.

'It doesn't matter what you say,' said Themis to her husband. 'Queen Frederika—'

'Themis! It d–d–doesn't do us any good.'

After a few days, Themis gathered the courage to go out on the street again to see what was in the shops. She reached the bakery she had patronised for decades and was shocked to see the notice on the shop door: '*Closed until further notice.*'

Themis remembered how Kyría Sotiriou had muttered her condolences for Panos that day after her return from Trikeri, and the look of pity and sadness she had given her as she dropped her few drachmas of change on to the glass dish. She realised even then that the baker's wife would not have spoken with such depth of sympathy unless she was on the left.

A casual comment a few years before had left Themis in no further doubt that the baker and his wife had both voted for the centre left party (as she had herself), and she had also heard a rumour that the wife's brother had died on Makronisos.

It was enough to put them both under suspicion and she assumed they had now been detained by the new regime.

During the following days, new government instructions went out prohibiting long hair for boys and short skirts for girls. Andreas was furious to be taken for a haircut and even crosser when Sunday church attendance was made compulsory for children.

Closer to home, some of the teachers from the children's school were detained and there was no attempt to conceal the reason. The justification for their arrest was openly publicised: they were 'subversives who must be prevented from contaminating juvenile minds', or so read a notice outside the school.

Around four in the morning, a few days after the children had returned to school, they heard a hammering on the door. It came from the floor below but was so loud it woke them all up.

Against Themis' will, Giorgos opened their door by a few millimetres. He heard the voice of their neighbour, a lawyer, and the higher-pitched tone of his wife. It was not possible to make out what she was saying but she was pleading.

'They're arresting the l-l-lawyer!' said Giorgos, shutting the door carefully.

Themis walked quickly towards the living room and slipped out on to the balcony so that she could watch what was happening. A police van was parked down in the square and she could see that their neighbour was not the only one being escorted away. An elderly couple from opposite were also being bundled into the vehicle, along with two other people from another apartment building whom she did not recognise. From behind the lemon trees they could watch in safety. Themis' heart was beating hard. With her records somewhere out there, she knew she could easily be with them and, from now on, every footstep on the stairway, and each knock on the door would instil great trepidation.

The King soon publicly endorsed the coup, declaring in his statement that previously democratic institutions had been undermined and that the interests of the people had suffered. He accepted that the new government was seeking a return to democracy.

The King's statement horrified Themis. She learnt that so many had been arrested that they were being held in football stadia. There was nowhere else large enough to accommodate them all. Some had already been sent back to the prison islands.

'What did I tell you? They're traitors! The monarchy is *not* on the side of the people. They've sided with the army. With a dictatorship. And all because they are afraid of true democracy, of the possibility of a leftist government. And you know why that is?'

'P-p-please, Themis,' Giorgos appealed. He hated to see his wife stirred to such anger.

She could not contain herself and left the apartment to cool down. In the hallway she bumped into Thanasis, but brushed past without speaking to him. 'Themis!' she heard him call out, as the outer door shut behind her. She knew what his views would be and was not in the mood to hear them. She needed to feel the air on her face.

The benches in the square were all occupied. Some boys were kicking a ball around and a woman was walking her dog. Everything looked so peaceful but this was far from the reality.

For the sake of her family, she must stay calm. She walked to a bakery she had never been to before and bought a loaf for their dinner. There were only two days to go before Good Friday and they were also selling *tsouréki*, the sweet Easter bread. She bought some of that too and broke a piece off as she left the shop. The sweetness briefly cheered her.

On her way home, she passed the church of Agios Andreas. It was packed with people and the music of the priest's voice drifted out into the street. Even Themis, who had not entered a church for some years, paused to enjoy a moment of calm.

The next sound she heard was very different from the gentle liturgical chanting. As she opened the apartment door she heard a strident male voice. It was coming from the radio and was describing the country as a 'sick person' strapped to an operating table.

'If the patient were not fastened securely, the government could not be sure that it could cure the disease.'

She saw Giorgos and Angelos sitting close to the radio and Themis stood to listen, each phrase shocking her progressively more.

'The aims of the new Government are the social training of the country . . . Communism is in conflict with our Helleno-Christian civilisation and those we deem to be dangerous communists will be tried by security committees . . . Five thousand have been arrested.'

'Can we turn that *off*,' she said, her voice trembling. 'I don't want to hear it.'

'That was the leader of the coup, Colonel Papadopoulos,' said Giorgos quietly. Themis felt as though ice-cold water was running through her veins. The persecution of the left was happening all over again. Politicians were being put in prison and even the former Prime Minister, Georgios Papandreou, was being held in a military hospital.

Giorgos tried to say something reassuring, but Themis did not respond. She crossed the room, put the bread on the kitchen table and began to make the dinner. For the first time in more than a decade she felt afraid.

An hour or so later, she took a dish to the upstairs apartment for her grandmother and Thanasis, but did not want to have any discussion with her brother on the rights and wrongs of the military coup. For her it was entirely unjustified.

During the Easter celebrations that happened in the following days, the King attended the midnight ceremony along with military leaders. Themis did not go to church but the three younger children accompanied Giorgos, Thanasis and their great-grandmother. In those days she could not avoid the often-repeated words: 'Christ is risen' and 'Hellas is risen'. The State and the Church seemed to have become as one. Themis feigned a headache and lay on her bed in a shuttered room until her family returned.

The new regime constantly issued edicts and the words 'We decide and we order' preceded each one of them. The colonels took the theme of resurrection for themselves. 'Hellas is reborn!' came the constant refrain from the radio.

Themis was shaken to the core by the speed with which the coup had happened. The forthcoming elections had finally promised the social justice that she fought for nearly two decades before. Now, overnight, freedom to express political views had been swept aside and opposition crushed.

In past days, she had not been able to bring herself to pick up a newspaper. Nikos also found the right-wing press unbearable.

'Look!' he moaned. 'Look at it!'

'Try not to be so angry, Nikos,' said his father. 'We have to get our news somehow.'

'But look at it! Look at that grinning photo of Papadopoulos!

There's obviously something wrong with this newspaper. There's not even a hint of criticism of what's going on.'

Themis was laying the table and glanced down at the front page. She could see that Nikos was right, but at the same time wanted to avoid a dispute developing between father and son.

The following day the paper did not even appear.

'I was right,' announced Nikos, with a note of triumph. 'It was being censored!'

The publisher had shut it down in protest.

'Brave woman,' said Themis.

'At least someone is resisting,' said Nikos. 'There's been enough apathy. I hope there'll be more actions like these.'

Themis felt a flutter of anxiety in the pit of her stomach.

Political parties were soon dissolved, freedom of the press was suspended and several foreign journalists were expelled. The arrest of Andreas Papandreou, son of the former Prime Minister, caused a huge outcry too, and soon rumours of extreme torture of dissidents were circulating.

'Do you think there could be war?' Anna asked her mother.

'No, darling. I'm sure there won't be,' Themis said without meaning it.

Without *Kathimerini*, they now had to depend on other newspapers for their news. One of them reported that Brigadier Pattakos, one of the leading figures of the Junta, had visited the island of Yiaros where over six thousand prisoners were being held. He had announced that many of them would soon be released.

I'll believe that when it happens, thought Themis. And how will anyone know if it does? They tell such lies, these people.

A few days later a list of more than two thousand detainees was published that included trade unionists, doctors, journalists and artists.

'Even Ritsos!' she exclaimed. 'A gentle poet!'

'Well, the right doesn't think he's so gentle,' Nikos reminded her. 'He's dangerous enough with his pen, and his work has been getting banned for decades.'

'That's true, *agápi mou*,' said Themis. 'But it's not a reason to lock him up.'

In the second week of May, Andreas Papandreou was formally charged with conspiring to commit acts of treason. Along with his father, he was accused of plotting to overthrow the monarchy.

Only a few weeks had passed since the coup but day-to-day life had already resumed a strange normality. It was too soon for Themis' liking, and she was agitated that there had scarcely been any resistance. At the same time, she was grateful that she could continue to shop and cook for her family and that the children were back at school.

'What's happened to me?' she asked herself one morning, as she did up her blouse in front of the mirror. She was wearing an old dress to do the housework and noticed her thickening waist and greying curls. 'Have I become complacent?'

She was disappointed with herself but suddenly realised that there was still passion within her.

'If I didn't care about politics,' Themis said to Giorgos, 'I could just carry on watering the plants and enjoying this lovely summer air. But I can't stand what's going on. It's all so wrong!'

Giorgos tried to keep his wife calm. He sometimes even hid a newspaper if he thought there was an image that would provoke her and had done it that day with a picture of Frederika at the consecration of the new head of the Church of Greece.

'The royal family *and* the Church are holding hands with the colonels,' said Nikos furiously. 'Why do they do that?'

Around the table, everyone looked at each other but nobody had an answer.

For a few months, things continued superficially as before, but in December King Constantine attempted to overthrow the colonels. He gathered troops loyal to him in the north of the country and claimed that the navy and air force were with him too.

'It's civil war,' said Giorgos, as they all listened to the radio. 'There are troops getting ready to fight each other.'

Themis found it difficult to decide which side she despised more. She would not fight for either and hoped that her children felt the same.

This new crisis passed. The leader of the Junta, Colonel Papadopoulos, acted swiftly to crush the attempt and, within a day, the royal family was forced to flee to Rome. They were now in exile.

Giorgos no longer concealed the newspaper when it contained photographs of the royal family in their furs and jewels. Themis felt no pity for them. On the contrary, she felt a sense of satisfaction that they were experiencing what it was like to be far from home and unable to return. This had happened to so many Greeks in the past and was continuing to do so, even now.

'They've released Andreas Papandreou!' Giorgos announced one day as he came into the apartment. If there was even a glimmer of good news, Giorgos always told his wife straightaway. He was excitedly waving his newspaper.

'That's all very well,' she said, 'but there are plenty of others still locked up . . . What about all those other prisoners?' she said. 'Theodorakis? Ritsos?'

The composer and the poet were both adored by the left, but scorned by supporters of the Junta.

'We have nothing to celebrate until those two – and everyone like them – are free,' she said adamantly.

Giorgos quietly sighed. He yearned for his wife to be contented. That was his real wish in life. The Junta was now firmly in charge and most people, unless arrested or persecuted, now went about their usual business.

In the years that followed, Themis, like many, kept her political opinions hidden. During this period of dictatorship, they seemed as useless as the old-fashioned linen and lace that Kyría Koralis had made for her dowry; they were stored in a chest.

In spite of the iron grip of the colonels on politics, the country's economy kept growing and there was a widespread economic boom with living conditions for most people continuing to improve. Supermarkets were well-stocked and days of famine a distant memory. The Junta operated a quiet and efficient repression sometimes so subtle that it was hard to protest. Vigorous objection to the regime was voiced abroad but Themis believed that there was nothing she or anyone else could do within Greece itself.

Almost a year and half after the colonels took over the country, Kyría Koralis died in her sleep. She was ninety-seven years old. In the last few days of her life, she told Themis that her job was done. In her final few years, the roles of caring and being cared for had reversed and Themis had lovingly looked after her. Her long life had been filled with the joy of her grandchildren and latterly her great-grandchildren, and she accepted sadness and loss as, what she described to Themis, 'part of life's tapestry'. Her death was without suffering. She had never lamented lack, but celebrated plenty instead. There was a very small gathering at her funeral. Pavlos could not be contacted and all her friends had died some time before.

The younger children cried inconsolably, but Themis reassured them that their great-grandmother had lived the longest life anyone could hope for, and would continue to love them all from what she referred to as 'another place'. All eight members of the family lit candles in her memory and the little church of Agios Andreas was bathed in a golden glow.

After Kyría Koralis' death, Thanasis was alone but his hours of solitude were never burdensome, with one or other of the children visiting him each day. Living in such close proximity in a *polykatoikía* offered great benefits to them all. He had retired on a full disability pension and was always there to help his nephews and his niece with homework.

On the day of Kyría Koralis' forty-day memorial, there was another funeral. The former Prime Minister, Georgios Papandreou, had died. Much against Giorgos' will, Themis went with Nikos to the centre of the city. The two of them stood patiently in line outside the Metropolitan Church, and eventually it was their turn to pay their respects.

They then followed the procession to the First Cemetery. For Themis it was an anti-Junta act rather than a show of admiration for a politician who had shown himself to be against the communists. The crowd was a huge and politically mixed one, and it demonstrated that the regime was popular with neither the left nor the right. By crushing democracy they had alienated politicians on all sides.

Along with hundreds of thousands of others in the swelling crowd, Themis chanted, 'Freedom! Freedom!' It was a roar, a cry for help, a call to the outside world. And it was heard.

For the first time in eighteen months, the sense of futility she had experienced lifted. She and Nikos stood with arms linked and she took her son's hand and squeezed it. She could feel the beat of his pulse as if it were her own.

There were many arrests that day but the pair of them were already back home when this news came through.

Chapter Twenty-Three

THROUGHOUT THE LATTER days of his schooling, Angelos had continued to be ambitious and achieved top marks in all his final examinations. The discovery that he had a grandfather in America had lodged itself in his mind and he decided that he would like to go and study there. Perhaps he would meet his long-lost relation. Angelos wanted to be rich, to have a house with many rooms and a car. Perhaps many cars. One day he announced his intention.

'You've spent too much time with your uncle,' teased Themis, who never really imagined that he would go.

It was true that Thanasis had let his nephew watch dozens of American films. The small wooden box in the corner of the room had introduced him to other worlds and changed his aspirations. Even before he had taken the final exams, he was applying for university courses in business in New York and Chicago. When the letter offering him a scholarship arrived, Themis struggled to contain her sorrow. Her son was leaving for new opportunities in a country that imposed no restrictions on civil liberty, she told herself. Why would she discourage this? It was a triumph for the family, a great joy, something for Giorgos to boast about in the *kafeneío* and she silently reprimanded herself for feeling sad.

During the months that led up to his departure, when Angelos was going through the long process of filling in forms and applications for visas and a passport (a very exacting task under the Junta), there were several moments when Themis felt the urge to tell him the truth about his father. Without mentioning it to Giorgos, she had gone to the telephone exchange and looked up the name 'Tasos Makris'. There were several listed, but the sight filled her with revulsion. For a moment, her pencil hovered over a scrap of paper she had taken from the counter. Then, with a sudden decisive movement she threw both back into her bag and snapped it shut. She did not want even to write down the name. She knew how Giorgos would react, in any case. He regarded himself as the boys' father and would never willingly agree to destroy the solid edifice of their family.

The day came for Angelos to leave. Giorgos had just bought their first car and they drove down to the airport near Glyfada in the September sunshine with a full boot and two suitcases strapped precariously to the roof. Out of the corner of her eye, Themis could see Angelos sitting between his two little brothers on the back seat. They were playing a game, squealing and laughing and tickling each other.

Angelos' excitement was palpable as he gave his mother a perfunctory hug and waved them goodbye at passport control. Themis insisted that they all wait in the car park until they had watched his plane take off and climb steeply into a clear blue sky.

'How do you know it's that one?' asked Andreas.

'I just do . . .' she said, turning away from them all to conceal her tears. She felt a physical pain in her heart.

In due course, a letter arrived from Angelos describing his daily life and painting a warm image of America. Only then did she admit to herself that his decision had been a good one. At least she had one child who lived in a free society.

After Angelos had left, Nikos seemed to acquire new motivation. No longer was he in the academic shadow of his brother. After a year of labouring on a building site, Nikos returned to school to study for his final exams. His years of obsessive drawing then led him to an apprenticeship with an architect and his employer, who saw the rough sketches that he sometimes absent-mindedly drew in the office, encouraged him to take up formal study.

'You're a fine draughtsman, Nikos,' he told him. 'But surely you would like your sketches to be realised?'

Nikos feigned indifference but through his work at the architect's office he came to understand that something more satisfying was almost within reach. Athens was full of construction projects during these years. Everywhere he looked there was a new apartment block going up and most of them were in the same style, designed for speed of completion and low cost. The city was being stripped of its old character even as they watched. Nikos wanted to combine beauty with functionality and his drawings often incorporated an element of classical detail that lent them elegance and grace.

On a large drawing board that leaned against the wall of his bedroom, Nikos had conjured up a fantasy version of Athens, keeping the nineteenth-century buildings in place but sweeping away everything built since that time. In a neatly drawn schematic, with everything perfectly in scale, he envisaged an Athens reborn with a balance of ancient and modern. He had mapped it out like a chessboard with squares and tree-lined avenues and each apartment block surrounded by gardens.

He washed it over with watercolours, differentiating the

buildings in various shades of sandy gold. Nikos' ideal city was dreamlike.

'If you could rebuild this city, it would be paradise,' said his mother.

It was obvious to them all that his hobby should become a profession and both employer and parents encouraged him to apply for a college place. Fired with ambition, Nikos sat the entrance exams and effortlessly passed.

Themis remembered her sadness over his every failure at school but now felt a surge of joy. She was his parent, but in spite of this, she heard a phrase going round in her head: 'Your mother would have been so proud of you . . . She would have been so proud . . .'

She had watched Nikos obsessively drawing, both night and day, for so long. Whether a picture of his family or a fantastical building, Themis knew where his prodigious talent came from.

The Polytechnic building was at the very beginning of Patission Avenue. It was a familiar landmark, and Themis' pride that Nikos was entering the gates was immense. Her son was twenty-one when he finally enrolled and a new decade had begun.

Nikos became a serious student and applied himself fully to every assignment, approaching his work with an idealism that impressed even his professor. He was deeply motivated: by the belief that buildings should be beautiful as well as functional, and he already saw it as a mission to share his vision with his younger siblings.

Andreas was doing his homework one evening and his books were spread across the table. One of them was open at an engraving of the Parthenon showing how it would have looked two thousand years before.

'We have the most perfect building in the world at the end of our street,' Nikos commented. 'It should set the benchmark for every other building in this city!'

'Beauty is for everyone,' he continued. 'It's not just for the rich. Why should less fortunate people live in cheap and ugly places?'

'There's no reason!' Andreas agreed with enthusiasm.

It was in an equal society that Nikos believed and it motivated every stroke of his pencil.

Listening to her son, Themis realised that her beliefs were no weaker than they had been in the past even if the opportunity to take action had lessened with time. She saw in Nikos the same fire that she had seen in Aliki.

Four years had passed since the coup, and the streets of Athens were adorned with posters commemorating the anniversary: 21 April 1967. The slogans sickened Themis as much as the military parades put on to celebrate it, with events that included the youth movement. She went upstairs to take Thanasis some shirts she had ironed for him and glanced over at the television which, as usual, was on in the background.

The uniformed youngsters took her mind back to the days of EON and she recalled how much Margarita had flaunted her navy-blue suit. It was more than three decades earlier but the similarity of the scene struck her with force. Another decade, another dictatorship.

Themis stayed in that day and did not turn on the radio, even to listen to music. It was a day to keep the shutters closed.

Ways to express dissatisfaction with the regime were minimal. Newspapers were still censored and every time she saw the Junta's broadsheet promoting its economic successes and reputation abroad she wanted to rip it from the stand and trample on it. Even such an action was too subversive to contemplate. Anyone who stepped out of line was labelled a communist, and those who wanted to get a decent job needed a clean record. Both Themis and Giorgos were conscious of this with their children.

Someone, somewhere, still had her records and the authorities had already sent plenty like her to prison. Themis hated the regime, but for the sake of her family she contained any expression of it. During these years, if one of her younger children complained of some new measure at school (having to keep his hair very short particularly infuriated Spiros) she responded blandly or buried herself in a domestic task to hide her reaction. At such moments, she felt a pang of shame. It was against the very same fascism that she had fought, but now she was too cowardly to voice opposition or sing revolutionary songs. Memories of marching through the mountains, a rifle slung over her shoulder, fingernails black with dirt and her stomach hollow, flooded back.

She knew she was not the only one guilty of inaction. Over time, many like her who were bitterly opposed to the Junta had lost their will to express their opposition to it. Under the colonels, the economy had continued to grow and wages had risen. When they met one night for Andreas' Saint's Day party at the end of November, Thanasis commented on the copious number of dishes on the table. Themis understood what he was hinting at. For many people, social stability, good schooling for children, buses that ran on time and adequate food were more than enough to keep them happy.

While the flame in Themis seemed to diminish, something was growing in Nikos. She could see it in his eyes and in his nervous mannerisms. He spent less and less time at home, working most evenings in the library and scarcely sleeping in his bed. He had grown thin and rarely smiled.

'Your boy never comes up to see me these days,' complained Thanasis.

'We hardly see him either,' said Themis. 'He's such a serious student. I worry that he works too hard.'

'It's good that he's so determined to succeed. After his start in life . . .'

'Thanasis, please don't mention that,' reprimanded Themis.

Thanasis said nothing more. Occasionally, when it was just the two of them, he brought up the long-distant past. He reminisced about their family: their mother, father, Panos and Margarita. Decades had gone by since their mother's departure, but Thanasis liked to revisit the bad times and Themis was the sole member of the audience. He had no surviving friendships from childhood and he had formed none in the intervening years. His sister and her family were the only people he ever saw these days and their familiarity with his scars made them blind to his disfigurement. The lines that marked his face had never lost their colour or depth, and each time he ventured out people looked away or crossed the street to avoid him. Thanasis would feel the rest of his face redden with anger and shame.

One warm spring day, he was walking towards a small group on Patission Avenue. A woman with a child was talking to a soldier on the street. They seemed familiar with each other, smiling and laughing, flirting perhaps. Generally, he avoided looking at people of the opposite sex, but this woman was arrestingly beautiful and he found himself staring. She had long glossy hair, the colour of chestnuts ready to fall from the tree, her full lips were painted scarlet and she wore a vivid green coat, tightly belted to em- phasise her waist and short enough to show her knees. The three of them occupied the middle of the pavement and Thanasis could not pass.

For a moment he stared at this vision of a modern Aphrodite but was suddenly brought to his senses by the scream of the small boy. The child then proceeded to bury his head in his mother's skirt and began to wail with such volume that other people in the street hurried to investigate. A small group formed around mother and child and the young corporal turned towards Thanasis.

'You! Get away from here. Now,' he ordered. 'Keep away from these people. And don't bother them again.'

Thanasis, his legs shaking with fear and fury, turned away, his ability to walk almost failing him. His stick fell from his hand and clattered to the pavement.

He knew the danger. If he bent down to pick it up, he could easily topple but equally he knew he could not get home unaided. He hesitated. A second later the soldier was standing before him, nose to nose and Thanasis could feel his breath on his face.

The younger man gave him the merest push and Thanasis fell heavily to the ground. He lay still, remembering more than one occasion in his own career when he had kicked a defenceless man and braced himself for a boot in the ribs or the groin. It did not come and then he heard the muffled sound of footsteps. They seemed to be getting further away, not closer.

Thanasis tried to manoeuvre himself into a position to get up but had no leverage and realised that his shoulder was in the wrong position. It was only then that the pain overwhelmed him. Several people stepped around him as they passed, though he had no strength to cry out. Someone nudged his stick closer with their foot but he could not reach out for it. They must think he was some drunk who had passed out in the street.

He could not measure how much time had passed because his watch was on the same side as his twisted shoulder, buried beneath his body. Was the soldier still standing by, mocking him with his eyes?

Suddenly there was someone bending down close by. The voice was familiar.

'Uncle Thanasis! Are you all right? What happened? Let's get you up!'

Thanasis did not reply. He was dazed, disorientated.

'Your head is bleeding!' Nikos said, seeing the pool of magenta that had already dried on the pavement. 'We need to get you home.'

It was only when Nikos tried to move Thanasis that he cried out in agony.

'It's my shoulder,' he said weakly.

Nikos immediately thought of the butcher, Hatzopoulos, in a nearby sidestreet. He once heard his great-grandmother say that she had never bought meat anywhere else.

'That man kept us alive during the war,' she would say, and once described how he had sometimes given them offal and offcuts during the occupation. Now the family's help was needed again.

'I'll be back in a moment,' Nikos whispered gently to Thanasis.

Soon, with the help of the butcher's burly son, Thanasis was being carried very gently towards the square. It was only two hundred metres away but it took them ten minutes at least to reach the front door and another five to carry him up the stairs. Thanasis had become very thin as he aged and each could have lifted him single-handedly but they were determined to minimise his discomfort and bore him like a porcelain figurine.

Themis had begun to fret about Thanasis when he did not appear for the evening meal. He rarely went out for longer than fifteen or twenty minutes and he was now an hour late. She went on to the balcony and looked out over the square. Perhaps he had gone to sit in the early-evening warmth.

'Should we send one of the children out to look for him?' she asked Giorgos. 'It's so unlike him.'

'I'll t-t-take a stroll up the street,' he answered, as ever sensitive to his wife's concerns.

As he opened the door to let himself out, Nikos appeared with the Hatzopoulos boy. Giorgos did not see Thanasis at first but then gasped as his brother-in-law came into view.

Themis hastened to his side.

'Thanasis! Nikos! What on earth . . .?'

The younger children had gathered round, all asking questions at once. Thanasis was pale but clearly conscious and they knelt in a row along the sofa where he had been laid out. Themis was fetching warm water and antiseptic to bathe his head, and one of the children was told to fetch the doctor who had moved into the neighbouring building. Against his corpse-pale skin, Thanasis' scars shone out more vividly than usual.

The doctor came running in and examined his head and then his arm.

'I think we should take you to hospital,' he said.

'I don't want to go to hospital,' Thanasis said quietly. 'Can't you fix it here?'

The doctor had passed the time of day with Thanasis when they had met in the square so their acquaintance was superficial, but the former army surgeon understood his reservations. He expertly splinted the arm himself and later brought in some strong painkillers. The head wound was superficial, a graze but nothing more, and he was satisfied that Thanasis was not concussed. He would come in and see him on a regular basis.

Thanasis spent a few days sleeping in the crowded family apartment so that Themis could keep an eye on him. The children fussed around him, enjoying the novelty of having their uncle so close. On the first day, Andreas picked him some flowers from the square, a gesture that so profoundly touched him that he felt the unfamiliar sensation of tears meandering down the creases in his face. Eight-year-old Spiros took over the job of cutting up his uncle's food and Nikos entertained him with card tricks.

During his period of convalescence, Thanasis resolved never again to leave the building. Once the perpetrator, he had become the victim. Everything he needed was here: family and food. There was no need to go out into a hostile world when he could see what he wanted of it on the small square screen of his television. Thanasis watched news bulletins, but most of the time lived in the gentle world of domestic comedy or American musicals and romances. At least he could watch people falling in love even if he had never experienced it himself. It would be enough. He found all the fresh air he needed on his balcony where he sat each afternoon reading. Even he had lost his appetite for newsprint and had begun to devour books. This need was satisfied by Nikos, who borrowed what he could for him from the university library.

'I have never known him happier in all my life,' Themis commented to her husband.

'He seems contented enough,' agreed Giorgos.

The recent past seemed forgotten and Thanasis no longer felt vulnerable. Everyone within the family circle accepted him, loved him, tolerated him, looked after him. The scars on his face that had always throbbed were calmer now. It almost seemed as if they began to fade.

Chapter Twenty-Four

W HILE THANASIS WITHDREW from the world and isolated himself from the fetid air that permeated the streets of his city, Nikos became more embroiled in an increasingly tense political situation.

In his first years at university, he had focused on his assignments, determined to excel. Once he had proved to himself that, despite his late start, he was equal to his fellow students, Nikos became more sociable. With his quick wit and strong views, he was always at the heart of conversations.

With his new friends, he found himself in underground bars, away from the constant scrutiny of security police who were ever-present in all their lives. His card tricks further broke down barriers with his new *paréa*, as they smoked, drank and listened to rock music. In whatever way conversation began, it always returned to the same theme: the Junta.

Several of Nikos' fellow students were members of a communist underground movement, *Rigas Feraios*, named after an eighteenth-century revolutionary. Many of its members had already been arrested. In this company, Nikos felt himself on fire. He was learning the skills that would help him to revive the beauty of his city but now he had the chance to revive something more significant: the civil liberties of its citizens. Their fundamental rights had been completely suspended.

Surrounded by groups of young men who were all similarly passionate, he quickly formed friendships and grew close to a group of law students. Their views opened Nikos' eyes ever wider. Their studies in another faculty made them all the more aware of the injustices of the military regime and they talked angrily of the emergency laws that had been instituted. The colonels had given themselves random and unchecked powers. How much longer would they tolerate this? The Americans were said to be supporting them. What action were they going to take?

These past months Nikos had grown a beard and his wild curly hair had grown almost to his shoulders. His generally unkempt appearance meant that he was often a target for security police checks. Each time it happened, they took his name and had once even taken him to the station. Their motivation seemed purely to harass him but he refrained from telling his parents. He did not want to worry them.

'Law under the Junta is a travesty,' Nikos told his mother one evening while she was preparing their meal.

She nodded in agreement, but said nothing.

'We're sleepwalking, *Mána*. All of us. It's more than half a decade now,' he said.

Themis carried on with what she was doing, feigning lack of interest. Nikos continued too.

'My siblings won't remember any other way of life,' he said. 'And it's getting to the point when even *I* can hardly recall things as they were.'

That day Nikos had come once again face to face with the authorities when he was stopped arbitrarily in the street on his way home from a class. The two policemen turned the contents of his leather satchel out on to the pavement and gave Nikos a good kicking as he stooped to rescue his papers. He was not detained but even before he was up from the ground they shouted at him: 'Get your hair cut!'

Absent-mindedly, Themis turned on the radio. She liked to listen to music when she was cooking and thought it might soften Nikos' anger or, at the very least, distract him a little.

Sound crackled through the speaker, but through the interference, came a voice they both recognised. It was Colonel Papadopoulos giving orders or issuing warnings – it did not matter which, she did not want to listen. Themis immediately fiddled with the dial to find some music, but it was too late. The sound of the harsh military barking provoked an immediate response in her son.

'*Mitéra!* What are you doing listening to these people? Why? *Why* do you? Isn't it enough that they're ruining our lives? They've taken away our freedom to think and speak and *breathe!*'

Themis had entirely underestimated her son's brewing frustration. But it was her apparent indifference to his sense of injustice that had really infuriated him. Suddenly he was next to her and pulling the plug from the wall to silence the radio.

'*Why* are you so apathetic? *Why* can't you see what's happening to this country? We're dominated by fascists and Americans! And you don't seem to *care*! Neither of you! I am *ashamed* of this family!'

Nikos stood quivering with anger but Themis was shaking so hard that she had to sit down. She could feel the physical heat of her son's passion.

Giorgos had come through the front door in time to hear the final moments of his son's tirade.

Themis was struggling to contain her tears. She knew that Nikos had no idea how unjust his accusations were but at the same time she did not want Giorgos to be too hard on Nikos.

With her whole being she wanted her son to know how hard she had fought, with her fists, with her sweat, with her blood, with her very essence. She had even killed. She had risked everything to combat the fascism to which he referred.

Giorgos knew how deeply his wife felt and came round the table to comfort her. As he did so, Nikos shrank away, rightly fearful of his father's wrath. He knew how protective he was of his mother.

'Please don't say anything, Giorgos,' she asked him quietly, knowing that they both held fast to an agreement that the children should not be burdened with Themis' past. Silence protected this family. If Themis spoke out to defend herself, then so many other truths might come tumbling out.

The three of them looked at each other.

Nikos reached out and touched his mother's arm.

'I'm sorry, *Mána*. I'm really sorry. It was wrong of me.'

His contrition was genuine and his brief apology enough. The situation defused, he left the apartment and Themis and Giorgos were left alone.

It was then that Themis allowed herself to cry.

'H-h-h-how d-d-d-dare he speak to you like that?' said Giorgos. 'A s-s-s-son to his mother? If you h-h-hadn't restrained me . . . I-I-I . . .'

Anger was rare in this gentle man but, when he was roused to it, it was hard for him to contain. His stutter worsened and he could scarcely get out his words, so enraged was he that Nikos had shown such little respect.

'But it's how things seem to him, Giorgos,' Themis said quietly, defending their son. 'It must look as if we approve of the regime. We never say anything against it.'

Themis heard the door and quickly dried her tears on her apron. Thanasis and the younger children were coming in and it was time to eat. A letter had come from Angelos that morning and it was the family tradition that one of the three younger children read out his news. Anna finished eating first so she slit open the envelope and along with the pages of transparent airmail paper pulled out a postcard.

Dear everyone,

Everything is going well. I started my internship last month and am now living in the centre of Chicago. It is a very exciting city – you can see it for yourselves on the photo. I work in one of those very tall buildings, on the eighteenth floor, to be exact, and have marked my window with a cross!

One of the boys grabbed the photo from her and Anna protested.

'Andreas, don't snatch, *agápi mou*,' said his mother. 'Pass it round so everyone can look at it, please.'

I am enjoying my job, working as a junior accountant in one of the big firms. They have promised to promote me when I pass the next set of professional exams and they are already paying me well (much more than I would earn in Greece). I have even bought a car! It's white and fits at least four people on the back seat and has huge wheels. Everyone here has one and I go on trips at weekends with . . . my new girlfriend! She is called Corabel and she works as a secretary in the company.

'Corabel?' interrupted Thanasis. 'Is that a name? It's not a saint I've heard of . . .'

'Don't be silly, Uncle Thanasis,' giggled Anna. 'She's American, not Greek. He hasn't found a Greek Orthodox girl!'

'And you've seen enough Hollywood films to know they have strange names over there,' teased Andreas.

'Let her continue!' urged Themis.

'Shall I start again from the beginning?' asked Anna.

The family groaned collectively, so she picked up from where Thanasis had interrupted her.

. . . Her family come from the West Coast so she has a very different accent but I manage to understand her! We get very little holiday here, but in the summer we will take a vacation and drive across to see her parents. The roads are amazing – very straight and very wide and very smooth.

Love, Angelos

Themis could not deny it. There was no doubt that her twenty-three-year-old son was living the American dream, with opportunities beyond the reach of anyone in Greece.

'He sounds happy, doesn't he?' said Giorgos, getting up to clear some plates.

'I haven't finished,' said Anna impatiently. 'There's a PS!'

'Come on, then, Anna,' said Themis. 'Read it out.'

Anna was enjoying being the centre of attention in this noisy family and was now reading with an American accent.

'*I tracked down our grandfather,*' she drawled, trying to imagine how her brother sounded these days. '*He lives in Salt Lake City. I got a very short reply to my letter. He said he would come over to see me one day.*'

'Salt City?' said Spiros, pouring salt on to the table and shaping it into a pile.

'Spiros! Stop doing that!' Themis murmured half-heartedly, her mind not really on her son's bad behaviour. She was momentarily annoyed by the thought of her father and the obvious lack of interest in his old family but the moment soon passed. After more than three decades of absence she felt little connection.

Nikos' place at the table remained empty but when he came in later, he picked up the letter that was still lying there and read it carefully.

He saw his mother on the balcony and went out to sit with her.

'You've forgiven me, haven't you?'

'Of course, *agápi mou*,' she said. 'All you have to remember is that things aren't always as they seem.'

He was puzzled by her comment but the moment passed. He had something else on his mind. His brother's letter.

'He seems to be doing well, doesn't he?' said Nikos.

'It's nice to know how happy he is,' she responded. 'And a new girlfriend too, that's . . .'

'It's more than four years since he left . . .'

'I know. I just wish he would come home and visit. He did promise,' said Themis.

'Four years,' emphasised Nikos. 'And not once has he ever mentioned what's really going on in that country.'

'He sends us his news, doesn't he?'

'I don't mean that, *Mána*,' said Nikos, aware that he must keep his voice low.

His father was napping on the sofa just inside the doors.

'I mean the *real* news. Vietnam, for example. America went in and slaughtered people who didn't agree with their politics.'

He knew his mother did not follow the news carefully these days but she had heard that many US troops had been withdrawn and a peace agreement reached.

'All that's over now, isn't it?' said Themis.

'The action might be, but even when it was happening Angelos never referred to it. Thousands of innocent people died! And now there's something new. Nixon is implicated in some kind of cover-up,' he said, his voice rising. 'It's full of corruption, that country.'

'Shh, *mátia mou*,' urged Themis.

'I know my father is sleeping,' he said. 'But it's America that supports the colonels, *Mána*. They interfere here just as they interfered in Vietnam. They meddle wherever they want and nobody stops them.'

Nikos had said everything he had to say, so he stopped.

'But Angelos is happy there,' said his mother. 'And he was never interested in politics, was he?'

'That's true,' said Nikos. 'He's gone to make his fortune and I'm sure he'll succeed.'

'I'm glad that you're so different from one another,' said Themis, taking her son's hand and holding it firmly in her own.

Nikos got up, kissed her forehead and went back into the apartment. His father was just waking.

Themis put the conversation to the back of her mind until a few months later when Nikos came home very late one night. It was early in 1973. She was tidying and about to go to bed but immediately noticed something strange about him. In spite of it being a cold night, he reeked of sweat, and she could see, even in the low light of the living room, that his hands and face were streaked with dirt. His trousers were torn at the knee.

'Nikos?' she asked. 'What happened?'

Her son was wild-eyed. There was a look of fear in his eyes, but at the same time she sensed his exhilaration and recognised the combination from her own distant past.

He was still out of breath from the exertion of running, but eventually answered.

His mother had brought him a glass of water.

'I was helping out some friends,' he panted.

'What do you mean?'

'At the Law School. They've had enough of the Junta's interference and they were protesting. I joined them.'

Themis adopted her customary silence, whilst listening intently.

'It's almost six years, *Mána*. Six years since they took away student rights. We're not even allowed free student elections. The ones they staged last autumn were a sham.'

'So what happened at the Law School?' she asked gently.

'There was a demonstration and the police came. And they were violent. One of our group is in hospital. He'll be OK, but he is badly bruised.'

'And you?'

'I just caught the edge of one of their batons. Nothing more,' he said, making light of his wound.

Nikos drained the water in one gulp and handed the glass back to his mother.

'People have had enough,' he said.

Themis carefully washed up the glass and went to bed, listening to the sound of Nikos in the shower. He was whistling. Perhaps it was a revolutionary song.

The following day it was reported on a radio bulletin that a demonstration at the law faculty had been resoundingly crushed.

The summer was even hotter than usual and the streets were quiet until the sun went down. Only then did people go out. High temperatures sat like a weight over the city, sapping the energy to stage demonstrations against the Junta. Nikos spent plenty of time with his uncle during those months. The upstairs apartment was a retreat from the noise of his own home where his growing siblings seemed to dominate the space. Andreas and Spiros, now thirteen and nine, were almost constantly engaged in a continual wrestling match, making it impossible to study. They called Nikos and their uncle the '*yéroi*', the old men, as they sat on the balcony, facing outwards over the square like friends in the *kafeneío*.

What they talked of was a mystery to Themis, but whenever she saw her son helping his uncle down the stairs for the evening meal she was touched by the strength of affection that existed between them. She could only assume that they never strayed into political discussion.

When autumn came, the rhythm of life changed. Nikos was attending university classes again and the teenagers started a new academic year too.

One evening in mid-November, when Nikos came in Themis recognised something new in his mood.

Giorgos was outside on the balcony pruning two lemon trees planted many years before by Kyría Koralis.

'What's happened, Nikos? Tell me.' Giorgos overheard his wife ask.

'Don't say anything to *anyone*, especially my father, but there's a strike going on at the Polytechnic and I'm going to join in. And don't tell me not to,' he announced with determination.

Giorgos appeared. He had heard his son's words and they had irritated him, particularly the reference to himself.

'It w–w–won't do any good,' he said. 'So why even b–b–bother? The Junta will always win. They have a whole army behind them.'

Nikos found Giorgos' mild manner irritating at the best of times and this was the wrong moment for him to encounter such apathy.

'I'm not even going to listen to you,' he almost spat. 'How can we be so different? How can you be my . . .?'

Giorgos had turned his back. He knew what might come next from Nikos' mouth and did not want to hear it.

'I'm going to the *k-k-kafeneío*,' he said, addressing Themis, and left immediately.

Themis had always known that her husband's sympathies were not wholeheartedly with the left but she suddenly felt annoyed by him. She was left alone now to face Nikos.

Nikos was not ready to drop the matter.

'I am sick of this family being so *spineless*! I know you hate the Junta, *Mána*. And I know why you are always silent. It's *cowardice*. And I don't want to be like you—'

Themis felt her temperature rising. Like a *bríki* with coffee that had heated to boiling point, her anger now overflowed.

'Stop!'

The firmness in his mother's voice arrested him. Her voice was generally so calm.

'Please, Nikos, stop,' she said. She was burning from within and could feel it even to the roots of her hair. 'You have to stop *now*.'

She gripped the back of a chair to steady herself. In front of her she saw not a child, but a twenty-five-year-old man accusing her of cowardice, she who had given everything, almost to her last breath.

The passion of the moment took her. Was it not time he knew? And knew *everything*?

Defying all that she had agreed with Giorgos, she began to speak in her own defence. It was impossible to restrain herself for a moment longer.

'Listen. I fought for the left in the mountains, Nikos. I killed. I was captured and I spent months in prison. Months in exile.'

Nikos was open-mouthed.

'What? You're only telling me this now? *Why?* Why didn't you say anything before?'

Nikos pulled out a chair and sank down into it. Themis took the seat opposite him.

'Why?' he repeated. 'Why didn't you say?'

'It seemed better to distance us all, that's why,' she said. Nikos reached across the table to touch his mother's hand. 'Your uncles were always arguing, and then it was me and Thanasis later. And then there was Margarita. She was . . . more on the right. Politics can be venom, Nikos. I didn't want you to be poisoned.'

'I still don't understand why you said nothing,' said Nikos, his throat almost dry with shock.

'Because your father and I didn't always agree on what was right and I thought it was better to say nothing.'

'But why—'

'It's dangerous to be on the losing side, Nikos, so isn't it better not to be on any side?'

'No! If you don't take a side, then evil wins.'

'Sometimes evil wins whatever you do,' she said, thinking of Aliki. The day of her execution was still so clear in her memory.

Both of them were calm now.

Suddenly she knew she had no right to keep the truth from the young man who sat opposite her. She was his mother, but so was Aliki. To deny him the right to know this was to deny Aliki's right too. Her right to be remembered.

'There is something else I want to tell you, Nikos. I think it's fair that you know.'

'You were a communist!' he said with admiration, squeezing her hand. 'And you fought! I would never have imagined . . .'

He had seen his mother in a new light and there was a detectable hint of joy in his voice.

'*Shh!*' Themis said softly. 'Please keep your voice down.'

Even now she did not want the other children to know, and certainly not her neighbours.

'Your mother was a heroine of the civil war,' she continued.

'It sounds like it,' he smiled. 'And I am proud, even if I knew nothing of it until today.'

'That's not what I meant,' she said, looking very directly at him. 'I'm not talking about me.'

For a moment, Nikos looked confused. So who was his mother talking about?

Themis saw all the colour drain from his face and now she took his hands in hers. His skin had an icy chill.

'Your mother was a *true* heroine,' Themis told him gently. 'She died for her beliefs and for her principles.'

Shock had grabbed Nikos by the throat and strangled his words, making his mouth so dry that his voice would not function. Not a single syllable could escape.

Themis continued to talk gently for a few moments, trying to read Nikos' expression as she did so. He was listening intently.

'Her name was Aliki. She loved you very, very much and made sure that you were going to be looked after. She was a true friend to me when I was in need, which is why I became your "mother" and why I love you as though you are my own.'

The revelation had come crashing down on Nikos like a meteor. There had not been the slightest warning of such an announcement and he was unprepared. Themis could see this and was beginning to regret her rashness.

He had a dim memory of some other place in his early life, but not of another mother.

'Aliki,' he repeated hoarsely.

'Yes,' said Themis. 'I will find a photograph I have of her. A photograph that was taken of us both. And I also have a beautiful drawing that she did of you. I will show you.'

'Not now . . .' said Nikos.

He could scarcely take in what he had just been told and the words went round and round in his head: his mother was 'a communist heroine'. She had been executed.

Suddenly he stood up.

'I must go,' he said agitatedly. 'My friends are waiting for me. I am sorry I called you a coward. And now I understand why I can't be one either.'

He quickly kissed her on the forehead and a moment later he was gone. He had not even bothered to take his jacket, which hung on the back of his chair, nor did he respond to her goodbye.

Themis got up and opened the balcony door. She just caught the silhouette of her son disappearing round the corner. He must have run across the square. That Nikos had been in a hurry to leave was evident and it was understandable that he might want to digest what he had been told or perhaps share it with his *paréa*. She pictured him going to meet them in a *kafeneío* or, perhaps later on, in one of the bars he frequented. His friends were on the left, but she hoped he would be cautious about his choice of confidants. Being the son of an executed communist would not help to gain him employment under this regime.

She knew that her words had shocked Nikos and was certain that he would need time to take it all in. No doubt he would soon return with a barrage of questions and would undoubtedly want to know who his father was.

A small part of her felt a sense of relief that he now knew about his mother. There had been so few times in the past two decades when it had seemed right but if there had ever been a moment, it had to have been this. As the sense of elation gradually faded, the possible impact of her revelation on the rest of the family began to nag at her. She would, of course, need to tell Giorgos what she had done and this was something she feared. After that they would have to decide what to tell Angelos. Even though he was far away, he would need to know some version of the story.

Themis came in from the balcony, went into the bedroom and, from the back of her locked bedside cabinet, took out the photograph taken on Trikeri. Scrutinising it closely, she realised that Nikos had become more like Aliki with the passing years. Pehaps he would be in the mood to see it when he returned.

Far from needing time to assimilate the news, Nikos had decided on immediate action. The discovery that his mother, his true mother, had been a heroine, inspired him. He would ask a thousand questions later, but for now he felt as if there was revolutionary blood coursing through his veins. He was the offspring, the son, of a martyr and perhaps this was why he felt so compelled. It was not just a desire to protest, but an obligation.

The demonstrations at the Polytechnic that had begun earlier that week had gained momentum. Support for the students had swelled and high-school pupils, factory workers, teachers and doctors were all now joining in, chanting slogans in and around the building.

It weighed on Themis' conscience that she should tell Giorgos as soon as possible that Nikos now knew about his mother and why she had felt such a need to tell him. All evening, she had silently rehearsed what she would say when he came in from the *kafeneío*, but courage failed her when he did. The three younger children were all in the apartment and she must tell him when they were alone.

That night, Nikos had not come in when they went to bed.

413

This was not unusual in itself and they all imagined that he had gone out with friends ('To h-h-hear some of that terrible music,' suggested his father, who disapproved of heavy metal even though he had never heard a note).

The following morning, Themis saw that Nikos' bed had not been slept in. Perhaps he had stayed with a friend.

When evening came, and once again his place was empty, Themis' anxiety reached a new level. She casually switched on the radio after their meal and heard that there was a group of students and subversives demonstrating in the centre of the city. People were being advised to stay away.

She knew immediately that Nikos would be down there. She both feared for him, knowing that he would be in the middle of things, and admired him. Giorgos had heard that there had been violence against the demonstrators and that some of them were being attacked by the police.

'They j-j-just want to disperse everyone,' said Giorgos. 'But Nikos is a fast runner. He'll g-g-get away.'

One of their neighbours who had passed close to the centre told them that the slogans being shouted were a huge provocation to the authorities.

'They're yelling "Torturers", "Down with the Junta!" and "US Out!",' he said. 'What good will that do?'

Themis did not answer.

Nikos, just as Themis had imagined, was in the city centre with his friends, chanting into the faces of the security forces, who were trying to make the crowd, which had swelled to many tens of thousands, disperse.

The air was thick with tear gas sprayed by the police. In retaliation some of the demonstrators lit fires in the street. Despite choking on the acrid air, Nikos continued to shout. His passions, as those of all the others, were high.

The demonstrators were aware that there were dozens of police, but they outnumbered them by a huge ratio. Surely there was safety in numbers. The adrenalin gave them almost limitless courage and they already felt themselves free from the tyranny of the Junta. The old regime would fall and a new society would be built on the foundations of their defiance.

It was late at night now and outside the grounds of the Polytechnic Nikos became separated from his group. In the murky atmosphere he could not see how close he was to a policeman whose arm was lifted high into the air. Suddenly, he felt a weight come down on the back of his head and he screamed out in pain. Turning around, he saw the baton ready to strike him again. This time he ducked the blow. Weaving between the mass of people, he made his way towards the entrance to the Polytechnic.

A *crack* of gunfire suddenly cut through the dense wall of noise. From somewhere, the demonstrators were being shot at. It was impossible to see the source and around him protestors scattered, running in any direction they could, panicking to escape this unexpected terror. It was chaos.

Still feeling dizzy from the blow, Nikos could see that the Polytechnic's gates were being shut from inside. He told himself he must get inside as soon as he could, but his body was moving slower than his thoughts.

Then he felt a sharp pain in his side, as if he had been kicked hard in the ribs. He was almost doubled up but nobody heard his cry. All around was a deafening cacophony of sirens and shouting.

As Nikos approached the closing gates, one of his friends caught sight of him and grabbed his arm, roughly pulling him inside a second before they were bolted and padlocked.

The scenario excited the students. There was already a sense of triumph along with a stirring of collective memory. The siege of Missolonghi was on their minds, the moment when the Greeks had defiantly stood up against the cruel Turks and refused to be bowed. For Nikos, this was the true '*Óchi*!', the true 'No!', the refusal to accept the situation any longer. This was the thought going through his mind as he slumped quietly to the ground. '*Óchi* . . . *Óchi* . . .'

Most of the students inside crowded against the barricaded gates and no one noticed Nikos lying there. Their attention was focused on what was taking place in the street. They had heard a low distinctive rumble. To the horror of everyone who stood there, a tank had positioned itself outside with its guns trained on them.

One of Nikos' friends saw him, blood pooling around his body, and pulled him further away from the mêlée. Panic-stricken, he told one of the others to get help but it was already too late. When a young doctor reached him, his life had already drained away through the hole in his side and the gash in his head. The medical student closed Nikos' eyes and found a blanket to put over him. For now, there was nothing they could do with the corpse. It would have to lie there while they waited and watched the tanks that were positioned in front of the main and side gates in the street outside.

Back in Patissia, Themis could not sleep. She was listening to the radio, half awake, when an announcement came that the Polytechnic had been occupied. 'It is expected, however, that this situation will be resolved soon,' said a clipped military voice.

In the early hours of Saturday morning, she managed to retune to another station. It was one that was broadcasting from within the university grounds. It seemed that the students already sensed victory and she felt proud knowing Nikos was out there. Giorgos was fast asleep, oblivious to the unfolding events.

Eventually Themis dozed off on the sofa, with the volume turned low, and when she woke at five it was to a continual hiss from the radio. Sitting up and rubbing her eyes, she tiptoed into the bedroom and had another hour or two of sleep, filled with confused nightmares of fire and falling buildings. Even Margarita had made an appearance in her subconscious.

It was Spiros who woke her.

'*Mána! Mána!* They smashed down the gates! A tank smashed the gates! Of Nikos' university!'

'Where did you hear this?' she asked, springing out of bed immediately.

'Uncle Thanasis just came to the door. He saw an announcement on his television and thought we ought to know.'

Themis was still half-clothed from the night before and it took her only a moment to put on her skirt and find her shoes.

'Where are you going?' Spiros asked, seeing his mother throw on her coat and pick up her key. It was only seven in the morning and she did not usually go out at that time.

'I'm going to see . . .'

Then she was gone.

Chapter Twenty-Five

THEMIS RAN. SHE knew every paving stone of the road that ran down towards the Parthenon. There were several road blocks that day and many soldiers on the streets but they allowed her to pass. They did not seem to care about a middle-aged woman who looked as if she was late for a train. They would have had to run to catch up with her in any case as she skirted round their cordons. Fear fuelled her speed.

Over the heads of the soldiers and policemen who were all standing around, some of them smoking, some even laughing, she could see that the gates of the Polytechnic had been crushed. The mangled wreckage lay there, tangled up with flags and debris. The entire area was littered with abandoned flyers, lifted by the wind like autumn leaves. These manifestos seemed futile now.

No one got in Themis' way as she stealthily bypassed a group of uniformed men to get a closer look. Her heart was pounding from exertion and fear, and the coolness of the November day was not sufficient to prevent sweat dripping down her back.

Through the twisted metal bars she could see the remains of whatever had been used to try and create some kind of defence and for a moment this held her gaze. Then she saw something else. There were some bodies laid out on the pavement. They were not the wounded. They were the dead.

Two of them seemed bulky, the third smaller. From the latter, protruded a boot. Its familiarity pierced her like a blade. She had polished its brown leather so many times.

Themis pushed her way past a young soldier who was in her way.

'You're not permitted in this area,' he barked at her. 'These here are waiting for collection.'

He referred to the corpses as though they were goods in a warehouse.

Themis did not even hear him. She did not care for orders at this moment. Very carefully, as if not to wake him, she gently folded back the blanket. She saw the face of her son, calm, tranquil, handsome. On one side of his head, the long, thick curls were matted with blood.

Themis sank to her knees. The soldier did not try to intervene as she lifted the body into her arms. Nikos was slight and it was no effort to hold him, lifeless and still. Her grief was so profound that at first she could not weep. She gently kissed his face as she had done every night of his childhood.

The soldier was in his early twenties and knew his mother would do just the same. He turned his back on them and listened to the woman talking gently to her son. She whispered to him and then she was quiet for a while.

'I want to take him home,' she said to the soldier, her face now streaked with tears and blood.

He did not reply, but Themis gave him her address and she watched him put it in his top pocket. She would go home and wait, hoping that he and his colleagues would show even the smallest shred of kindness.

Themis walked back to the apartment very, very slowly. No one stopped her. She passed through two road blocks, and soldiers stepped out of her way as though she were a ghost. It was as if the world had gone silent. All she was aware of were the paving stones under her feet. One step and then another and another. She was in no hurry to arrive home. The more time it took her to get there, the longer it would be before she had to share the terrible news, with Giorgos, with Anna, with Andreas, with Spiros, with Thanasis. When that moment came, she would take the burden of their grief on her shoulders, with all the guilt of someone who was its cause. Never in her fighting days had she had to confront anything with such courage.

She did not even have to wait until she reached the apartment. Anna was walking across the square. She had gone out to find her mother and her brother. News as well as rumours were flying around. Common to them all was that the army had killed and wounded an as yet unconfirmed number.

Anna saw her mother from a distance and immediately noticed her slow and painful gait. Even her downcast gaze told her that something terrible had happened.

'*Mána!*' she said, hastening towards her. '*Mána* . . .?'

Themis' expression was enough to tell Anna.

'Nikos . . .?'

Themis looked down. She could not look into her daughter's eyes.

Anna gasped. She held her mother and the two sobbed where they stood in the square. Other people passed and glanced at them with curiosity. Such naked emotion was rarely seen on the streets. Attracting attention to yourself was ill-advised under the regime.

Giorgos had seen them from the balcony and came hurrying down. He shepherded them both across the square and into the hallway of the apartment, and supported Themis up the stairs. None of them spoke.

The door to the apartment was open and the two boys were standing waiting. Two pairs of chestnut-brown eyes looked at her expectantly.

'Where is Nikos?' asked Spiros, innocently.

Anna shook her head slowly.

'He's not coming back,' she answered to her brother, tears coursing down her face.

The boys grabbed each other and began to sob.

Anna heard the customary sound of her uncle's stick rapping on the door and opened it.

Thanasis had been watching his television all morning and did not need to be told what had happened. He was soon weeping uncontrollably, his already crumpled face ghoulishly contorted.

Nikos was the person who had brought him back to life. He felt so impotent that he was unable to do the same for him now, his beloved nephew, with whom he had shared so much time and conversation and who had showed him so much love.

Anna helped him towards a chair and Thanasis sat bowed with his head in his hands.

The room was almost silent, save for the sound of sniffing and the occasional gasp of someone drawing breath.

A while later, a sudden knocking sliced through their mourning. They all jumped. It stopped for a moment, then resumed again, this time more impatiently.

They looked anxiously at each other, knowing that it might be the authorities hunting for anyone who sympathised with the protesters. Not content with having slain an unknown number of innocents, it was possible that they were looking to round up others who had taken part.

They had no choice. The security police had a reputation for kicking down doors if they were not opened. None of them wanted that.

Giorgos went towards the door.

'Be careful, *agápi mou*,' whispered Themis, standing behind him.

When he opened it, Themis recognised the face of the young soldier who had spoken to her down at the Polytechnic.

The soldier recognised her instantly and addressed his words to her.

'Kyría Stavridis, I submitted your request. Your son is being brought home.'

'*Efcharistó*,' Themis said, almost inaudibly. 'Thank you.'

There was silence for a moment and she could see that the soldier had turned away and was already going down the stairs.

'When will that be?' she called after him.

'He is here now,' came the reply.

Giorgos leant over to look down into the stairwell. He could already see some movement in the hallway. Then came the heavy clip of boots on the marble as other soldiers came up. Within a moment they had reached the Stavridis door, bearing a makeshift stretcher on which lay a still, human shape beneath a grey blanket.

'Where . . .?'

Giorgos and Themis led them into the apartment. The children were comforting each other, their heads bowed. Only Thanasis watched as they brought Nikos' body in and laid him on his bed.

Two of the younger soldiers wanted to take the stretcher away with them, but the third said there was no need. He addressed the comment to Themis as if there was something generous in his gesture.

Once the door had closed behind them, Themis ran the tap.

She wanted to bathe Nikos' body and clean the blood from his face.

The children went upstairs with their uncle. He would bring them down again when Themis had finished the task.

With Giorgos' help, she changed their son into a clean shirt and a pair of flared trousers, which he had recently bought.

Even in death his curls were glossy as they dried.

As she worked she paused to examine the wounds. The bullet in his side had made a neat, circular hole and it was impossible to know whether it was this that had caused his death or the much larger wound in his head. She imagined herself back in the mountains with her friend Katerina and the others, cleaning gashes or trying to prevent a life from draining away. Thinking of the other dead that she had prepared for burial almost thirty years before took her mind away from the fact that this was her son. She could not allow herself to face that it was him, her precious boy, Aliki's Nikos, who lay on his bed in a sleep that would last an eternity. No, she did not allow her thoughts to dwell there.

She was oblivious to Giorgos, who stood and watched as she did up the shirt buttons. She had placed a piece of rag on the wound so that no blood could seep through. Even at such a moment, Themis was practical.

Giorgos brought two dining chairs into the bedroom and placed them one on either side of the bed. Themis sat down in one of them and bowed her head. She was thinking, not praying. No God, no Virgin Mary, came into her thoughts. It was just her and Nikos, replaying their last conversation. She told him that his mother would be proud of her warrior son. She told him over and over again, that she had loved him as if he were her own and promised that he would never be forgotten.

Then she wept quietly, bringing her chair closer to the bed so that she could take his cold hand. She had no sense of time passing and perhaps one or two hours went by. She only looked up when she heard the door opening and Thanasis came in.

'Can I sit with him?' he asked.

He put his arm around his sister before taking the other chair, crossing himself many times as he did so.

They both sat for a while and then Themis left the room. Giorgos was just coming in. He had been upstairs using Thanasis' phone to call Angelos.

'It's impossible for him to get a flight in time,' he said. 'But he'll try and be here for the forty days.'

Themis nodded. She could not bring herself to ask how Angelos had responded but understood that the conversation had been brief.

The children were back in the apartment, sitting in a row on the sofa like birds on a wire. They were all still crying. The closest that death had ever come to them was when their great-grandmother had died. They had all been very sad, but this was what happened to people when they were old and stooped, and their hair was grey and their skin wrinkled like fruit forgotten in a bowl.

Only Anna wanted to go in and see her brother. It was curiosity. Would he still look the same?

The sixteen-year-old walked in and to begin with she kept her distance. Her parents must have made a mistake. It was impossible that her big brother was not going to leap up and roar. She remembered the game 'sleeping lion' which Nikos had often played with his younger siblings where he lay silently and then suddenly roared, sending them screaming from the room. They had even sometimes had complaints from the man who lived below, whose afternoon rest they had disturbed.

She went slightly closer and leant in, to see if she could see his chest rising and falling.

In spite of his total stillness, the girl left the room telling herself that her brother was simply asleep, slumbering like a wild beast in a far-off land.

Giorgos, who was on reasonable terms with the priest, organised the funeral for the next day. The colonels were still denying that there had been any deaths but the whole city knew this was a lie. The service for Nikos was not the only one taking place that day.

Immediate family and neighbours, including the Hatzopoulos family and the Sotirious, who had been released but never reopened their shop, almost filled the tiny church of Agios Andreas. A few friends of Nikos arrived and stood in the shadows at the back. Even now the authorities were hunting down perpetrators of the Polytechnic strike, along with demonstrators, and a few of Nikos' *paréa* had been too afraid to come.

The flicker of candlelight illuminated all their faces as they listened to the chanting priests. Their voices floated incomprehensibly over Themis. She was lost in her sea of grief, the casket in front of them all a moment-by-moment reminder of the harsh reality of death. She noticed the priest sprinkle it with holy oil and then a phrase cut through into her conscious mind.

'*All is dust, all is ashes, all is shadow.*'

With these words she agreed. It seemed as if the rest of her life would be this way. At this moment she felt herself nothing more than a shadow. Nothing seemed real.

When the priest chanted: '*What now is shapeless, ignoble, and bare of all the graces*', it was all she could do to restrain herself from shouting that their Nikos would never be ignoble. He was a hero, in death as he had been in life, just as his mother had been, she

425

who had no grave, no marble to protect her bones, no place to be remembered except the barren island of Trikeri.

She no more subscribed to the words of the Church now than she had before this day. They were all obliged to listen and watch for what seemed like hours, hypnotised by the liturgy and the ritual, but all the while Themis was talking to Nikos in her mind, telling him everything she knew about his mother, how she had been a great artist, a woman who had defied the guards and laughed in their faces when they pressurised her to sign a *dílosi*. She told him how all the other women admired her, how selfless she was, and how she had saved Angelos without hesitation.

'Like you, Nikos, she was beautiful and strong and courageous,' she muttered under her breath, too quietly for Giorgos to hear.

During the service, it occurred to Themis that Aliki had never received burial rites. In her mind the priest was doing this for mother as well as son. Both of them deserved the dignity of a kind farewell, whatever their faith had been.

'*Kýrie eléison, Kýrie eléison, Kýrie eléison* . . .'

They all fell under the spell of the words.

'*Lord have mercy, Lord have mercy, Lord have mercy.*'

Each person inside the tiny church was calmed by the rhythm and the repetition, as though they had the power to heal. Even if they did not listen to the words themselves, the sounds they made soothed them like a balm.

The children were like a row of marble statues. They were suffering deeply over the loss of their brother but the change in their mother had also profoundly affected them. Even the expression on her face was unfamiliar. Life no longer had the certainty that they were used to.

The friends of Nikos who had been at the back of the church left first and had evaporated into nearby streets before the family emerged. Two soldiers stood on the street corner observing with interest.

The casket was taken to the Second Cemetery of the city where they gathered around the tomb to say a final goodbye.

When they returned home, a neighbour had brought in the traditional *kóllyva* that she had prepared. The children hungrily devoured the dish of mourning: wheat and sugar, nuts and raisins. For two days now they had not eaten anything but bread, rice and oranges. There was not much else in the house.

The old life seemed to have vanished overnight.

Chapter Twenty-Six

GRIEF SAPPED HER physical energy so much that Themis could scarcely get out of bed. She slept for most of the day, only getting up to sit at the table with the children, but they could hardly look at her. Her weight had dropped away so rapidly that she resembled a crow, her face thin and drawn, with a black dress that flapped loosely around her. Anna was doing all the shopping and cooking, and skipped school for a few weeks.

Even when, eight days after Nikos' death, Giorgos told his wife that there had been a change in regime, Themis showed no interest.

Following the disastrous outcome of the demonstration at the Polytechnic, a hard-liner, Brigadier Ioannidis, had ousted the hated Colonel Papadopoulos, claiming that order needed to be re-established. He accused the current leaders of corruption and put in his own men.

'What difference does it make?' said Themis wearily.

'They're saying he'll take even more brutal measures against any opposition than his predecessors,' said Thanasis. 'And you know Ioannidis' reputation, don't you?'

The new leader of the Junta was head of the notorious military police, a man who had already authorised so much terror, including the brutal crackdown during and after the recent Polytechnic uprising.

Thanasis' tolerant attitude towards the Junta had vanished in an instant after the shock of the previous week. He now regarded the leaders of the current and former military dictatorships as murderers. They had slaughtered his beloved nephew and for this they would never be forgiven.

Every day over the following weeks, Themis took the bus to the cemetery. Sometimes Giorgos would come with her but her grief demanded solitude and she did not want company inside it.

When Angelos came from America for the customary forty-day memorial service, Giorgos hoped his wife's spirits would lift and that she would be cheered by the visit of their long-absent son.

They all noticed immediately how different he looked. It was five years since he had left and everything about him had changed. He had thickened around the waist ('Blame this on the portions of food,' he laughed, patting his stomach, 'and the burgers!'). His weight did not bother Themis. She associated this with good health and prosperity. What she really disliked, however, was his haircut. It was short all over, with not a curl to be seen. But his presence seemed to cheer his siblings.

'You even have an accent!' teased Anna. 'You sound strange when you speak Greek. Say something in English! I want to hear you talk like an American!'

'Howdee, young lady!' said Angelos, emulating a Hollywood star.

The children all howled with laughter. It was as if their big brother had gone to the moon and been turned into an alien.

Angelos stayed for only two days but during that time he talked only of his new life, hardly drawing breath between descriptions of Chicago, his office, his colleagues, his car and the basketball team he supported. Corabel, the girlfriend, came frequently into the conversation and he passed around a photo that he kept in his wallet. She was blonde and curvy with huge lips and a wide smile.

When Angelos was out of earshot, Anna commented to everyone that her brother's girlfriend looked like a character from an American cartoon she had watched on her uncle's television. It was the first time the children had seen their mother smile since Nikos died.

Angelos seemed so in love with his new homeland. Everything in America was the biggest and the best, and he saw nothing wrong with US involvement in Greek politics.

'It's a well-run country,' he said as they ate. 'Not everyone likes Nixon, but at least there's no place for communists to hide with him around.'

Themis got up and quietly left the room. She had neither the will nor the energy to respond to such a sentiment.

'I suppose he did his grieving in the US,' she said to Giorgos as they returned from taking Angelos to the airport. They had all noticed that he had expressed little sorrow and seemed unbothered by the absence of his brother.

After the memorial service was over, Themis had told herself that she must try to rise above her sorrow, for the good of the family. Even if it was just for appearance's sake, she must make the effort. The combination of her grief for Nikos and the guilt over what she had told him was a great weight. She would always imagine that her revelation about his mother had driven her son into the fray.

The arrival of the new year brought little sense of renewal for

Themis. The only excitement was when Andreas won the coveted cross in the Theophania diving competition in January. It was in the local swimming pool but many older boys entered too and the family was proud that Andreas, at fourteen years old, was one of the youngest ever champions.

Spiros had made a crown out of cardboard for his brother and he kept it on throughout dinner. Everyone tried to keep conversation light and Themis had even done the cooking, making the apple cake that everyone loved so much, using her grandmother's recipe. They all wanted to believe that normal life was returning and chatted about how the priest had got soaked through when he threw the cross into the water, how one of the other boys had fought Andreas in the water to take away his prize and they all teased him about the attention he had received from a group of girls.

Towards the end of the evening, though, conversation grew darker. Even at the happy and traditional event they had gone to that morning, they had been aware of the presence of armed soldiers. They began to talk of the increased repression that Brigadier Ioannidis had instigated. It seemed in some way that sacrifices made by the Polytechnic victims had not only been in vain, their protests may even have led to a worse state of affairs than before. The regime continued to deny that there had been deaths and still hunted down anyone whom they suspected of being involved.

'That man is a monster!' Anna said.

'It's best not to say those words, even behind your own closed door,' urged Thanasis, who well knew the sinister tactics of the police. 'You never know who your neighbour is, or if they have the same views as you. If they overhear and they're not on your side, you could find yourself on a list, so be careful.'

'But he was the one who sent the tank!' she protested. 'That killed our—'

'Anna, please,' interjected her father.

Themis winced too. She knew there was a danger of both Anna and Andreas becoming politicised following their brother's death and, despite being only ten, Spiros could easily be influenced by his brother.

They all knew Ioannidis was a dictator, even though his style was to work behind the scenes. He had placed plenty of informers within the army to eliminate any soldiers who were not loyal and the small steps towards liberalisation that had been instigated by the deposed Papadopoulos were reversed. There was a new reign of fear.

In spite of herself, Themis could not challenge the status quo. With a mixture of sorrow and despair, she accepted that this was the way they now lived. All she wanted was to shield from harm the three beautiful children who came and went each day into the streets of Athens. She had given up the fight and found herself discouraging even her own children from voicing any criticisms of the Junta. Through the rest of the winter and into the summer she kept her sons' hair short and encouraged her daughter to wear her skirt long. The boys were enthusiastic pupils, Anna was studying very diligently for final school exams and all three went to church with their father.

Then, just when Themis thought that this oppressive regime was going to continue for ever, the cold-blooded Ioannidis set out to achieve his long-held ambition to unify Cyprus with Greece. In mid-July he staged a military coup on the island to depose its democratically elected president, Archbishop Makarios, whom he regarded as a communist. It was a step too far. Greece's interference gave the Turkish government an excuse to invade Cyprus, claiming it had to protect its citizens living on the island. The result was a huge loss of Greek Cypriot territory and lives. The Junta was forced to fight back, and the entire male population of Greece between the ages of twenty and forty-five was called up.

Within a week, the conflict was over, a ceasefire agreed and Cyprus was sliced in two, with tens of thousands of Turkish troops remaining in the north. It was an unmitigated disaster for Greece but Themis, like many others, felt a sense of satisfaction at Ioannidis' humiliating blunder.

One hot day in July, windows all around the square were open. Thanasis had his television on and as usual the volume was turned up high. This was the hour when everyone slept, but he would ignore neighbours' complaints today. Something had happened that he had to tell his sister.

It was unheard of for anyone to knock on the door at this time but Themis meandered blearily towards the door when she heard the rapping. It was Thanasis. Unusually, he was smiling. Ioannidis' catastrophic failure in Cyprus had heralded his end and Thanasis needed to share the news that power was being handed back to politicians.

'It's over,' he said smiling.

'What's over?' said his sister with incomprehension.

'Military rule,' said Thanasis. 'It's over. Finally, it's over.'

Thanasis came into the apartment and told Themis to put on her radio.

It was true. The Junta had collapsed. Democracy was to be restored.

At first it was almost impossible to believe and Themis sat listening without reaction. It was so unexpected that now it had happened it was hard to take in.

Giorgos rushed in mid-afternoon and Themis held out her arms to him. They silently embraced. The belief that Nikos' death may have played a role in the downfall of the Junta was in both their minds and, for the first time, Themis truly felt that he had not died in vain.

Over the next few weeks, Themis watched with a new sense of hope as a former Prime Minister, Constantine Karamanlis, returned from self-imposed exile and established an interim government until elections could be held in November. Political freedom was reinstated and the Communist Party was legalised. The speed of change surprised them all.

At the first democratic elections in a decade, Themis voted for the communists, but she was among a small minority, and Karamanlis, with his new centre-right party, New Democracy, was voted in as Prime Minister.

Soon after, he held a referendum on the monarchy. Themis and Giorgos did not agree about the royal family. His parents had been very sentimental about them and he had been brought up with a portrait of King Constantine's grandfather on the wall. Themis knew that he would vote in favour, and decided it was best not even to discuss it. She was just happy to be able to vote, and her vote would cancel out his. In December, when the country decided decisively in favour of the republic, Themis was thrilled.

'At least that meddling woman won't be back,' she said. Even after all these years, she resented the way that Frederika had so blatantly interfered in Greek politics.

The abolition of the monarchy was a significant change but it was not enough for Themis.

'What I am waiting for,' she said to Giorgos, 'is for someone to be punished, for someone to *pay* for their crimes.'

'You d-d-don't think it would be better just to forget the past? And m-m-make a new start?'

Themis did not conceal her scorn.

'That was never *their* position,' she said. 'The right always saw things through to the bitter end. And now I want to do the same.'

'That s-s-sounds vengeful,' he said.

'It is, Giorgos,' answered Themis. 'It's revenge that I want. Don't you understand?'

Many people had chosen exile for the past seven years rather than live under the colonels, and during that time had campaigned against the Junta. Most were now returning to Athens, as were those who had been forcibly exiled. They returned from the islands with horrifying stories of abuse and torture, and were living witnesses to the horrors of the Junta. They had no fear of speaking out now. Like Themis, they felt that something was unfinished and that there should be some kind of recognition that crimes had been committed.

'At last,' she muttered to herself one day when she was alone in the apartment and listening to the radio.

It was January and the Junta leaders had been arrested. Separate trials were going to take place of those who had staged the coup, those responsible for the action at the Polytechnic and those who had been torturers for the regime.

Themis was impatient but she had to wait six months until procedures began. There were dozens of defendants, but there was only one in whom Themis was really interested.

Themis, who had never liked television before, went up to Thanasis' apartment each day and insisted that they watch as much of the proceedings as were being shown. Together they sat on the sofa, mesmerised by the grainy black-and-white images projected into the apartment. It was electrifying to watch the accused, their every feature and expression shown in close-up. From time to time

Ioannidis stared directly into the camera and Themis felt as if his cold eyes looked straight into hers. The apparent callousness of the man chilled her to the core and occasionally she had to look away. Both he and Papadopoulos wore expressions of total indifference and Themis hoped that their obvious arrogance would destroy their hopes of acquittal.

She sat through every possible moment of the first trial, where both Papadopoulos and Ioannidis were found guilty and sentenced. The second trial obsessed her more. It was of those accused of perpetrating the crime at the Polytechnic, foremost among them being Ioannidis himself.

After a two-month trial, the man she blamed for the death of her son was found guilty. Themis sat next to Thanasis, waiting as though they were both in the court itself. Both of them hated the man equally and when he was sentenced to life imprisonment they quietly embraced each other. They were still sitting like this, reflected in the glass of the television screen long after the programme had changed.

Themis was initially disappointed that the psychopathic individual, whom she held responsible for the murder of her cherished son, did not receive the death penalty.

'Perhaps death is too good for someone like that,' she said to her brother.

Thanasis nodded. His throat felt so tight that he could not trust himself to speak. Themis continued.

'I hope that every day for the rest of his life he will wake up in a prison cell knowing that he will never have his liberty, never walk the streets again, never see the sunshine. Maybe that's worse than execution.'

She remembered her own time in solitary confinement and, satisfied by this thought, she wept with both pleasure and pain.

She still partly blamed herself for her son's actions but the ruthless monster responsible for his demise was finally punished. A deep sense of catharsis overwhelmed her. At last, some justice had been done for the innocents and the idealists who had died that November night.

Chapter Twenty-Seven

1976

THE THREE-YEAR MEMORIAL of Nikos' death was to take place in a few months and Themis was hoping that Angelos would return for it. It would be the first time he had been back to Athens since the forty-day service, though his letters came as regularly as ever, charting his steady upward trajectory: an office on a higher floor, a bigger pay packet, promotion to a better position, a new apartment and a flashier car. The letter twelve-year-old Spiros had just found in the hallway this morning announced that his big brother had proposed to Corabel, and photographs of the couple at their engagement party tumbled out of the envelope.

'Look, *Mána*!' Anna cried out, grabbing the one closest to her. 'She's so *pretty*!'

It was Spiros' turn to read from the pale blue airmail paper but he stopped in order to pick up one of the photographs that were being passed around.

'*Theé mou!* Look at her big boobies! Andreas! Look!'

'Spiros! S-s-stop it! N-n-now!' snapped Giorgos.

'Don't talk about your brother's fiancée like that,' interjected Themis. 'It's *very*, *very* rude.'

All the children were sniggering now and a crooked smile even passed across Thanasis' face.

Themis held an image of the couple in her hand and glanced at it. Spiros was right. Corabel's low-cut dress emphasised that she was well endowed.

What would be considered indecent in Greece was obviously acceptable in America, she thought to herself. She also noticed that her son had put on even more weight. The couple could only be described as overweight.

'Carry on reading, Spiros!' Themis instructed, when the mayhem had died down. They were all smiling now.

He put on his impression of a radio announcer's voice and continued. It was a description of all the food they had eaten at the party.

'*Pretzels* – what are they?' he asked.

Everyone shook their heads, so he continued.

'*And we barbecued the biggest steaks that I have ever seen. And Corabel's mum makes the best cheesecake.*'

'Cake made from *cheese*?' exclaimed Andreas. 'That sounds *disgusting*!'

Laughter ricocheted from wall to wall. In the warmth of this shared moment of humour, Themis felt the intense joy of the present. The feeling was an unfamiliar one. The agonies of the past had cast a long shadow over her, but perhaps it was going to fade.

Giorgos had never given up trying to encourage her into a more positive frame of mind, constantly reminding her that the children were all doing well, and how lucky they were not to have any money worries.

Themis appreciated the higher standard of living that they all now enjoyed. There were often outings to local tavernas and the cinema (Themis insisted on seeing Aliki Vougiouklaki's films as soon as they were released) and they were even planning to restore a small house in Tinos that Giorgos had inherited from an aunt. A telephone now sat proudly and prominently on a specially purchased table in the hallway, and they also had their own television, and the previous month had bought a new fridge and a vacuum cleaner. They would even be able to afford to send Andreas to study in London if he passed his exams. He had told them it was his dream.

'We even have a decent p-p-prime minister,' Giorgos said to his wife one day.

Themis smiled. 'I didn't vote for him, but I admit he's not doing a bad job.'

Themis still wore mourning. Over the past year, Giorgos had suggested that she should exchange her dark clothes for something a little brighter and one day made the mistake of buying a new blouse for her, white with blue flowers.

'Thank you,' she said politely, kissing him on the cheek. She then put it discreetly in the back of her cupboard. When Giorgos asked her a week later why she had not worn it, she replied curtly: 'I'm not ready, Giorgos. I will know when I am. But it's not yet.'

Until she felt the moment was right, it would be a betrayal of Nikos. Month by month she had torn a page from a calendar but this merely represented the vanishing of time, not emotion. The death of her son was still fresh in her mind and she did not want it to be otherwise.

With less than a month to go before the memorial service, the October days were short but there was still warmth in the air. Themis was on the balcony one afternoon when she heard a ring on the bell. She leaned over the railings hoping to see who it was but could only make out a head of silver hair and a dark blue jacket.

The man then glanced up as if he could sense her gaze and Themis was almost certain he had spotted her.

Since the legalisation of the Communist Party she no longer feared unexpected guests or cold callers, but in spite of this her heart began to beat with anxiety.

She went to the door and pressed the intercom.

'Who is it, please?' she asked very formally, an audible tremble in her voice.

A voice crackled through the speaker.

'Tasos,' came the answer, almost impatiently. 'Tasos Makris.'

A chill went down her spine. It was more than twenty-five years since she had heard that name and she had never imagined she would do so again.

There was no choice. He knew she was there and she had to let him in.

Her trembling finger pressed the button that opened the outside door and, a second later, she saw a ghoulish shadow dancing on the wall. This man from her past was climbing the stairs. Immobile with shock and fear, Themis stood at her apartment door. Even now it would not be too late to disappear inside and refuse him entry. A moment's hesitation lost her this opportunity and suddenly he was standing in front of her: Tasos Makris, almost unchanged from the last time they met.

'Themis Koralis?'

'That was my name,' she answered. 'Stavridis now.'

They stood awkwardly on the threshold for a moment.

'Can I come in?'

'Yes . . . yes. Of course.'

Makris followed Themis into the apartment. It was so rare for anyone but family to come in and it felt awkward to have a stranger in the home. Neither Giorgos nor the children were expected until later.

Themis offered Makris the armchair in front of the dresser. It

was the one that Thanasis sat in when he came down to see
them.

There was little light in the apartment and the curtains were
partly drawn. Themis decided she would leave them as they were.

'Let me make you some coffee,' she said. 'With sugar?'

'Without,' he responded. '*Sketo.*'

She turned away, wondering if he too could hear the pounding
of her pulse. The awkward silence was only punctuated by the
sound of clattering china and glass as Themis shakily went to work
with refreshments. She slopped sugar carelessly into the little pan
along with the coffee, not bothering to stir. Biscuits? No. She
wanted to keep hospitality to a minimum. Even before the water
had risen to the boil, she poured the murky, tepid mixture into
two cups and, with her back turned to her visitor, used these
moments to compose the questions that she would ask.

With coffee and glasses of water now in position on a small
tray, she walked slowly back towards the low table in front of
Makris and set them down. Once seated, she allowed herself to
look at him properly for the first time.

He was lean and dapper. She took in his well-cut suit and highly
polished leather shoes, neatly manicured nails and the flash of an
ostentatious gold watch. His hair was still impressively curly, even
though silver-grey now, but his moustache had streaks of dark. His
face was lined but no more than Giorgos', and his eyes were the
same as she remembered them. She recalled the last time she had
seen them. On Makronisos.

'How did you . . .?'

He anticipated her question and answered immediately.

'Koralis. In the phone book.'

'But it's in the name Stavridis.'

'Well, there's a Koralis in the building,' he answered.

It was Thanasis' name that had led him here and she did remember telling him, even all those years ago, that her family lived in Patissia.

'I tried a few wrong addresses,' he said. 'But I got here in the end.'

He gave her a smile. Decades earlier she had found it charismatic, but now she felt nothing. This man may as well have been a stranger in a crowd for all she cared. For so many reasons, she did not trust him. On Makronisos, his role had seamlessly shifted from being a victim of torturers to being a torturer himself. Even now a fascist element lurked in society and Themis could not be certain that he was not part of it.

Makris had many questions for her but, unsure of the man's reason for being here, she evaded them, answering vaguely and without commitment. Yes, she was married and she and her husband had three children. No, she did not need to work, as her husband had a good job. Yes, he was a public servant. Yes, one of her children had gone to live in America and was doing well. No, they did not really travel themselves. All her answers were true.

Behind Makris, in the shadows, were several photographs. These were of her wedding, the baptisms of the younger children and the photo of the young and handsome Thanasis when he graduated from the police academy. In addition, there were two sizeable framed images on the wall: one of Angelos in his academic gown, quite pompous and proud, and one of Nikos, taken when he was in the school football team.

Themis had a clear view of them as they talked and it seemed that they were trying to catch her eye. The likeness between father and sons was striking. Behind the halo of curls in front of her, Themis could see theirs, thick and black, and dark eyes that looked into hers.

She asked a few bland questions. Where did he live? Was he married? Did he have children? What did he do?

The answer to the last question was the only one that mattered to her. It came as no surprise that he had stayed in the army, eventually becoming an officer and retiring when the Junta fell. Many senior-ranking members of the army had evaded trial and prosecution by leaving at that moment. He had literally done a *volte face*, Themis thought, betraying all those ideals for which they had fought in the mountains. She wondered how many of her comrades might have died at his hand and how many people he had brutalised between then and now.

Makris took a sip of his over-sweetened coffee and put it down again, his expression betraying that it was undrinkable.

'*Loipón*. So,' she said expectantly, to fill the silence. It was the prompt Makris needed. She wanted him to go very badly but at the same time knew he had come for a reason and was impatient to know why.

'I want you to know that I saw you on Makronisos,' he said, leaning forward.

'Oh,' Themis responded, blandly.

'But I thought it would be better for you if nobody made the link between us.'

'I see,' said Themis. It was an obvious lie. It would have been worse for him than her.

'And I wanted to explain that I had signed the *dílosi* so that I could rejoin the fight,' he continued.

Themis listened but did not believe a word. His self-justification sickened her, but he had yet more to say.

'Instead of letting me go free, they kept me on Makronisos and made me supervise the new prisoners. It was the worse punishment they could have given me.'

'But then you stayed in the army afterwards,' Themis pointed out politely.

'Yes,' he replied. 'I wasn't qualified to do anything else and it was a good job.'

His explanation was shallow and his tone light-hearted.

Something she had learnt during her life was that if you allow someone silence, then they fill it and tell you something you might want to know. That was exactly what Makris did.

'I have started a new career now. I decided to go into local politics. Maybe in the longer term I'll aim higher. New Democracy . . . What do you think?'

His choice to join the centre-right party did not surprise her at all, but Themis was not prepared to engage in jovial conversation with this man. What she did think, though she had no intention of telling him, was that she now understood the reason he had come. He wanted to befriend her, to make sure that she would not betray him to people in his life who knew nothing of his past. Neither being an ex-communist nor an ex-torturer on Makronisos would help him in an election campaign.

She shrugged her shoulders and mumbled that she did not take much interest in politics these days. She did not wish to prolong the visit any further.

Makris then commented casually on the fact that she was in black.

'You're in mourning,' he said. 'One of your parents?'

'No,' she replied. 'They left us a long time ago.'

'A relation?' he asks.

'No,' she said. 'Not a blood relation, at least.'

It was the truth.

Right from the moment when Makris sat down, she had decided what she would reveal and what she would withhold. Nikos, Angelos and Aliki would not be mentioned by name.

Themis felt no emotion for this man. Neither passion, nor pity was stirred. All she wanted was for him to leave and by starting to tidy the cups she made this clear.

Suddenly Andreas and Spiros burst in through the door to dump their schoolbags and get ready for football practice.

Makris and Themis stood up. The likeness between the old man and their two elder brothers was very strong, but neither boy gave Makris a second glance.

'Children, please greet our visitor,' she told them. 'Mr Makris.'

The boys gave his hand a cursory shake and ran to their rooms to change. A moment later they were gone.

Themis did not sit down again. She needed Makris to leave before he turned round and noticed the photos. Even more importantly, she wanted him gone before Giorgos returned from work.

'I must be getting on,' she said. 'It was kind of you to find me.'

'It was very nice to see you, little fox,' he murmured, clearly hoping to raise a smile.

She did not give even a flicker of response to this reference to their past.

Until he was in the hallway, there was still a chance that the portraits would catch his eye, so she led him briskly from the room. He followed and did not look back.

Without another word, Themis opened the door.

'Goodbye,' she said, firmly.

Makris held out his hand but she did not take it. He looked momentarily puzzled and then turned away.

Themis shut the door immediately and stood with her ear pressed against it, listening to the sounds of footsteps descending the marble stairs. Hastening out on to the balcony, she stood and watched from the shadows. She could not resist. Just beneath the apartment she noticed a large, black Mercedes Benz. It had already moved off and was now purring down the street sending a cloud of exhaust fumes into the sky. It must have belonged to Makris. It did not surprise her. Everyone said that politics was a place where there was money to be made.

She went back inside and quickly cleared the cups and saucers. In her mind was a vision of this man driving back to Metamorphosi, where he lived, his gloved hands on the steering wheel, occasionally admiring himself in the driver's mirror or glancing down at his wristwatch to check the time. Themis had a feeling that it was a Rolex he had been wearing. She hoped that she would never see him again.

She was still drying the crockery when she heard the sound of a key in the lock. It was Giorgos.

He gave Themis a peck on the cheek and they both greeted Anna, who had come in just behind her father.

'How was your d–d–day?' he asked Themis.

'It was fine,' she said. 'Nothing out of the ordinary.'

'And y–y–yours, Anna?'

'I have so much studying,' she moaned.

'You'll manage,' smiled Themis. 'You're a clever girl.'

'Will you help me, *Babá*?' she asked. 'It's to do with interpreting blood samples. It's all figures.'

Anna was now at Nursing School and her father happily sat down to help her out.

'Of c–c–course, *agápi mou*,' he smiled, and sat down next to her.

Themis put a dish in the oven for their evening meal and wandered across to the dresser. She picked up the various photographs and dusted the frames. Then she removed the image of Angelos from the wall and gave the glass a cursory wipe, afterwards doing the same with Nikos'. Before replacing the latter on the hook she looked into his eyes and kissed his forehead. How ashamed Nikos would have been of such a father.

The disturbing visit and the forthcoming memorial service perhaps prompted Themis that evening to unlock the slim drawer in her bedside cabinet. She wanted to remind herself of the sweet face of the sleeping Nikos and to touch his lock of hair. While the drawer was open, she also ran her fingers across the embroidered heart, the thread still so silky after all these years. Tasos Makris had missed out on so much, she almost pitied him. Locking the drawer again, she replaced the key on the shelf and went back into the kitchen to serve dinner. Father and daughter were still at the table, contentedly poring over numbers.

A week later, the three-year memorial took place. Angelos could not make it.

The cemetery was tidy and the graves well swept. Avenues of the dead stretched away in every direction. Next to many, oil lamps flickered and several women were on their hands and knees cleaning and polishing. When she passed the area most recently used for burials, Themis noticed the diminutive grave of a child with still-fresh flowers on the mound of earth. A marble slab was yet to be laid. Next to this was the tomb of an army general and a plaque next to his bust read: 'Serving his country on Mount Grammos, 1949'. Adjacent to that was a couple who had died within months of each other, aged ninety-eight and ninety-nine respectively. As she did on every visit, Themis paused to reflect. Whoever you were, if you lived in this part of Athens this was likely to be where you would spend eternity. Your actions and beliefs, the cause of your death, the length of your life, made no difference to your destination. The Second Cemetery in Rizoupoli held the bones of every kind of person. As it was for the living, the dead did not always choose their neighbours.

Giorgos' ancestors had been wealthy enough to purchase a burial space and Nikos' name was now etched into the marble slab, which also covered the bones of Giorgos' parents and grandparents. The black-and-white photographs of the older generation had faded, but Nikos' colour image was still fresh. It was the same photograph as on the wall of the apartment, and his youth and good looks stirred anyone who passed. Nikos' face would forever be unblemished.

As family and friends gathered by the grave, the words of the priest floated in the air around them, but their focus was on the recently engraved plaque. Themis had long ago decided not to adorn her son's grave with a poem or a promise that he would not be forgotten. It was unnecessary. '*Our beloved son who died for his beliefs, 17 November 1973*' said it all. A butterfly was fluttering about close by and landed on the flowers that Themis had laid. She did not believe in God but she paid attention to such signs and left the graveside knowing that Nikos was at peace.

That night, she stepped out of her mourning clothes and put them in the laundry basket. The following day she would wash them and put them away. It was time to cast aside her *penthos*. She found the blouse that Giorgos had given her at the back of her cupboard and stood in front of the mirror doing up the buttons. Shedding her dark clothes would make no difference. Her grief for Nikos would always live within her.

Chapter Twenty-Eight

1985

POLITICS HAD SEE-SAWED in recent years between left and right, and Themis had been happy when the country got its first ever socialist government in 1981. Andreas Papandreou, the Prime Minister, began to face up to resentments that had lingered for almost forty years and officially recognised the courage of those who had resisted the Nazis during the occupation.

He also gave communists who had fled the country at the end of the civil war permission to return and lifted the threat of persecution.

The day she heard, Themis thought of Panos and Aliki and those with whom she had fought. Only with such people could she celebrate this moment. She reflected on the news with a mixture of joy and sadness. It was too late for so many.

More than with politics these days, she was preoccupied with the lives of her children. There were so many events and milestones.

Anna had long since qualified as a nurse and was soon to be married, Andreas had a good job in the biggest bank in Greece, and Spiros, who was in his final year at university, was hoping to follow his father into the tax office.

At the end of October, news arrived from further afield. Two

450

letters arrived on the same day. One had a German and the other a US postmark.

After their grandmother's death, Margarita had continued writing occasionally to Themis. She shared the letters only with Thanasis as neither Giorgos nor the children were very interested in them, having never met her.

This time, Margarita's letter did not come from divided Berlin. In recent years, her occasional missives had become little more than veiled descriptions of austerity and dissatisfaction, but this time there was a different tone. Margarita had married for the second time and her new husband was the manager of a large State-owned printing company. She had moved to Leipzig to be with him.

He has some grown-up children who often come to visit with their children so life is busy at weekends.

We had just a few guests at the wedding and I enclose a photograph with me and Heinrich, our best man, Wilhelm, and two of the grandchildren, who were flower girls. We had a lovely day and went on a short holiday to a lake near Dresden afterwards. It feels like a new start and I must confess it's nice to have moved away from Berlin. I can't say much but it really was a very depressing place to live.

Leipzig is the city where a famous composer called Felix Mendelssohn was born and the buildings are beautiful. Even the village where we live outside the city has a fine square and everyone takes great pride in keeping the place clean and tidy.

My German is now good enough for me to work in the reception at the factory! I am there a few afternoons a week and it will give me rights to a pension and other benefits, which the government here is very generous with. My husband will retire in five years' time

*and I will stop working at the same time so that we can enjoy our
retirement together.*

Themis still pictured her sister as a dark-haired beauty in her
twenties. Now her eyebrows knitted together, as she tried to
recognise the Margarita she remembered in the face of the silver-
haired sixty-year-old. Her features were recognisable, though in a
thinner face and she seemed to have shrunk to half the size. She
looked more Eastern European than Greek now but was still
beautiful, if in a different way.

Margarita had never openly complained about Berlin but Themis
had always read between the lines and it was always obvious that
her first marriage had not been a happy one. In the previous letter
she had mentioned that her divorce had come through and her
former husband had immediately married his mistress, who
promptly gave birth to their child.

For the first time in decades, Margarita sounded content.

'Happy, finally,' said Thanasis sparingly.

Themis nodded in agreement, silently reflecting on the irony
that it was her sister, rather than herself, who had ended up living
in a communist state.

The letter from the US was equally unexpected. It was not on
the usual airmail paper but instead was heavy, with the address on
the envelope almost obscured by the number of stamps that had
been needed to send it. As was traditional with Angelos' letters,
they would wait until they were all eating together before opening
it. It was Spiros who now opened his big brother's 'missile', as he
called it.

'It's a parcel!' he exclaimed. 'It's not a letter!'

He carefully made a slice through the tape that sealed the package
and pulled out an elaborate concertina of card. It was dove grey

with an ornate arrangement of silver ribbon and shiny rosettes. Very gingerly he handed it over to his mother.

'It doesn't look as though it needs me to read it,' he said.

'It's an invitation,' beamed Themis.

With great difficulty (because her English was minimal), she began to read out the announcement of a forthcoming wedding.

Mr and Mrs Charles Stanhope
are proud to announce the marriage
of their daughter Virginia Lara Autumn
to Mr Angelos Stavreed

She stopped reading.

'Stavreed?'

'I think he's changed his name to a version that's easier to pronounce. In America anyway,' said Spiros.

'But that's not our name!' exclaimed Giorgos indignantly.

'Virginia? Who's Virginia?' queried Anna.

Themis shrugged.

'You can carry on reading it,' she said, passing it to her son. 'I can't manage this swirly writing.'

Spiros continued, paraphrasing.

'They're getting married at All Saints' Church, Bel Air and afterwards there is a reception in the Sunorama Hotel in Beverly Hills.'

'. . . But wasn't he engaged to Corabel?'

'He's never mentioned Virginia before,' said Anna. 'What happened to Corabel?'

'And are we invited?'

'Of course you're invited, *Mána*,' Spiros reassured her.

All their names, including Thanasis', were squeezed in a row across the top.

'Where is Beverly Hills?' Themis asked.

'In Los Angeles,' answered Thanasis knowledgeably. 'On the west coast of America. It's a very, very long way away.'

'Uncle Thanasis knows all about Los Angeles,' teased Spiros. 'It's where all the film stars live!'

Thanasis smiled, unashamed of his favourite hobby. He revelled in the knowledge of American stars that came with watching television.

'And when is it?' Themis enquired.

'September.'

'September? Then we've missed it!' she said with exasperation. 'It's already happened!'

'Don't worry, *Mána*, it's for *next* September!'

'You mean in a year's time?' Themis shook her head.

A son who had changed his name, getting married on the other side of the world, in almost eleven months' time? She was bemused.

'Well, we have p-p-plenty of time to think about it,' said Giorgos with a wry smile.

'Was there a letter with it?' asked Themis, hoping for more explanation.

Spiros shook the package, but nothing else fell out.

'You'd think he would have written to tell us what he was planning . . .'

Themis was hurt that her son's marriage should be announced to them so bluntly.

A few weeks on, another letter arrived from Angelos.

I hope you will come for our big day! It will be very unlike a Greek wedding but I am sure you will have a great time. Virginia's family are Catholic so I have had to convert. But on the whole we believe in the same things so I don't think you will find it too alien.

Themis did not mind in the least about the religious aspect of the wedding. She minded much more that he was getting married so far away, to someone they had never heard of until the invitation had arrived and that his name had already been Americanised. It seemed a crime to deny his Greek roots in that way.

The following September, with their children's encouragement but not their agreement to attend, Themis and Giorgos both boarded an aeroplane for the first time. Acquiring passports and visas had been trying enough, and after nearly two days of travel and several changes of plane, they arrived exhausted in Los Angeles.

They were greeted by a smiling Angelos in his gleaming new red Cadillac. He was excited that they had come and impatient to show them his new life.

Themis' first observation was that he had put on even more weight than she had expected, but she covered her disapproval. 'You look well, *agápi mou*,' she said.

'When will we m-m-meet Virginia?' asked Giorgos.

'Today,' answered Angelos, brightly. Themis noticed that he now spoke Greek with an American accent. Despite her curiosity, she did not pluck up courage to ask what had happened to Corabel.

When they got to his home, a pretty house with a lawn out front, Virginia was waiting to greet them. They realised that they had already been living together for some time. Giorgos disapproved, but Themis felt that she was in no position to do so and greeted the perfectly coiffured blonde with warmth.

It may have been the jet lag, but their enthusiasm for almost everything except the climate was lacking.

The wedding was in three days' time, and they spent a few hours each day with their son, mostly meeting various members of Virginia's family and eating meals that they could not finish.

'It's n-n-not as if the food tastes of anything!' Giorgos complained to Themis. 'So why d-d-do they give you so much it spills off the plate?'

It struck them both as a waste, but also the reason that so many people seemed almost obese.

The night before the wedding, there was a formal dinner. Themis had brought some of the linen that she had been given by her own grandmother. It seemed appropriate to pass it on. The table-cloth and pillowcases were finely embroidered with delicate lace edging but she could see immediately Virginia opened the parcel that it was not to her taste.

'It's so . . . *quaint*,' she said.

Angelos looked mildly embarrassed. The expression on his fiancée's face said more about her feelings for the gift than the words that Angelos used to translate. Themis understood that the well-meant gift would be put in the back of the cupboard as soon as she and Giorgos had left. This was clearly the implication of 'quaint'.

Virginia's mother, sisters and aunts all wore bright colours to the wedding and Themis felt dowdy in her pastel-blue dress and jacket, even though she had had it specially made by a Kolonaki dressmaker. The man-made fabrics people wore in America were as unfamiliar to her as the ubiquity of blond hair. The food, the whiskey and the music were similarly alien, as was the language. Both Themis and Giorgos tried to speak a little English, but the Californian accent made it almost impossible to understand what people replied and, although the Stanhope family did their best to make them feel at home, Themis and Giorgos felt out of place from beginning to end.

Themis kept wondering how Nikos would have viewed the gathering and wished he was there with them. Although the boys would not resemble each other so much now (Angelos would probably be twice Nikos' size and his hair was clipped shorter than ever) it would still be evident that they were brothers.

It became clear to Themis during conversations that Angelos had written Nikos out of his own history. Virginia and her parents knew only of his three living siblings.

Apparently Nikos did not fit the image that Angelos wanted to cultivate, and when she listened to the political opinions expressed by the Stanhopes she realised why. They were staunch supporters of Ronald Reagan ('Uncle Thanasis would definitely approve of him,' quipped Angelos, 'a Hollywood actor turned Republican president!').

Themis and Giorgos stayed on in Los Angeles for three days after the wedding but were relieved when the time came to leave and even happier when they eventually arrived back in Patissia. They faced a barrage of questions from their children. Was it the land of plenty that they imagined? Was everyone glamorous? Did people drive round in huge cars? On three-laned highways? The answer to all their questions was a simple 'yes'. America had seemed like another planet. Even Thanasis was curious to know what the United States looked like in 'real life', but what he really wanted to know was whether his father, Pavlos, had turned up.

'I don't think Angelos invited him,' said Themis. 'He hasn't met him since he moved there so . . .'

The next letter from Angelos announced that Virginia was pregnant with their first child and in the following half-decade, every letter was accompanied by the announcement of a pregnancy or a photograph of a new baby or a toddler taking first steps or attending playgroups or on swings or in the swimming pools of flashy hotels. They were not framed and placed on the dresser. Themis was still annoyed by Angelos' lack of loyalty to his brother's memory. Perhaps one day if she met Nancy or Summer or Barbara, she would change her mind, but for now they seemed no more than distant relations. When they received a note one day saying that another baby had arrived, they were shocked by the name. Nikos.

'Why now?' asked Themis quietly to Giorgos, as her eyes ran over the lines. 'I hope this boy knows what he has to live up to.'

She was mildly affronted by Angelos resurrecting his brother in this way.

'I am sure he h–h–has his reasons,' said Giorgos, putting his arms round her. 'It's nice that he wants to r–r–remember him.'

Themis had her own theory. She suspected that the birth of a son had brought out the more traditional side of Angelos. She could think of no other reason for him to revert to a Greek name for this child.

Themis was not upset for long. She contemplated this baby thousands of miles away in a cot. Perhaps he had very curly hair.

Anna, Andreas and Spiros all married over the following years too and Themis soon found herself with five grandchildren who all lived in the city of Athens. She was a model grandmother and everyone relied on her for childcare. Given that they had all stayed in the same neighbourhood and within ten minutes' walk of each other, this was never hard to arrange. The old table was full again and hungry children jostled to fit. Only Uncle Thanasis had an 'official' seat. Even when the stairs became an enormous effort, he came down each day. Everyone loved to see him in spite of his crookedness, and the smallest children liked the fact that his food had to be cut up for him just as it did for them.

When he did not appear as usual for dinner one day, Themis sent Anna's oldest up to check on him. He returned ashen-faced.

Within seconds Themis was in her brother's apartment but she could see immediately that he had gone. A catastrophic heart attack meant that he had not suffered. In death, she caught a glimpse once again of the good-looking boy he had been and knew that he was totally at peace.

Themis' affection for Thanasis had grown immeasurably these past years and she mourned him deeply. Her brother's unequivocal love for Nikos had swept away all other memories of their conflicts and differences. He was laid next to Nikos, and Themis made sure to tuck their mother's embroidered handkerchief in his pocket before the burial. She had found it in his hand the day he died. For a second time, Themis took the bus each day to visit the *nekrotafeío*.

After forty days she stopped. She had to clear out Thanasis' apartment. Her brother had few possessions, so it took only a short time. She left his old television where it was and the only thing she kept for herself was his stick. It had become such a part of him and now it stood in the corner of her living room.

Anna and her husband gave up their rented place in a nearby street and moved into Thanasis' former apartment with their three children. The place was cramped but no more so than it had been when Themis was growing up there with her siblings. The children ran up and down the stairs to spend time with their grandparents and Themis cooked enough for them all. The doors were always open and there were tolerant neighbours who rarely complained about the noise. Anna was nursing full time at the Evangelismos Hospital and relied on her mother to keep her family filled with *gemistá,* and *spanakórizo*. Themis vainly hoped that if they were eating tasty food made with produce from the *laikí,* they would not be tempted to grab something from one of the fast-food restaurants popping up all over Athens.

Since suffering a mild stroke that had left him slightly immobile, Giorgos was unenthusiastic about going out and mixing with other people. Themis spent much of her time caring for him but frequently went out with her children and always sat at the head of any table. She was the matriarch and still full of energy.

These days, usually with one or two children under her feet and school collections to do, Themis had no time to read the newspapers and if she had the radio on, it was to listen to music.

One day in the summer of 1989, Anna came in to see her parents on her way from work. Giorgos was ill that week so she brought in some fresh spinach from the market, knowing that her mother had not been able to get out that day. Themis had mentioned that she wanted to make *spanakópita,* spinach pie. They drank some cold lemonade together and then Anna left.

It was a hot afternoon and the ingredients for the filo pastry stuck to Themis' hands. Eventually she put a cloth over the mixing bowl and left it to rest before preparing the strong, green leaves that Anna had so thoughtfully purchased for her. She took them out of the newspaper in which they had been wrapped, put them in the sink and ran them under the cold tap, splashing her face with water as she did so to cool down. Once she had dried her hands, she picked up the scrunched front page of *Eleftherotypia* to throw it away. Something caught her eye. It was a word in the headline: *Symmoritopólemos.* Bandit war. She winced. It was an expression she loathed. Would she ever be able to put those memories behind her? Forty years on the word brought back the pain of being sadistically lashed, *sym-mor-í-ti-ssa,* 1-2-3-4-5. With each syllable a soldier had brought down his whip hard on her bare back. '*Synmorítissa!*' 'Criminal bitch!'

Leaning against the kitchen worktop, she ran her eyes over the article. Next to the word she hated so much, *Symmoritopólemos*, was another. *Emfýlios*. Civil war. This was the very first time she had seen those years of conflict described in such a way. In a gesture of reconciliation, the government had proposed a law to formally recognise those five years of vicious conflict in which her brother had perished and her comrades had died as something other than a 'bandit war'. From now it would be officially referred to as a conflict between the government army and the communist army. Themis saw the drops of her own tears falling on to the page and smudging the type. After all this time, it had been recognised that she, Panos, Katerina and so many others had been soldiers, not brigands. This was a huge step towards the healing of old wounds and something she had never imagined could happen. A coalition that comprised both the centre-right and the Communist Party was currently in power and had proposed the change, and it was not going to be contested by other parties.

She looked across at Giorgos, who was asleep in his chair and wished she could share her joy with him but he would never fully understand, especially now. She sat down at the table and spread her hands across the page to flatten out the creases. There was something else she wanted to read and with almost total disbelief she took in the implications.

In a paragraph on the same crumpled page, the journalist referred to the files on communists and detainees. All these records were still held by the security services but were now to be destroyed. Themis knew hers had always been there, somewhere, gathering dust in a cabinet. All these years it had hung over her like the sword of Damocles.

Only the briefest details on this decision were given. For the next hour or so she occupied herself with cooking and soon the intoxicating smell of her spinach pie drifted out of the balcony

461

doors, rose and entered the open windows of the floor above, summoning Anna's hungry children down. All the while, Themis thought of what she had read.

For the first time in many years, she bought a newspaper each day and surreptitiously scoured the pages for more details. When there were none, she immediately disposed of the paper in the bin. In the following days, articles began to appear that reported some opposition to the impending destruction. Some believed it was a magnanimous gesture of forgiveness, others claimed it was the gratuitous destruction of a historical archive, others said that such an act protected all those who had collaborated or informed. The files were said to contain detailed notes on people's comings and goings, eavesdropped conversations carefully transcribed and lists of every suspects' acquaintances. It seemed that millions of people had been happy to exchange fragments of information for even a minimal fee. There were even some government ministers who were insisting that their own files should be located and saved. Themis was obsessed by the issue but said nothing to Anna, or to Andreas and Spiros when they called in to see her and their father.

It was 29 August, the anniversary of the final day of the Battle of Grammos, the last day of the civil war. More importantly for Themis, it was the date of the death of her brother. As she did each year, she went quietly and alone to light a candle in Agios Andreas.

There was no one in the church and she stood for a moment contemplating how it might have been to die on those mountains. Did Panos know at that moment that the war was lost? Did he die in pain? No matter how many years had passed, she always asked herself the same questions.

The temperatures were soaring that day and as she emerged

from the semi-darkness she was momentarily blinded by the sunshine. She did not see old Kyría Sotiriou, who still lived in the neighbourhood, coming towards her. At first, she just heard her voice.

'Kyría Stavridis,' she said breathlessly. 'Kyría Stavridis! Have you heard?'

Themis stopped.

'Heard . . .?' she said.

'They've done it . . .'

The elderly woman was struggling to breathe and Themis realised that she was overcome with extreme emotion.

'Do you want to sit for a moment?' Themis asked, leading her to the bench just by the door of the church.

'They . . . They . . . They've burned them. They're all gone . . .'

For a moment, Themis wondered if she was talking about a forest fire. Some of them had been devastating in recent years, possibly started deliberately and, in this heat, trees could easily go up in flames.

With one or two more gasps, Kyría Sotiriou finally managed to get her words out.

'All the files have gone. Millions of them. They're gone.'

It was unspoken between them, but Themis knew that Kyría Sotiriou had her own reasons for celebrating this.

The older woman sat there, shaking her own head from side to side, as though she still could not believe herself what she had just heard. Themis could scarcely take it in either.

After a few minutes, Themis helped her up and they walked together to the corner where they went their separate ways.

As soon as she was back in the apartment, Themis put on the radio. Her hands were shaking so much that she could scarcely turn the dial from her usual music channel to the news. She knew that, on the hour, someone would read the headlines. It was ten minutes to two. She helped Giorgos to drink a glass of water and then sat at the table and waited.

Sure enough, the newsreader confirmed what Kyría Sotiriou had told her. Names, evidence, records had been incinerated. Eight million files had been destroyed in Athens and a further nine million in cities around Greece. A reporter gave a first-hand account from a factory in Elefsina just outside Athens, describing how truckloads of files had been loaded into the furnace. There had been protests from people wanting to retrieve their own files. For Themis, it was the ultimate act of forgetting. Her final release. It was almost beyond belief.

That night the temperature in Athens hardly dropped from the daytime high and Themis went to bed feeling almost feverish.

She had a vivid dream. She was standing in front of a huge conflagration. Fire was licking hundreds of metres into the air and men in overalls were stoking the pyre with armfuls of cardboard files, carelessly chucking them on to the flames. She could feel the heat as pages and pages with lists of names curled and rose into the air, disintegrating into small shreds of ash that were blown away by the wind. When she tried to catch a piece the fragments melted away. Then she saw an entire sheet rising into the air. It was a photo of Panos. He was in army uniform, smiling and strong, his hair made fair by the sun and his skin darkened by exposure to the elements. She wanted to seize it in her hands but she could not grab it in time and it floated out of her reach. Then she saw a drawing of Aliki. It was an exact likeness. She was radiant, just as she always had been. Both these images were lifted up higher and higher, dancing and twirling in the breeze, further and further out of reach. Finally the blaze died down and embers were all that remained.

Themis woke. It was still dark in the bedroom and she lay there for a moment before quietly getting out of bed to avoid waking Giorgos. Desperately needing some air, she went out on to the balcony.

Dawn was just breaking as she stood watching a brightening sky.

Epilogue

2016

Nikos and Popi were silent for some time. The young people found it almost impossible to take in what they had heard. Before today, they had known so little about their family. Most of all, their grandmother was not the person they had imagined. She was so much greater.

'And all the time we didn't think you cared about politics,' said Popi. 'I didn't even know how you voted.'

'I did get a little disillusioned with everything,' Themis admitted. 'I felt I had done my bit really.'

'Your "*bit*",' Nikos said, smiling at her understatement.

'At least they recognised it as a civil war,' added Popi.

'It was a big moment,' agreed Themis. 'I just wish Panos could have known it, and Aliki and everyone else who gave up so much.'

Nikos was particularly thoughtful. It was almost more than he could take in.

'I knew very little about my Uncle Nikos,' he said. 'I'm really shocked. *Yiayiá*, you know we have a big portrait of him in our house.'

'Of course I didn't . . .' she said with a smile that betrayed her surprise. She had not been to the US since Angelos' wedding.

'There's a technique that can enlarge a photograph and make it look like an oil painting. So Dad commissioned one from a picture of Uncle Nikos and now it looks like something from an art museum. It's the same image you have on your wall but transformed into something really grand.'

With his hands he indicated its size: almost one metre high.

Nikos could see that his grandmother was pleased by the idea.

'It's in pride of place. The "hero in the hall", we call him,' continued Nikos, smiling.

Both Popi and Nikos were full of questions about what they had heard.

'How did you survive childbirth in those conditions?' asked Popi. 'My mother tells us it is the most painful thing a woman can ever experience . . .'

Themis shrugged.

'There was no option, *agápi mou*. A baby has to come out somehow. And the support of other women kept me alive, as I told you.'

Nikos had a burning question.

'So my grandfather isn't really my grandfather?'

'No, Nikos. But Giorgos brought those two boys up as his own. And he was the best father anyone could have.'

'But Tasos Makris? Did you ever see him again?' he asked.

'No . . .' said Themis with enough hesitation to raise a doubt in her grandchildren's minds.

'But do you know what became of him?' asked Popi, detecting the smallest of cracks.

'Yes, I do,' Themis answered.

Makris was Nikos' grandfather, so she felt it was unfair to withhold the truth, given that she had told them both everything else.

'Your mother met him, Popi.'

'Really? She's never mentioned it,' said Popi with bemusement.

'That's because she didn't know it was him.'

1999

One September day, Themis was clearing plates after lunch and Giorgos had moved over to his usual chair to watch the new colour television. He had the volume high, which Themis would turn down as soon as he fell asleep. Suddenly she heard the almost musical sound of glasses tinkling together on the draining board. Then the door of the dresser fell open and a framed picture of Andreas' family slid towards the edge. She ran over to save it from falling to the floor and automatically straightened the photographs of Nikos and Angelos that were slightly askew on the wall behind. She knew it was illogical even as she did it. Only when the windows began to judder violently did she react as she knew she was meant to. It was an earthquake.

In more than seven decades, living almost continuously in Athens, the regular vibrations of seismic activity beneath the city had become part of her life. She knew well that a small tremor had been enough to destroy the mansion where she was born.

Everything around her was vibrating now. It was like being on a train that was trundling through a station. The light fitting that hung from the ceiling was swaying and the television flickered, though Giorgos did not seem to notice.

Themis hurried over to help him from his chair and with great difficulty got him to move. Their building was constructed many years before engineers had found a way to defy the movements of tectonic plates but Themis took the standard precaution of getting them both underneath the dining table. It was a huge struggle but she knew this was the only safe place to be.

Anna had come running down to make sure they were all right. Her children were out playing in the square so she was anxious, but knew they were safer out there than if they had been inside. As long as they followed the standard drill to find an open space and stay there, they would be safe. She cowered under the table with her arms around her parents and waited.

They knew the movement might return either with a stronger or a lesser shock, so they paused a few minutes in anticipation and then agreed that for now the tremors seemed to have stopped.

'I'll go and stay out there with the children,' said Anna to her mother. 'If there is another quake, you must get back under the table.'

They both helped Giorgos back to his seat and then Themis put on the television again. The film that had been on had been replaced by a news report, showing early footage of the damage caused by the quake.

Themis watched with dismay. There were graphic images of collapsed buildings and victims being ferried on to stretchers and taken away for emergency treatment. The epicentre had been close to Parnitha, a region north of Athens, and the journalist was listing some of the places most badly affected. Kifissia and Metamorphosi were among them.

When Anna returned with the children, she called in to check on her parents. It seemed that their neighbourhood was undamaged, but the screams of ambulances rushing up and down Patission Avenue were enough to persuade her that she should go to the hospital to see if there was anything she could do.

'Reports are saying that there could be thousands injured,' said Themis.

'I'll go right away,' said Anna. 'Will you give the children something to eat later?'

'Of course, *agápi mou*. Don't worry.'

Themis and Giorgos continued to watch the TV, mesmerised by the images of buildings that seemed to have crumbled like pastry, leaving ugly metal rods protruding in every direction. Distressed families stood about anxiously as firemen and soldiers attempted to lift slabs of concrete to find the missing.

Minute by minute, events unfolded in front of them. It was a real-life drama, not an artificial one, and happening not far away.

'It's terrible,' said Themis. 'Terrible.'

Giorgos was watching with a blank expression. He did not seem to register the seriousness of the situation.

For several hours, there was continuous footage of the dead and wounded, and then politicians and fire chiefs began to appear in front of the cameras. Several large factories had collapsed. If the earthquake had happened at night, said one politician, the workers would not have been affected but at three in the afternoon meant it had been catastrophic.

As he said this, two men passed in front of the camera carrying a stretcher. The body had his or her face concealed with a blanket but the arm hung limply down to the side.

'Shall we turn it off, Giorgos?' asked Themis. 'I think we have seen enough now. Do you want me to turn to another channel?'

Giorgos had already nodded off to sleep, so Themis switched off the television and went out on to the balcony. The plants were dry. It was a very hot September day and she began to water them.

She needed to do something to take her mind away from a tragedy that she could do nothing about.

As so often, her thoughts strayed to Nikos. Would he ever have allowed the construction of a building that was going to collapse in an earthquake? She doubted it. He had wanted better houses for everyone, not worse.

Anna, meanwhile, was at the hospital. She had done the right thing to go. There were dozens of people waiting to be treated, some mildly injured but many much more seriously, and every pair of nursing hands was needed. She was immediately assigned to the team dealing with those requiring the most intensive care, and soon the ward was full.

She dealt with several women first, cleaning wounds caused by falling masonry. She and another nurse worked together.

Anna wondered whether it was like this in a war zone, with the constant arrival of the wounded, having to prioritise one dying person over another, working with too few resources and trying to remain calm and not listen to calls from those in pain.

Her fourth patient was quieter. He was an old man. She was unsure if he was even alive at first because he was so still. He had a dressing on his head but blood was soaking through.

She spoke to him and his eyes opened wide.

'Can I remove this?' she said gently.

He did not reply so she went ahead.

As she peeled away the bandage, and carefully cleaned the deep gash on his forehead, she noticed his halo of silver-grey curls on the pillow. All the while that she went about her work, Anna was studying his face, mesmerised by the set of his eyes and the depth of their colour despite his age. He must have been so handsome as a young man. His was the kind of lean, sculpted face that never lost its beauty. What really struck her, though, was the sense of something familiar.

She noticed his shallow breathing and realised that he was struggling. His fathomless eyes seemed to plead with her.

'Do you need some water?' she asked.

The old man could not speak and she ran to find a doctor. All of them were busy tending to patients, most of them with more obviously life-threatening injuries.

'I'll be there in a minute,' said one doctor.

'You'll have to deal with him on your own,' said another crossly. 'There just aren't enough of us.'

Anna hurried back to her patient. She tried to lift him so that he could sip a glass of water and he gazed up at her, even now trying to say something. She soaked a spare bandage and squeezed a few drops on to his lips, instinctively taking his hand and holding it. Leaning in to try to hear him, Anna thought she heard the word 'fox', but it could have been his final breath escaping. His pulse seemed to weaken.

After a few minutes, without letting go of him, she leant over to see whether she could detect a heartbeat. His head had rolled to one side. He had gone. As gently as she could, she closed his eyes with her fingertips.

Anna looked at the colourless, waxy skin and thick hair and thought how strange it was that it would keep growing for another few days. She had seen many corpses in her nursing career, but suddenly recalled the very first time she had seen a dead body. Nikos. She realised that the man she was looking at reminded her strongly of her brother. Age seemed to melt away in death. She could not stop herself from staring. Once again she took his hand. It was impossible to let go.

After some time, one of the other nurses came across from the opposite side of the ward. She had noticed Anna sitting motionless, gazing at the face of her patient.

'Are you all right? What's happened?' she asked with concern.

Anna could not speak. She was struggling to control her emotions.

Finally, a doctor appeared.

'If this one has gone, there are plenty of others who haven't,' he said brusquely. 'I'll deal with this.'

Anna did not move.

'Down at the end,' instructed the doctor. 'Second from the left. The patient needs stitches in her arm. She'll bleed to death if you don't get a move on.'

Anna got up. When she looked back, the face of the man she had failed to save was obscured by a sheet and his bed was already being wheeled away to the morgue.

All night and for the whole of the following day Anna worked ceaselessly as hospitals all around Athens struggled to keep up with the flow of major and minor casualties.

She did her work diligently but her mind kept wandering back to the old man. It was impossible to get him out of her mind.

When she was relieved of her duties, she took the bus home and wearily climbed the stairs to her apartment. She called in on her parents before going to her own place.

It was more than twenty-four hours since she had left. Her father was, as ever, sitting in front of the television. Anna sat down for a moment and watched. The screen was still showing images of the areas affected by the earthquake but there was more hard information now: they were still trying to locate the missing from beneath the rubble, the estimated number of dead was many more than one hundred, and thousands of houses and businesses would need to be rebuilt. Accusations were flying. Why had so many died? Amidst the personal tragedies, there was one element of good news. The Turkish government had come to Greece's aid, helping them with rescue attempts and expertise. The gesture of friendship from an often hostile neighbour, an act that reciprocated Greece's response to a similarly damaging earthquake in Izmir only three week earlier. was welcomed. 'Disaster Diplomacy' said one headline.

Themis appeared from the bedroom. She was happy to see Anna.

'You must be exhausted, *agápi mou*,' she said. 'Did you work all night?'

Anna nodded.

'Let me make you something,' she insisted.

'I'm really not hungry,' Anna replied. 'And I must get upstairs to see the children.'

Before she went, however, there was something she needed to tell her mother.

'I know this will sound strange,' she said. 'But I looked after a man. An old man. With silver hair . . .'

'That doesn't sound so unusual,' her mother interjected. 'It sounds as though a lot of elderly people were affected.'

'He wasn't just any man, *Mána*. He looked exactly like Nikos.'

Themis tried not to react.

'What do you mean?'

'Just that,' she said emphatically. 'When I looked at him, I saw Nikos.'

Anna had not given a thought to how her mother might respond and realised now that it might have been tactless. Twenty-five years had passed since her brother's death but sometimes it seemed no less raw. She knew how sensitive her mother was to his memory.

'What was his name?'

'I don't know. Most people came in without any form of identity.'

'You didn't ask?'

'No, *Mána*. And he wasn't in a condition to say his name.'

Themis was agitated.

'You mean you don't ask a patient their name? Doesn't it have to go on their notes?'

'Sometimes it's not appropriate,' Anna answered. 'And this man was dying.'

Anna noticed her mother blanch.

'It was a very strange thing, that's all. I felt as though I was treating someone I knew.'

Themis had sat down.

'Enough,' she said sharply. 'Enough.'

Anna could see that her mother was crying.

'There's been too much suffering,' Themis suddenly said. 'Turn the television off, would you? You must need a break from it all too.'

Themis picked up a book and flicked idly through its pages. In reality she was watching her daughter.

On her way out, Anna paused in the hallway to look at the photographs of her two big brothers.

Themis remembered Makris telling her that he lived in Metamorphosi and knew with certainty he had died.

Anna turned to look at her mother and their eyes met. She could see the pain written on her face. Perhaps one day she would ask her more, but now was not the right time.

'I must go,' she said. 'I'm sorry if I upset you.'

'You didn't, *agápi mou*,' she replied. 'I promise, you didn't.'

For days after, the newspapers were dominated by the earthquake. One of them reported that a mayor in an area of Northern Attica, a suburb badly damaged by the earthquake, had been killed. There was no photograph and little detail, merely a quote from a fellow member of his party describing Mayor Makris as 'a man dedicated to public duty'.

Then a week later came a damning front-page article about the faulty construction that was being blamed for the extent of the human tragedy. The number of fatalities and injured were both much higher than they could have been. Themis' eye was drawn to a list of those who were suspected of taking bribes for rubber-stamping substandard plans. At the top of it was a familiar name: Tasos Makris.

2016

Both of Themis' grandchildren were visibly shocked. Nikos wanted to say something, but he was not sure what. He understood why his grandmother had mentioned nothing about this before and he also knew that he would never mention it to his father. It would destroy Angelos Stavreed's own sense of who he was and where he came from. There was no point.

Popi played with a crumb of baklava that remained on her plate. Nikos took awkward gulps from his water glass.

The waiter came over and gathered their cups and Themis dipped into her purse for a note.

It was time to leave.

Nikos took his grandmother's arm to help her up and they all went out into the street.

She linked arms with them both, enjoying their youthful warmth as they strolled.

It was Nikos' first visit to the church of Agios Andreas and he was struck by the beauty of this ancient building that nestled so discreetly between a souvlaki takeaway and a shop selling cheap Chinese goods.

Themis led them to a pew in the back corner and they sat and watched the handful of people who came in. Most of them were old ladies, dressed just as Themis, with the uniform hair, clothes and shoes of their generation. Themis was more keenly aware than her grandchildren that beneath their faded hair and papery skin, each of them carried thoughts and burdens unique to them.

The other women lit their candles, kissed the icon, crossed themselves and sat to pray. The priest had already gone. He would return later to lock up.

The three members of the Stavridis family made an unlikely trio sitting beneath the icon: the old lady in her polyester dress and loose cardigan, the girl with the savage asymmetrical haircut and dense rows of studs and rings in the semicircles of her ears, the besuited American boy, as clean-cut as a proselytising Mormon.

Their outward appearances said little about the reality. The old lady in the mass-produced floral print had once worn army uniform, traversed ravines weighed down by ammunition and killed for her beliefs. Even Nikos' well-cut suit was no more than a costume. He would normally be found in jeans and a faded sweatshirt. Most of his waking hours were absorbed by teaching political economy, a subject that he passionately believed could make the world a fairer place. Perhaps only Popi was as she seemed, an angry young woman continually protesting at the state of her country.

Nikos took in everything that was going on around him with wide-eyed interest: the eyes of the saints that looked down from the walls, the strings of silver charms that asked for a cure or said thank you for an answered prayer, the intricately carved wooden screen.

Nikos' father had not introduced his children to Orthodox traditions. Angelos had baptised his children in the Roman Catholic faith, though they had never attended Mass after their first communion.

Both of the grandchildren were deep in thought, still trying to assimilate everything Themis had shared with them.

Eventually the three of them were alone in the church and in the low light felt free to talk.

'I have never seen you as a warrior, *Yiayiá*,' said Popi, squeezing her grandmother's arm. 'But you were.'

'That's an exaggeration, *agápi mou.*'

'But I've been living close to you for my whole life, and had no idea what had happened to you!'

'I was always good at silence,' said Themis. 'I learnt it early. And later on, I learnt about compromise.'

'I am sure my father doesn't know anything about what you went through either,' added Nikos.

'Your father doesn't even know who his father was,' said Themis with some regret.

'And there is no need to tell him now,' said Nikos. 'At least that's what I believe. Don't you agree, Popi?'

Popi nodded.

'I always got the impression that my father felt he had disappointed you,' said Nikos.

'But he's made a huge success of his life!' exclaimed Themis. 'He runs all those companies! And made so much money!'

'I think he felt inferior to his brother,' said Nikos. 'And I think that drove him.'

Themis had never imagined that Angelos saw things this way.

'Uncle Nikos was part of a huge change, *Yiayiá*. His death made an impact on history,' urged Popi, in agreement with her

479

cousin. 'Greece might still be a dictatorship if it wasn't for people like him.'

'Well, I certainly didn't realise that your father had looked at the past in that way,' said Themis to Nikos. 'And I had no idea that his brother's death had such an effect on him . . .'

'I think he had a change of heart at some point. Why else do you think I was named after him?'

In this half-light Themis felt free to confess, to her grandchildren, if not to God.

'I still feel guilty,' she said. 'If I hadn't told him about his mother . . .'

She still imagined her beloved boy's death was the consequence of her impetuous revelation.

There were many other burdens she carried too and even after many decades all of them still weighed heavily on her. Why had she not noticed Fotini's desperation? Had she betrayed the communist cause by signing the *dílosi*? Should she have told Giorgos what had driven Nikos into such danger?

In the absence of God, nothing relieved her of these regrets. She envied those who enjoyed priestly absolution.

Themis took some coins from her pocket, dropped them in the wooden box and picked up a handful of slim yellow candles. A dozen or more had already been lit in front of the icon and she used the flame of the closest to light the first.

'This is for my comrade Katerina . . . and this is for Aliki.'

She then handed candles to Popi and Nikos and they took turns to light them, as she directed.

'For my brothers, Panos . . . and Thanasis. And one for my grandmother, of course,' said Themis, as Popi held hers out to a flame.

And, as young Nikos dug his into the sand: 'And this one is for Nikos.'

The last of the candles Themis placed herself, at the centre of the others.

'Fotini,' she said, simply.

The three of them sat down again and contemplated the seven golden flames that illuminated the darkness. A pleasing scent of tallow filled the air.

'Beautiful, aren't they?' said Themis, not expecting an answer.

Instead, Nikos had a question.

'Why do you light these candles when you're not religious?'

His grandmother pondered her ritual for a moment.

Popi turned to look at her too.

'Yes, why do you?'

Themis smiled.

'It's my way of keeping those wonderful people alive,' she answered.

'And does it work?'

'I believe so, Nikos,' she said. 'There is a line I have always held on to. It comes from that poem Fotini copied out all those years ago.'

'How does it go?' asked Popi quietly.

Themis paused a moment.

'*Those who are loved*,' she quoted. '*They shall not die . . .*'

THE END

Note on the title

"Those who are loved" is a line from one of the best known poems in Greece, *Epitáfios* by Yannis Ritsos (1909-1990). In 1936, during a strike by tobacco workers in Thessaloniki, several men were killed and when Ritsos saw a photograph of a mother weeping over her son's body, he was inspired to write his long work about love, grief and social justice. A few months later when a dictatorship was imposed, copies of the poem were burnt within sight of the Acropolis. Some twenty years later, the poem acquired new fame when parts of it were set to music by Mikis Theodorakis and recorded to great acclaim (1960) first by Nana Mouskouri and then by Grigoris Bithikotsis.

A lifelong communist, Ritsos supported the resistance against the Germans and, in the closing stages of the civil war and beyond, was interned in a series of island detention camps (1948-1952): on Lemnos, Makronisos and Ai-Strati. In April 1967, the Junta arrested him and imprisoned him firstly on the island of Leros and then on Giaros; from October 1968 until October 1970, he was kept under house-arrest at the family home in Karlovasi on Samos.

Among many other awards and distinctions, he won the First State Prize for Poetry (1956) and the Lenin Peace Prize (1977). He died in 1990 and is buried in the cemetery of Monemvasia, the peninsular town in SE Greece where he was born and raised.

Acknowledgements

With thanks to:

My phenomenal publisher, Headline, especially Mari Evans, Patrick Insole, Jo Liddiard, Caitlin Raynor, Flora Rees and Jess Whitlum-Cooper,

Peter Straus and all at Rogers, Coleridge and White, Literary Agency, for looking after me so well,

John Kittmer, for so much, but especially for sharing his knowledge of Yannis Ritsos,

Emily Hislop, for her razor sharp eyes and insightful edits,

Alexandros Kakolyris, for taking me to the most powerful and significant places in this story,

Popi Siganou, for leading me on countless adventures into Greek history and culture,

Thomas Vogiatzis, for helping me to understand the Greek way of thinking,

Fotini Pipi, for invaluable questions, translations and fact-checking,

Ian Hislop, for his uncompromising comments,

Vasso Sotiriou, for holding my hand in Athens,

Katerina Balkoura, for finally getting me to Makronisos,

Will Hislop, for support and understanding,

The London Library, for providing the tranquil surroundings in which to write,

My writing companions Victor Sebestyen, Rebecca Fogg, Diana Souhami and Tim Bouverie for their camaraderie.

Kostis Karpozilos and Vangelis Karamanolakis for the information on the burning of the files and for showing me an original *dílosi*,

Roderick Beaton, Richard Clogg, Stathis Kalyvas and Mark Mazower for writing my most treasured books on Greece. Also, the numerous other academics and historians on whom I depend.